War (

BY THE SAME AUTHOR

Fiction
Local Colour
Visible People
Caltrop's Desire
Human Interest
John Ross
Born of Man
Time of Our Darkness

Poetry
It's About Time
The Assassination of Shaka
Hottentot Venus
Love Poems, Hate Poems
Apollo Café
Season of Violence
Selected Poems

Drama
Cold Stone Jug
Schreiner

Criticism
Southern African Literature: An Introduction

War Child

Stephen Gray

Serif
London

This edition first published in 1993 by
Serif
47 Strahan Road
London E3 5DA

Copyright © Stephen Gray 1991

The moral right of the author has been asserted.

All rights reserved. No part of this publication
may be reproduced, transmitted or stored in a
retrieval system, without permission in writing
from the publisher.

British Library Cataloguing-in-Publication Data.
A catalogue record for this book
is available from the British Library.

ISBN 1 897959 01 X

Typeset by Photo-Prints Ltd, Cape Town
Printed and bound in Great Britain by the Bath Press

*To my father, Ginger Gray –
very much alive –
health and happiness*

It is chiefly due to underwater divers that the true docile nature of the manta or devil-ray has become known. Mr Townsend and his family came across the animals some distance out from the shore and, during the course of a few days, he and his children actually succeeded in taming it. Each day as they went out, it would come to meet the boat as soon as it heard the sound of the outboard motor. It became so tame that his daughter and others were able to ride on its back. Mr Townsend succeeded in filming a good part of their contact with this animal. When their film ran out they had to make a long journey to buy more; on their return they were sad to find that their gigantic and unusual friend had moved on.

JLB Smith, *High Tide* (1968)

1

Silver Town had changed beyond recognition. I would have to ask the way.

Running down the slope of the mountain there used to be a hairpin pass. As the native buses of those days, with their brakes tight, bumped on the shoulders of the raw, brown track, their passengers could gasp and wonder at the shine of the bay. If you were blessed enough to own a car, you had straps to hold. If you met an oncoming vehicle – which was unlikely on the deserted descent into the remote paradise of Silver Town – you would have had to slam on anchors, and skid, and reverse up a bank of shingle. Courtesy demanded that a climbing car had right of way. Much apology and local news was exchanged over boiling radiators on the treacherous bends of that pass.

I was born in Silver Town, Cape Province, South Africa, in 1936. To be more precise, Silver Town was where I was taken after I was towelled into a sufficient amount of life in a Cape Town maternity ward, after which I was kept behind the glass walls of a new invention – an incubator. I presume, like most babies I enjoyed being the necessary centre of attention. My mother's accomplishment was cause for much gentle celebration. Despite what anyone might say, she was pleased to have a quiet, thoughtful infant. She made the very best of me. I was to be her and my father's only child, their son and heir.

When my mother, with me wrapped up on her lap in a blue blanket, which I gather I hugged around me for an overlong period, sat beside my father in her bucket seat of the four-square Austin model they owned – one of the six cars in Silver Town – and father swung off the main road, using the mechanical arm to indicate, although there wasn't another vehicle in sight between Cape Town and Mossel Bay, and she said, as she always said, 'Be cautious, Andy, oh please' – and this time, because of their special burden, she would have put her free hand up to his shoulder in an appeal – then, I fancy, being so pleased that they had left Silver Town as a family of two and were returning as three, father drove meticulously. But he would also have been so proud that any ascending car would have had to give way.

After they'd crossed the railway tracks, the first building in Silver Town they would have come to was the trading store, where the native bus ground to a steamy, dusty halt every Saturday morning. Then the Silver Town post office on the right, a square box with a counter so high that the post mistress, Miss Bester, had to lean right over to serve children those half-sized, wartime paper-saving stamps of aviators and sailors. The big red drum of a postbox, with its ornate initials for the king – G.R. – was also too high for a child to reach. The initials were adorned with red feathers, my mother explained, to remind us that the king used to write a lot of letters to the colonies, enough to fill the box every day. This she always said within earshot of Miss Bester. Miss Bester was nobody's royalist and defended herself by pretending to have no understanding of English. Silver Town gossip maintained that she had connived to assist in acts of sabotage. That's why the postbox was sunk in cement, like a fortification.

After the post office the frequency of buildings increased. They were on both sides of the gravel road, almost more than a child could count on both his fists. Yet I knew every one, each in its own detail and each in relation to the whole. Silver Town had never been planned; it fell into place haphazardly under the remote control of a council over the mountains. Evidence of the council appeared only on Friday evenings before a fishing weekend. There was the town's only meeting place, a church hall which some benefactor had thought to build in wood, and the butchery alongside, both facing Mrs Feverall's tearoom café next to the rambling hotel and the bar which her husband ran. The bank next door, with Barclay's Dominion, Colonial and Overseas on a brass plaque, open only two mornings a week when the clerk appeared with much ceremony from inland in Silver Town's seventh car, an armoured one.

The petrol station followed, a corrugated iron shack with, on the apron, one pump and two glass columns above it, and an airhose at an awkward angle. The rusty sign read Marfak Lubrication, which seemed to be the garage's name. Because of the run-down appearance of its owner, whose hovel at the back was pressed under a stack of empty green bottles – because he was reputed to have Coloured women to his all-night parties – I used to have to cross the main road before the garage corner. On the other side Miss Kettley's Beginners School clustered under the pine tree – a tree that held a swing, made by my father from a burst tyre thrown out of the garage, suspended by two ships' chains. After the school with its gravel pavement running from one puddle to the next, where the wind churned up the Christmas thorn branches of Miss Kettley's hedge, Silver Town burst its bounds, and was no longer a village. It simply petered out into the sand dunes.

The way through the dunes was most easily taken following two roads, the Lower or Sea Road and the Upper or Lagoon Road. The subtle differences between the two were enough to divide the town. The lower road led past the original gabled farmhouse after which the district was called, Oudeskip, in turn a name that recalled a shipwreck of a few centuries earlier and of which various archaeological parties had claimed to have found traces. Oudeskip farm had seen its days of glory when in the 1890s it accumulated the ramshackle workmen's houses that ducked through the undergrowth towards the sea, now boarded-up farmers' dwellings that made a primitive health resort. Around the corner, behind a screen of wattles, where the road levelled out along the swamp that lay in the last hollow before the harbour, was the shanty settlement where, as the white lords and ladies of Silver Town remarked, everything ended up – corrugated iron, carcases of old trucks, jetsam, fencing posts, bed-frames, junk. This community within the community had started as a satellite of Oudeskip, and for most of the year disappeared under canopies of yellow mimosa blossom that hid everything from view. Seaward of the Pits, as it was named, the lower road edged along above the beach, reinforced and tarred for all of a mile and a half, which constituted a dyke. Then you ended at the golf club.

The other way of getting to the club, and the more scenic route, was via the upper road. Never more than two miles distant from the lower one, it could not have been more different in terms of social implications. On the upper road the relatively recent invasion of English had come to rest. Silver Town was formally established after the Second Anglo-Boer War by Sir Ronald Silver himself, a secretary of the Union Parliament. He annexed the acres of lagoon on the west side as a retreat for duckshooters, where they could keep clear of Afrikaners. There were never many ducks while we lived in Silver Town. The upper road led directly to the Silver estate, nestling under the next mountain. The inside of that domain was virtually unknown, except to rowing parties from the city, several of the more competent type of maids imported from Saint Helena, and a few disused cows. My parents were tenants in the lodge at the entrance to the Silver estate, and even we rarely ventured up the avenue. Fortunately the upper road forked half a mile above our squat home, and our leg was advertised as private. The public road curved on a gravel bend that generated pale dust if a car chose to speed, continued over some patches that flooded at high tide and, as if losing hope in the dunes, did a last heave up to the plateau which was the parking area of the club. Then along the dyke to the harbour.

That was the Silver Town of my childhood, the geography of the world that expanded for me from the walls of my chipped, blue cot, across the living room carpet and out of the French windows, across the sandy lawn sunken like a green playpen in the midst of wattles and sighing, dusty milk-bushes. My world was remote, but it was my own. I never knew how distant from the real world it was, and would not have cared to know. Silver Town constituted me. For my parents, I suppose, the years in the gatekeeper's lodge of the Silver estate were a dead-end. For me they were the basis of an existence which has led me far and wide, so that I now return to Silver Town across a gulf of memory, a stranger.

The route through the mountains, this shiny, foggy four-lane highway, is my way back. Where the pole with a wooden sign pointing down to SILVER TOWN used to be, there is nothing. No notice about shark-oil. Silver Town is connected to the outside world nowadays by this dark, cloudy military road, cutting its clean way through the mountains. I overshoot it by several miles to a point at the foot of the new pass where there is space for an offramp, buttressed on red rock three hundred feet above the lagoons. I come to a halt dangerously on the curve, knowing that everything will be changed, knowing that what I wish to recover could not have survived across five decades. There is already a huge lump of regret in my throat.

The shining, expanding lagoons of old Silver Town, coloured by the dye of decaying vegetation, rippled over the surface by the sluggish rhythm of the ocean. I can hear the ocean, over the dunes, out past the lighthouse to the west and the harbour the other way, angry, slow. The lagoons seem to me diminished. My hired car makes crackling, cooling-off sounds. Along the highway, coming like an apparition, is a donkey cart loaded with firewood. For a moment I thought the old, dark man was coaxing his animal along, hurrying to meet me. Over the side I look for grey shapes like drying tablecloths, basking in the lagoons. Memories I have totally absorbed pop afresh inside my head.

'Good day. Excuse me, is this the right way to Silver Town?'

'Ja master,' he says, 'jus' carry on.'

'It's not Credence or Saint George's Bay?'

'No.' He makes a corkscrew movement at a cloud of drizzle coming over us from the mountains. 'Silver Town is down there.'

I thank him, and freewheel a few yards to complete the curve in the road. There I can light a cigarette in safety. In the rearview mirror I see him hunched; he looks back once and disappears.

Before the cloud engulfs all, I can see that, thanks to intrusions like this road, the very topography of the lagoons has changed. In that regard the ecologists should have an opinion. The lagoons were an extensive system, always in flux, uncharted except by bait-pickers – an interlocking, multiplying retreat for migratory birds and fish alike, so rich for a child hardly able to see over the bulrushes. Now they seem all poured into one bronze-coloured sink, choked with salt.

The cloud over Silver Town had come as a relief. I should have known. Contemporary South Africa is not the only country where an old world backwater could not bumble on for ever. Silver Town today has no more branch line, but this coastal security road. The trading store that acted as the market centre of some thousand black people has gone. A squat Pep Store with cut price dishwashing liquids and unisex jeans has taken its place. The old post office is a standard brick affair, with everything on it in two languages. The hall is locked and unpainted. The tearoom and hotel complex, that leant over the cliff, with its terraces and bignonias, has gone. There is one long Sasol station advertising clean-burning fuel. Where Miss Kettley's pine tree grew is an undecorated oblong block of service flats, next to a Greek café with a sign marked Disco pointing up the sanitary lane. Bungalows and Mexican-style beach houses spread after that, quite grandly in that amphitheatre of rock, with gardens fitting around them. The grid of new streets is predictable: Strijdom Street, Pioneers Bend, Protea Lane, Seaview Drive.

The view is now for property holders only. I walk down a footpath which used to lead to the old quarry. It is now called Lovers Lane. At one point only is there a view of Oudeskip, a peeling white gable among the tallest eucalyptus. Oudeskip is now a separate centre, intersected by a brown grid of roads. New development is taking place with some raw square plots. The Pits area has been removed, they tell me, and resettled at a new township three-quarters of the way down Long Beach. They have their own bus service.

The upper road no longer executes that sharp turn above the gatehouse. By now I wonder if I have the courage left to walk up that overgrown track. Instead, in all of two minutes, I am down at the golf club, which has a marked-out parking lot for several hundred cars. Evidently surfers congregate there from all over the world. The old tarmac road on the dyke has buckled off like a scab, and now we glide on this engineer's smooth dream, past the beach and the picnic spots to the improved harbour.

The harbour never was functional for larger ships. Today the wall shelters a hundred pleasure cruisers and speedboats. These are for the idle middle class and the serious deep-sea fishermen and, because it is a weekday, seagulls roost on them, despite the cut-out black birds twirling on the sheets to scare them away. Silver Town bay, on a sunny weekend, must be noisy with waterskiers. The old harbour-master's building has been converted into a yacht club with a sundeck, members only. The fishermen who harvested the sea have been moved elsewhere.

I go back to the Greek café for a take-away toasted sandwich, and bite into it in the main street of Silver Town. The hot cheese sticks in my mouth. I cannot completely put the pattern of the new town over the old. On any given day in my childhood I could stand there and see the writhing arms of Miss Kettley's Christmas thorn; the one-legged seagull waiting for one of the garage hands to feed it; Mr Lotter, the butcher, whose wife had cancer, pulling a sheep's-head out of the window; the farmers' bakkies outside the bar, loaded with black workmen waiting to go home; Mrs Feverall's Alsatian with the eczema, lying half down the steps; Miss Bester closing for lunch, walking with the keys in her hand. Maybe an old four-square car would trail a cloud of dust down the road, and all of us – the seagull, the Alsatian called Brutus, myself the pupil – would shift to let it steam through. Maybe it was going further along the upper road to visit my mother. I was reeling at my sense of recall.

The sky was lowering now, peeling off streamers of rain. I foolishly thought that should I get caught I could always take shelter under Miss Kettley's pine tree, or even crawl, crawl, through the daisies and under her balcony. And hide, so scared, because I knew I was apart in this world – with the footsteps of the other children, banging on the boards, above my head, and Miss Kettley with her stick, tapping, and all of them calling for me, 'Jimmy, Jimmy, where are you now? Come out, we can see you! You liar, you lie, you lie!' Mr Lotter's daughter Lettie, with her red, scrubbed knees; Mrs Feverall's grandson, my own age but six inches taller; Miss Kettley's own favourite grandnephews who thought they owned the place. And Miss Kettley herself, tapping on the brick border, saying, 'Jimmy, we really can see you, therefore you're not invisible.'

'What's invisible, Miss Kettley?' little Jenny Green would ask, and Miss Kettley replied, 'Invisible, Jenny, is the opposite of visible, just as courageous is the opposite of frightened.'

'You mean that we can see him plain?' said Michael Longford.

'Quite plainly,' Miss Kettley corrected him. 'Liars have every right to be ashamed, and you know what liars get, don't you, Jimmy?'

Mouths washed out with soap and water.

'I am not lying, I am not lying!'

'Soap and water,' said Michael Longford, 'and we'll hold your head under the pump.'

'It's not a lie,' I said, crouched before them. 'It is not, it is not.'

'You haven't seen anything like it, so there,' said Jenny Green.

'I shall have to tell your mother you have an overactive imagination.' With that Miss Kettley wheeled the other children, who were staying late that day as a cloudburst was coming, back to the house. That way she appeared to have won the battle. She had not succeeded in dislodging me.

As the rain came down, I could hear Miss Kettley phoning from her office above me. 'Hello, Mrs Esslin. Yes, I know how very trying it can be. But he's a disruptive force. He absolutely will not obey.'

I do not know the actual words she used. Presumably my mother apologised on my behalf.

'I feel pity for you, Mrs Esslin, but you are aware I have to run a school. Yes, it's the tablecloth story again – '

I turned round to the site of Miss Kettley's Beginners School. Of all things, the long vegetable garden had been occupied by a state funeral society. I walked along the verge of the upper road I used to take home after school. With the memory of that particular afternoon's wet misery inside me, it seemed that I was following my younger self. I had left my satchel behind and half-walked, half-stumbled. I was defeated and inarticulate. My leather shoes had to have the laces of the left one coming round the left side so that I didn't trip. The sole of the right one had split under the toe of the sock, letting in grit and moisture. And I was hurt in a basic way, because Miss Kettley and those children were all wrong. They had no right to be so cruel. I knew that I was distinct from them – that I knew things they didn't know, and would never know – and that I profoundly needed to be left apart from them with my knowledge. I was not a liar, but I was fast becoming Silver Town's most withdrawn child.

And how spiteful and unsympathetic that old gargoyle could be. Adults treated non-conforming children like that then. It was a case of agree with your elders, or be ostracised until you do agree. How I loathed that awkward, grey-haired lady, with her mashed face and raised shoulders, her frozen hip and that shiny cane that preceded her. And how indifferent I became to her prods and jabbings.

Those lonely walks home – the other children lived in the village or down Oudeskip way. On that late afternoon the rain was blotching drop by drop onto my shirt, and my one shoe, the right one, was accumulating sludge. I snuggled for a while under a mimosa, breathing the damp freshness. I was becoming the kind of child who had chronically to deceive. My place in their world was shrinking.

And what a boundless, expanding, microscopically interesting other world I was claiming. The way the side of the track eroded, where the foreman of the distant council failed to construct a culvert. In rainy weather a vast milky-brown puddle would accumulate, and leap up and paint the landlord's car – about the only car that went right down the branch of the road – and how the thick, tawny drops would stain the boulders. How, for me, the puddle meant stepping stones that I could walk blindfold. How I'd arrive home with scummy rings round my socks. There was some fatal power of fascination in all moving things for me.

On the afternoon of my desperate humiliation those absorptions seemed to have lost their vitality. I walked sombrely, soaking up rain. My solitude was my refuge, and I preferred that. I was the only crook and cheat in the school; there was no matter of injustice. I had actually told my story and not been believed, because they didn't want to hear or believe it. I would not tell it again. I realise how powerful, binding these decisions were on my part. Indeed, I have not told and shared that story with anyone since. I don't know that I can share it even with myself.

But the one I wanted to hide from least of all was my mother. She was out on the track with her big black umbrella, waiting for a sign of me. She was carrying her torch, although it was long before sunset. We were a family of two in those days, and I was her young squire, her watcher and her champion. I felt bad that she was carrying a torch, which meant she was afraid I might not come home at all.

'Well, there you are, Jimmy-boy,' she said. 'You didn't go off the trail this time.'

I nuzzled up to her.

'Miss Kettley's in a steam again,' she said. 'She telephoned. Heavens, you are completely soaking wet.'

I walked alongside her, under the umbrella, within the range of her reassurance.

'Oh, Jimmy,' she said, 'you've left your satchel again.'

I knew there was no ill-temper in her voice. I started to walk so that she would follow me. My right foot was binding round in its sock; it would disappoint my mother to take it off now.

We continued a bit to the hump in the road.

'I'm sorry, mummy,' I said.

'Oh, Jimmy,' she said, 'what are we going to do? Miss Kettley might be an old bag, but she does do her best.'

That was my mother all over. Part of her personality always said to leave things well alone.

'But Miss Kettley said soap and water,' I protested.

'Well, Jimmy-boy,' she said, her calm, rational voice lapping round me, 'you are growing older now and must set a good example. Miss Kettley comes from Scotland, and they have absolutely no imagination at all. So just be a bit forgiving, if they don't cotton on.'

I gave up, taking the umbrella from her and holding it above her head, touching the mimosa branches. I wish my father had been there. If he had, I would have told him. Sometimes I ached for my father, who was away at the war.

Below us was our home, the white cottage built at the gate of the Silver estate. We could stay on at a special low rent while father was gone. It had been designed as much like a ship as a house could become. Although the ground floor was square, it was set at an angle on the plot, so that from the gate you had the impression it was a prow berthed there. The wooden fence around it held back the land, the flowerbeds were the shoreline, and the lawn itself was the ocean. When the rain poured down, the house really did look as if it were afloat, for the foundations were below sea level. A path ran to the veranda like a gangway. Set back like a bridge on the first floor were square rooms, one with a porthole, and the rest of the roof was a deck surrounded by rails. Supposedly the house had drifted in past the lighthouse, through the heads, and was temporarily grounded. My mother told me that when they first moved in my father took down a lot of masts and flags.

Not much was left of any of that by the time I arrived back there, a middle-aged man. The wooden gate had long been replaced by a metal one in a concrete wall, and the name, Peter's Lodge, had gone. No Hawkers was the notice. But I had followed my mother and my younger self this far, and wasn't going to turn back.

The first thing that hit me on entering was a grimy dachshund. Through the wet grass it came at me, barking and clawing down my trousers. I sidestepped and sidestepped, but it cannoned at me. Finally, I kicked it, not hard, on the nose, and thereafter it followed me obediently to the veranda. The antique bougainvillaea creeper had developed tons of weight over the trellis, so that I had to duck to reach the front door. But the door was the same: dark wooden panels with a bulging metal door handle. Instead of reaching up for it, it was now at the level of my chest. I rang the bell.

I heard it ring in the kitchen. The dog behind me snuffled in a hurt fashion. The front door had a hatch in it, rather like a cuckoo-clock's.

I could hear an occupant shuffling to the door. When the hatch opened, for a moment I thought old Miss Kettley was still alive. As it turned out, it was a woman called Mrs Hopper and she had moved into our house, Peter's Lodge, from Cape Town, only nine years before. I thought she was going to close the hatch on me.

'Excuse me, Mrs Hopper, my name is James Esslin, and I very much wanted to see the house – please, if it wouldn't be a disturbance.'

'But my husband is not home yet.'

'Well,' I sputtered, looking for some argument. 'I've come from England. This is my last day in Cape Town, and I thought I'd just hire a car, you know, and drive down. I honestly didn't mean to disturb you.' The offended dachshund looked as if it was reassembling its energies. 'Oh please, just for a moment.'

She seemed to overcome her mistrust. 'Well, keep it short. I'm very busy, you know,' she said. The door opened. 'Oh, but look at you, you're covered in pawmarks.'

'It's not my day,' I said.

Mrs Hopper closed the door, scooping her grey hair up the back of her head. She was tightly bound in a dressing gown. She wore slippers with pink pompoms on them. The dog must have chewed those pompoms. She looked most distressed. Then she said something that showed she wasn't scared of me at all; in fact, she was quite welcoming.

'So you lived here, hey? You better dry out a bit in front of the fire.'

The fire in the living room was no longer an open hearth which led up the chimney to become a funnel over the top deck. It was a grill of electric bars. I stood before it gratefully. On that same spot I had stood before my kneeling mother and stripped off my soggy clothes, while she arranged them on a drying horse. I could smell those curled shoes drying against the fireguard, feel mother patting me down with a soft, absorbent towel.

'Well, Mrs Hopper,' I said, as the trousers behind my knees began to warm out, 'it's very nostalgic for me. Thank you for letting me in.'

'I wouldn't let that dog in the house or he'd be over everything. It was all right when we had a servant, but nowadays – my husband and I only have the girl coming in once a week, and she can never cope.'

'Yes,' I said. They had added a sun-porch off the old, rather dark living-room where we were. Mrs Hopper kept busy with needlework. Her treadle machine was swathed in a new kind of cheap dress fabric.

'Yes,' she said, completing a thought of her own, 'we like it here, except in the winter. Too damp, man. My husband put everything into buying it. He's retired, you know. But he can still do odd jobs. Our children come out, you know, with the little ones – on Christmas Eve, you know, and stay till the 5th.'

'You don't feel cut off here?' I asked.

'Oh no,' she said, weighing her pockets down with her

hands, 'oh, not really. It is a bit off the way. But Silver Town's such a going concern. New houses going up every day. My husband, he's a building contractor, retired now, so it's just the place for pocket money.'

'Well, some people can afford it,' I said.

'We don't let him in the house,' she said.

Mrs Hopper was so alone that she must have secretly rejoiced to have a visitor. In the kitchen the radio was playing a never-ending serial for lonely women. She heard it too, and went to switch it off.

She returned. 'Of course, you must find it all very changed,' she said, 'coming back so long after. But lots of people have had it since your time. I don't know who all.'

'We rented it from the Silver estate,' I said. 'They all dead now.'

'Deader than a dodo, if you ask me,' she said.

'Yes,' I agreed.

'My husband likes it here, Mr Esslin, but I can tell you – to be perfectly frank – I've never had such a long weekend in my life.' She stood there bitterly. 'I'd much rather be back in Tamboerskloof. At least there's a trackless trolley.'

I turned round to get the heat more on my knees. 'Yes. My mother used to find it isolated, too. But then she had me for company. My father was away at the war most of the time.'

'My husband went to the war, too. If you ask me, that was the highpoint of his life. You should just try him. He went to Tobruk just to collect medals. You'll never hear the end.'

'It was my father who was there, not me, Mrs Hopper. I was only – six or so,' I said.

'Well, he sounds like six when he talks about it,' she said. 'God spare us if there's another.'

'Another what?' I said.

'War,' she said.

I made a few affable gestures to convey that I was comfortably dry.

'You want to look around? Just don't mind the mess.'

'Thank you,' I said, and to my relief she didn't offer to accompany me.

Mrs Hopper's husband, the retired builder, had made extensive additions to the house, doubtless to accommodate the children and their children between Christmas Eve and the 5th. My bedroom alongside the main bedroom was a store full of ladders and paint buckets. The main bedroom, full of Hopper family photos in gold frames, was much the same, except that where my mother's single bed, which was tied with wire to my father's single bed, stood against the end wall was a settee in a style that they would not have countenanced.

Mrs Hopper was standing in the passage, quite unsuspicious of me.

'Can I – go upstairs,' I said, 'just to have a quick look?'

'We don't have many visitors,' she said, whatever that meant.

I bounded up the stairs and saw Mr Hopper had broken a new door into the study room, my father's den filled with sunlight. The adjacent bedroom still had its metal door open onto the huge deck. Mr Hopper had ripped up the old bubbly tarpaper that grew so hot and melting you couldn't walk on it. That deck, across which wind blew and rain swept, was more like a prison yard than a veranda. Towards the old Silver estate I saw a suburb had proliferated along the winding avenue that used to lead to the all-powerful sanctuary. Where the lagoons swept in under the bulrushes were banks of reclaimed land.

It was all gone. There was no point in coming back. Peter's Lodge was squalid, badly-kept, unexceptional. The lagoons had been contained. There wasn't a bait-picker or a caddy in sight, nor a water bird – the birds that used to migrate to Europe from our own front lawn. Silver Town was a wretched place, with no particular spirit – it was now merely an extension of modern South Africa. I was perplexed, I felt displaced. I should not have come back. I had the impulse to hurl myself down the stairs, into the broom cupboard underneath – I did that once – and to yell words, dark words.

Then there'd be my mother again, patient and calm and amused, standing in the light and saying to me, 'It's all right, Jimmy, come back, come back. Tell me all about it. I won't hurt you.'

And I'd stumble out of the broom cupboard, wounded and distressed, because there were things I knew – and had always known – which other people did not know. Where she was wrong was that if I told about them they would hurt other people, they would hurt her – and that was the last thing I was able to do. We sat in front of the anthracite fire, and my mother arranged my hair with a tortoiseshell comb. And I said nothing.

'Tell me, Jimmy-boy,' she would say, 'what do you mean by tablecloths? Tablecloths are in the house, like Aunt Rosemary's; not in the lagoons. Look, there's our tablecloth, the plain one with the red and white checks.'

'They're not tablecloths,' I'd say. 'They're fish, fish as big as tablecloths. They can't fit in here.'

'You mean they're square and big like that? And they haven't got red stripes, now, have they, Jimmy?'

And I'd say nothing more.

'Well, we'll have to ask the fishermen; they know these things. I'll ask Mr Olivier in the morning.'

I felt the comb in my hair.

'All right, don't tell me then,' she said, smiling – the way adults get when they know they can't understand and lose interest and begin to play anxious games with you. 'Shall we have Marmite toast tonight, or Bovril? Come on and lay the table. Jimmy, don't just sit there.'

She'd go into the kitchen and I'd look up to the mantelpiece at the portrait of my father in uniform, and I knew he'd believe me. We could talk without words.

I closed the door and bolted down the stairs to where Mrs Hopper was waiting.

'Ah, Mr Esslin,' she said, 'I was wondering if you'd like a cup of tea, before you get all wet again.'

I thanked her, but said no. I had to get out of there, move right away until none of it touched me any more.

'All changed, all gone,' she said. 'Isn't it?'

'Well yes,' I agreed. I was panicking.

'Then don't look so bad about it, Mr Esslin. Wait until you're my age. You said you actually grew up here, is it?'

I repeated that I had.

'Oh, then if you grew up here, that's much harder to take.'

'If only I could find something that would let it all jell. Do you know what I mean?'

'All broken, all gone,' she said. What a morbid disposition

she had. 'My husband says there's still a lot of stuff in the garage. You better try there.'

With that she led me through the kitchen – new egg-timer, new sink, new table and chairs, ironing board. Only the bars on the window remained. The bars were to keep me inside. She opened the back door, and let me pass.

The muddy dog launched itself again.

'Oh, voetsak!' she yelled after me.

I ducked under the lean-to as fast as I could, as if I were in flight – from the house, from the dog, from the woman in her pink slippers. The dog's kennel stood on bricks in the walled sun-trap of the yard. Some of Mr Hopper's soggy laundry was on the line, looking as if one boring afternoon he'd been strung up there.

I opened the door of the closed-in garage, still a huge, dark space. My father's car had stood all those years on the sand, leaking oil which made a paste on the grit. With the process of time, it firmed up into a shiny floor. I felt my way along by the pencils of light coming through the wooden walls. I reached the work bench and turned, to the right. My eyes were taking a long time to adapt, but I now knew that over there, in the deep corner, was what I was really looking for – a jumble of wooden beams and stakes originating in the old mast and yardarm that once stood proudly on the roof.

Then – and I knew it would happen – I distinctly felt another presence in that murky, endless space. Someone other than myself was there. I wasn't sure whether it was in the present time, or in the past which kept bursting within me. I felt so strongly it was there that I knew it was soon going to talk to me. I stood rigid, waiting for it. I brushed my hand down my front, I suppose in a last-minute effort to appear as ready as possible.

I must have placed my hand on old board, because ants started crawling up my cuff. I waited, looking from one slat of light to the next. And out of the dark several things began coming clear – dangling from the roof beams the rusty lanterns that weren't used except during storms; the droop of the rotten canvas sail; the platform of firewood, sawn and chopped so that the red ends showed in a pyramid. Still I waited.

As I turned to the deep corner the electric light came on and a voice did say, 'Ah, so there you are.'

'Yes, oh yes,' I replied with relief. It was obviously Mr Hopper, come back from his odd jobs.

'My wife said I'd find you here.'

'Yes, excuse me, prowling around like this. How you have tidied everything up, made improvements.'

'Yes,' he said in his drawling way, 'glad you like it. Reroofing, replaced some of the timbers. Was all quite worm-eaten. S'pose it's come up in the world since your time. We like it a lot, you know. Peaceful.'

'So Mrs Hopper was telling me. You really have made it quite the modern workshop,' I said. He had neat plastic trays for nails and screws, implements across the wall hanging from hooks, a power drill and lathe that accounted for the shavings underfoot. 'It used to be, you know, just a store.'

'Still some junk in the corner round there,' he said.

'Yes, used to be the mast and stuff. The old man who originally built this house had it all decked out. The porthole was his idea.' And then I came to the point. 'My father got from him a boathook, a sort of gaff. Any idea if it's still here?'

'Oh, the really nasty one. Yes, it's there. Don't think I touched it. I mean, we bought the place voetstoots, but that bit doesn't feel like mine.'

The gaff was more like a weapon used by medieval jousters than a piece of maritime equipment. The stem was still varnished and springy. It was about twelve foot long, and even now needed an effort to control it. At the end of that swathe of power was a central spike with teeth moulded into it, a hook as grasping as a shark's jaw. Other spikes came out of it in a calyx, like the crest of a pineapple. It was not merely an implement for catching anchor chains or sail sheets whipped overboard, but a machine of destruction. Along the beautiful bronze flukes of its lines, flesh had opened and blood had been released.

'Should have a licence to own a thing like that,' said Mr Hopper.

I swung it round. 'Today, I suppose,' I said, 'they'd just make it out of stainless steel.'

'There's no workmanship today,' agreed Mr Hopper. 'Look at the bite of those points. An artisan, an artist made that. Don't get that no more these days.'

If that implement was a work of art, it was a sinister and vile one. I knew what it had done. It had destroyed my world.

'Better put it away now,' said Mr Hopper.

How pleased I was that he was there. I was the interloper now, a guest in his garage. The gaff was his. He brought everything back into perspective.

'Unless you want it. Go on, you can have it. Belonged to your family, did it?' he said.

I hesitated, with the gaff in my hands. I was tempted to take it. But the fight had gone out of me. 'Couldn't get it on the plane,' I said feebly.

Mr Hopper took it from me, stacking it back in the jumble round the corner. I had a huge, draining sense of relief that he had decided for me.

'Well then, yes, my wife insists you have some real South African tea with us,' he says. 'Sounds like you made a good impression on her.'

'I've come a long way,' I said, 'and unfortunately I must be going. Must turn in the car.'

With great rudeness I was out of there, not even stopping to say goodbye. I kneed the sloppy dog, waved to Mrs Hopper standing behind the glass, pointed to my watch that I was late, and was gone.

Within minutes I was out of Silver Town. I had had no forewarning that my casual return to Peter's Lodge could do anything to me; I felt confused, sore, irritated. All I was certain of was that the further I got out of there, the sooner I'd be at rest. Why it disturbed me so, I will have to try to explain. I can evade it no longer.

Even while I accelerated up the new military pass, peering into the misty Cape with its slow, curling darkness, its darkly-coloured grey rocks, I knew how distorting my memory had been. For years now, if I'd remembered Silver Town at all, I'd thought of it as a shining, sweet paradise. It was uncomfortable to learn that that paradise was a blighted one – a dark, murderous one – which, without my even knowing it, haunted me still. I had no choice: Silver Town would be mine again, till the end of my days.

2

Before the war, life in Silver Town was full of absorbing pleasures – for me, at any rate. If it wasn't, I made this known by screwing up my blotchy face and sulking. I didn't scream or cry much; I was a peace-loving baby who managed to explore for myself.

At first my exploits were limited to the Persian carpet in the living-room, where the sun poured in through the French windows like honey out of a blazing jar. On that carpet I could reach out a flat hand, locate a footprint of my father's in the nap, and straddle it. Like as not, once I'd assumed possession of the patch, I'd leak over it. My mother would like as not throw up her hands and rush forward. She carted me in her elbow to a roll-over on the kitchen table, which was close to the bin in which nappies were thrown. Mother, to me, was a warm mouth full of safety pins.

Father, to me, was the pair of shoes and socks that came home in the evenings, attached to the knee that bounced me up and down, watching the carpet go looping the loop. This was a faultlessly regular routine. Soon enough I learned to wriggle my way off the knee down to the shoes and socks, where I could do my teething on a piece of coal.

'Ah, get that out of your mouth, honestly,' mother would say, throwing the coal in the grate and moving the fireguard across. Or at least that's what she must have said, being my mother, and he, being my father, would have replied, 'Price of coal's going up, dear.'

Weekends were even more social. The maid would spend most of the Saturday mornings getting me ready for an expedition into the hinterland, tying me down in the pram with sweaty concentration. What should have been a simple operation was not. There were, first, numbers of poppers and straps and bands that had to go round me in case I burst out of my clothing and, second, a like amount of halters, harnesses and belts before I could be declared equipped. Then, when the maid – she was a good body called Euphemia in those days, before I could speak and wore her down to being Phemie – had accomplished the strapping-in to her own satisfaction, I was wheeled, tethered and uncomplaining, to mother, who undid all the harnesses and halters and belts to get back to the original strap or band or popper that was wrong.

There was a wooden bridge not far from Peter's Lodge, planned to span the marshes for a road that was never built, between the Silver estate and the golf club. I had no complaints about the wooden bridge, except that it ran on a slope. Going down it was never a problem; in fact, I'd noticed that everyone who pushed got excited about it and laughed a lot, for my benefit, as we went onto the gradient. I suppose they had to let off steam. All this performance would result in the struts marking off the limits of the footpath flashing past at a terrific rate.

Either my mother was pulling the pram up the steps of the bridge, bump by bump, and was tired, or my father was hauling and was weary, but, anyway, before we got up onto the sloping wooden track trouble had started. The result was that, once the pram was on the bridge, neither was pushing. While they spooned and made up, gazing at the romantic view from the prominence, the pram took off on its own. If there was a brake on the thing, it had failed me. I got rather a lot of the sensation of wooden struts passing me by. There was a lot of running and shrieking and recrimination. I began to see the point of the harnesses and belts and halters, the way I was dangling from them over the edge.

For long periods I preferred Euphemia taking me for a walk. She fussed less about me and left me to my own devices. As we rumbled past any white people who might be loose on a weekday, the fact that a stout black lady was pushing had the effect of forestalling their attempts to squash my cheeks. With Euphemia I was somehow part of another, less disturbing world which slipped invisibly by. When she stopped for conversation, though, it tended to be for a much longer time, and conducted at a higher pitch. When the wind was behind her, Euphemia had a voice that could carry right from the lagoons to the Pits, where she lived. I had too, but I kept it in reserve.

Yet Euphemia had the failing of using my perambulator as a transport. She loaded it with fish from the harbour, with sacks of squirming prawns from the bait-pickers, with lost golf balls that she sold back to the caddies, and once – this I can hardly forgive her – with a pumpkin from the native market. This orange monster, wedged between the rests across my knees, was destined to be driven to the Pits, which meant a winding, corrugated descent all the way past Oudeskip. During that illicit journey I learned more about strategy than before, because there was no way my physical strength alone would dislodge it. I tried prising it off with crossed knees, with fists balled. I tried punching, biting, butting it with my forehead.

'Ow, Master Jimmy,' she said in her sweeping way, 'you very naughty boy today.'

I was trying to tell her how radically I wanted that pumpkin to bounce off me onto the sharp stones at the side of the road, and smash into a great slew of yellow and pips. Its presence meant that I was squashed and humiliated beneath it.

At last, after summoning all my energy and losing much strength by converting it into a burst of sound, Euphemia untied me and extricated me from underneath the foul pumpkin. She bent forward over the pram and slung me over her shoulders, bringing the blanket beneath me and tying it around her. I fell exhausted into a warm, comfortable sleep against her back, hearing the four-wheeled carriage groan with the weight of the pumpkin being pushed out in front.

This new arrangement did not last very long either, for these manoeuvres had upset the equilibrium of the pumpkin itself. By the fuss Euphemia was making, I gathered that it had, indeed, bounced out of the pram of its own accord, precisely onto the sharp stones. Thereafter Euphemia balanced the major portion of the pumpkin on her head. From my point of vantage I could see yellow streaks working their way down her turban.

Eventually Euphemia's son, Meshack, came out of the Pits at her call and they assembled her trophy in the dust, and he took it through the wattles.

'Ow, Master Jimmy,' she said, straightening me on her back, 'you getting a big boy.'

But I was too far gone to reply.

Thanks to Euphemia I first met my contemporary white babies of Silver Town. Most of the madams sent their maids to the village, after they had done the breakfast dishes, for minor shopping at Mrs Feverall's. She kept a good check on any goings-on in the main street, so the routine was quite orderly. Alongside the tearoom café was a vacant plot in the middle of which grew three mature eucalyptus trees. They reached up into the sky so determinedly it seemed as if they wanted to settle up there.

Beneath these trees the black nannies of Silver Town would assemble. Euphemia and I often took our places among them. For us offspring it was a welcome breather, since our tacklery was loosened for us to sit unimpeded among the eucalyptus roots. Most of my generation had preferred crevices and basins there, which we endlessly examined while the talk went on soothingly above our heads.

Most of the information in Silver Town was exchanged in this way, and a lot was settled. All the nannies had husbands working in the big city, so news occasionally came in from one or another spouse who had written. The post office was opposite, so it was easy to tell which one had just received a letter at ten o'clock when the mail was sorted. What followed once the envelope was opened and the contents worked over by the best reader was usually also above my head. If the letter contained a postal order, we would know about that, too, pretty soon.

When the gums were flowering these nannies' unions were not so pleasant for me. The flowers gave off gummy knobs that used to trickle down the back of my dungarees. The sticky pink pistils would shower all over me, giving me hay fever. This was tolerable up to a certain level, but about three knobs in my nappies, and ten sprinklings of pistils, combined with being in the sun for a certain time would drive me to sneeze. The sneeze itself was a fearsome event for me, acute internal pressure causing spastic body movements. There was no stopping such a sneeze – my stomach would lower, my chest inflate, throat constrict and, when the point of intolerability was reached, this wretched explosion would burst out of all openings. In its wake I experienced semi-consciousness.

If that was the source of my complaint about my life on earth, the same could not be said of my early experiences with water. Water was my return to soothing preconsciousness where I belonged. Darkness, wetness, fluidity – those were the substances of my dreams and of my delight. The bathing routine always took place in a tub which stood on four curved legs out on the deck veranda. More care went into preparing my bathwater than ever went into mowing the golf course or reinforcing the harbour wall. The tub was metal, rubberised with a pink coat on which I had an opportunity to do some teething.

Unless I sat upright in the one corner, holding on tight with the skin of my buttocks by surface tension, I would slide into the centre, kick merrily, and go under backwards. Under was really where I wanted to be, where I could turn over and shuck off all the ungainly parts of my body, nuzzling forward into a dark crevice. The feeling of being marooned out of my element would leave me, and the solace of being able to move in my true fashion would be mine.

But gradually, against my will, I was gaining traction below, and the hold on the rubber walls seemed to compensate for what I'd lost. As in most things, I did not complain. The most important decision of my life – be a live man or a dead fish – was taken right there, evening after evening, in the tub overlooking the sunken garden with its milk-bushes and spiralling birds.

Time moved me on. The next decision to take was whether I would walk or not. I was reluctant to decide affirmatively. In my mother's eyes I could do little wrong, so it was of no great worry to her that I chose for far longer than was normal to continue to haul myself around on one elbow, using a crab-like sidekick. My father was more concerned with comparisons with other children of the neighbourhood. He used to hold me upright, wrenching my back straight, and say, 'There's a clever little lad.'

It must have disappointed him, the number of times I belly-flopped forward, and went into my trail of crazy circles towards my mother, sitting patiently across the carpet, darning the holes I wore through the one elbow of my jacket.

'Let him be, Andy,' she'd say as I grasped her ankle. 'He's quite happy his way.'

'Well, I would like to see him try, before I go,' he'd reply.
'It's only a phoney war, so you don't have to sign up at all,' she'd say.
'With employment opportunities as they are now,' said my father, 'a war really is needed.'
'We're doing all right, Andy.'
'Yes, but I would like to see him try and walk, Sarah, you know.'
'Appeasement always works, Andy. Anyway, who knows if they'd call for South Africans? You're so restless. Anyone would think you're actually bored with our life in Silver Town.'
'Sarah, my dear, all I'm saying is that if your Britain does declare war, and if I do go to help it out of the soup, I'd like to have seen my son walk.'
'I suppose you crawled perfectly straight. I suppose Jimmy doesn't get any of his behaviour from you. Before your mother died, you know, she told me you crawled in such a deurmekaar fashion she thought all you'd be good for was tumbling in a circus.'
'All right, Sarah, I was just wondering, that's all,' he said.
She calmly took a mouthful of needles and pins from me.
Every night at six we listened for the chimes of Big Ben. Neville Chamberlain was making his agreement with Adolf Hitler that there would be peace in our time. Chamberlain broadcast that message and we heard him on the A programme. We stayed close to the wireless on the bookshelf in the lounge. Mother was delighted and called Chamberlain a good man; father was dubious and called him a fool.
Later that night, once they had kissed and made up, I crawled as gracefully as I could into their bedroom, and my father picked me up and held me upright with his steely arms, and said, 'You're doing all right, soldier.' My hair was standing at forty-five degrees, which is what caused that remark, I suppose; I was saluting my mother, who lay there in her nighty, accepting everything as it was and wanting nothing to change.
She flopped forward into father's lap, and I nestled on her, and that way we made up a family group. My father closed the circle by giving my cold foot a rub before replacing my worn, tired bootee. His gentle hands, containing my foot, and

his thumb massaging up my calf. My mother's placid breathing.

The world of Mr Chamberlain and his umbrella was very distant from us – six thousand miles away across the oceans. It was connected to us by the mailboats that kept the network of empire in communication with London, and by the latest weekly flying boats. From London, with about three weeks' time lag, came all the pictures that belonged to the radio voices in the form of the *Illustrated London News*. Mother cut out many photos and stuck them on the mantelpiece. That gallery meant a lot more to her than to my father, not merely because she was British and he was South African, but because they said there would be no separation between them. The great upswing in the debate about the fortunes of the century had the effect with us of father renewing the lease on Peter's Lodge for another three years, and he turned his time to making improvements.

Father's hands worked transformations. For a start the lean-to over the car was to be replaced by a more solid garage. Because permission would not be granted by the council for a permanent structure without plans, and plans were expensive, father decided he could get away with just two walls and the planks from the lean-to.

The first I knew of all this expansion was a truck arriving from the shore, which poured out a whole dune. The pram fell into disuse for a while, Euphemia and my mother were let off taking me on promenades. There was my very own beach right on the property. I took to it avidly. Shortly before, my aunt who lived in the Caribbean had sent me the money to buy a bucket and spade for Christmas. These became of immediate use.

I had found my true milieu – out in the sun with my hat on, among the men – and my vocation – haulage contractor. I surprised myself by taking my first steps as well. No one witnessed this, so I kept it to myself, but it did help to get the bucket along with the greater height one gained in standing up.

None of this operation was without its trials. The top layer of sand was fine and dry and easily movable, but lower down it became sludgy. If I dug too far, it would turn into water. Then, once father had the planks of the lean-to stacked against the fir tree, they let loose a plague of insects – grasshoppers and caterpillars, ants and old grubs that were all trying to escape. These could be collected in an old methylated spirits bottle and disposed of later. But the greatest difficulty of all was snakes, and this I told no one about either.

The snakes had come out of hibernation in the old lean-to and for a while slept on undisturbed in a hollow under the car. Fortunately for them, the car was out in the open under a tarpaulin, and father had no need to drive it. Then one of the snakes took to the sandpit which, I suppose, was warmer on the surface, and she made her home along the boards that formed the rim closest to the house. At that stage, as far as God's creatures were concerned, I was already given to live and let live, and her company there disturbed me not in the least. To tell the truth, I was rather relieved to have someone there to keep me company.

I knew she was guarding me, because occasionally her eyes would open and her tongue flicker. But she disapproved of my experiment – seeing how selected insects would manage to survive without air. Her view must have been a distorted one, because her head was so low on the ground. Sometimes I lay flat and looked at her, and she looked back at me, and we were very lowly together. I respected her not because she was an eight-foot hooded Cape spitting cobra, but because I was privileged to know her. When I pulled myself up on the boards and took my first lopes along the sandpit, my foot coming to rest where her tail tapered out, she turned around and watched, and was full of admiration.

But for the most part she was inactive, and I had my building operations to contend with. The fury of my days was not the snake, but my efforts to imitate the men in my life – father with his sunhat and trowel, up to his ankles in foundation trenches and cement, and Meshack, Euphemia's son, passing bricks and straining with the wheelbarrow. The routine was for Meshack to leave the wheelbarrow most of the morning against the boards of the sandpit, and me to get busy filling it for when they would next need some sand for the cement. It was hot, sweaty work, out there in the sandpit, loading a wheelbarrow. Meshack would come and help fill it with the big shovel and take it from there.

One day when the two walls were up and only the timbering was to be done, my father took me out for a walk. This I regretted, because I missed my snake in the sandpit. Nevertheless, there were many compensations in being carried around my father's neck. I didn't see long distances well, but even through the blur of colours and light I knew that altitude gave me an advantage. I could see over tree-shapes and on top of rocks, and my head was just above the level of the bulrushes along the lagoons. My hands crossed tightly on his forehead. The brim of my hat kept flopping over my eyes, but I couldn't let go to brush it back; then the breeze would come to lift it, and I would see a wind-ruffled water surface. I forgot all about the snake in my domain. Father, laughing and fooling, put me down on the shore of the lagoon, where the washed sand is speckled with green weed. Stints and sandpipers were almost within grasp, but I settled for a bit of fruit box which was useful for digging.

'Where's Mummy?' is what I wanted to say, for it was unusual to be without her or without Euphemia.

As if in answer, he explained to me, 'Mummy's ill today. Poor Mummy. It won't be long now till she's better.'

I didn't understand the words. I began to get in a state of uncertainty. I thought my father had kidnapped me, was taking me far away from home, and that we'd never see it again. Soon it was going to get dark and we'd never find a way back. For the rest of our voyage of discovery around the lagoon I kept very quiet so as not to distract my father in his efforts to retrace his steps. When we got home it was twilight, and I saw the sandpit with the dark, curled shape of my snake in it.

The next day I caused my mother's return to active circulation. It happened like this. Euphemia's son, Meshack, was loading the wheelbarrow with planks alongside the end of the sandpit, where my snake lay withdrawn, minding her own business. My own experiment with the methylated spirits bottle was reaching a conclusion – bugs and grubs and even ants were piled on the bottom, sharing a common funeral. Meshack was not of very great stature, being only thirteen and fed on pumpkins and such-like all his life; you would never have thought he was Euphemia's own blood son, he being so spindly. Of all the nannies who met under the gum-trees, Euphemia held the record. I knew that perfectly well; I could get lost climbing around her. But Meshack, who had brains and a pleasant outlook to compensate, did not take after her. So spindly was Meshack that he couldn't get the wheelbarrow round, and the guard in front of the wheel hit the boards containing the sandpit. The sandpit was such a depleted place, compared with the days when it was a whole white heap, that the boards gave way and collapsed inward.

I was not in a crawling vein, so I just let it happen. Father was of no use – he was sitting in the car, pumping the pedal and trying to get it to start. Euphemia was hanging nappies on the line in the yard, talking to Meshack in their language. Mother was up, because I could hear the drain flush when she let the soapy water out of the hand basin in their bedroom. I suppose her dressing gown and pale hair were moving in a blur behind the frosted glass window. She had been like that for many days.

She opened the window. Meshack was yelling, 'Snake, snake!'

From under the boards my snake was crawling towards the bottle, and I knew I should not have been storing up all her food. She was waking up and very hungry, and I'd taken away her supply. Meshack was shouting to Euphemia and my mother was shouting to my father. My mother's voice was very low, as if she'd been a dead person, but she hadn't died – she had influenza. All of them were shouting in great confusion, and they were shouting at me. My snake had woken up completely.

Oh, she was a proud snake, she was beautiful. Her head came right up as if there were a bend in her body, and from her brown neck she could open out a hood with a black lining like an umbrella, making her much bigger than she'd ever been in the corner. And she could dance with it, swaying from this side to that, her head perched on top of the hood, looking down at me with her eyes wide open and her mouth open, and her tongue quivering like a blade of grass. She had such strength that when her tail came round, it clipped the bottle. She was angry about that.

Then I noticed, amidst all that noise, how continuously tired-sounding mother's voice was. She had been coughing and her throat was sore. But now, for the first time in my life, she was talking to me – not just prattling away, or humming tunes, or singing words from Gilbert and Sullivan, but saying words to me. Further, she was very serious about my hearing them, as if I had to reply to them. She could speak actual meaning to me, and I must respond, because it was meant for me alone. She was saying that I must not make a jerk with my hands, that I must crawl, slowly and casually, backwards towards her.

So I had to leave my snake that was so beautiful, that was singing to me across the bottle, and crawl backwards to my mother. I was leaving my world of sand, I was leaving my beautiful snake. I knew what a companion she was, and I would not see her ever again. I had no choice, because my mother was speaking and I understood her and had to obey.

When I backed over the fallen boards at the edge of the sandpit and was in the open, my mother's arms grabbed me. I thought she was going to say what a heavy boy I'd become. She was breathing deeply and painfully, clutching me, squashing me, running to the kitchen steps. My father was running after my snake with the long boathook in his grip. Euphemia came outside, and Meshack had a piece of gutter.

Then father brought my snake to show us, hanging on the end of the boathook with its tail curling upwards, as if she wanted to climb onto the boathook, and Meshack brought her head, and we all went inside. Mother kept on hugging me and pinching my cheeks and changing my nappies, whispering in her sore voice. But she wasn't talking to me anymore, just generally talking, saying I was such a big boy. And that's the story of my snake.

There was a sequel. Where one Cape cobra was to be found, so was her mate. This meant that for the rest of my father's holiday, and for a long time after that, I was not allowed outside unless I was already in the pram. Every night there was a search through the house for the mate, especially in my blankets and under my cot. Father fixed the flyscreen door at the kitchen so that it couldn't get in, and Euphemia kept the windows closed. Father used to lock the French windows, so that none of us went out when he was away at work. The women left the snake's mate to my father, who was a South African and would know how to deal with it. The other snake was so alerted it moved on to the Silver estate, and was eventually beheaded in their stables after the fall of Warsaw.

All during the early days of its reign, however, I found I could divert everyone's attention from snake hunts by giving a display of walking. This I did first when neither my father nor my mother was expecting it, when the wireless was on and mother was writing a long letter at her desk to her mother; she lived near Big Ben.

Father was braiding leather thongs into a stockwhip, which could catch snakes as well. He used the knob on the corner of the sofa. I decided I should just stand up and hold the rope of leather above my head. My mother spoiled it by rushing to catch me and dumping me back on the Persian carpet.

But I did it again, and this time they watched. By reaching for the leather rope, I could sway, rather as my snake had done, but I had arms and legs to hold me, so I could let go and stand there, wobbling, and then roll over to the carpet.

They wanted me to do it again, but I wouldn't. The first person outside Peter's Lodge to hear about the first step I took was my distant grandmother, who also got letters about how I could traverse from the sofa to the dining-room table using the stockwhip, and come back again, and how, when the stockwhip was stored away, I could do all that without it.

My father worked for Mr Pennington-Worthy, the same man who was our landlord. His nearest office was in the farming dorp that controlled Silver Town, which was too small for a branch of its own. So father always had to do favours for Mr Pennington-Worthy, who was too old to do things for himself. If Mr Pennington-Worthy wanted my father for anything, he would stop his car at the back gate and hoot, and my father would go out to find out what it was. Otherwise father would drive up the pass to work in the farming dorp every morning and come back in the evening, and listen to the wireless with my mother. Between his departure for work and his return at night, the time was more or less ours. Although we lived in the lodge of the Pennington-Worthy estate, we never went into their property because Mr Pennington-Worthy didn't like other people's children.

One night I knew that was where my parents had gone without me, because mother came in with her hair curled in a Toni Perm and father was washed and in his dinner jacket, and Euphemia stayed on very late with me. Euphemia sat on the sofa and fed me mashed banana and cream. Euphemia never used to sit there, so I knew it was a special night. And we listened to the wireless, which was a great treat for Euphemia.

Meshack came in, looking very spindly, and Euphemia gave him some bananas and told him to go home; her sister who worked for the Longfords was very ill, but she couldn't come. Meshack sat at my mother's desk and listened to the wireless. It was music. He never used to sit in the house at all. I strolled over to him and gave him some cream, and Euphemia had to clean up because I spilled it. There were so many cars passing the house with their headlights on; Euphemia could count them, but I couldn't.

After the ball Euphemia had the next two days off to go to her sister's funeral, and I was all alone with my mother who told me about all the people who had been at the Pennington-Worthys, Lady Duncan included, and how she and my father had danced and danced, and she showed me how they did it. Mr Pennington-Worthy was very pleased indeed with my father and had a big job coming up for him. The main thing was that the lease was indeed renewed on Peter's Lodge, and father had the sum deducted from his pay.

I understood nothing of this except by my mother's tone of voice, which was a happy one for a long period.

3

Hard on the heels of walking came learning to talk. Talking would give me some chance of commenting on most of the things I heard.

I was retarded in finding the ability. There was some deep maladjustment within me from the start. Babies, I think, are necessarily so dependent on adults for their every need – food, water, hygiene, comfort, basic skills – that they have to collaborate or fail. I loathed this dependency, for there were other sirens luring me beyond human society. Even at that age I had decided my residence among my elders and betters was provisional. Besides, my other world was one in which speech was not needed. It was a world where howling and screeching and hissing and chirping and snorting would do. My other world was the world of my dead snake, secret, brooding, waiting on me.

I learned about it first from Euphemia. My mother got an irregular morning job, fixing up the bookkeeping at the golf club, so I spent a lot more time in Euphemia's care. My father would drop my mother off at the club on his way to work, and mostly Euphemia and I would do the clearing up and the washing, and then strap up to go and visit her. It started as a passing remark Euphemia made as we were approaching the wooden bridge.

'Haai, there's the little man,' she exclaimed.

We broke out into a trot. She had never moved as fast as that before; I was immensely impressed. She hauled me out of my harnesses and under her arm and we tottered in fright across the bridge. Down the steps at the other end she collapsed with exhaustion, and I had to help her reassemble the pram and everything.

We recomposed ourselves and arrived in our normal stately fashion at the door of the club. I was disembarked and went on ahead, down the shiny tiles of the entrance hall, to tell mother what had happened. Euphemia followed with the folded pram.

Ransom, the doorman, came to meet me and, clutching his trousers, I exhibited my rattle. Then Euphemia knew it was all right and would go round the back for tea in the kitchen. The doorman picked me up, and we would go through Mrs Van's office with the telephones to one of the back rooms where mother worked. She had a desk and a wastepaper basket and a grey carpet on wooden floorboards. Mother would sit high up on a stool, with account books open across the desk, and write in them in ink.

I wanted to tell mother about Euphemia and the little man, but all I knew at that stage was how to call mother's attention.

'Yes, Jimmy-boy,' she crooned, 'so you had a nice, nice walkies.'

No, I thought to myself, it was not nice, and something is wrong with Euphemia.

'Euphemia get you here safely safely?' she asked, though why she asked I do not know; it was self-evident.

Euphemia got me here after a manner of speaking, I wanted to say.

'Well, we'll get some lovely tea for Jimmy-boy,' she said.

Euphemia saw the little man, I wanted to say.

Then the conversation went awry as Mrs Van came in with a tray with tea and cake on it.

'Oh, he's getting such a big boy, Mrs Esslin,' she said, 'aren't you, Jimmy? Honestly, you must be so proud of him. My husband and I been trying, but we can't have one like that,' she said. 'We only have daughters galore.'

My mother crumbled a piece of fruitcake in half and passed it to me. 'He never refuses his food these days,' she said.

'Got a good appetite, have you?' said Mrs Van. Her name was actually Mrs van der Westhuizen.

At that point I evidently squashed the cake, and part of it toppled into the wastepaper basket.

Mrs van der Westhuizen leaned down for the piece and wiped it clean on her handkerchief. She passed it to me, saying, 'Waste not, want not, that's always the best with so many mouths to feed.'

Euphemia saw the little man, I wanted to tell Mrs Van.

'He's not talking yet, is he?' she said.

'The baby book says he should start about now,' said my mother.

'Then they never stop for one minute,' said Mrs Van. 'I've heard more than I can take from my three, I can tell you. They're like budgerigars.'

'My husband's a bit – you know, on the quiet side. So maybe that's come through from him,' said my mother.

'I wouldn't worry about it. They all get more or less right in the end,' said Mrs Van, offering to pour some more tea.

All I could do was sit it out, squashing fruitcake into my cheek, taking big, airy slurps out of the cup. The little man was going to remain a secret between Euphemia and me.

On the way home I noticed that Euphemia avoided the spot where she had seen the little man by wheeling me right the way round the Pits, where she dropped off some left-over chops from the club, and told everyone she had seen the little man. She repeated the news at the nannies' circle the next day.

This all meant that Euphemia had to take precautions. She was smart at not spreading the alarm among her employers. In true nanny fashion she had it sorted out. Mrs van der Westhuizen's nanny, who worked for them near Oudeskip, used to take the youngest Van der Westhuizen daughter on promenades, so why shouldn't those two special nannies team up and outface the little man. It would appear quite normal for Mrs van der Westhuizen's nanny to walk Little Marie that way, since Mrs van der Westhuizen was a friend of my mother's at the club.

So the morning came on which Euphemia and I were to rendezvous with Bathsheba and Little Marie at the gate at quarter to ten. We all set off in tandem for the lagoons. Little Marie was a cross child and, in spite of what her mother claimed, didn't say much, which was just as well, because she spoke only Afrikaans. The nannies were speaking their language, getting nervous and agitated, keeping close, so that the prams rubbed together every so often, and Little Marie would look at me and fend me off. 'Voetsak, voetsak,' she said, which is the Afrikaans for go away. That much I knew.

Owing to the nature of perambulation, with the vehicle sticking out in front of the one who propels it, Little Marie and I had ringside seats on what was to follow. We felt at once privileged and vulnerable, especially when the nannies stopped talking altogether and slowed right down. We were where the pathway crosses a bit of dune. Usually that patch slowed even the most vigorous pusher, but this time the wheels were really binding.

Then Bathsheba had a failure of nerve, turned Little Marie around and they ran off. She had decided it was safer for her not to accompany us. Euphemia was absolutely furious with her because, without Bathsheba and Little Marie, her courage was not up to continuing alone. Presently Bathsheba was persuaded and came sliding back with Little Marie, who bumped right across me and said, 'Voetsak, voetsak!'

And once more we proceeded uphill to the outlook. The group fell very silent indeed, except for the scrape, scrape of my mudguard and Euphemia breathing. Little Marie kept her peace, straining in her seat as if she knew her delicate balance would make her pram easier to push.

Just then Bathsheba had another failure of nerve, but she disguised it as tiredness, sinking into the sand with a sigh and mopping her forehead. Little Marie told her to keep quiet.

Then, when Bathsheba was refreshed and there was no alternative, we reached the brow of the dune. All four of us stared forward intensely. I thought it must be a kind of gnome we were looking for, like the ones with red hats and big noses near Oudeskip. But those were statues put there by someone in relation to a garden; here the landscape was completely unkempt. The reeds were all flattened where some heavy creature had broken through. Even the spill of water looked unshaped, being a frothy brown colour, with the skeleton of a tree floating.

But the little man who made Euphemia so frightened seemed not to be in evidence. If he had, we would all have been tumbling down the dune and screaming. Euphemia's uniform would be broken and her doek falling off.

The two nannies took a few paces forward to confirm. Their fear of the little man had reached us as well, and Little Marie began to call for them to come back.

I told her to shush or she'd anger the little man. If he came out he would eat Little Marie, which is what she deserved for making a disturbance.

'There, Bathsheba,' Euphemia was pointing, 'that's where he was. By the stump, by the stump. He was so big –'

'Yes, yes,' Bathsheba huffed and puffed.

'And his tongue – so long –'

'Yes, his tongue, his tongue.'

'And his back, his back. It was this long, crooked.'

'Yes,' Bathsheba agreed.

'And his little legs, Bathsheba, his little legs were only this long. Ah, it was terrible.'

'Yes, his legs were only so long,' she agreed.

Euphemia paused, and Bathsheba took the lead.

'And he was standing right there, Euphemia? With his legs only so long, and his back, and his tongue – which was so very big?'

'Yes,' Euphemia sighed, 'right by that stump, on the left side. And if you had seen it today, Bathsheba, you would be dead.'

Little Marie thought this was enough now; her disappointment was getting the better of her. If she couldn't see something horrible, really appalling, she would like to move on. This she told Bathsheba.

The relationship between Little Marie and me was worsening, because I was content to wait there. Maybe he would appear in due course, and maybe she would see him, and be convinced, and be struck dumb. I felt sorry for Euphemia, because I knew how much she wanted once more to see the little man.

We left the crest of the dune with much stopping and starting. Mainly it was that the two nannies had to return with us in secrecy. I was no threat to security. Little Marie was the risk. Bathsheba and Euphemia decided the whole affair could be converted into a surprise for Mrs van der Westhuizen at the club, and had nothing to do with searching for little men along the lagoons. Bathsheba told Little Marie over and over not to tell; she would get cake for tea if she complied.

We went up the drive of the club and to the portals. It was the first time Little Marie had been there, and she became very awed, gazing at the tiles on the floor, and the palm trees in pots with wooden baskets around them, and the numbered lockers for the golfers' gear. Little Marie's mother was answering the phone in the office and hadn't heard us yet.

Little Marie became scared of the waiting, and Bathsheba looked as if she wanted to go. She ran along with Little Marie. When Ransom came, I just followed him, and Euphemia went and, when Mrs Van had finished on the phone, he told her that Little Marie was there.

'What, you mean Little Marie's here?' She jumped up from the switchboard. Even she called Marie little, because she was actually the big Marie in that family, Little Marie being named after her. I could never understand this because Mrs Van was called Stinnie by her friends.

'Oh, yes,' said the old doorman.

'But she's not meant to be here. And she's with the nanny?'

'Yes, they went to have tea in the kitchen,' said old Ransom.

'Honestly, Ransom, I told her never, never to come here.'

'Yes, madam.'

'Children aren't allowed, Little Marie knows that perfectly well. And next thing I lose my job because of Bathsheba!' said Mrs Van.

Then my mother came out of her office and I waddled over to her, and she picked me up.

'Do you know what's happened now, Mrs Esslin? Honestly, I'm sick and tired of it. Why do they never do what I tell them? I'm so sick of it I could just cry.'

'Don't let it worry you, Mrs van der Westhuizen,' said my mother.

'Ransom, you can go now,' said Mrs Van.

'Yes, thank you, Ransom,' said my mother and Ransom went.

'Honestly, Mrs Esslin, Jimmy is all right because he's no trouble. But if Mr Wolpe hears Marie's come, he'll blow a gasket,' said Mrs Van.

'Oh, Mr Wolpe doesn't mind well-behaved children. I know it's the rule of the club – '

'That's just the point. Mr Wolpe hasn't met my Marie yet. If she comes in here, that palm tree's out of its bin in two ticks. She'll have the phone lines down by eleven o'clock. She's a fast worker.'

'Yes, well, we'll be on the alert then,' said my mother.

'Honestly, you just stick at one child – that's enough. I should have stopped at two. Another one is too much to take.'

She commenced her search for Little Marie, under the desk with the lunch reservations book, behind the palms, in the toilets. Ransom came out and told her Little Marie was in the back.

'I expect the kitchen's in a mess now, too,' she said, and went charging round the outside.

I settled down restfully in my mother's office. I couldn't see that any of the fuss had much to do with me.

'Look, Jimmy-boy,' my mother said, passing down to me a picture of the new king, who was smoking a pipe sitting in an armchair. 'That's King George, and I got him framed at last. He's going to hang there where his father was. It's really about time I changed them round, don't you think?'

While my mother climbed up on her stool to get the old king down, I held the new king in my hands. She was a good three years behind with this exchange but, as she always explained to any visitors to the Royal Silver Town Golf Club, she was fond of the previous king, loath to let him go.

Mr Wolpe came in and saw my mother about to fall from the stool. He rushed to help her.

'Oh goodness, thank you, Mr Wolpe,' she said, blowing on the old king. 'Phew, he's awfully dusty.'

He took the current king from me and passed it to my mother, who hung it and, with Mr Wolpe's help, she climbed off. She pulled her dress down at the waist and was blushing.

Mr Wolpe didn't look at her, but at the picture, which he straightened on the wall.

Then he looked at me, because I had been so helpful.

'And how are you doing, Jimmy Esslin?' he said.

All was well with me.

Mr Wolpe had big ears and a big nose, and I thought he must be related to Euphemia's little man.

'You've got a fine little boy there, Mrs Esslin,' he said, reaching down to pat me.

'Well yes, Mr Wolpe,' said my mother. 'He needs a lot of care. I do hope he doesn't disturb any club members.'

'Gooder than gold,' he replied. 'Only children that misbehave disturb the members.'

'Thank you, Mr Wolpe,' she said.

'Rules are made to be broken,' he concluded, 'in exceptional cases.'

My mother sat down and gazed at her picture on the wall.

'Do put in for a crate of Alphen Burgundy, Mrs Esslin. The Hermanus team has booked for Saturday night,' he said.

'Yes, Mr Wolpe,' said my mother.

'Better add that champagne, as well,' he said. 'Can't stand colonial wines myself, but they seem to be suitable for the members and their guests.'

'Anything else, Mr Wolpe?'

'No, that'll do. Thank you, Mrs Esslin,' he said. He left, closing the door.

'Thank you, Mr Wolpe,' said my mother.

Presently the door opened and Mrs Van came in on tiptoe.

'Does he know about Little Marie?' she whispered.

'No,' my mother whispered back, 'and he really doesn't mind as long as they keep still.'

Mrs Van hussled Little Marie in to play with me on the floor. Little Marie had already been at the cake, you could smell it on her breath.

'Tea's coming any minute,' said Mrs Van, 'sh, don't say a word!'

'Hermanus are coming again on Saturday,' said my mother. 'Look at all the extra he's ordering.'

'Gosh,' said Mrs Van, 'that'll bring some life to this dump. Remember last time when they broke the stained-glass window? Oh, you weren't here yet then.'

'That's the worst of a tournament,' said my mother, 'they cost more than they bring in.'

'Well, as long as they've got some life, then they can have this dump.'

'If they don't drink themselves silly on Saturday Mr Wolpe won't be able to keep employing me.'

'Well, you're here to put that right, aren't you, Mrs Esslin? If you can't sort out the mess, I don't know who can.' She stretched down and stroked Little Marie for being so good. Little Marie was drawing herself a picture on the dusty glass of the old king.

I thought she shouldn't be doing that, so I pulled the picture away. Little Marie held onto it, and that is where the trouble began.

'You two leave the poor king alone,' said my mother, trying to rescue him. There ensued a tug-o'-war between the three of us.

'Leave it! That's Mrs Esslin's,' said Mrs van der Westhuizen.

The picture was wrenched out of my grip. Little Marie and her mother and my mother held on.

'All right, Marie,' said my mother. 'I'll give you a piece of paper to draw on.'

'Marie, listen to her!' said Mrs van der Westhuizen. 'Now you just behave yourself!'

Little Marie broke away with the picture and Mrs van der Westhuizen grabbed after her. 'No, that's Mrs Esslin's king, Marie!'

Little Marie was determined.

'I told you – give it! give it!'

Little Marie cringed and wouldn't hand it over, and got a big slap and my mother took her king and put him in her bag.

But now Little Marie was crying full pelt. That brought very concerted action from the mothers, and then the door opened. It wasn't Mr Wolpe; it was Ransom with a tray full of tea.

During the tea Marie proved herself a real traitor. She started to whisper to her mother through the cake.

'Wat!' said her mother, 'hoe sê jy?'

Little Marie swallowed, and whispered her secret more intensely.

'Ag, no man, Marie,' said Mrs van der Westhuizen, because cake was going over her hair. But Little Marie held her mother's arm and went on telling her story.

'Oh I see,' said Mrs van der Westhuizen, her eyes standing out with interest.

My mother was trying to find a piece of paper for Little Marie to deface, and a coloured pencil.

'Mrs Esslin,' said Little Marie's mother, 'tell me, did you know anything about this? So that's why Bathsheba had to bring her to the club.'

'I'm sure it was for a pleasant change, Mrs van der Westhuizen.'

'Yes, but do you know who she got the idea from? – Euphemia. She's been filling my child up with the most dreadful, dreadful –'

'It's quite safe if the two of them set off together. Not much can happen between your house and my house and the club.'

'That's what you think. You live on the wild end of town. Down my end there's nothing like that.'

'I think our end is perfectly respectable.'

'If you call a bunch of dronkies hanging round in the reeds respectable, I would agree with you.'

'You've quite enough of those of your own, down in the Pits.' She passed Mrs van der Westhuizen a refilled cup, and gave Little Marie the paper and pencil.

But Little Marie was not satisfied with the way the conversation was going. 'And,' she said in Afrikaans, stressing every word, 'he had big ears, big – like so.'

'You, of course, wouldn't understand, Mrs Esslin, not coming from this country, but do you know what Little Marie is telling me? I can hardly believe what I hear.'

'Yes, well, where I come from little girls don't tell such ugly fibs,' said my mother. 'So perhaps it's just as well I don't speak your language.'

'Oh, is that so?' said Mrs van der Westhuizen. 'Well, let me tell you the same thing holds good for you as for your king. Tell him I listen to nothing he says until he can say it in Afrikaans.' She and Little Marie sat in a huff.

'How could he possibly learn to speak Afrikaans? Do you realise how many, many languages there are in the British sphere of influence? – why, in India alone there must be over two hundred –'

'India!' said Mrs van der Westhuizen, 'India! The way they going now they making so much trouble your king won't have to worry about that many languages for much longer.'

'Well, Africa – just take British Africa alone. You Afrikaners aren't the only –'

'I didn't say he had to learn a black language. Afrikaans is different. It's spoken by his white subjects.'

'And by the drunks at the garage, you'll have to admit that as well.'

'Yes,' said Mrs Van. 'That is true, that is so. Fair's fair. But that's a very debased Afrikaans. I don't think your king need learn that variety.'

'An awful lot of people misuse English, too, Mrs van der Westhuizen, so you needn't take umbrage.'

'Ja, I suppose so,' Mrs van der Westhuizen agreed. 'But I must say, my husband and I, we speak a very good Afrikaans, we're very careful about that. Especially in front of the children.'

My mother passed me another sliver of cake.

'Ja, if you ask me,' said Mrs van der Westhuizen, 'it's these nannies that set them a bad example. Ag, if you could hear the stuff that comes out of my children's mouths.'

'Big huge ears and a back like so – crooked,' said Little Marie.

Her mother looked at her with a troubled expression. 'Ag, my child – what have the nannies been filling you up with now? It isn't suitable for you to hear such things, my child –' and she lifted Little Marie off the floor and hugged her.

'Well,' said my mother, smoothing her lap and sitting upright, 'whatever it is, it's done Jimmy-boy no harm. Nothing like a brisk, fast ride through pleasant countryside to put roses in the cheeks. He's flourishing much more here than he would in England.' She picked me up and held me.

'I suppose in England,' said Mrs Van, putting Little Marie's hair straight, 'they all a bit slower learning to talk.'

'Perhaps,' my mother conceded, 'children do grow up faster here, because of the climate. But at home every child has a far richer cultural life.'

'So does that slow them down or what? Here you got to learn to talk fast so that you can fend for yourself. Nobody coddles you in South Africa.'

'Well, I'll tell you one thing. In England they don't have little men with big ears hiding round every shrub. They don't scare children with that sort of thing.'

'Oh, so you do understand; you do understand some Afrikaans? Why didn't you tell me?'

'A few words, a few phrases. It's not that difficult.'

'So you did understand what Marie was telling me?' She gave Little Marie a stroke down her back.

Mother patted me on the shoulder. 'Not every single word. I'm not sure I want to. You should tell your Bathsheba that such dreadful folklore is not suitable for children.'

'My Bathsheba,' exclaimed Mrs van der Westhuizen. 'It was your Euphemia. My Bathsheba wouldn't dare.'

'Neither would Euphemia. She has her church and is very respectable. So let's just leave it there, shall we? We better break up, or Mr Wolpe –'

It was too late. Mr Wolpe had his head in the door, and Mrs van der Westhuizen scuttled into action. 'Only having our break, Mr Wolpe, and the telephone's not ringing.' With Marie clinging to her she squeezed out to find Bathsheba.

'I brought your Jimmy a piece of cake; it's quite fresh,' said Mr Wolpe.

'Oh, Mr Wolpe,' said my mother, putting me down, 'how very kind of you. But he's had two whole pieces already.'

'We'll keep it for tomorrow then,' he said, most obligingly.

'Thank you, Mr Wolpe, thank you so much,' said my mother.

'What's the matter with Mrs Van?' he said.

'Little Marie's going through a worrying time.'

'I see,' said Mr Wolpe kindly, 'then we mustn't be too hard on her.' He stood there, rubbing his hands.

'I better get Jimmy off, too,' said my mother, picking me up.

When Little Marie and I were all saddled up outside the kitchen, came the parting of the ways. Both Bathsheba and Euphemia were very sombre. We trundled down to the arch over the gateway. Then Euphemia turned to Bathsheba, and Bathsheba turned to Euphemia. Both had strict instructions: Bathsheba and Little Marie were to go along the coastal road, Euphemia and I over the wooden bridge. Little Marie had my mother's pencil in her fist and Bathsheba asked Euphemia if she could keep it. Euphemia said no, and put it in my pram.

The return trip wasn't too bad for me; after all, I knew it well enough. I woke at the wooden bridge when Euphemia unstrapped me, and we crossed in silence. On the other side Euphemia didn't even bother to look for the little man who was still waiting for her in the reeds. She just put on speed and didn't veer to right or left, and when we were home we started making lunch for my mother.

4

I had the words inside me, but I didn't know the way to articulate them. I was a child wrapped in silence. English in which all things began and ended for me, was not mine to wield. It was building up, though.

I remember now that singing appealed to me more than speech. If human beings had been made for opera, I'd have been an early performer. At times when my parents or Euphemia sang to me, I almost burst into song with them. I had little trouble understanding the words and could reproduce them from beginning to end. I could be the very model of a model major-general. Or there was my father leaning over my cot at night, mumbling in his rough voice, 'Baa baa black sheep,' and then replying to himself, 'Yes sir, yes sir, three bags full.' Euphemia strapping me up and singing, 'Nkosi sikelele Afrika.' They were all about equally plastic to me.

As it happens, I have to go on record with a first utterance that was only too typical of my heritage. I was standing and swaying on the Persian carpet in the lounge, while Pa was sketching a plan for a borehole and Ma was writing a letter to her mother, who once again received the news first. I said, probably because I was wet and fractious, 'Where's that Phemie now?'

My mother looked up. 'What did you say?' she said, thinking my father had spoken.

He merely replied, 'Hasn't she gone to get firewood?'

'No, of course not,' said my mother. 'I gave her early today to get ready.'

'Well then,' he said, putting aside his drawing board, 'I'll go and get some.'

'You know that she's got to sort Meshack out. I've let her take the old blue suitcase; she doesn't have one.'

'That's all right,' said father, 'I'll get some from the garage.' And off he went to fetch wood, closing the kitchen door and the screen door behind him.

I tried again. I screwed up my throat and clenched my fists and said, 'Where's that Phemie now?'

Mother looked up vaguely but I could not doubt that she had heard me. However, she must have thought it some strange echo of her own voice inside her head.

So I thought I'd better change my tune. I took my position alongside the arm of the sofa and sang out, loud and clear, 'Four-and-twenty black sheep baked in a pie.' I sung it so completely, without wavering and with such control of cadence and rhythm, that I thought she could only be delighted.

'Blackbirds, darling,' she said. 'Not black sheep – that would have to be a very big pie.'

The absent-minded way she'd said it really put me in my place, and I kept my peace.

She wrote in her letter, 'At last Jimmy-boy is trying to make some recognisable sounds. We'll have him singing God Save the King soon, loud and clear. You must know what his first words are going to be – Where's Mummy? He's at that stage of always looking for me everywhere. Things are going quite well at the club now, owing to what the heavy sozzlers spend. Thank the Lord Andy doesn't knock it back. And they get so South African when they're plonkers, just like a herd of bulls. That's another thing I loathe about South African men. But still, I'm freer now to do a job and they do pay adequately. We couldn't afford the nanny otherwise. The nanny is just off on her three week traditional holiday, so it's going to be difficult with Jimmy-boy. She has managed to place her son in a church school for them in Cape Town, if you don't mind. Andy's had his holiday, remember, so we'll see.'

'Four-and-twenty blackbirds,' I sang.

She added a P.S. to her letter, 'Jimmy really is coming on now, don't you worry your head about a thing. Promise.'

I continued rehearsing, 'Four-and-twenty blackbirds – '

My mother abandoned her letter-writing and joined me on the sofa, taking my hands in hers and clapping them together, 'Four-and-twenty – ' and I felt myself clapping with her.

'When the pie was open, the birds began to sing – ' she went on. 'Come on, Jimmy, don't give up now!'

'Wasn' that a dish to setta bore our King!' I concluded.

'That's right,' she exclaimed with pleasure, and I crooned back at her in my simple way. Those were more days of pleasure.

My father then came back with his arms full of firewood. They would have to decide whether or not to light a fire. The fire made part of the house glow while the rest was stonily damp.

'Listen to us now,' said my mother. 'He's got a singing voice just like yours, Andy. Thank heaven something's cottoning on.'

I couldn't stand the way they pretended that I was subnormal or handicapped. I would do things in my own way and in my own good time. So, instead of singing that same song again, I repeated what I wanted to say, 'Where's that Phemie now?'

'Well, I don't know, love; I didn't see her in the garage, I assure you.' He was quite irritated.

'Well, it is her holiday, after all. She can't hang around when she's got packing to do for two people. Can she, I mean, can she?' She was now irritated in turn.

'Look,' he said, kneeling with pieces of wood in his hands. 'I don't think we need her around as much as she is. We're both capable of looking after him.'

'He can hardly go to work with you all day. Oh, let's not have a fire. It makes so much cleaning,' my mother replied.

'I bet I can look after him as well as you could,' my father challenged her. 'Just a little fire; I'll clean it out.'

'I don't exactly like him hanging round my skirts all day. I do a job as well, you know.'

'Yes, I do know,' said my father. 'I only meant that, if you want some time to balance the books, I'm perfectly capable of taking him off your hands. Besides, when do I see him? – only when I come home.'

'Yes, Andy. Isn't that the way with most fathers in this society? I admit you're exceptional, but most of them don't know which end to change a nappy. If it wasn't for nannies and mothers, this country would come to a complete standstill.'

'He spends most of his waking hours not with me, not with you even, but with Euphemia. Lord knows what she pumps into his head. It certainly isn't what I think he should learn, you know that.'

'You're just like Mrs Van, blaming the nanny for your own deficiencies.'

'Where's that Phemie now?' I said.

'You see?' said my father, picking up the message. 'He doesn't want you, he doesn't want me.'

'Phemie's coming in a minute,' said my mother. Then she changed her mind. 'No, she isn't, because Daddy's going to fetch her tomorrow.' Then she looked amazed. 'Andy,' she said, 'you do realise your son is talking, even if you don't like what he says!'

Father lit the newspaper under the fire.

'Oh no, not now, Andy,' and she burst into tears.

My father blew on the flame. 'Well, if he's talking,' he said, 'we must celebrate somehow.'

During the ensuing fireside scene it was arranged that, instead of my going to the club for the morning, my father and I should drop mother off there and fetch Euphemia and Meshack and the blue suitcase, and drive them up to the dorp to collect the train from there. It was quicker and almost the same price as the native bus and would get Euphemia to her husband in Cape Town with a whole extra afternoon. That was the plan, and I stared at the flames, saying nothing.

There was never such a commotion as that morning, with mother packing me into our square Austin with provisions to last a fortnight and enough warm clothing to keep me sweltering. Several times she told father about how to undo me and do me up, even though he knew – he lacked practice, that was all – and how to feed me solids and, above all, to keep the windows up tightly so that my hat did not blow off at the first gale. He kept saying, 'It'll be all right, dear.'

At the golf club archway she was in tears, and came round to the back seat for the seventh time to tighten a strap on the baby seat, so that, finally, I could see no view beyond the leather upholstery and the silver ashtray on the level with my eyes. Only when Mr Wolpe and Mrs Van came to wave us goodbye did she resign herself.

'Ensure you don't damage the goods,' said Mr Wolpe to my father. 'Return them in the condition in which you found them.'

'Hello, Mr Wolpe,' said my father.

'Ah,' said Mrs van der Westhuizen, 'That's more than my husband would do. Jimmy, don't give your pa no trouble, see?'

'Where's that Phemie now?' I said.

'You're going to get Phemie,' said my mother.

'Ag, he looks just like a little Spitfire pilot,' said Mrs van der Westhuizen.

'The men are turning to,' said Mr Wolpe. 'That's a sign of the times.'

And we left them in a cloud of dust, my father waving and looking back to see if I was all right.

This was something of a false start, because we stopped again only half a mile along to pick up Euphemia and Meshack who, with the heavy blue suitcase, couldn't really walk all the way to the club. My father parked in the wattles, so close that the yellow bobbles were coming in the window. I thought I might sneeze. I heard Phemie's voice coming from the Pits, and soon she and Meshack were there, smelling all fresh and smoky from the wood fires. The car sank on its springs as that blue suitcase was loaded aft, and the doors opened, and Phemie came in the one door on my left and Meshack on the right, covered in yellow pollen. They were both dressed – I'd never seen them like that. Meshack had a grey suit on and shiny leather shoes, and a striped shirt and braces which he adjusted, and a cap on his head with a leather brim and a popper that held it up so that he could see properly. He showed it to me.

Euphemia had to take her hat off or the feather would have broken on the roof. She posed with it in her silky black lap, guarding it with her umbrella. So dignified was she in her clothes that she hardly had time to greet me. She wouldn't let me examine her hat.

My father said, 'Everything all right back there?' and he started to reverse out of the trees. The branches swished along the windows. I knew the Oudeskip road by the bumps and turns, which felt much faster in the car.

When we came to the eucalyptus trees, where father had to stop and look for other traffic, Euphemia and Meshack waved, rather like royalty but with more vigour. All the nannies were sending greetings and laughing, and Brutus the old dog was barking. A cloud of dust caught up with us, and we were off towards the railway crossing and the pass. That railway was for goods only and so Euphemia and Meshack couldn't take that train; it had to be the train at the dorp in the mountains, where my father's office was and I had never been before.

We were going up and round the pass when all my sandwiches and the bottle of fruit juice came tumbling off the back window ledge, falling where I couldn't reach them. Anyway, I got hold of one packet which I could see through the greaseproof paper was Marmite on white bread, and I couldn't stand Marmite and I couldn't stand white bread. So I shoved it towards Meshack, who put it in his side pocket as a present for the journey; he was so spindly and needed nourishment. He was so pleased he put his hat on me, so that I had two on now.

Euphemia was so serious about it all, I didn't play with her. Whenever we went round a big corner, she would say, 'Ow, master!' and clutch her hat. She didn't seem to be my Phemie. She had more important things than me to worry about, because she had to get Meshack to school.

Soon we came to the station. Euphemia unhitched me and carried me to the ticket office, and I was not to touch her handbag, and Meshack managed the blue suitcase. The train was already coming in and we had to run down the platform, to the end where all the black people were rushing forward to meet it with suitcases even bigger than ours. The train was already jammed, so you can imagine the jockeying and pushing. My father grabbed me from Euphemia and they were all going right to the edge to get a place, and the doors banged open and my father took me away, so there wasn't time for a real farewell. Meshack pushed and Euphemia cleared the people away with her umbrella. I realised she was Mr Chamberlain's wife. Now there was no Phemie and no spindly Meshack and just my father.

Whenever I was very down in the dumps with my father, he would turn me around in his big hands, throw me up in the air and catch me, and say, 'That's my boy, that's my boy!' He did this now. For those brief moments I was airborne I could see the engine giving a belt of steam and all the black people so packed in the carriages they had to lean out.

'That's my boy,' he said, and I thought I must be very respectful. This was the first time I had been alone with him apart from when my mother was ill, and the surroundings were not familiar to me.

We climbed back in the car. He didn't harness me in behind, but as a treat left me sitting on the bucket seat where my mother used to sit. There were no tying things there, so I had to grab the strap, and as he drove my father held me with his hand. He told me we were going to his office, just down the road, where we could play all day. When the car stopped he left me sitting there, and I could stand up and see the whole street from the front of his office. This was Pennington-Worthy's Soil Engineering, which had a shining glass window like a mirror. So much was happening in the reflection – cars banging and clattering, and a cart and horses. A boy with a bicycle came and parked it right alongside the car.

Then my father was swearing, because everything had gone wrong, and we couldn't go in the office. Three big black men, all covered in dust, climbed on the back seat. They put a box full of spanners and screwdrivers and wire on top of my blanket and nearly on the sandwiches that were left. They sat there talking under their breath, and got out and put more equipment in the boot which opened and closed with a wallop. One of them talked to me in his language, but I held my peace.

So we drove a long way this time, with the sun and the dust coming on the windows, with terrific bumps, and then my father would slow down. He was very annoyed, and said I must hold tight, and his hand came and rescued me from falling off the seat. He stopped once and stood me on the carpet on the floor, where I could hold onto the glove compartment and not fall so far. The three black men were laughing.

In due course we arrived at this farm. They pulled most of the tools out of the car and unloaded at the back, and my father picked me up and threw me in the air and said, 'That's my boy!' and I went back to the car.

Father closed me in and at first it was all right. Then it began to heat up. Due to the dust and the heat, I began to want to sneeze. I gazed at the world of glass all above me. I could reach the one pane with my fist. Behind that shining glass was my father. I wanted to sneeze, but strained and struggled to keep it within me. There was a lock on the handle of the door and in any case it was too heavy for me. My eyes were watering, heart pumping. Then he opened the door and the sneeze buried itself inside me.

The experience of being on a farm was too much for me. Only towards midday did I begin to get some sense of it. For a start, it was completely flat. There were no dunes at the one edge of it and no mountains sealing off the other end. My father's car was the tallest thing on that plain, apart from the windmill which his team had come to repair. The three black men were very good at it, because they were up on the struts before my father could say a word, and he climbed up after them with a ruler in his mouth. I took off my hat and threw it in the dirt because I couldn't see properly.

All around me were strange bushes. For the first time in my life they were shorter than I was, so I could see their tops and walk around them to the other side. Some of them had branches like my fingers, only green in colour. When I squeezed them they snapped open with green strings and a small bit of water which, my father showed me, was all the sheep had to drink, and that's why they had to get the pump working. Otherwise the sheep would die.

They had already died. There was a very big dead one, lying on the soil without moving. Crows around it were eating it. One of the horns had come off and was lying there on a piece of rock. Its face had shrunk and its mouth was open. All its stomach was falling with worms in it, and the crows were pecking at that.

Father had left the car door open on my side this time so that I could climb in. I sat there, but I couldn't get in the back to fetch my blanket. I didn't need the blanket, because it was very hot. It was hot on the glove compartment, and very hot on the steering wheel, and the leather of the seat was hot, so I couldn't sit there for very long.

I found a much better place where the shadow of the windmill fell on the ground, and it was like sitting in a wind because the blades went round and round very slowly as if they were patting me. Then I went back to the sheep, but I couldn't get across to the horn on the rock. The crows stood and watched me.

And when it was lunch time my father came and showed me the cement trough where the water ran in so that the sheep could drink before they died. And we had some lunch, sitting against the trough which smelled of new cement. My father didn't know some of the sandwiches were missing. He had such a big mouth he could eat practically a whole sandwich in one bite. Then we discovered it was the wrong packet, and he'd been eating my sandwiches and I was expected to eat his, and we agreed that we wouldn't tell my mother. So I got his sandwiches broken down into smaller pieces, and it was peanut butter which I liked a lot when they weren't hot. My fruit juice was boiling also, and sticky. My father sent the black men to look for my hat, and the one came back with it in his hand, and I threw it off again, because I liked the sun.

We were just finishing our lunch when the farmer came. He was driving a big open truck. The wheels were so large they came to the top of my head. The farmer was also very big; beside my father he looked like a champion. His face was all burned with the sun, and he wore an old khaki hat, and a khaki shirt and baggy trousers. He sat on the running board in front of us, and talked about his best ram over there. The farmer said that if the windmill was not getting water out of the borehole, he was going to sue Mr Pennington-Worthy. He didn't like Mr Pennington-Worthy because Mr Pennington-Worthy killed his best ram.

My father said that he and his team would have the windmill working by the afternoon at the latest, and then they talked about other things. It turned out that the farmer played golf and knew my mother because she worked at the Silver Town club.

'Oh, so that's your mother, is it?' he said to me.

'Yes,' said my father, 'she's only there temporarily.'

'Hang,' said the farmer, 'but she's a great acquisition for Silver Town. Keep Mr Wolpe in order, hang, I don't trust him. That's where I go when we retire; my son takes over this farm. You know the house with the blue roof just on the other side of Oudeskip?'

'We live over on Pennington-Worthy's side,' said my father.

'Hang,' said the farmer, 'and now he's president of the golf club, too.'

My father said, 'He has a lot of inherited wealth.'

'And you –' said the farmer, turning to me, waving his hat against his face, 'when you grow up you're going to take over Mr Pennington-Worthy's, hey?'

'Oh, there's no chance of that,' said my father. 'We're not related.'

'So what you going to do, hey?' the farmer asked me. 'Put in better windmills than your father does? This stuff's rubbish, man.'

'Where's that Phemie now?' I said.

'Never mind,' said the farmer, sighing, 'your father's the right sort. He'll go far. But why work for a British firm; why not work for SA Boreholes? They got American windmills now, the ones with the feathers painted on the tail.'

My father said yes, but his chances of promotion were better if he did long service with Pennington-Worthy Soil Engineering.

The farmer had a brown bottle of beer which he passed to my father, and now they were talking about fishing. When he retired the farmer was going to become a fisherman. He said after a whole life without water, he wanted water every day without end.

Somehow the brown beer bottle came my way, but I knew I mustn't touch it. My father held it so that I could get a grip on it, and both he and the farmer were watching me. The dent around the rim where the bottlecap fitted had a sour taste. In all of a rush there was a hot smell inside my head, and my father and the farmer laughed away. 'That's my boy!' said my father.

One of the black men came with his hat in his hands and asked my father's permission to climb up again, and the farmer said he jolly well better. Then the farmer and my father were talking about the war. The farmer was strongly against it, and so my father didn't say much.

'But if you work for the British, that doesn't mean you have to go and fight for them, also. Stay here, man. Then when they come back you'll own half the British interests. You've got no moral duty to go.'

Well, my father said, he'd see.

'No, you must listen to me. What has Mr Pennington-Worthy ever done for South Africa? You just work for him because you think you've got no choice. But when it comes to choosing, I'm telling you, you got only one side to choose.'

Maybe, said my father.

'There's only one, and that's South Africa. He sends all his profits to Britain. Keep the money here, I say. It's got nothing to do with us what they get up to over there.'

Yes, said my father, but he thought the Germans were coming here.

'They better think again,' said the farmer. 'If they want my farm, all my sheep are vrekking and there hasn't been rain since 1934 – they can have it.'

Yes, said my father, but the drought wouldn't last forever, and perhaps South Africa in better times was very desirable to them.

'Well, if they can get this borehole to work better than you can, then let the best man win,' said the farmer.

Then he opened another bottle of beer; he didn't have an opener so he had to do it on the bumper of his truck. It came out with a white head running down the side of the bottle. Just then, the one black man shouted from the ladder up the side of the windmill, and my father had to run.

The farmer sat down on his bumper again, and said that my mother was the new one working at the club. That was when I became homesick. I wished I was at the golf club with my mother. It seemed as if I had last heard her voice three weeks ago, and I was never going to hear her again.

'I bet your mummy's very occupied, hey?' said the farmer.

I just looked at him.

'Did you see how my sheep is dying?' he said to me, and with the beer bottle in one hand and me in the other, he led me to where the ram was, with its horn off on the rock. He prodded the carcase with his boot, and the crows flew off. He gave me the beer bottle to hold, and stooped to pick up the horn, and then took the beer bottle from me and gave me the horn to play with. Then he threw the beer bottle at the crows.

After that I climbed back into my mother's bucket seat and it was very sizzling there, the leather was sizzling and the dashboard was sizzling and the steering wheel and the gear lever and the carpet. I lay down and I think I was cooking. I moved where the window wasn't shining, but it was still sizzling. My eyes were full of water, but I wasn't crying. The inside of the car was hotter than the living room at home when the sun streamed through the French windows, but there I could escape to the shade.

Father came to get me, and my whole body was covered in sweat, as though I'd been having a bath in sea water. It was as hot outside, and nobody knew where my hat was. My skin was shining like glass. Father had kept quite cool, and he carried me to where the newly-cemented trough was. One of the three men came down the side of the windmill on a rope, not even bothering to take the ladder. There was no one up there now.

Then my father carried me to the bottom of the windmill and told me to grip my hands around his forehead. My arms went round but his forehead was slippery. He was going to climb up, with me clinging on behind.

'Don't tell Mummy,' he conspired with me. 'We're going to make you king of the castle, hey, Jimmy-boy?'

I gave my assent by clinging even tighter, so that he loosened my arms a bit and he showed me how I must hold his chin, not his throat. The farmer had just come back in his truck, and he strolled over and gave me a dusty pat on the back. The workmen stood well back. One of them had located my hat, and came running up with it, and the farmer put it right over my eyes. I couldn't let go to adjust it.

Father started climbing up the steps on the side of the windmill. Father was very strong and had a lot of energy, but he took it slowly. He was breathing beer fumes. Where my arms were holding him, I could feel his heart beating under his skin. It was hard and leathery, with pinpoints like splinters where he hadn't been shaving properly. He couldn't turn round, but he said, 'Here we go, Jimmy-boy.'

'Now let's see if it works this time,' said the farmer.

'Ja baas,' said one of the men, and they laughed a lot.

I was already high enough off the ground, being on my father's back, but when he began to climb the steps it seemed as if the dry, red earth was falling away from us. My father would rest his forehead on the steel ladder, and you could hear his shoes climb up one more step. Then he would make a lifting noise and his head and I rose up a whole step more. His shoulders were so round and strong and padded and big, it was as if I were cushioned on them, my feet digging into his belt at the back. I kept staring forward under his ear, and he took another step up.

This was his windmill, even though it belonged to Mr Pennington-Worthy and the farmer had bought it from them. It was his windmill from the way it creaked and groaned and got thinner. Father was blowing and sighing a lot, telling me through his teeth to hold on. I was throttling him and, with his forehead against a strut, he leaned into the ladder and pulled my sweaty arms from around his throat and lifted me up to his chin again. 'Hold there, hold there,' he said.

Then he got the rhythm of climbing up, and we went quite quickly up the side of the windmill. It was windy up there. You didn't get that breeze down on the ground. There was a wind coming straight over my father's shoulder, and my eyes were watering again and the brim of my hat came down; I couldn't see anything more than his collar, squashed under my chin. I could hardly breathe and I thought my arms were lengthening like elastic going to stretch past the point where it can shrink back. My father climbed so well and I held on so tightly, and the wind was going.

Then my father gave a big upward heave and his shoulders with me on top of them came down on the platform they have up there at the apex of windmills. A wooden platform that is quite strong, made of slats like floorboards. I wouldn't let go, but father was telling me to get off now, because he couldn't breathe; I was strangling him. He ripped my arms off and got rid of me in a lump on the platform. I didn't look at anything, but realised I hadn't fallen because I was on the platform in the centre, and the wind was blowing right up the side like a roller of air. My father pulled himself up beside me, and sat on the edge.

He said I must look over, and see how very far below the farmer and the workmen were, but I continued to fix up my hat. Every time I held it one way, the back would flap up, and if I turned my head the front came down across my nose. So I lay there with my head sideways, and eventually it blew off.

'Don't tell Mummy,' he said, since my mother was always furious if I lost my hat.

Then father crouched on the other side of the platform and undid the wire that was holding the pumping shaft. He threw it overboard and said it was going to work now. He stood up on tiptoe and swung the vanes over so that they weren't locked in with the tail, and gave the system a big wrench, and had to duck as it took off with immediate speed. The vanes made a terrific cutting noise with all the wind, and the whole structure swung round so that it was hammering above my head. The platform was shaking. And my father worked desperately on the shaft, and it was going down from his hands right into the ground and through the rock and deep into the earth, and down it would go, forced by the power of the vanes.

And then the whole windmill did a shuddering reverse, and the shaft stayed still and then slowly began to come out again with its heavy cargo of water. A misty brown colour settled over us from the very deep water that was running under the earth.

I gazed through the planks and I could see how it worked. In all that silver fretwork the shaft was the main thing and it went straight down. Underneath it the farmer was standing and so were the workmen, and they were all wearing hats. They were very small and short under their hats. Then my father showed me where the pipes ended, and how the rusty water was going through them all and tumbling into the new cement trough.

He put his hand on my back, and I could feel it was all clammy and strong, and he said, 'There you are, Jimmy-boy. How do you feel now?'

I said the only words I could say that weren't songs.

'Oh, don't you worry about her. She's in Cape Town by now, and you're safe with me. Don't you like it up here, and you see how dry the land is, and we're going to make it like the Garden of Eden.'

I was going to talk, but my mouth became full of the wind. I wanted to say that his windmill was a great success, and that he was the king of it all, and I was his son.

After that day, on the windy platform of a steel machine that was emptying the core of the earth onto the Karoo, with my father beside me like a great miracle, I took to the ram's horn. The ram's horn was always in my right hand, after that. It meant for me all the power and the strength of my father, of high places, of achievement, of being away from the fussy world of my mother and Euphemia and the other women in my life. The ram's horn, which I could gouge with and lever with, became in my hand my first implement for exerting myself on the environment around me. It extended my body into things which previously had imperilled and trapped me. It was my entry into independence of mind and will.

My father explained to my mother, when we eventually got home – after stopping a dozen times for the workmen to open farm gates, and after dropping them back in the dorp – that an old farmer had given it to me.

'So you saw a nice sheep, Jimmy-boy?' my mother said, trying to pull it out of my hand before bath time. 'Heavens above, Andy, but he's raw with sunburn. He looks as if he's feverish, Andrew – Andrew, how could you?'

'Well, it is pretty stinking up there, Sarah. And I had to fix that windmill on old Breda's farm.'

'You mean – you weren't – just at the office? But Andrew, that's miles away – no wonder he's so burnt. Oh my darling –'

My mother examined me from head to foot and now clutched me to herself. I was baked like an apple in its jacket.

'He is running a temperature,' she announced.

'Well, we'll camomile him, that'll take out the sting.'

Vrrm, vrrm, vrrm, I said. I was feeling sick, but determined not to show it. 'Baa, baa, blackbird,' I said.

'Now give me that filthy piece of horn,' said my mother.

But when all is said and done, I took it into the bath, and it, too, got the sting taken out of it.

Only months later, and from farmer Breda himself, when he came down to the club, did my mother discover I had been right to the top of a windmill with my father.

5

Euphemia came back from her holiday, I learned how to walk and talk – reluctantly, but it was only a matter of practice now. My mother took over the ordering at the golf club, because Mr Wolpe was fired for having his hand in the till. My father stayed away more, because he was putting up Mr Pennington-Worthy's windmills on even remoter farms. All this passed naturally without any stopping; we kept on living it through. We all knew our world would be disturbed; we didn't know how, we didn't know when. But the disturbance came in slow stages from outside, and we were powerless to resist it.

The first incident was a trivial one. Our Coloured postman came to the house as usual from Miss Bester's post office. He said hello to me, as I was playing in the geraniums, and I walked alongside him. Normally he put the letter from my grandmother with the British stamps on it in the box at the gate, so his coming in meant he had a parcel. He rang the doorbell for Euphemia, although the door was wide open. He pulled a large parcel out of his leather bag that Euphemia was to sign for. Euphemia couldn't sign, so she would put her cross and he witnessed it.

Euphemia came down the stairs with her feather duster, and said she wouldn't sign for it, as the parcel was for Mrs Pennington-Worthy and not for Mrs Esslin. This she could make out herself, because the name was much longer. The postman explained to her, but she wouldn't sign. Normally when the postman brought a parcel, she offered him a lime juice, but she wouldn't give him a lime juice this time. He must get it up at the big house from Mrs Pennington-Worthy herself.

No, he said, Euphemia must take the parcel up to the big house and he'd have his lime juice here. He was under strict instructions from Miss Bester not to go nearer the Silver estate.

Because last time he had gone up to the Pennington-Worthys with a parcel and to get his lime juice, Mrs Pennington-Worthy had tried to shoot him dead. Although he was wearing his uniform with the shiny buttons and his white helmet was fully visible from where the hedge turns halfway down the avenue, she thought he was a trespasser. In the end Euphemia said she would sign for the parcel and take it up the drive, because Mrs Pennington-Worthy wouldn't shoot a nanny with a red doek on.

And so, quite unexpectedly, the morning routine was interrupted by being inspanned in the old pram with the parcel and Euphemia fixing her doek high on her head like a cone. We set off on our errand, all to do Mrs Pennington-Worthy a favour, although I had never been up the Pennington-Worthy drive before and I'm sure Euphemia hadn't, either.

The drive had well-shaped quince hedges that, for an adult, stopped at eye level, and the gravel was swept and raked every day by two men, early in the morning, so that all the tyre tracks were erased. To avoid spoiling the gravel, Euphemia wheeled me along the grass verge which was quite broad and well mowed. Behind the hedge were orchards with some workmen in them, but a long distance away; you could just hear them pruning. We passed their shed which was like a garage, but it was made of stone painted white. Behind that were stables for the horses, but none of them were there because the snake had been. Then we came to the bend. Euphemia's doek could be seen from the main house itself.

We wheeled along quietly, and I had my fingers tight on the strings of Mrs Pennington-Worthy's parcel. It was from Britain; I could tell by the stamps. But there were many more of them than on a letter. It was probably a present for one of Mrs Pennington-Worthy's grandchildren from her mother in England.

Then Euphemia stopped and told me that it was from right there that Mrs Pennington-Worthy had shot at the postman, even though he had his helmet on, and now she changed her mind. So we went home along the grass, making no sound. Euphemia was sweating, and so was I.

When my mother came home in the afternoon, she said that Euphemia shouldn't have accepted the parcel in the first place;

it was nothing to do with her and it must go straight back to Miss Bester, whose job it was to get it to Mrs Pennington-Worthy. My mother said she thought the postman was just getting lazy, letting it off at our house so that he didn't have to go so far in that heat, and Euphemia was never to make her cross for a parcel that wasn't for Mr Esslin, or herself, or Master Jimmy. Euphemia didn't explain a thing about how the postman nearly got a bullet in his white helmet just past the stables, or any of the other circumstances; she was afraid to tell that we, too, had been on the Silver estate. It was a compact between Euphemia and me. All right, said my mother, big master would have to take it up to the house in the car in the evening. That was to be the end of that.

But then my father wasn't coming home that evening because he was far away, so what could be done with the parcel? It would have been much easier if he just took it up the next evening, but what if Mrs Pennington-Worthy needed it, and it had taken long enough with the shipping to get here. So my mother phoned Mrs Pennington-Worthy's Saint Helena maid and explained that a medium-sized parcel had been delivered to her in error and she couldn't get away; wouldn't she send one of the orange-pickers to come and fetch it.

We waited for the orange-picker to come on his bicycle. My mother went to the gate and handed the parcel over to him. In exchange he gave her a note, but he needed some string to tie the parcel to the carrier on the back. I went and got some with the scissors, and we secured it with him, and then he rode safely with the parcel up the drive. Now she's going to shoot him, I thought, because he was wearing a very dowdy cap. But she didn't shoot him, because he was not a trespasser if he worked for her and for Mr Pennington-Worthy.

The note was from Mrs Pennington-Worthy, and my mother read it aloud to me:

My dear Sarah,

You know perfectly well from the noticeboards adequately displayed around the estate that under no circumstances will Mr Pennington-Worthy tolerate trespassing. This has always been our policy. I'll thank you to convey this information to any nannies in your employment. As tenants Mr Pennington-W has informed you that your rental is kept at a bare minimum in order that you may cut down on trespassing from your end. I think in these days it would be safer for you to employ a white nanny. The fence of Peter's Lodge could do with a coat of paint.

Yours faithfully,

Alice Pennington-Worthy.

This letter upset my mother. She would do anything in the world not to offend Mrs Pennington-Worthy, whose brother was Lord Catchmere, who was in the British Parliament, which was bigger than our Parliament. The parcel was, in fact, from Lord Catchmere's wife, who was Lady Catchmere, not Mrs Catchmere. My mother was just Mrs Esslin.

'Jimmy,' said my mother, looking me straight in the face, 'what does this letter mean? Does it mean that Euphemia and you have been spotted on the estate?'

'No, mummy,' I said, quite truthfully.

'Doesn't it mean that you and Euphemia have been more than just strolling on the side of the road?'

'No, mummy,' I repeated.

'Well then, what does it mean?'

'It doesn't mean anything,' I said.

'Yes it does,' she said. 'It means that Mrs Pennington-Worthy must have stopped and seen you playing with Euphemia, and she thinks Euphemia is unsuitable for you. What were you two up to, Jimmy?'

'I was digging for moles on the lawn, mummy, with my horn,' I said.

'And did you have your trousers on?'

'Yes, mummy.'

'And your hat?'

'Yes, mummy.'

'And did she say anything to you when she looked over? Was Euphemia with you?'

'Euphemia was in her smart doek. She was helping me catch the mole.'

'Then why didn't she give the parcel to Mrs Pennington-Worthy there and then, instead of all this trouble?'

I said: 'Because Mrs Penny just looked over the fence and told her to keep it.'

'Well, I know she's a bit eccentric. But don't you be offhand with her, you hear? She's got two sons in this war and Lord Catchmere was invalided out in the last, so she knows all about it. Next time she comes, you say, Good morning, Mrs Penny, and behave like a gentleman. Do you understand, Jimmy?'

'Yes,' I said.

'But why was Euphemia wearing the red doek to play on the lawn?' she said.

'Because she likes it in the sun, mummy,' I said.

The affair of the parcel was not over yet. That weekend my father burnt the old coat off the picket fence with a blowtorch and scraped it, and I helped him paint it shiny white. My mother made rice pudding, and we had supper outside as it was so hot, and we could smell the paint.

Then it was Christmas, 1939, and Freddie the postman always had a big bag to lug around. This year it wasn't so bad for him, because he refused to carry all the parcels they got up to the Pennington-Worthys – Miss Bester cancelled their delivery service and gave them a private bag at the post office. We were now the last house on the beat, and the parcels I had were quite light. For every one I received, Freddie got a lime juice from Euphemia. The stamps were from everywhere: Jamaica, and from London, all with King George on them, and also some from South Africa from my father's side, but I knew those ones.

For Christmas my father cut a branch off the pine tree at the back, and set it in wet sand so that it wouldn't wilt. Euphemia and I found pine cones, which my mother and I painted white for snow with the paint left from the fence, and sprinkled with glitter, and tied them on with red bows. We had some tin candleholders that held twisted candles in red and white and orange, and the whole tree got strings of tinsel. My mother found a wooden angel with a trumpet that went on top. Behind the tree on strings above the magazine photos on the mantelpiece we hung all the Christmas cards that came with more stamps from everywhere. They went in front of the portrait of granny and the one of my mother and father and me on the golf course when it was full of white flowers, so many that you couldn't see the end of them.

The night before Christmas was Euphemia and Meshack's time. Euphemia came dressed again, like the time she went to Cape Town, and so did Meshack with his school cap. He was back for the holidays. They knelt down before the tree, and we knelt behind them, and we sang a hymn, 'Abide with Me', but I didn't know the words for that. Then my mother passed them their presents, and Phemie got the biggest one of them all – a new cooking-pot with handles – and Meshack got a scout's knife for cutting bait, but my father said he should have received a book. Then I had to open my presents, and I didn't want to disturb the tree which was blazing with all the candles on and the lights out, and wax coming off the candle-holders and the angel on the top of the tree with her long hair, blowing her trumpet. It was a clear sound, and she was saying, 'Come, Jimmy, to see what you have.'

I had a set of rails for my train so that it would go, and a signal station, and a colouring book, and a packet of crayons, and a new hat with a brim like Meshack's and – but it was parked outside – a tricycle with a brown saddle and big rubber wheels. It was parked outside because Father Christmas couldn't get it down the chimney. And we all sat on the carpet amidst so much wrapping paper, and admired the tricycle. That was the last time we had a family Christmas together like that, because my father went to the war and after that Euphemia went, also.

The ram's horn that had been my instrument became buried in a drawer, superseded in its function of extending my world by the tricycle. Inside the house I was confined to the carpeting, which stretched from the living-room through the hall in a square, and then in a strip down the corridor to each room in turn. I made a point of visiting the bathroom on the right, and the toilet, stopping at the verge, and crossing against the traffic to the verge of my bedroom and my parents' bedroom at the end. The stairs were carpeted, but obviously there was no riding there – the stairs meant dismounting and hauling it up by the front wheel, round the corner and up to the parking patch outside the spare room and my father's study door. Peter's Lodge was awkwardly built, but there was at least that over-night space that wasn't used and where the tricycle was under no one's feet. I slept soundly at night, thinking of my tricycle in a warm corner upstairs.

Outside the house was more difficult. There were the red tiles of the veranda running into the mauve bougainvillaea. Then steps. Then lawn. The lawn I found heavy going, and my knees would ache from standing on the pedals and falling over the handlebars when the front wheel stuck. I was allowed only where they could see me from the house. My progress on the tricycle was tied to one or another of the adults as if by invisible wires. If I went too far down the lawn towards the milk-bushes and the holding power weakened, sure enough my mother's voice would come floating out of the kitchen, 'Come back, Jimmy, it's too wild down there.' If I went round to where Euphemia was hanging the laundry, and then cautiously made for the back gate, stopping a lot casually to examine the wood-pile, sure enough, as I got to the groove where the gates opened, Euphemia would call, 'Jimmy-boy, you get run over.' If my father was home and standing on the deck balcony, so that I could bask in the magnetic field of his attention, and I went down to the letter box at the front gate, and then opened it to see if Freddie had come without my noticing, he, too, would go, 'All right, that's far enough, Jimmy. Better start coming back.' There's no counting the hours of trike-watching they put in for me.

But one afternoon, when my mother was alone with me and I could hear the phone ringing inside and her answering, the power of their magnetism snapped for me. I was off, through the back gates and into the public road, pedalling standing up, as energetically as I could go. I knew, as I made the decision, this was disobedience. It was a good track; I liked it. At least I went the safe way, in the opposite direction to the Pennington-Worthys.

My mother must have almost instantly felt I had defected, such being the power of her special sense of knowing. But the phone-call was from Mrs Van, who always took her time when it came to a discussion. 'Hello – oh Stinnie, it's you,' my mother would say, and the household came to a standstill for half an hour. This gave me a chance to get to the bend and, after that, take the downhill that went into the gully of stones where, after an experience of exhilaration and ferocious speed, I shot into the sand.

Then everything happened too quickly – I was disentangling the tricycle from my sleeve; a huge silver front of a lorry bounced towards me; brakes made a heavy stopping noise. The dripping, muddy bumper came to rest just above my head, and I knew it wouldn't advance any further. All the orange-pickers who worked on the Silver estate climbed off the back, and the driver jumped down right beside me and was shouting at me. To make it worse, my mother was running towards us.

The rewards of disobedience made a considerable impression on me. Instead of being comforted – because I had had a complicated fall and my shoulder was screaming in its socket, and the tricycle was bent completely round – I was abused by everyone present. Even my gentle, good-mannered mother was transformed. She quickly thanked the driver for stopping, then scolded me in a hard, cold voice. She dragged me and the tricycle towards Peter's Lodge. I had no conception of how strong she was. She was dragging me by the elbow with one hand and the tricycle by its handlebars with the other, and yanking us both forward up the hill. The workmen hooted and drove past us, shouting and waving, and mother was livid with them and gave me a backhander on the face, and resumed dragging me, and dragged the tricycle a bit. 'Get up,' she insisted, 'get up!' she said, prodding me from behind, and pulling the tricycle. 'Walk, you little swine!'

When we got to the garage gate which I had opened, she made me stand back, and she went through with the tricycle. 'Now,' she said, 'come in and close it. And don't you ever open it again!'

I closed it to keep the traffic out.

'Now, James,' she said, 'follow me.'

She led me through the front door, across the hall and up the stairs. At the top I thought she was going to park the tricycle, but she opened my father's study door and strode through the area I wasn't supposed to be in. I followed her, and she pushed open the door onto the balcony. She threw the tricycle outside and gestured for me to follow it. I turned round and looked at her, shaking inside to hold her dress and bury my head in her skirt and to ask her to stop.

'There, James,' she said, 'now, if you want to ride around, do it somewhere where you can't get out.'

And she closed the glass door and locked it with me and the tricycle outside. Then she unlocked and came out and locked the wooden door that led to the outside stairs and went back into my father's study and locked herself in.

I knew she was watching me, so I made no complaint. I pulled the tricycle upright and, although I was shaking from head to foot, got my leg over the saddle, my foot on the pedal and my other on the ground to give it a push. Any move I now made would take me from my mother, who stood there behind the glass. I gave a small shove, and put my weight on the handlebars, even though my one shoulder felt raw and blown up. All around me was the bright, white wall with railings, and ample room for tricycling. I thought, just to spite her, I should ride in a happy circle, as if nothing had gone wrong, showing no resentment of my new confinement. But when I peeked, she had gone.

I could hear her voice very distantly, 'Oh Stinnie, I am sorry – no, do carry on, it's nothing – you know.'

I rode very slowly to the opposite wall, and came to a halt. There I sat on my tricycle, experiencing very bitter desolation. From that afternoon onwards, I knew that everything I did or thought would have a different meaning; everything in my life had changed. I was a kind of criminal, reduced to being a true child in the hands of their incredible strength, a prisoner confined to playing on the balcony, which was hot and where the bitumen sheets buckled and meant that I fell over with the tricycle.

My mother finished her telephone conversation, but she didn't come up and release me.

In the evening my father stopped the car outside the gate and came out to open it. He didn't see me as he drove in and closed the gate, and parked in his garage and went into the house.

I thought he would come and release me, but he didn't. I banged on the glass door of his study, but there was no result.

Presently he came up with my mother and turned the light on. Mother had been crying, and he was very stiff. He opened the door. I was huddled in the corner, out of the light. I thought he was going to rush at me and hit me.

He crouched in front of me. 'Jimmy,' he said, 'that was a terrible thing to do. You do realise you could have been killed?'

I didn't say anything because I had forgotten how to talk.

'Jimmy,' he said, 'do you hear me?'

I looked at his trousers where his knees were underneath.

'He can hear you,' said my mother. 'And I hope he's ashamed of himself.'

'All right, Sarah,' said my father, 'I'll handle this.'

'We could do with a man about the house sometimes,' said my mother. 'He's too much for me, much too much.'

'All right,' said my father, not stooping forward, 'I said I'd do it.'

Mother sat down in my father's chair and blew her nose.

'Come on, Jimmy,' said my father, 'behave like a soldier. Pick up your tricycle.'

I obeyed him without a thought of rebellion. I righted the poor machine and wheeled it towards the glass door. He picked it up by the handlebars, took it across his study and parked it at the top of the stairs.

'Yes, come in now,' said my mother.

I stepped over the lintel and realised I shouldn't approach her.

'All right now,' said my father, 'it's all over.' And as I got to him at the study door he put his hand on the back of my head gently, and pointed me down the stairs.

Down I went on my own in the semi-dark and reached my room where a bit of light was shining from the corridor. I took off my shoes and stood on the floor, and started to unbutton my top. Then, because they didn't follow me, I undid my shorts and stood. I couldn't see where my pyjamas were and I climbed up on the bed, but they weren't there. So I lay on the bed and pulled the sheet and blankets over me. I lay like that for a long time before they came down and turned the bed-side light on.

Without saying anything, my mother reached for the pyjamas that were on the shelf and stood me up and took off my underpants, and put on the soft pyjama top and buttoned it. Then she put me down on the potty, and pulled on the pyjama pants and tied the knot in front. As she always did, she stroked my hair back and said, 'Now say your prayers, there's a good boy.'

And I knelt alongside her, and father stood in the doorway, not joining in until 'Amen'.

'God bless mummy and God bless daddy, and God bless this house, and Phemie and Meshack and Mrs Van and Mr Wolpe at the club.'

'No, not Mr Wolpe,' said my mother.

'Not Mr Wolpe,' I said, 'amen.'

'Amen.'

Then I hopped into bed, and my mother kissed me and tucked the blankets in, and my father kissed me and turned out the light, and I went to sleep.

A few days after that scene, my father got into his soldier's uniform. He called me upstairs. I thought we were going tricycling in the road, but instead of that he invited me into his study, and I thought that it was very serious. 'Come in, soldier,' he said, and I went and stood in the middle. It was strange that he called me a soldier, when he was the soldier of the family. His hair was cut short and his khaki trousers were very well pressed with knife edges.

'Jimmy, I'm going to the war now,' he said, 'and I want to show you where.'

He took from his oak desk a very large map of Africa with Europe above it, and laid it out on the floor. He knelt beneath it, and I came alongside, staring at it with my chin in my hands. Africa looked like my tricycle saddle with blue around it. A lot of lines cut it up, running this way and that, and some more detailed lines containing colours – big pieces of red, and pink, and red-and-white stripes.

'Those are all the British lands,' said my father. 'In any one of them I'll be safe; look, Kenya, and the Gold Coast, and Basotholand, but that's not far away at all.'

Then there was green for the Germans, but that was only a little, and purple for the Portuguese, and orange for the French and brown for the Italians. And there were some independent ones with no colour at all, or my father checked them on the colour key; there were Spanish, also. And we were down at the very bottom – a red triangle called the Union of South Africa. All the pieces of the jigsaw fitted together perfectly, just blue where there was a perfect lake in the middle, and you could see the rivers running from it with tiny tufts to show that they had reeds.

My father showed me that we were at the bottom because we were very far south – Silver Town was almost the very last settlement on the whole continent, even further south than Cape Town and near Cape Agulhas, where the ships had to turn the corner and change their courses. Even then I felt how perilously Silver Town was situated, for it seemed to me that the whole weight of Africa was resting on us and it was only because of the mountains that we could hold it up. But father said that was not a factor; all weight pointed inside the earth, downstairs, like the shaft of the windmill, not just down a piece of paper where it was spread out flat for airway pilots to see at a glance. Yet Silver Town seemed very insecure to me.

My father put a cross with his pencil to show where we were, because Silver Town was too small to have its name on. There was only the Cape of Good Hope, and the next place was Port Elizabeth. Then he put a cross where he was going, which I thought would be near PE, but he leaned right over and pulled the map round and put the cross on Italian Somaliland, which was big enough to have its name spelt out. He said it was too far away to come home every weekend.

Now, it may be a trivial thing, but at that time I was also learning to conjugate by singing a song that went, 'I scream, you scream, he, she or it screams for ice-cream.' I thought if I started singing it, since he was not going to come back that weekend, it would lead us to getting an ice-cream before he went. So I began humming in a voice laden with innuendo, 'I scream, you scream, we all scream –'

But my father was not in a susceptible mood. He got his ruler to work out the distance between the two crosses. He said it would only be approximate because he didn't have the cross for Italian Somaliland correctly. And even the cross for Silver Town was wrong, which puzzled me; it was right here and we who lived in it should know where it was best of all. It was where the Pennington-Worthys were, and the harbour, and Miss Kettley's school, and the gum-trees, and the golf club right on the dunes that you couldn't miss. But my father said he was going to leave all that behind, and I had a very empty feeling about how cut down Silver Town would be without my father.

'Is Mr Penny going to the war?' I asked.

'No, he's much too old,' said my father.

'And me – can I go to the war?' I asked.

'No, not you, Jimmy – you're much too young.'

'And Meshack? What about Meshack?' I asked.

'Not Meshack,' he said, 'he's too dark in colour. They're only taking whites between certain ages, and some Coloureds.'

'Then why doesn't mummy go? She can look after me at the war.'

'No no,' said my father, 'mummy has to look after you here at home. They are taking some women, but they're women without little boys like you.'

'Is Mrs Van's husband going, because he's got three children to look after?'

'No, he's not going, because he's a neutral. He doesn't agree with the war, though many Afrikaners do,' said my father.

My logic was relentless. 'And Phemie?' I said. 'What about Phemie?'

'Oh Phemie,' said my father, 'well, I don't think Phemie would make a very good fighter, do you?'

I thought Phemie could have done quite well, but I said, 'No, I suppose not.'

Then my father finished measuring the distance between the crosses and did some calculations on his slide-rule, and told me what the results were.

I tried again, very timidly, with 'I scream, you scream –'

This time it worked, and my father fetched the long stock-whip which was useful for so many things, and tied it to the column under the handlebars of my tricycle. We set off down the road with his pulling me on the rough patches. We came to the stony bit where I had my accident. He shook his head a lot, and kneeled down beside me with the shiny handlebar with its dent not far from his hand, and he said very solemnly, 'Now look, Jimmy, you must really never do that again. It's not fair on mummy. With me away you have to look after mummy and help her, and not give her trouble. Do you understand me, soldier?' he said.

'Yes,' I said.

'Good,' he said. He reached for the handlebars and, where it was dented, he massaged it as if his hand would make the metal better. 'Mummy's going to need you a lot, so you will look after her?'

'Yes, I promise,' I said.

'Good,' he said. 'Shake on it.' And we shook hands.

Then he pulled me uphill, and sometimes he pulled so well that my feet spun round on the pedals or the whole front would lift up and I didn't have to pedal at all.

We got to where the main street begins and my father stopped for a breather. It was so hot, he said, he could do with an ice-cream, too. It was good to be there because I hadn't been for a while, and you could see very well over Silver Town's coast from the rocks.

We went right up the middle of the road as if we were very important. Mrs Feverall's tearoom café was the only place for ice-cream, and we parked outside next to Brutus who was lying off the steps, scratching himself. We didn't go into the hotel but along the veranda to the tearoom, and Mrs Feverall served us herself with a cone of chocolate for me and a white one for my father, and he wanted to pay her.

No fear, she said, she wasn't going to charge a man in uniform. And Mr Feverall came out through the beaded curtain and shook hands with my father. No charge, he said. And they laughed about going to this war.

'Keep them off the shipping routes,' said Mr Feverall.

All right, said my father, and they came out onto the veranda to wave to us. We weren't going anywhere really, except to the post office to post a letter to my grandmother to say thank you for the Christmas presents, but Mr and Mrs Feverall waved again as we came back past. We stopped once more, because it was difficult to eat the ice-cream with the handlebars wobbling about, and Mrs Feverall said, 'Just you show 'em Andy, that's our boy.'

'Thank you for the ice-cream,' said my father. 'And for Jimmy's, too.'

When we came back to the rock at the end of the street to finish our ice-creams, the most wonderful thing happened. For ever more I associated it with my father. A couple of cranes was picking up food in the dry grass, right close to us. My father was so pleased and crouched down, and put me on his knee, and studied them. They were taller than I was, with long grey necks, and completely unafraid of us. My father helped me with the cone that was going soggy. The one crane lifted its head and looked at us out of the side of its face.

Then they took off. They needed so much space to get up a run that their wings came directly over us, so close you could reach up and touch them. Those huge grey wings unfolded and beat into the air. Their heavy legs swung back and tucked underneath, and they just stroked the warm air and flew over our heads. That supple, grey, feathery flight meant my father to me.

Within days he was gone. Because my mother didn't drive, Mr van der Westhuizen offered to come with us to the station in the dorp and to bring the car back with us; he wasn't in favour of the war, but he would do that for us personally. We fetched him on the road outside his house. Mrs Van and her mother and the three girls came out. He had a big bottle of beer for my father to drink on the journey. It was wrapped in a brown paper bag so that no one could tell. My father drove off up the hill and we all waved until we couldn't see them anymore. Miss Bester was outside the post office, but she cut us dead; she didn't approve of Mr van der Westhuizen helping us.

It was a long drive, so hot that it seemed on the worst bits of the pass the car itself was sweating. It was a drive I wish we'd never made. Although I didn't realise it at the time, Italian Somaliland was indeed a long way away. In all those years I was to grow in the absence of my father, waiting for him. I wish I had been able to stop the clock as we reached the top of the pass, that I'd gone into hibernation and sat out all the years to come, resuming life on my father's return.

What affected me on the drive was the formality of all the adults. My mother would brush her hair back and look at my father, and say nothing. He would take his hand off the wheel and straighten his very smart beret in the mirror. Mr van der Westhuizen would clear his throat and look past me. Their dispiritedness touched me like a cold hand.

The train was very late and we waited on the platform with some other men from all over the district who were in their uniforms, huddled in the sun at the one end. The front coach was reserved for them. There had been an incident of a troop-carrying train being blown up; I suppose that is why they were protecting themselves. Some Coloureds with their families all dressed up were at the other end, where they were also catching the train to go to the war.

When the train came chuffing in, it had bits of ribbon on it. The men in front were already crammed in tight and riding on the part in between the coaches, so we had to push my father to squeeze him in, and somebody gave him another bottle of beer, so he had more than enough to last him. My mother gave him a lot of kisses and Mr van der Westhuizen helped with his suitcase – the same blue suitcase – and we played last touch, last touch, with my mother holding me up.

'Thank you, Van,' said my father. 'You just take the car if there's any trouble. Sarah will know what to do.'

'Don't worry about a thing,' said Mr van der Westhuizen. 'Send us a postcard when you get to Cairo.'

'All of the north's crawling with Germans,' said my father.

Then my mother held me up for him to kiss me and her for the last time, and our heads squashed together, and my mother said, 'Just you see you come back in one piece.'

And my father said, 'Don't worry, I'll show them.'

Then the train pulled out and some people cheered, but most of the soldiers were asleep from the long journey. Mr van der Westhuizen drove us down to Silver Town and unplugged all the wires in the car so that the battery wouldn't go flat while my father was away.

6

It was arranged that while my father was gone, my grandmother would come out from Great Britain to keep my mother and me company. In the end she couldn't, because of the Battle of Britain. But she did manage to arrange for my mother's sister to travel from Jamaica; it would be good to reunite at least some of the family. This was Aunt Rosemary, who sent me the colouring book.

When eventually Aunt Rosemary pitched up, we didn't have to get Mr van der Westhuizen to plug in the car, because she insisted on arriving in style by taxi. I was pleased she was with us, as it had been a long time with my mother, and Euphemia was sulking. When Aunt Rosemary unpacked her grand clothes she gave a bundle of laundry to Euphemia, and she sulked some more.

'Well, Rosemary,' my mother said. They were walking arm in arm in the garden. 'All this way, missing shipping disasters. What an adventure. Oh, how lovely to see my little sister, safe and sound!'

'It was rather incident-packed up north, yes,' said Aunt Rosemary, giving my mother a kiss. They laughed a lot, and Aunt Rosemary lit a cigarette.

'Jimmy thinks you're terrific,' said my mother, 'I can tell.'

'Do you, Jimmy,' she turned around to me, 'do you really?' And she turned to my mother again, saying, 'Oh Sarah, you are so very lucky. We weren't married long enough to have one. Poor Bonzo, I miss him awfully, you know. If it hadn't been for that terrible, terrible death-bend, he'd be alive today. Poor Bonzo.'

'Oh frightful, Rosemary, but at least it was quickly over,' said my mother. 'Of course it must have been a terrible shock for you.'

'At least you've got Jimmy for some consolation,' said Aunt Rosemary.

'Never mind,' said my mother, patting her arm. 'You'll soon be right as rain.'

'It was all so sudden,' said Aunt Rosemary, putting her hand on her forehead and faltering.

'Yes, Euphemia, we'll have tea on the lawn,' said my mother.

'She's a lowering one; where on earth did you get such a mammy?' said Aunt Rosemary.

'Yes, but she's an able body,' said my mother, 'and very good indeed with Jimmy.'

'That may be so,' said Aunt Rosemary, 'but from henceforth when you're at work I shall look after Jimmy.' She picked me up, blowing out smoke. 'Oh, you are a handful,' she groaned, because she was very frail.

After tea, when Aunt Rosemary had produced all her photos of Bonzo and said the house was very tiny, and Euphemia was doing the washing-up, I asked Euphemia why Aunt Rosemary said the house was so small.

'Ow Jimmy,' said Phemie, 'because she's a very big lady.'

'She can't be, now that Bonzo's dead,' I said.

'Ow, but a lady like that is big wherever she goes,' said Phemie.

After that Aunt Rosemary brought out the present she had for us. We cleared the dining-room table of all my mother's sewing things and Aunt Rosemary put the present down. It was a very big tablecloth, white and silky in colour with bright embroidery over it, with fishes and pineapples and birds, which she had inherited from Bonzo. She wasn't very big, Aunt Rosemary, because she couldn't reach over the table to spread it. My mother had to pull it out to get it over the ends.

My mother exclaimed that it was more like a shawl, but Aunt Rosemary said, no, it was a tablecloth for special occasions, and we were to have it. She didn't mind if I spilled egg over it because Euphemia could always wash it. Euphemia picked me up to look at it, and we all said it was wonderful.

'What's that?' said Euphemia, pointing with her free arm to a shape.

'A yellow bird,' I said.

'Oh, that's just a parrot, we have lots of those,' said Aunt Rosemary.

'That's a fish,' I said, placing my foot on it.

'Clever boy,' said Aunt Rosemary, 'I can see we're going to get on so well.'

'Oh, it is lovely, so exotic,' said my mother. 'It's incredibly generous of you. Are you sure you want to part with it, Rosemary?'

'Well, it can stay here for now, can't it, and every time I see it out of the corner of my eye it will brighten my day and remind me of Bonzo,' she said.

'Yes, and I'll use the card table for my sewing, don't you worry,' said mother.

'And every time we all see it together, we'll have a party, won't we?' said Aunt Rosemary, lifting her gin and tonic.

'Cheers,' said my mother, who didn't really drink, but was having a gin and tonic for the occasion.

Aunt Rosemary was an intruder in our lives, but soon it seemed as if she and her brilliant tablecloth had been with us for ever.

Then the first postcards from overseas came from my father. For some months he had been at a basic training camp in South Africa, but the card didn't show a picture of that – only a protea like the ones that grew on Silver Town mountains. This one showed a really tropical scene of a lake. My mother read it to me many times, and Aunt Rosemary read it, and then I got it for my collection. My father had a very tiny handwriting, but he put at the bottom in capital letters, LOVE TO JIMMY-BOY.

Aunt Rosemary spent her mornings with me so that Euphemia would have more time for the housework. Aunt Rosemary had a good idea for what to do in the mornings, because she was a watercolour artist and could paint in all styles. She was fascinated with art, and that's why she had sent me the colouring book. She didn't have outlines to fill in; she made them herself, softly with a pencil. Silver Town was going to get its first distinguished artist at work.

The first morning wasn't such a success. We set off for the main street with me on the tricycle and Aunt Rosemary was very weak after Bonzo's death. She couldn't get me up the hill to a decent viewpoint, and we came home again. Aunt Rosemary had a shoulder bag and an easel to carry, so she couldn't pull a tricycle that well. I didn't feel like assisting, because I would rather have been with Euphemia.

'But he can pedal all the way to the tearoom café,' said my mother. 'Euphemia just gives him a shove in the sticky patches with her foot.'

'Euphemia may be an artist at that, but I have my type of art, which means equipment to lug,' said Aunt Rosemary.

'Then stick to painting the wooden bridge for a week or so, until he gets used to you,' said my mother.

'Oh, very well,' said Aunt Rosemary, lighting a cigarette and blowing the blue smoke out of her nostrils.

'He gets that from Andy,' said my mother. 'Won't do a thing he doesn't want to do.'

'Well, when I eventually meet your Andy, I'll show him a thing or two. It doesn't pay to be obstinate.'

'Oh, but he's a good man, even if he doesn't measure up to your Bonzo.'

'Absence makes the heart grow fonder,' said Aunt Rosemary. 'Isn't that what they always say, Sarah?'

'Yes, sister,' said my mother. 'But at least Andy is still alive and I do love him, you know.'

In this way the days went by; Bonzo about to come back from the dead as the ideal gentleman, my father always about to send another card that bore no clear indication of where he was, Euphemia doing more and more housework and never getting to the nannies' meetings, myself wrapped in contemplation over the new balance of power.

Aunt Rosemary and I spent the mornings at the wooden bridge, which she painted from a number of angles. I got quite used to carrying her paintbox and helping her adjust her lightweight collapsible easel and her canvas stool. She would put out her drawing paper with pins and sketch her outline and mix the paints with a few drops of water on her fingers, and wipe them on her rag, and select one of her brushes. The next thing was her cigarette lighter and she set to work with smoke pouring out from under her straw hat. I wasn't to go on the bridge then, because she couldn't paint me moving about so much. Once she was smoking, any area out of the periphery of her vision was mine.

Another postcard came with a palm tree on it and LOVE TO JIMMY-BOY. When my mother finished her letter I wrote love back. This was in red crayon and it didn't look the way he wrote.

Aunt Rosemary said, then, that I was getting very impatient playing when she was working, why didn't we get the car roadworthy so that it would be a bit more exciting for me. She knew perfectly well how to drive.

'But wouldn't that remind you of poor Bonzo's end too much?' said my mother.

'Oh, not a bit,' said Aunt Rosemary, 'a touch of fresh air would put roses in our cheeks. Oh, be a sport, Sarah – I'll pay for the petrol and the grease, and keep the tyres pumped.'

'But our roads are full of death-bends. What if you and the boy should have an accident?'

'Oh Sarah, we'll only tootle. You always were the cautious one. He gets his lack of adventurousness from you, you know.'

'Oh Rosemary,' said my mother. 'He's all right; you know it's you who's getting restless. Don't use my little son as an excuse.'

'There is very little I haven't painted around this side, my dear. I'd give anything for a bit of maritime scenery.'

'Yes, well, we'll fix you up with that in due course,' said my mother.

But Aunt Rosemary was very obstinate. She must have got it from Bonzo. Presently Mr van der Westhuizen came and plugged in my father's car, and Aunt Rosemary filled it up at Marfak Lubrication, and everyone in Silver Town came out to see us drive by. Aunt Rosemary had her easel sticking through the window and a long scarf that blew out of the side, and she used the hooter to disturb Brutus.

This is when I began to take to Aunt Rosemary. She had a passion for finding exotic corners of Silver Town. We went down the Oudeskip road to the harbour. There were lots of fishing boats, and she set herself up right in the middle of the quay and painted exactly what was in front of her. Mr Olivier, who was in charge of the harbour gates and had to see that nothing went wrong, came out with his hands covered in bait and, when the easel blew down, splotched it all over her drawing paper. He helped her to a more sheltered place. Aunt Rosemary worked with a lot of inspiration there, doing deep breathing whenever she'd finished a sheet.

'Come on, Jimmy,' she said, 'don't be wet. In, in, in . . . and expel, expel. In, in, in . . . and out it comes. Good boy. Make a man of you.'

Behind her floppy straw hat I had more than enough space to explore. On the concrete were salty puddles, dried out with crystals forming on the sides, and bits of fish that, if I threw them right into the air, a bird would swoop down and catch in mid-flight.

Once Aunt Rosemary agreed that my mother could send one of her watercolours to my father. It had to be a miniature one, because of the postage during the war and there wasn't much room in his tent. We chose the small one with the quay and the red and green fishing boat with the eye on its prow. It was called ST 163. That would make him homesick, all right. And it was a very long time before a card came back from him, saying he recognised it exactly and how talented Aunt Rosemary was.

One morning Aunt Rosemary decided to set off with me in tow for the side that was called Long Beach. We parked on the edge of the road, and had to go right down a big dune before getting to the sea itself. That was where the line fishermen went, and you had to keep away from them because they liked to concentrate. There were two white men with very strong rods out on the rocks. Aunt Rosemary was going to paint them.

We set up her camp quite near the rocks, where these two men were fishing. Aunt Rosemary's folding stool went too deep in the sand, so we had to move a bit back where it was firmer. Then she put her hat on, and the smoke came out and she was at work. We were really in the middle of nowhere; all there was to paint was the thin line of rocks with the swell breaking and the two upright figures. I knew we were disturbing them, because one of the fishermen was putting down his rod and coming to shoo us away.

'Go and play, Jimmy,' said Aunt Rosemary, and I pulled my hat round my ears and played with a mussel shell.

The fisherman was coming towards us, and Aunt Rosemary bent down to do a lot of work, her scarf hanging right across her shoulders. I played with my shell busily.

He was coming up to us. He stopped right in front of Aunt Rosemary's easel so that she couldn't see past.

'Morning,' he said. 'Nice day.'

'Isn't it absolutely gorgeous,' said Aunt Rosemary. 'Manage to catch anything?'

'Only some harders,' he said. He spoke exactly the kind of English Aunt Rosemary spoke.

'They must be a local kind of fish,' said Aunt Rosemary.

'Very good fried,' said the fisherman. He was old, about Aunt Rosemary's age, but not as old as the other man who stayed on the rocks.

'Well, I hope you bring in a lot more, then,' said Aunt Rosemary.

'As a matter of fact, we wondered if you didn't have an old blade in your kit. Our little knife got carried off.'

'Why, of course,' said Aunt Rosemary. 'I use this penknife to sharpen my pencil.' She rootled in her paintbox and eventually found it, and lent it to him. 'You won't be long now, will you? I may have to use it myself.'

'You an artist?' he said, looking ever so pleased with himself.

'Only pencil, and watercolour,' said Aunt Rosemary. 'But it calls for such quick work.'

'Shan't be long,' he said, hopping off in his boots.

'What a nice man,' Aunt Rosemary said to me. 'Fancy, he lost his knife. Well, he didn't lose his manners, did he, Jimmy?'

I went on polishing my shell.

'You know, Jimmy-boy,' she said, 'most of the men who come to Silver Town are so uncouth, it really is a pleasure to meet a well-mannered one.'

She lit another cigarette and drew a few clusters of rock with her pencil, and filled in some wavy lines for the sea. She said you had to be quick with a wave or it would move away; she always caught it.

The fisherman came back with her knife.

'Oh I say, can I see?' he said, stepping alongside her. 'Won't lose your stride?'

But Aunt Rosemary was shy and put her hand over the paper. 'Not until I'm finished,' she said. 'Then, if it turns out all right, I'll let you have just one peep. Watercolours can go terribly wrong if you're interrupted.'

'I say, I'm sorry. Got a frightful bird's-nest on my brother's line, and you came to the rescue. Awfully good of you,' he said.

'Anything to help a fellow mortal in distress,' said Aunt Rosemary.

'Actually, we're not doing too well today. Thought of going round to the golf club side.'

'Oh no,' said Aunt Rosemary, 'please don't. Then I shall have nothing to paint, and the light couldn't be better.'

The fisherman shielded his eyes. 'Yes, it is a fine light,' he said.

'That's what I like about Africa. Everything's so crystal clear.'

'I say, you're not painting us, are you?'

'I hope that doesn't offend you. But you do look so splendid out there.'

'I say, I don't think we've been introduced,' he said. 'Roy Westerley's the name.'

'And I'm Rosemary Paul. Let's pretend we were introduced all along, shall we?'

'Oh yes,' he said. 'Well, I better get back to a spot of fishing. Don't want to distract our lady artist, do we?'

'Yes, off you go,' said Aunt Rosemary, watching him clump along.

She lit another cigarette and was back at work, quickly before the light changed.

I thought it was time to help myself to my bottle of juice, but Aunt Rosemary was very absorbed and pushed the bottle aside with her foot and said, 'Let's wait till they come, Jimmy, and we can have a party.'

I couldn't work out how she knew they would come again. Yet she was right, since, by the time she had finished the last strokes of her very fine watercolour, the two fishermen had waved and waved to us, and she had waved back. They were coming with all their tackle.

'Oh, bet you must be thirsty,' said Aunt Rosemary, uncorking her bottle, and you could see how thirsty they were.

Roy Westerley introduced his brother, Tom. Tom had a beard and was a bit bald, which made him the older brother.

'Ah, I could do with a spot of that,' said Tom.

'Well, Jimmy wouldn't mind if you share his, would you, Jimmy?' she said, passing Tom my bottle.

'Let's have a little preview,' said Roy.

'All in good time, my man, don't be so forward,' said Aunt Rosemary.

Tom drank my bottle down to half way and gave it back to Aunt Rosemary and smacked his lips.

'Rosemary Paul,' said Roy. 'Well, it isn't always we have the chance to encounter a watercolourist in these uncivilised parts. Silver Town's not what one might call Bohemia.'

'Westerleys of the Elgin Apple Farms,' said Tom.

'Oh, I thought you must be. I've only been here a few months, but everyone knows of the Elgin Westerleys,' said Aunt Rosemary.

'It's so difficult for us to get away, but I assure you this is not our usual catch,' said Roy, holding up a string of harders, a bit bigger than sardines.

'Usually we get yellowtail and tunny, but they're not running at the moment,' said Tom.

'How lovely,' said Aunt Rosemary. 'And how big are they?'

''Bout this size,' said Tom.

'No, this size – this size,' Roy held his hands out wider.

'Well, you'll find my little watercolour awfully small, then. But I'm better as a miniaturist,' said Aunt Rosemary. She picked the cover off her page, and showed it to them.

'Oh awfully good,' said Roy.

'Yes, very accomplished,' said Tom. 'I like the way you've caught – the movement, you follow me?'

'And the light,' said Roy. 'Course, that's the important thing. I say, can we walk you back to our car? We left it on the road.'

'That would be lovely,' said Aunt Rosemary, and we decamped.

'That your child?' asked Roy.

'My sister's,' said Aunt Rosemary. 'She lives in Silver Town. I'm merely a visitor.'

'Where d'you come from, then?' said Tom.

And Aunt Rosemary said, in her husky voice, 'Jamaica.'

'Oh, Jamaica,' said Roy. 'Suppose you know the big sugar family there, the Vennings?'

'The Vennings – do I know the Vennings,' said Aunt Rosemary.

'They used to say, in Jamaica, anything that wasn't owned by the Vennings was owned by the Pauls.'

'Oh my goodness, those Pauls,' said Tom.

'I wasn't one of them for very long. My husband was the last son, you see, and he died rather tragically. But that whole set's crumbled now; very badly hit by the war.'

'Yes, the war,' said Roy, and he took Aunt Rosemary's easel under his arm, and Tom took all the rods and the string of fish, and Aunt Rosemary took her stool and I took the bottles. Aunt Rosemary walked alongside Roy, and as the wind blew I could hear her laughing, and her scarf billowed out behind her. It was the first time I'd heard her laugh. I didn't mind that they'd drunk all my juice.

After that Aunt Rosemary never talked of Bonzo again. Bonzo just disappeared. I used to sit at the table over Aunt Rosemary's cloth, and think that Bonzo had touched it. But all she talked of now was Roy, Roy. Even when she and my mother crouched over the wireless when the reception was bad, she would talk of what Roy said and what Roy did. My mother kept saying, What a catch, what a catch!

It was easier to remember my father because my mother and I now shared the same room. With father gone, my mother had both beds to use, and my cot went alongside under the window so that I would wake up fresh and early. When the telephone went, Aunt Rosemary, who was in a single bed in my room – the bed we brought down from the guest room upstairs – would rush to put on her slippers and get it, so that my mother could have some more rest. 'It's only Roy,' she'd say, scurrying down the corridor.

My mother would lie asleep for a while longer, then pick up her watch from beneath her bedlamp, where my father's portrait stood behind the perspex, and say that she wondered if Roy was coming to fish again.

Roy usually pitched up on a weekday when my mother had to work, and she would give Euphemia and me strict instructions about what to do if he ever actually came to the house. He had to have fresh tea and cake or, if it was later in the morning, Euphemia must get the key from Aunt Rosemary and unlock the liquor cabinet and get a lot of water with ice. But

Roy never came to the house, since Aunt Rosemary said it was too tiny for him.

Aunt Rosemary and I met Roy Westerley at the parking place one morning. He had a sports car with upholstered seats in front, and the roof came right across and strapped back behind where I used to sit. It was an MG made before the war. Roy said, 'Hello, Jimmy-boy,' and we were very excited, because Aunt Rosemary had wanted to go to the shark-oil factory for so long, and now we were. Roy started the car with his crank and jumped in over the door. We went so fast through Oudeskip that Aunt Rosemary had to clutch her hat, and Roy did a double declutch, and then we were past the native store and going along beneath the railway lines where there wasn't any traffic.

'Stand by to get out and push,' said Roy, but there was no need. The MG was good and had lots of power. It wasn't really a road at all, but the lorries used it sometimes when the train didn't come, because there was a lot to cart away from the shark-oil factory, and there was also the working quarry, which was what the railway line was really for. Roy drove very well, leaning over the wheel and looking out with his goggles on. There was a place where the car had to go right alongside the railway line and the wheels went bump, bump on the wooden sleepers.

When we got to the shark-oil factory it had closed down, due to the war, and we could have our picnic on the big concrete blocks on the side of the jetty from which you could look right down on the waves. There was an old fig tree growing through the blocks, so we laid the cloth underneath it where it was coolest. It wasn't Aunt Rosemary's embroidered cloth, but an ordinary one with red checks that could get dirty. I knew to get my need for a drink in quickly and had some juice immediately. We had an excellent picnic.

Afterwards, when it was two o'clock, the whistle went at the quarry where the men were working, in spite of the heat and the world situation. You could hear the rock landing in metal coaches with an explosion. But the sea was louder at the foot of the concrete where they used to drag the sharks up to make shark-liver inside the shed. All the shark boats were moored over at our harbour now, where they were being converted. Roy put me on the highest point and showed me our harbour, but I couldn't see it. They had some coffee and I finished another cup of juice.

Aunt Rosemary and Roy went for a little walk to digest. I could hear their voices behind me in the gully where they were going down to sea level, but they only climbed along the side, and they weren't resting at all. It was very energetic climbing and Aunt Rosemary stood on the edge of a rock and Roy, who was very strong, picked her up and let her down where he was standing, and she held his hand so as not to topple over. I had my colouring book, but it was too hot and the pages were full.

Then Roy put his arm around Aunt Rosemary and pushed her against a rock, and her hat came off, because he was very tall and heavy. I thought he was going to squash her against the shells on the rock. Her little white arm came up his blue shirt and she held him so that they didn't fall. Roy put his legs apart so that he was the same height as her, and she was taking something out of his mouth with her mouth.

Then Aunt Rosemary was shouting at me not to fall off the edge, and Roy said, 'Get back, get back!' and they came running up to rescue me from falling over.

Aunt Rosemary was breathing with the climb up, and held her hat in her hand and saw that I was quite safe.

We packed up the picnic and on the way home there was another kiss, ending just as badly. Roy was driving through a sticky patch and, just as we were through it, decided to switch off to let his engine cool down. We sat there with the engine clicking as it lost its temperature. Roy put his arm around Aunt Rosemary, and Aunt Rosemary's hat came off again. Roy said, 'Will you really, Rosemary dear, come and discuss it with Tom and his wife? They'd be awfully pleased.'

Aunt Rosemary said, 'Yes, yes.'

Then they couldn't kiss anymore because the quarry train came past with a huge puffing and blowing, pulling a whole lot of loaded trucks. The trucks were giving out yellow dust that made a whole storm over us, and the wheels were rattling over our heads almost. To get out of the dust Roy tried to start the car and it gave trouble, but it did start, and the trucks were rumbling. And now the back wheels of the car were stuck in the sand and sinking in fast. Roy was furious, and the train went on and on with only a guardsman at the end, hanging with a red flag to tell us to be careful.

When the train was gone Aunt Rosemary was covered in dust from head to foot. She looked as if she was wearing face powder. Roy was also covered in dust, sweating through it in streams.

'Dreadfully sorry,' he said, 'but you'll have to get out and push.'

Aunt Rosemary protested, as I think it was the end of her lovely day, and she said she'd only push if I helped. So I helped her.

We stood at the back bumper in the sand up to our knees, and I pushed so hard I could feel my shoulders burn, like the time when I fell off my tricycle. And Aunt Rosemary pushed mightily, too. Then the wheels threw up a lot of sand and dust on our bodies, and we were covered in it, and the car rocked and rocked and slid back into the two holes.

Roy got out a sack which he tore in two, and packed a half under each wheel, and we pushed again, standing in the middle where there was less dirt chucked up. And the car's tyres bit into the sacks, and it rocked and rocked, making a huge effort.

Aunt Rosemary said it was hopeless. She was absolutely covered in filth. She said she couldn't push anymore, and we shouldn't have come.

Roy packed some stones and bits of wood from the bushes growing there under the tyres and stamped them down. Aunt Rosemary said we should never, never have gone there, especially in an MG, it was far too low. Roy said if it hadn't been for the train stopping him we would have got through.

Aunt Rosemary said with those stones underneath she was going to stand back with me, just in case we got shot, so it better work on its own this time. We went and stood right behind a clump of bush, out of the firing line. Three herdboys came up; they had a whole flock of white goats grazing in the tunnel under the railway. Aunt Rosemary bribed them to help with the car, and Roy climbed out over the door to show them where to push. She was a good aunt, because she joined in once more, and this time the car got out. Aunt Rosemary paid the herders some more with sweets, and they were revving so much I thought I'd be left behind. I wouldn't have minded if I had been. I was tired of the picnic.

I was tired of Aunt Rosemary's romance, too. Everything centred on her – cooking to build her up, ironing for her so that she looked smart, and endless evenings before the wireless during which she and my mother sewed and cut patterns. The war and Aunt Rosemary became the same to me, and I wished the war would stop so that Aunt Rosemary would go and my father would come home.

In due course the excitement that regulated the lives of the two sisters came to a head. Aunt Rosemary was to be married, and Roy was coming to claim her. He made one terrible mistake, which almost had the whole performance called off – he came to our tiny house, the gatekeeper's lodge on the edge of a mysterious estate – and was very embarrassed at how small and unsuitable it was. Aunt Rosemary had forbidden him ever to go there, but he arrived by surprise one morning with a basket of apples for us. Euphemia gave him tea on the veranda and shook her broom right under his nose. I gave him back the basket, but he said we could keep it, it looked as if we needed it.

Aunt Rosemary came out with her hair hastily done up and no lipstick on, and said he must forgive her, and it all came out. With the wretched war on her sister didn't have the money to buy even proper bread and meat. So they decided to have an austerity reception at the golf club after the wedding, where my mother could get everything with some per cent off. It was not a bad deal for Roy, getting a whole wedding reception in exchange for a basket.

But while the listening to the wireless and the addressing of invitations was going on, and mother and Euphemia went out and spring-cleaned the whole of the golf club, in other words, while the centre of attention for a protracted time was Aunt Rosemary and not me, I was free to begin to discover my own way.

When Aunt Rosemary came into the lounge, and Euphemia and I were listening to the wireless, and she swooped around in her wedding dress, and she was going to drive my mother and herself to the church in the dorp inland, and she said would I give her a special wedding kiss on her forehead and had I seen, had I seen the list of guests who could be drummed up at such a gloomy time, I just gave her a messy kiss and went back to my own drawing on the Persian carpet.

'I'll never forget you, Jimmy-boy,' she said, 'you've been such a faithful ally.'

'I'll never forget you, too,' I said.

'Look after him well, Euphemia,' said Aunt Rosemary.

'Yes, madam,' said Euphemia, staring at the new teacups Aunt Rosemary had given her for all her attentions through those months.

And then she went to her wedding, and we only had photographs of her and Roy with the big wedding cake after that.

7

I was old enough now to go out on my own, but too young to be delivered to Miss Kettley's school. Boundaries were set on my explorations, but in time I managed to wear down most of these. I discovered that if most of my settings forth were to culminate in the golf club or, after visiting there, back home, with a suitably casual report to either my mother or Euphemia, anything could happen in the territory between them. My mother extended her job to a full-time one, Mondays to Fridays, so I was a free being for the time after lunch as well. During these months, you could say, the good people of the village became my extended family, and I became their communal responsibility.

Taking the route up to the tearoom café was different now. I could always hang around Mr Lotter the butcher's, when he opened his shop with the cool marble counter, behind which he stood in his blue and white apron, with a white hat splotched with stains. Mr Lotter always seemed to me part of his meat. Sometimes his daughter, Lettie, would sit in the sawdust, her panties getting bloody.

I handed over the note about three chops on account. He overturned a measly bunch of liver and kidney, looking for the chops. He opened the fridge door to see if they were hanging there on their metal hooks, but they weren't. 'Come,' he said, 'and I'll pick you some fresh ones.'

We went into the backyard where the cutting up of a pig was in progress. He slaughtered on Thursday mornings, to be ready for the weekend meat rush. The dead pig had come apart in his assistant's lap, as if it were lying there, exhausted. Mr Lotter pulled out of it a string of ribs, and then the carcase seemed to be much smaller, and he dragged the ribs back to the shop.

As we passed the bedroom door, he bent down. Although I was making no noise, he told me not to clomp-clomp with my shoes. His wife was behind that door. 'Ah, sh, she's very sick today,' he said, and I looked at the panelling of the door. I thought Mr Lotter must sit on the bed with her in his lap and try and put the pieces back.

In the shop he chopped off three nice ribs with his cleaver and wrapped them in brown paper and passed them over to me. I thought they were going to take one more breath, expanding in my tiny fists, and then relax so that I could carry them more easily.

Then I would deliver the morning's commission and see how Euphemia was, and go to lunch at the club with my mother. We would sit at a table almost out of the main dining-room, under an aspidistra, and sometimes Mrs van der Westhuizen would join us, or the new manager. Ransom was also fired, like Mr Wolpe, because my mother caught them both with their hands in the till.

'And how did you get on today?' my mother would say.

'Ah, very nicely,' I would reply.

'And did you get the chops from old Mr Lotter?' she said.

'Oh yes, I got it,' I would say.

'Poor Mrs Lotter,' my mother said.

'She's very sick,' I said.

'Ill,' she said. 'Sick is when you're sick in the tummy. Now eat up, there's a good boy.'

If there was an urgent errand I'd do it for the golf club as a favour. One afternoon Miss Kettley had to have a receipt for some eggs she had supplied and a big fat cheque for last month.

'That old bag can't get her chickens to lay unless she shows them the actual cheque,' said Mrs Van.

'Come more from sparrows than chickens, I reckon,' said Mr Lever, the new manager.

'Yes, whenever they poep Miss Kettley gets half a dozen small ones for free,' said Mrs Van.

'Oh Stinnie!' said my mother, and I caught the joke, too.

When I got to Miss Kettley's she was standing in the hocks with a paper bag, waiting for the eggs to come.

'And what do you think is so very funny?' she said, tapping me with her cane.

'Nothing, Miss Kettley,' I said.

She towered over me, her shoulder bones coming out of the top of her grey blouse. 'Then why are you squirming, boy? I don't see the joke!' And whap, she hit me on the shin.

'No, at the club they say you have very nice chickens,' I lied.

'Oh, you're from the club, are you? Have you brought my money?'

'Yes,' I said, handing the cheque right over without a crease in it. 'It'll make them lay.'

She inspected it ferociously through her glasses, and then stared back at me with contentment. 'You must be Sarah Esslin's boy.'

I nodded that I was.

'Good, you're the one we'll take next year. You're not up to standard yet. You'd pull down the others terribly the way you are now.'

'I'm sorry, Miss Kettley,' I said.

And she gave me a friendly tap on the seat pants and said I was to go post haste. And off she went, calling out, 'Kip kip kip . . .' to encourage them to blow out all their eggs. I hid under the Christmas thorn hedge on the street, and every time she went 'Kip kip', I just laughed and laughed.

Sometimes when Freddie, the postman, was very drunk and Euphemia had seen him sprawled on the beach near the Pits, I had to go to Miss Bester's post office to fetch the post for my mother, and also for the golf club. Miss Bester liked nobody in Silver Town and nobody in Silver Town liked Miss Bester. But her humour had improved now that there was so little mail. Miss Bester was very aloof, and when she wasn't in the post office she lived in single quarters and you could see her light burning and her standing behind the curtains at night.

We would hang around in the vestibule of the post office, waiting for her to sort – a bunch of fishermen with their boots still on and fish scales on their thick jerseys, and a delegate from the nannies' circle over the road, and Petrus from Mrs Feverall's, and usually one of the people who ran the native store, and old Brutus would come across to poke his nose in. Always Miss Bester would say to whoever asked first, 'No, there's nothing for you.'

Often there was something, because I could see my father's handwriting and I knew the stamps, and I would say, 'Please, can I have that one?'

And she would say, 'I told you, it's not for you.' That was just because she was political and didn't like to help the army.

'Is there any mail for the golf club?' I queried.

'The postman will take it later,' she said.

'He's gone fishing, Miss Bester,' said one of the men, thinking that was a big joke.

'Sies, he'll catch it in the neck when he gets back,' she would say.

And everyone would laugh a bit.

Then, when I was desperate, because I knew she was swindling me, and all the people were served with their letters before me, and my spirit was finally broken and all I could do was rely on the authority of my mother, who would have to get off work – her hours were the same hours as Miss Bester's – and challenge her personally, she would flip the letter over the counter and say, 'It must have crawled inside another one. So take it.'

And I ran down to the golf club, almost tempted to take the short cut through the quarry. I was also forbidden to open letters because my mother could do it so neatly with a paper-knife.

'Honestly, she's such a nuisance, even if I do say it about one of my own race,' said Mrs Van. 'Fancy not giving the boy a letter. I mean, it's paid for; look at the stamps all over it. Does she think she's not paid to do that?'

'She's just upset about Freddie being on a binge,' said my mother.

These days my mother was looking miserable, and Mrs Van tried to cheer her up now that Aunt Rosemary had gone.

'I wonder what that glamour sister of yours is up to. Doesn't she write?'

'Oh, why should she – she's only just up the road,' said my mother.

'Well, she doesn't come and visit you, does she, Sarah?'

'It's the petrol shortage, Stinnie; she'd come if Roy could lend her a horse – you know Rosemary.'

'Yes, she did well for herself, hey?' said Mrs Van 'All right, then it's your husband. You miss him a lot, don't you?'

My mother put down her spoon and nodded.

'Shame,' said Mrs Van, and she turned to me, automatically picking up my jelly spoon and feeding me, although by then I could feed myself. 'Listen, Jimmy,' she said, tipping my cheek full of jelly, 'don't let your mother get like this, you see? You meant to make her happy.'

I gurgled and said yes.

'Oh Stinnie,' my mother said, smiling, 'Jimmy is my treasure.'

After lunch I ran off, but I had forgotten to take an order to Mrs Feverall's for some goods that hadn't been delivered, so I had to go back, and my mother put her hand on my shoulder and gave me the stamps cut off my father's letter, and I went to Mrs Feverall's.

A few weeks later Freddie came round with the post to get his lime juice at Peter's Lodge, so everything was all right, but it was just bills in envelopes with shiny windows.

Once the pink flush of babyhood had left my skin, it went a pale white, and now the erosion of summer and autumn was turning it brown. With my hat pulled down more firmly than ever, now that my mother was with me, we strode out quite often on the weekends to the harbour to buy fresh fish, which was cheaper. Past the Royal Golf gates I always ran ahead to the seaside road, banked powerfully at the edge of the beach with gravel and tar that the waves reached on a really rough night. Down, down the brown side I would rush until the clumps of grass and sourfigs gave way to the level sand.

If there were no boats in and the wall wasn't bustling with people and carts, we'd more or less stop for a swim, changing in the morning glories. Sometimes Mrs Van would join us in her old-fashioned bathing costume with the long black skirt, with Little Marie and one or two of her daughters – they were too frightened to swim – and then they'd talk all the time.

If we went to the harbour, the Coloured fishermen would joke with my mother; they were very familiar with her from the club. They always tried to sell her the biggest fish, and she'd always pretend to be shocked, because did they think we had a fridge big enough for a yellowtail. Trippers from Cape Town who could get petrol came down to buy fish, as well, and they'd put them in their boots and go and have lunch at the club, where they got solid food, thanks to my mother's ordering. And the prices were still pre-war.

Once when there was trouble in the kitchen at the golf club I remember I ran a very important errand for my mother. The phone had broken down again, so I had to take a note to Sergeant Thoroughwell who had come out of retirement to help us through the war. He lived at the most inconvenient place for a police station, right past Oudeskip on the other side. It didn't matter to him, because he had a patrol van which he could drive anywhere. I found old Mrs Thoroughwell and gave her the note, and also told her the story of how one of the caddies had stolen the dress of the chief cook, Mrs Kreli, when she was in her uniform and had her back turned away from the big kitchen door.

And Mrs Thoroughwell showed me her photo album, which was of Sergeant Thoroughwell standing with the fish he had caught – a blue marlin on the winch, and other really deep-sea fish. She said you had to go out really far to catch fish that big, because it was too shallow for them around Silver Town. But I had reason not to believe her; I knew about even bigger and stronger fish right in the Silver Town lagoons. They were the ones like tablecloths, my private friends.

When Sergeant Thoroughwell returned with only a few stinking snoek, he came immediately to the golf club in his van and arrested the caddy they'd all kept locked up in the fridge where the vegetables were. He was taken to the magistrate in the dorp for imprisonment and a fair trial. The cooks were all pleased with that, but Mrs Kreli never got her dress back. One of the other caddies must have passed it on, once the actual thief had been caught. So he wasn't red-handed, just guilty. Mr Lever said it was already traded for a bottle of brandy, because nobody was hiring the caddies and they couldn't get brandy in any other way.

No one went to the lagoons at our end of Silver Town. With the beaches of the whole Indian Ocean, plus the bay to the east towards Credence, there was little interest in any lagoons. Only the bait-pickers went there to supply the fishermen, and that's how they made their brandy-money. After them it was left to the wild birds, more or less.

The lagoons were a semi-salt area, not that different from the sea, and the tide worked in them so they were always clean. They were going to make the lagoons a nature reserve because nobody had any use for them. They were just a way for the stained river to lie about before it seeped through the dunes at the end of the golf course, where the lighthouse was. This immense shifting basin was more or less entirely mine.

It was also where my friends, the manta rays, came to breed in the autumn. The lagoons were appealing enough for them. Everyone thought it was too cold for them in Silver Town and that they stayed up in the Red Sea, but this was not so. They glided in past the lighthouse, over the sandbars where they were much the same colour, and the lighthouse-keeper would never see them. And then they'd be hidden in the salty brown water where they could graze peacefully.

Sergeant Thoroughwell didn't have to go right up to the Equator to catch a manta ray that would be a record, because they were occasionally in the Silver Town lagoons. If anyone talked of preserving the lagoons, they said it was just for the pelicans and flamingoes. But I thought it must be for the mantas. Even though the back of the golf club lounge and the bar protruded right over the one part of the lagoons and all the bird-watchers had binoculars, nobody knew about the mantas. Because they were my friends, I kept up a point of honour for them – don't tell.

'Oh no, you'd never get devilfish,' said the barman, when I was helping him pack beer bottles into those wooden crates. 'You get the sandsharks, though. You know why Mrs Ryan wears rubber shoes; 'cause she stepped right on a stingray, and it sent a shock through her ankle, and it went septic. But that was a long time ago, before you were born, Jimmy-boy. Should think the ray's died from stinging Mrs Ryan by now.'

He went on counting – seventeen dozen, eighteen dozen.

'Only place you'll see the big mantas is in the *Children's Encyclopedia*,' he said. 'Now, off you go, mate.'

I can recall my first sighting of a manta ray or devilfish with perfect clarity. I had been doing everything I was forbidden to do – escaped from Euphemia, trespassed around the Pennington-Worthy fence where it said No Trespassing, paddled under the cover of the bulrushes past the back of their orchards, where a tractor was going so that they couldn't hear me, waded past their private beach, leaving footprints under the water, where you could see the bay window of their low white house and Mrs Pennington-Worthy with her pistol, and then nipped over the jetty of their boathouse and taken my own route through the reeds where on successive explorations I had worked down a pathway that looked like a coot's passage. I was very nimble-footed and sped along the shining, secret earth to my destination.

This was in a glade which couldn't be seen from the mountain pass, from the Pennington-Worthys' house, the lighthouse or anywhere else in the universe. I don't think anyone knew about it any more, or at least those who did were now dead and buried in Silver Town's main cemetery. There was only one inhabitant of that glade at the time, and he was so hidden under corrugated iron and sacking I didn't know about him until my third or fourth visit. He lived beyond the pale; if he came into town, people threw stones at him, so he just kept out there.

The glade was at an opening in the reeds where wild grass spread like a carpet of fibres over the sandy shore. The grass led up to the only palm tree in Silver Town, a very antique one with half its branches falling off in a poor state of repair.

All the dead people used to come to that glade, because one of them must have planted the palm tree. They certainly built a wooden platform from the same wood as the bridge, but this was purely an observation post; you couldn't cross it to anywhere. The wood needed tarring, because above the water it was drying out in the sun and becoming grey and powdery. That was the warmest water of all, because it lay very flat on the fawny sand where all the mussels breathed and sent up puffs as they were digging. I just stood in the pale water in my underpants so that my shirt and shorts didn't get dirty. I put my clothes in one of the joins of the observation post. The first time I knew anyone was there was when I paddled out and they were gone.

He was standing on the grass, a very buckled figure. In his one hand was my shirt and in his other my shorts, with the scout belt dangling. I thought for some reason he was going to bang them together. He had a funny skin, as though old car-oil had been thrown on him in patches. He said, 'Goh 'way, boy, goh 'way, boy.' This was exactly what they said to him when he strayed into town, on account of his vileness.

I said, 'I can't go away if you've got my clothes.'

'Goh 'way, boy,' he said, 'got no jobs for you.'

'I don't want a job, Mr Jensen,' I said.

But he was still talking to the people who pitched him out when he went to their houses begging. 'Give me bread, missus, give me a piece of bread.'

'There's no missus here,' I said.

'Give me weeding work, klein basie,' he said, and then went on with, 'Goh 'way, boy.'

'Give me my clothes and I'll go away,' I said.

'If I come to your mother's house, will she give me weeding, will she give me bread?' he said.

'She's already got a big strong gardener from up country,' I said, which was a lie, as she did the gardening herself.

He threw down my clothes and went away.

When I got home, very well washed-down and fully dressed, my mother assumed I had been with Euphemia all afternoon. Euphemia thought I had been with my mother. There was a loophole in their plans for me. I was not a communicative child, so that when my mother asked if I had had a nice time with Euphemia, all I said was yes, and when Euphemia asked if it had been all right at the club, I also said yes.

This simple approach to a complicated situation caused some trouble, for in truth I had two supervisors whose most careful co-ordination had gone awry. Mother would check with Euphemia to find out what we'd done, and Euphemia, confused, would say the usual, or Euphemia would check with my mother, if she dared, and my mother would say it was none of Euphemia's business, and they'd both get very cross indeed, and Euphemia would end her work silently and go without saying goodbye, and my mother wouldn't talk, either. Then the wireless would announce something that made my mother even more silent, and I began to wonder if any of us controlled what we were doing. The long evenings would settle in with a few lights on, and I'd plan a return visit down my pathway to Mr Jensen's.

The dream I played for myself, over and over, was the dream of my first encounter with the mantas. In my dream I was climbing the high struts of the observation post at the glade, and the sun was ragingly big in the sky, throwing light in handfuls on the lagoons. The higher I climbed, the stronger the wind blew. On the old mouldy platform at the top, where the planks were loose in their bolts, I could crawl forward on my stomach. The wind would rustle and tickle on my back, as I pulled my way across on the grey wood. And caught in a rush of wind and sun, I would gather my courage and lunge forward off the observation post into the bright air, my body bunched out like a flying creature. And with the most gentle wing-flaps I would cruise, cruise there over the shining lagoons with the great flying rays. And no one would stop us or hurt us, because we were in a private world which was invisible to them.

I did try to describe that world to my mother. In all honesty, trusting her, even if I didn't have the vocabulary, I tried. One evening, when I was sitting at her knee and she was cleaning porridge off Aunt Rosemary's tablecloth, and the material was resting on my shoulder like a cloak, I said, 'Mummy, I saw the little man.' That much I would tell, even if I couldn't give her a time and a place.

'What little man?' said my mother.

'You know,' I said, 'Phemie's little man.'

'That's nice, darling,' she said, and went on cleaning.

'No, I did see it,' I said. 'Don't you believe me?'

'Of course I believe you, Jimmy,' she said. But she didn't believe me. 'You know what happens to liars and swearers; they get a mouth full of carbolic soap.'

'You didn't say Phemie must get soap when she told you about the little man,' I said.

'Yes, but Phemie's a grown woman, and she should know better than to fill your little head with stories,' said my mother. 'She wasn't lying, she was just imagining.'

'What's imagining?' I said.

'It's when your worst dreams come true, and if Phemie's dreams are like that, she should keep them to herself,' said my mother.

'And if I have a dream, mummy?' I said.

'Well,' she said, 'tell me all about it.'

'All right,' I said, 'I'll try.'

Then she collected up the tablecloth and we swung it over the dining table and it came to rest on the surface with great silky folds. I truly did not have the words to describe that.

'It's like a tablecloth, mummy,' I said, and she said it was bedtime.

Many days later the conditions were right again for Euphemia to be thinking I was with my mother and vice versa. I was off around the fence and through the bulrushes as quickly as I could go, because I didn't have much time. I got past the Pennington-Worthys' beach with my footprints closing over in the water, but the lagoon was very dismal and cloudy, so no one could track me anyway. The mussel holes were closed over with a drift of sand, as it had been quite stormy the night before, and they kept to themselves. Eventually I got to the glade, and it was undisturbed.

There was not a sign of Mr Jensen, and the old palm tree sighed as though it were doing a floppy sword dance up there. The observation platform was unvisited and I slipped off my clothes and waded out.

I have absolute certainty about what followed. I knew what I was going to meet. I had neither fear nor doubt. My duty was clear to me, and without even thinking about it I had to go. I had no other reason to be out there in the bare reaches of the lagoons, the brown, snaky waters above my knees. I was shivering, because the water was no longer warm. To the one side the reeds were pressed down with heavy birds' nests and on the other the debris of trees was knotted up over networks of channels and streams. I glanced back once, and the glade was safely behind me. And what I had come to meet was ahead in the grey, tinny lagoon that stretched forward.

By the soft ripple on the surface of the water I knew that it was coming towards me. I held my arms out before me, because I knew that was the proper greeting. And the ripple slackened and, although I couldn't see clearly, I knew the manta had seen me because she was slowing, she was cautiously deciding if she should move forward to encounter me. Then she decided, and the front ridge of the ripples built up and she curved and then she touched me gently, and the ripples went behind me, and she was at my feet.

Then I put down my hand and touched her, first where she was barked against my one leg and then down the knobbly verge of her wing. My hand felt very tiny and frail against the coarse surface. Despite her hard rind I knew she was soft and gentle inside, not very warm, but through that covering you could feel her. She had to have protection from what she might swim into, and to hold her on the great voyages she took from the Red Sea before reaching the Silver Town lagoons. She was hard bone and rough skin, but where I stroked her she was warm and yielding inside. I said, 'Poor manta, my manta. Thank you for coming to see me.'

She slid a bit along my leg and it felt like the hull of a boat, only she was living. She was so strong that, unintentionally, she pushed me over, and I crumpled on my knees alongside her, passing my hands over the forehead part to where her back was less knobbly and more sleek. I kept my head right up, so that there was no chance of not seeing her in case any of her back rose out of the water like an island, and I grabbed and held the bony part, and then she slid right under me and was gone.

'Manta, poor manta, thank you for coming.'

I waited a long time for her to return that day, but she didn't.

8

After that first encounter I was a different person. The world changed accordingly. Everything, now, depended on being free to attend to the manta ray; nothing must come between her and me.

The second time I crawled to the glade, I was early for the appointment. She did not come, although I stood there in the murky water, shivering, for at least an hour.

The third time, I tumbled through the undergrowth, slipping on tree trunks and the mushy ground where the reeds had become trodden and crooked. The very secrecy of my pathway was, I think, part of its great pleasure. As I tunnelled my way towards the old palm tree this time, I knew there was a danger. The Pennington-Worthy grandchildren had come round on horseback – girls of ten and twelve and fourteen, with black riding hats and the smartest leather breeches and mud-splashed boots. The one on the big horse walked it to the water's edge, right near the observation tower, with birds reeling in complaint, and when no one was concentrating the horse went into the shallows for a roll, and the bridle and saddle got soaking wet, and the rider responsible beat it angrily with her crop. Their noisy, splashing presence would keep anything at bay. For some yards into the water it was their property and they could disturb what they pleased.

When it was completely safe my manta came in, and I met her. This was the second encounter. 'Thank you, poor manta, for coming,' I said. She lay there very flat, and the water was clearer, so I could see her long, horny forehead and the flipper she used on the one side to close her mouth over. And her eye, which was bigger than my fist. I called her a she although I could not be sure, but it must be the she-mantas that come in to breed, while the he-mantas wait outside the sandbars. Subsequently I learned this was incorrect.

'Poor manta,' I said, and I must have given a sudden movement, because she was off, pulling up her back and diving forward, full speed ahead. Like a streak of light she was gone out to where the ripples didn't show. But soon, through the choppy water, I saw the smooth island of her back approaching and her wings break the surface for a few inches at the tips, and that was the first time I realised how very big she was. And she floated to rest at my knee, and I stroked her.

She was in a poor state from all her voyaging, covered in weed and dirty bits of growth. I dug my finger into a patch of this stuff, and it was like parting very wet hair. I should have given that part a good scrape, but I didn't want to hurt her.

The third and later encounters blur for me. I know there were more because once, by accident, I lay on her back as she swivelled around on the floor of the water, and I had my hands clenching her top jaw and she lifted me up and we went for a ride. She had great speed and strength. Knowing I was small and no good in the water, she glided just under the surface and I held on, gasping for air. It wasn't so satisfactory because in the deeper area I came off and was winded, and coughed out water through my nose, and had to wade back to the observation tower.

I huddled on the grass, coughing and panting, my body so strained that it would take hours to recover. I didn't have that amount of time, so I ran and ducked and fell to get back home before my mother returned from the club. Euphemia filled the bath in the bathroom and had much to say about the condition of my clothes. Because I was a filthy child she gave me a slap, which she wasn't meant to do.

'You been playing with the caddy-boys at the club, hey?'

'Yes, Euphemia,' I said.

'They dirty boys, you hear,' she said, throwing the towel on the linoleum.

I didn't say anything to Euphemia when she was in that mood, but I ensured I was spotlessly clean, behind the ears and round the neck, too, before my mother came. Euphemia said nothing to her about the mess I was in earlier, so that Euphemia was a kind of ally.

The changing of the guards took place. Euphemia picked up her brown paper bag that was full of scraps my mother had rescued from the golf club kitchen, and my mother locked the back door and the front door.

Then, for a terrible moment I thought I had been spied on, I thought my mother had been told.

She said, 'You know, Jimmy, you're in for some changes now. You're not such a little boy any longer, and to think you'll live to see them.'

I thought it was going to be the usual speech about responsibility that meant a tightening of routine.

'You're going to have to, have to be on your guard at all times.'

'Yes, mummy,' I said.

'Sir Pierre van Ryneveld says it is an absolute scandal Silver Town is undefended. They could sail right in, and nobody'd be any the wiser.'

I thought she meant the mantas, and a painful ache opened out in my chest. This aching sadness stayed with me for several days, even though what she told me had nothing to do with my secret appointments at the glade.

When I next went to the golf club I could see the difference. A motor boat from Mr Pennington-Worthy's boathouse was laying buoys on my side of the lagoons. They had about eight yellow ones. With a heave the anchor would go over and tug the buoy into the water. They were making an obstacle course across the deeper part, and everyone at the club was talking of the men coming.

Most of the community was in the bar on the Saturday when they did come in. The barman spotted it first, and everyone raised their hands to shelter their faces from the glare. Down the sky it came and you couldn't see it again until it was between the mountains. Then it was a very clear aeroplane with its nose pointing below, and you could hear the engine banking, and it turned to touch down in a splash on the runway of the lagoon, and Mrs Feverall said, 'Jolly good show.' The men from the north had come to inspect Silver Town. They would defend us after that.

All through the day their flying boat rested at anchor on the lagoon. The three senior men who had red on their hats had the very best meal the Royal Silver Town Golf Club could provide, and champagne as well, which was in short supply, and they made good speeches. I sat behind one of the potted palms, having my jelly, getting up every little while to see how the flying boat disturbed the lagoons. If they ate too much of the food, they'd be too heavy to fly out, and we'd be stuck with them. The word they kept using was commandeer and, after a while, even Mrs van der Westhuizen was commandeering things left, right and centre. She was going to commandeer the flying boat and take us all for a joyride, and make more noise than ever on the lagoons.

My mother was pleased because they were going to commandeer the old storeroom, and the room next to my mother's office, for the surveyor they were leaving behind. Until they were ready and his survey equipment came from Kenya, he would sleep in a tent in the dunes next to the putting green, where if he walked to the crest he could see out over the bay and keep watch.

Then Mr Pennington-Worthy arrived and everybody stood up and said how sorry they were he couldn't have enjoyed the meal, and he shook hands properly. I don't know why my mother didn't ask him where my father was, but she offered him some ice-cream, and he never ate ice-cream. So I commandeered some ice-cream when it came back to the kitchen and was melting.

Mr Pennington-Worthy did take coffee, but he liked it black and without any sugar, and the others took sugar to keep them sweet. They had the table half-cleared, and my mother and Mrs van der Westhuizen were very busy helping. On the table they unrolled a big map, which was of the Silver Town coastal area, and they discussed where the best fishing was, and that was all right, because it was all on the bay side. Then the one with the bushy moustache said, 'There,' and he drew a line along the deep-sea channel which led to Silver Town harbour, 'that is where the currents carry the best fish!'

They couldn't fish at night, now, as there was going to be a curfew. All the fishermen would have to be back in the Pits at sunset and couldn't use their trawlers until sunrise. My mother said that was very hard on them, but the man with the bushy moustache replied that it would be harder still if they got blown out of the water.

Mrs van der Westhuizen said it would be a good thing to have a curfew as so many women were alone in Silver Town.

That would stop the gangs of caddies roaming after dark. As long as they stayed in the Pits, that would be all right. My mother said those were just no-good layabouts, but she didn't see why the decent fishermen had to suffer on their account. Mrs van der Westhuizen turned on her and said, 'Sarah, you just don't know these things. It's better as the major says.'

'Curfew means safety,' said the major, the one with the moustache.

'Means what?' said Mr Pennington-Worthy.

'Safety, safety, Mr Pennington-Worthy.'

'Oh, safety. I thought you said suffering; I'm a bit hard of hearing,' he said.

'Mrs Pennington-Worthy let her pistol off too close to his head,' said Mrs van der Westhuizen to my mother, and my mother smiled.

'Out here in the colonies,' said Mr Pennington-Worthy, 'no precautions are too severe.'

'None to spare, yes, I can see that,' said the major.

'Severe, severe,' said my mother.

'Look here,' said Mr Pennington-Worthy, 'I'm the one that's a trifle deaf. Battle of Passchendaele. You don't know how they were going off, pop-pop-pop!'

'I do beg your pardon,' said the major.

'Would you have some coffee, sir?' asked my mother.

'White, thank you,' said the major, and the other two military men who smoked lit their cigars.

'Keep Silver Town clear by night,' said Mr Pennington-Worthy. 'If the situation gets any more aggravated, we can run a fifteen-foot fence round them.'

'Can't that wait until we get some Germans?' said my mother. 'It seems to me you're over-preparing a bit.'

'Not the Germans,' said the major. 'We've got quite enough trouble without them as well.'

'Well, who then?' said my mother. She was angry.

'The local rowdy element,' said the major. 'Without that you'll never get a peaceful night's sleep, madam. The Germans are an altogether different story. Our latest intelligence is that they haven't the U-boats to get down here!'

'Thank goodness for that,' said Mrs van der Westhuizen.

'In that case, what on earth are you defending us against?

This has always been a very peace-loving community.' My mother put the coffee pot down. 'I'm quite sure you have no brief from Sir Pierre or anyone else to start impounding our own population; it's disgraceful!'

'Now, leave it to us, my dear,' said Mr Pennington-Worthy, 'don't you stick your pretty little nose in something that's not your business!'

My mother was so angry she turned on her heel and strode to her office.

'I'm sure we're right behind you, every step of the way,' said Mrs van der Westhuizen, and the major stroked her arm.

Then she went to see how my mother was and I ran with her, because I knew my mother wouldn't be furious with her in my presence.

My mother was on her stool with her hands clenched, and she said she was spitting fire.

'Sarah, honestly, I know how you feel, but it's for the best,' said Mrs Van. 'Please don't make a scene or they won't take the rooms, and the club can do with it.'

'Oh, oh,' said my mother, making a big sniff. 'Nothing to do with us – well, who else but us is it to do with? Jimmy, please get my handbag – it's in the dining-room.'

I went to the dining-room table where still most of the meal was not cleared away, because it was a private luncheon and they didn't want the waitresses overhearing. I took the strap of my mother's bag.

'Not upset, is she?' said the major.

He was talking to me, and I didn't know whether to nod or not. She was upset, but she didn't want them to think she was.

'You young Esslin's boy?' said Mr Pennington-Worthy.

Yes, I nodded.

Mr Pennington-Worthy leant towards the soldiers and told them my father was one of the first men in the district to volunteer.

'Good show,' said the major.

'Do you ride horses, Master Esslin?' said Mr Pennington-Worthy.

I nodded no.

'Pity,' he said, 'or my grandchildren could have taken you out. They've got a spare pony, and no one to exercise it.'

107

'Can I go now?' I said.

'Tell your mother what a splendid asset she is to the community,' said Mr Pennington-Worthy.

Yes, I nodded.

'And thank her for the lunch; really splendid to turn out a feed like this, under such difficult conditions,' said the major.

He and the other two military men and Mr Pennington-Worthy went through the folding doors to the bar where half the people of Silver Town shook their hands and offered them drinks, even though it was after two o'clock when the bar was meant to close, and Mrs Feverall said, 'Jolly good show,' when they accepted.

I took my mother her bag and she drew a handkerchief out of it. She was sitting opposite Mrs van der Westhuizen.

'And just you remember what I said, Jimmy. Mrs Van doesn't believe me, but I am convinced Britain is a just land. I think it is very unjust that perfectly good British subjects who have done nobody any harm should be treated as if they were the enemy.'

'All right, Sarah,' said Mrs Van, 'but you'll be the first one to complain if all those unemployed men in the Pits start stealing your property, like they stole that dress.'

'They won't, because I'll tell them I'm on their side,' said my mother.

'Fat lot of good that'll do,' said Mrs Van. 'You think Sergeant Thoroughwell can get to you in time if you do need help?'

'Help from what, Stinnie, for goodness sake – have you also gone off your head?'

'All right,' said Mrs Van softly, 'but I still think you should have my husband's old .22. You defend what you have and just leave the whole rest of Silver Town to the UDF.'

'Oh, I wish they hadn't come,' said my mother. 'Just because somebody's taken some notice of Silver Town for the first time in its history, you all get so excited you lose your common sense.'

'Well, it will put us a bit on the map if we have our own gunboat. And they might even dredge the harbour a bit. Man, think of all the meals we can serve.'

'Oh, Stinnie,' said my mother, 'haven't we served enough already?'

Sergeant Thoroughwell drove up outside on the gravel with his van and the three military men climbed in. Mr Pennington-Worthy had the door of his car held open, and the chauffeur closed it, and they all drove off with the flag of Mr Pennington-Worthy's factory flapping on the bonnet.

I went outside to watch them go along the coastal road. I stood around with all the caddies who had no one to play golf today; the war was too important for golf. One of them tried to swap me a golf ball for my brown jersey and I said no, and he said two golf balls, and I said I didn't play golf.

The waitresses, who had been talking in the kitchen all this time, came out and cleared the dining-room, and everyone looked at their watches, because most of them work only half shifts now. My mother was getting them to hurry up, as there was going to be a banquet that night and, in preparation for it, they had to put up black curtains in all the windows. When it was getting dark I helped them by checking from outside if there were any chinks, and tapping on the glass when there was one, and they would join it together with a safety pin.

I went to sleep in my mother's office. When it was time for everybody in the whole town to go home, except the three military men who were sleeping on the sofas they had commandeered, Mr Lotter the butcher gave us a lift in his bakkie. The new manager of the club had given my mother a torch with black tape on it, so that it showed only a cross of light. We went up the path and the veranda to the front door with it on, making a very feeble light, and it was very dark inside.

The next day we got up very early to see the Sunderland go. It took off wonderfully well, and that was the last we saw of the three military men, including the major. They even took the buoys out of the lagoons so that it was certain they wouldn't come back.

After that, life in Silver Town went back to normal. The curfew was held for a while, which meant dinners had to be served early in the club to get the staff home in time, but no fences were erected around the Pits or anywhere else. We got quite used to the bell at the church hall tolling at eight o'clock and my mother and I were always in bed by then. We burned only a small night light, and so with the curtains drawn we were perfectly inconspicuous.

At night in those dark days I still slept in my cot against the wall in my parents' room, since my mother said it used less electricity. Lying there, waiting to go to sleep in that dim atmosphere, I came to know by close inspection every inch of the main bedroom of Peter's Lodge. If I turned and lay with the pillow in another direction, I could stare through the struts of the cot – it wasn't really a cot, but a half-bed with raised edges to keep the mattress from sliding off – and contemplate my mother in her bed, reading with her book held at an angle, her night-dress knotted in a bow across her throat with a little gap underneath and her pale hair resting on her shoulder.

After I had stared at her for a long time, until my eyes were going dry with concentration, filling myself with her beauty, she would say very softly, 'All right, nighty night now.'

And my eyes would close without my even noticing and the sound of the wind outside, rocking the house, rattling on all the doors and windows that gave access to the huge outside, would go soft and distant and suspend itself.

In the morning when the sunlight poured through the black-out curtains and the birds were going and the darkness seemed lost for ever, I'd wake after mother, hear her in the kitchen, unlocking the door for Euphemia, or running a bath from the plumbing that always had wind in it and sounded like a steam-engine, and remember the last sight I had had of her, reading with a bookmarker sticking out with a frayed edge, and see the book laid on my father's bed next to hers, always kept made up and never used, except as a space on which to put the ironed laundry or my colouring books before they went in the cupboard in my room.

The surveyor who had the tent on the links arrived. Although he was a soldier in uniform, pretty soon people ceased to think of him in that way. He was our guardsman, stationed on a golf club lawn under a sand dune, meant to defend an entire valley with all its multiple waterways, scantily spread mixed population, and all else that lived in it. No one knew how he would accomplish this, but that didn't matter, as he soon merged into the scattered social life of Silver Town and just became Blackie Rousseau, the man sent from Bloemfontein, not very well qualified, whom people took fishing or stood drinks at the golf club bar. He was engaged to be married and had had to leave his girl behind in Pietersburg, so we all felt sorry for him.

It wasn't too long before Mrs van der Westhuizen and my mother had fitted out the room for him in the club, although this was a great inconvenience for Mr Lever who had to store stuff outside where it might get stolen. Blackie Rousseau was an Afrikaner, so his English wasn't completely up to scratch, but Mrs Van said his Afrikaans wasn't either, so that cancelled out. When there were no bookings for an early dinner at the club, which there seldom were those days, my mother and Mrs Van would see that he had a plate full of cold meat and potato salad and some dessert on the trolley with the gauze over it to keep the flies off. That way he could play the wireless and eat when he wanted, even after the barman had gone home to Silver Town.

Sergeant Rousseau had to share the van with Sergeant Thoroughwell, so the van had a lot of exercise in the days before Sergeant Rousseau's jeep came. If I was running past Miss Kettley's with a message and the phones were down again, I'd see Sergeant Rousseau do some champion reversing in the van, sending dirt flying all over the place, because he had to get up to the native store. Sometimes, if I went from the clubhouse to the main beach, I could hear him coming, and the van would leap over a dune and scramble past me, and I'd wave and he'd wave. When Sergeant Thoroughwell drove, he was more sedate because he was older, and usually he had someone locked in the back so he didn't want to bump their heads. There was a lot of rounding-up of the drinking element going on. Once, when Blackie Rousseau was driving the van, I thought he'd give me a lift up to the post office, because Freddie had been arrested, but he said he couldn't because it was a police vehicle and he wasn't allowed to take passengers unless they were going to the magistrate. When the jeep came, the situation eased.

I was sitting in a patch of oxalis, which made those yellow and green colours quite fresh against the sandy ground and the dark stems of the wattles, none of them flowering now. Temporarily I had been deserted by all adults. I had an overwhelming sense that my world was coming to an end. I can't explain it. Being as conservative as any child and as frightened of change, I felt that I should resist anything that intruded into my world. I was listless and depressed. Maybe this was because I had acquired a reputation for backwardness. I was slow of thought, unyielding, not willing to break down into the channels prescribed for me for growing up. I sat, as I say, among the oxalis in a slow panic, afraid that my world was being taken from me bit by bit.

I took off and ran with this unnamed fear inside me. I was over the wooden bridge, ducking past the hedge around our house and under the Silver estate sign. I was splashing across the beach of the inlet with my sandals stuck out of my pockets, and along past the boathouse where the mooring buoys were collected in a bunch for use when the next flying boat came in, past the dead trees and into the reeds. My path had not been disturbed; in fact, most of it had sprung up like elastic, the parting being tugged upwards towards the sun where the feathery heads could wave above in the light. My heart driving in my mouth, I arrived at the lone palm tree, which was my sanctuary.

Little Mr Jensen the hunchback was there, but I ignored him. He was coughing and lumbered towards the observation platform, but I said, 'Leave my things!' and he said, 'Don't you play with da fish, boy, they devilfish and they going to get you!'

And I said he should mind his own business. Yet it was reassuring that, as I strode out into the lagoon, he guarded my things.

I had to wait for a very long time, around a corner out of sight of Mr Jensen. I had to wait and wait, the grey water swirling with sand about my knees – the level was exactly at my navel, and it rose with a dim echo of the ocean outside and then drained back. Then the miniature tide would heave past my legs and, if I stood still, it rose up my skin again, staining it a tan colour. There was really no need for me to make any movement, for they would come of their own accord. I was there to meet them where they could come.

This time I was surprised. What followed confirmed for me that my world was far preferable to any world of theirs. Even now I hesitate to write about it, for fear that giving up the secret cancels out the fact that it existed. It was so purely, entirely mine – the scene that I could not explain and did not question. These things happened for me alone, and only I was able to experience their meaning.

This time, when they finally sensed my presence and made a few invisible turns in the lagoons, they sped along, and the incredible speed with which they came only increased the excitement. Yes, and the surprise is that I, who had fallen in love with a lone she-manta, was now surrounded by them – there was more than one, and the other one was a male, her permanent mate, or perhaps it had been the other way round all the time, and I'd befriended the more outgoing one, and he'd kept his shy female partner behind, quietly watching us from the gloomy lagoon bed. At all events, they were a huge pair and they came from different directions and met about my legs, nuzzling, almost bouncing with me between them. They were definitely a pair because just to one side of them was their new baby manta, who had slid out of one of them and unwound and flown like an underwater bird.

And even the little one came to inspect me and, young though it was, its wingspan was much longer than I was tall. And this was the first time, too, that the water was clear enough for me to see how they were guided through the vast oceans and had cruised from the Red Sea, all the way down to Silver Town bay, because they had a family of pilot fish with them, and the pilot fish went wherever they went, showing them the way to Silver Town lagoons.

And I looked back for a moment at Mr Jensen, doing a kind of loony dance of his own, and wished he hadn't seen me. As I was floating alongside the manta I knew, she swooped me onto her back and soon I was out of sight. All I knew was how hard I had to hold on, as she stuck quite close to the surface and, with my hands on her soft, gummy upper jaw that was far too big for my grip, I clutched and clung on and we were away. And the other big one had his wing-tips up like fins, but my one flew with me on her back, and we went slightly sideways, and if I changed my weight she changed hers, and we went sideways the other way, until we had gone so far Mr Jensen couldn't see us any longer.

9

One mid-morning my mother took a tray of tea out to Blackie Rousseau in the garden of the club. He had a bundle of posters the government had sent him. He unrolled one for my mother to inspect. There was a Japanese soldier on it, with spiky hair and a big mouth. He was carrying a machine gun and the whole of Silver Town was burning behind him. Mother read it out, and it said, Do you want them here?

'Mr Pennington-Worthy thinks they'll go the other way, to Table Bay and Saldanha,' said Blackie.

'They couldn't get a submarine up to our harbour. It's about ten foot deep most of the way,' said my mother. 'Look at how the fishing boats lie during low tide.'

'They've got very flat submarines,' said Blackie.

'Won't you have a cup-cake?' said my mother.

Blackie pulled out a straw chair for her, although it wasn't proper for my mother to sit with the guests.

'Are you all right in that poky little room, poor Blackie?' she said. 'It must be awfully lonely for you at night. Still, we're so proud of you, the way you look after us.'

'No, it's fine,' said Blackie, chewing up half a cup-cake. 'Mrs Van brought me some wild flowers.'

'I noticed,' said my mother. 'And your girl in Pietersburg, do you have any news of her? Isn't it terrible how the war separates us all? And this is such a big country – you'll never be able to get back to her.'

'No, the minute I turn my back she gets married,' said Blackie.

'Oh,' said my mother, 'you must be very disappointed.'

'Yes,' said Blackie. That meant he preferred being in Silver Town now.

'Has she married – a friend of yours?' my mother enquired.

'Yes, my best friend,' said Blackie. 'What do you think of that?'

My mother had Blackie's army beret in her hand and was stroking fluff off the edge. 'Well, I think that's terrible and faithless. I suppose you feel neither of them is worth being your friend anymore.'

'He didn't sign up, you see. Oh, I'll tell them what I think of them, soon as the war's over,' he said.

'I should think so,' said my mother.

Blackie bonked me on the head with the rolled-up poster and I felt deeply insulted. My mother turned to me and offered me a cup-cake. I indicated that I was not hungry.

'He's getting a big child now, Mrs Esslin,' said Blackie. 'Should be going to school soon.'

'Miss Kettley won't take him until next year and, poor fellow, there's nothing for him to do in Silver Town.'

'Yes, I can see that,' said Blackie.

'It's difficult with an only child,' she said.

'Oh yes,' said Blackie, taking his beret. 'You should see my family – phew, there's a lot of them.'

'Do you want to have a large family yourself?' asked my mother. 'One day, when you've found a girl who doesn't run off when your back's turned.'

'Hell yes,' said Blackie, 'a whole dozen, so they'll never get lonely like Jimmy?'

'You'll have to wait for the peace for that,' said my mother.

Blackie sighed and clocked me on the head again with the poster. He was going to take me on his rounds.

Mother fetched my hat and screwed it crookedly on my head, and Blackie roared off with me on the front seat of the army jeep. There were a lot of poles in the back and noticeboards. We stopped on the dyke above the Pits and Blackie took on some labourers. Right opposite the track to the Pits, where the road takes a dip, they embedded the poles and hammered on the noticeboard and with a big pot of glue the first poster went up. All the people living in the Pits came out and stared at it. There was Mrs Kreli's husband, and all the fishermen, and the people from the garage pouring down through the wattles. They all stood around and pointed at the Japanese man with the red mouth and Silver Town burning in the background.

'Yes,' said one of them who worked at Mrs Feverall's, 'do you want them here?'

One of the maids said she wouldn't mind, and they all laughed. Blackie was furious with her and told her she didn't know what she was talking about.

Then we went to Long Beach and put up another poster near the warning about the undertow and no bathing. Only one old-age pensioner, who was the caretaker of Oudeskip cottages near where Mrs Van lived, came across, and he helped us, standing back and saying no, he didn't want them here, thank you very much.

Blackie drove us up to the trading store where the bus turned and they sank two holes where all the passengers wait, and in went the poles and Blackie climbed up the stepladder and personally knocked in the nails to hold the noticeboard. I sat and watched him while he glued it really straight and rolled the poster down the surface. Miss Bester was watching us from the post office. Blackie said good morning to her and so she had to talk, and she said there was no post for him anymore.

'It's none of your business,' said Blackie.

'Doesn't look as if there's any post from his father, either, these days,' said Miss Bester. 'Maybe he's forgotten them.'

'That's also none of your business,' said Blackie.

'It's my business if Freddie has to deliver them,' said Miss Bester. Freddie was on the beat again because he was the only one who knew where everything went.

Blackie handed her a rolled-up poster, which she was meant to put up in her window, facing the street, and he gave her some loose lengths of army tape.

At Mr Lotter's butchery Blackie went in with a poster and Mr Lotter came out with the black assistant who killed the meat, and Mr Lotter admired the poster with Blackie, and the black man went and stuck it in the window in front of the calf's head.

We crossed over to Mrs Feverall's and she said it was a pity Blackie had no more noticeboards or she would have been able to put it on the balcony of the hotel, and they could sit behind it, keeping watch. But in the end Mrs Feverall stuck it on the panelling at reception where it kept watch over them.

The only person who wouldn't take a poster was Miss Kettley. 'Such an ugly sight for the children, how could they think of such a thing?' She tapped her stick on the gatepost and Blackie rolled the poster up again.

'I'm sorry to worry you, Miss Kettley,' he said, 'I didn't mean anything by it.'

'But look at it, young man. You have eyes, you have feelings. Those are tender children in there,' she said.

'Yes, I know that, Miss Kettley, but the orders came through,' said Blackie.

'I suppose you've shown it to that Esslin boy,' she said, coming to inspect if I had been exposed. Many copies of the grinning Japanese were lying right under my feet in the jeep.

'Women don't look after their children in this day and age,' said Miss Kettley. 'I think you'd better come to school, the sooner the better.'

Blackie said, 'Excuse me, Miss Kettley, but the moment your children go in the street they going to see the poster. You can't hide them from it.'

'My children,' said Miss Kettley, 'don't go in the street.'

Blackie threw the poster back in the jeep and we drove up to the church hall. Nobody was in charge of it, so he just stuck a poster on the outside window. The bank wasn't open that day, either, so we slid one under the door.

Then we drove back to drop the labourers off and Blackie paid them, and went back to the club and rolled the rest of the posters up, putting them in his room next to my mother's office.

The awesome drawing of the Japanese on the poster merged in my mind with the threat of being sent to school at Miss Kettley's. I realised in a perverse way that, were the Japanese to come in their submarines one night, up the channel which was so seldom used and into the harbour, and were the man in the poster with his spiky hair and red mouth to stride up the Oudeskip road, with his uniform ablaze and his eyes hollow with shouting, that would at least postpone my education.

What did postpone it, however, was not the Japanese. When the posters were beginning to blister and peel, and the sensation they caused was all but forgotten, and some of the noticeboards had been used in the Pits as firewood, I caught scarlet fever. My mother told me there were so many cases of it that Miss Kettley had had to close her school. It was in the air. Keeping me away from other children had not prevented me from contracting it as well. I sank into scarlet fever like a destroyer capsizing down to the bottom.

The first night of my fever the doctor came, probing into my mother's house with his masked torch, mud all over his boots. I could see the squelchy patterns he left on the corridor carpet and taste the disinfectant on the thermometer. He put his hand on my forehead and I cried helplessly because I thought it was my father come back to my sickbed. His hands were not like my father's, and my father did not roll my pyjama top up and sting my chest with the cold end of a stethoscope.

I thought the stethoscope was a strand of seaweed trumpeting in the surf. The sheets were wound around me like wavelets and I fought with them, sinking into the fiery mattress. He was called Dr Walton, but in my pitiful debilitation I thought he must be a Japanese. He gave me an injection and a big white pill, which I swallowed with cold water, and it stuck in my throat, making a ring of pain which swelled and swelled. I thought my throat had developed a hood like a cobra.

My mother paid the doctor, which was very expensive, as he had had to come from over the mountains. Silver Town was not big enough. Dr Walton told her to phone him every evening free of charge, until I got better, and then she warmed up some dinner for him. My mother kept the door open in case I cried out.

On the ceiling I could see the only friendly element in my universe, the circular shadows of the night lamp creeping up the black-out curtains and turning into wings, gliding very peacefully across. At the corner they swerved without bumping anything, and came back again.

I could hear my mother's voice, much calmer now, talking to Dr Walton, who had news of Aunt Rosemary who had delivered a pair of twins. That was her tablecloth they were sitting over, with the spoon of the gravy dish clicking in the bowl. 'Well, well . . .' my mother was saying, 'fancy that. Good old Rosemary. Roy'll be pleased. He did phone, actually, very excited.'

I dragged my blanket down the corridor, avoiding the footprints the doctor had left. I stopped in the lounge doorway near the light, because the house was very sombre and cold these days. If I kept close to the light it was as if it would warm me. I had to have a drink to still the rings of pain in my Adam's apple.

Dr Walton was going to the war, too, for service in field hospitals in the desert; his papers had come through. His wife was maintaining the practice. She would really know what to do with scarlet fever, and she'd be busy with all the children in Silver Town. His wife was also called Dr Walton.

My mother grabbed me up but didn't kiss me, because she didn't want to catch it. She held me far away on her knee at the table, and Dr Walton ruffled my hair and said he had to drive off to the Oudeskip wing, where everybody had also succumbed.

'I must be going,' said Dr Walton. He packed his stethoscope into his black bag and clicked it closed. He stood up then, and let himself out. We could hear his car warm up outside, and drive away cautiously over that road, because mother said his lights were hooded with black tape to prevent the car being seen from the Far East.

Feeling terribly ill, I grabbed my mother's arm tightly. I asked her what it was to die.

'Oh Jimmy, you're not going to die,' she said, 'not on account of some lousy fever. No one that we know's going to die.'

'That's what Blackie told me,' I said.

'He did not, Jimmy. Really you tell such stories. He didn't even know you had scarlet fever until I told him this morning.'

'He did. He said that about the other children at Miss Kettley's. They all going to die,' I said.

'Oh what nonsense, Jimmy-boy. If he did say that, I shall reprimand him. He had no right to scare you like that.'

'Maybe the Japanese will get scarlet fever if they come, and they'll all be dead,' I said.

Mother shaped up my pillow, prising me off her arm. 'That is a thought,' she said.

The scarlet fever took many days to work itself out. Mother phoned Dr Walton in the evenings, describing the progress of the symptoms. To be with me she took off work on all but the Wednesday, which was stocktaking. She was frightened she would catch it, too, and then there would be no one to look after us but Euphemia. My mother wrote desperate letters to my father, knowing that, if at all, they would take weeks to reach him, and that by then the fever would be over.

One night the bad dream spilled into a sequence of horror which rearranged our lives in that tranquil, lost backwater of Silver Town. As I was dozing and my mother was reading in her bed, it started with a knock on the front door. I looked up at her; she had heard it but was not reacting. No one ever called as late as that. She was undecided whether or not she should ignore it. We were the only two people in the house, everyone knew, and the only light on was my mother's reading lamp, with a heavy veil over it. But it was a strongly moonlit night, as we could see from the light coming in through the chinks in the curtain.

I said, 'Knocking, Ma,' and she shushed me.

We listened some more, mother trying to go back to her book. But then there was definitely a knocking on the front door.

'It must be Phemie,' I said.

'Phemie would call out to tell us it was her,' she said.

I was going to say more, but my mother hushed me. Then she whispered. 'It's very late, Jimmy, go to sleep.'

'It's the Japanese,' I whispered back.

'Oh, don't be silly. Blackie would blow the siren at the club,' said my mother.

I sat up straight, and my mother was still undecided.

'Maybe someone has broken down on the way to the Penningtons,' whispered my mother.

'There wasn't a car,' I said.

Now my mother was in her dressing gown and slippers. She smoothed my hair down and pushed my head sideways. She took the torch and went very quietly to the front door. She must have stood there for a long time, for there was silence.

Then the wind blew and again there was a knocking and a shuffling that sounded like branches being dragged. I knew who it was – Mr Jensen, the little old man, keeper of the mantas.

Mother had the hatch open on the front door. She shone the torch out of it. This I could tell from the way she was saying, 'No, I won't give to anyone unless I can see them.'

Mr Jensen was a hunchback so he didn't like to be seen, anyway. He must have kept out of the light. My mother was saying, 'No, I've got no weeding. And it's eleven at night. Whoever you are, come back in the morning.'

But then there was a bashing on the front door and he'd found the bell, and my mother must have been a few feet from it.

'Stop that,' she said in a high voice, 'or I'll call the police!'

'Please ma'am, please, please,' Mr Jensen was wailing.

'I don't open the door to strange people,' said my mother.

Mr Jensen was bashing at it, falling around and making a horrible noise.

'No, do go away,' said my mother. 'I told you, come in the morning when you're sober.'

'It's the caddies, ma'am, they beating me!' He gave a crunching bang on the door panel.

'Well . . . stop that!' I could hear the metal of the end of the torch on the frame around the hatch. 'Stand up straight so that I can see you and I'll – I'll give you some bread. Stay there, just stay there,' and my mother closed the hatch. I heard her dash into the kitchen and open the breadbin.

Trouble was coming from the road as well, on my side of the house. A bunch of caddies was there. They were crashing around as if they'd got caught in our fence. They had sticks to beat Mr Jensen. I stood on tiptoe underneath the curtain material. One came right up to the window with a stick across his shoulder, and he sighed and pressed his face on the glass. There was no fire in him, but he was very far gone. It was a golf club he was carrying, and he wasn't going to smash the glass; he was admiring himself, patting his hair. I could see through my illness that he was quite ordinary.

They were after Mr Jensen, not us. Mr Jensen had come to take refuge on our property. I wouldn't have liked to have been him with that mob after me.

My mother had a wedge of national loaf from the kitchen and, as I got to the hallway, I saw her squeeze it through the hatch out to Mr Jensen. We didn't like national loaf because it was full of fishmeal.

He was carrying on, 'Let me in, let me in, ma'am,' but he took the bread. I saw his hand pulling it, with the crust coming off from the pressure.

'Now go away, go away,' said my mother.

'But it's Jensen, ma'am, let me in!' he persisted.

'I've given you all the bread, so go to your pondok and sleep it off.'

'Ma'am, they're going to kill me,' he said.

Mother closed the hatch and the next problem was that I was up and witnessing this. 'Go, Jimmy, to bed!' she ordered me.

'The caddy-boys are coming to beat him,' I said.

She flung herself down on the seat beside the telephone and opened the directory. 'What on earth do you mean?' she said.

I pulled the blanket around me, indicating that I would stay and protect her; I would not obey her.

'Oh, he's just a poor old wreck,' she said, 'but I shall reprimand him for waking us up. He's very unfortunate, Mr Jensen.' She drew her arms around herself, and I could see that she was wondering if she should phone.

'They going to beat him,' I said.

'Ah, that's enough from you,' she said.

The torchlight came down the silk of her knee. 'I suppose Sergeant Thoroughwell has gone night fishing again,' she said. She picked up the phone and started to dial Mrs van der Westhuizen's number. They would be home, because little Marie had scarlet fever, and so did her sisters and her grandmother. But the receiver was dead in her hands. She put it down. It never worked when you wanted it.

Then we heard the gang beating Mr Jensen outside. They pulled him through the bougainvillaea creeper on the veranda onto the lawn. There were some bumpings, and he was squealing to be let go.

Mother and I waited there. She was thinking that she should let them settle their differences. I was sorry for Mr Jensen; he was the only person who also knew about the mantas. He had never done me any harm.

Now Mr Jensen was wailing and shouting. The others were stamping and swearing. When he got hit, Mr Jensen would go silent, then start wailing again and get a hit.

My mother was more furious than she was frightened. They went over her flowerbeds and around the side of the lounge; they weren't going back into the street. She tried the phone again, but it was hopeless. We could hear them trample next to the fruit tree, and then Mr Jensen bellowed, and mother was truly enraged.

She opened the lock with one hand and, her dressing gown gleaming in the moonlight, went to stop them. I followed her. Outside it was very bright. At the bottom of the garden under the milk-bushes was the sleepy heron, its head on one side, listening. I could see the electricity wires clearly against the moon.

They stopped beating Mr Jensen when my mother was there. All she had in her hand was the masked torch and she held it out, pointing at Mr Jensen's face.

The man with the golf club raised it over his shoulder, as if he were going to give it a good swing, belting Mr Jensen down the green.

'No, I don't want you here,' said my mother. 'So please leave!'

'Oh ma'am, oh ma'am,' wailed Mr Jensen.

'Not you – them!' she said. 'Get out of my garden and don't come back. Until eight o'clock in the morning. You understand? At eight o'clock sharp you can fix up the damage you've done,' said my mother.

The gang of men stood quietly.

'You want to spend the rest of the war in jail? Is that the only thought in your heads? – you should be helping one another, not beating him down. What did he do – take your money? Mr Jensen, why are these people after you?'

Mr Jensen hauled himself up. 'No, ma'am, I only wanted a piece of bread.'

'I gave you that. Is that why they're beating you? Share it with them, Mr Jensen.'

'No, ma'am, he's taking all the money for bait,' said the man with the club. He lowered the club as if it were no good anymore.

'He doesn't take anything, he begs. Don't you know what a beggar is?'

The one who straightened his hair in the bedroom window signalled for them to go. Two of them sauntered off through the garden.

'Share and share alike. He's not fit to get a licence like you are.' My mother stood her ground. 'Answer me,' she said to the man with the club.

'No, ma'am,' he said, 'a beggar has what he's given, he doesn' jus' take it. We got no money, we got no bread, the children is hungry, ma'am, and the licence means the season's finish, ma'am. And he takes it when we wasn't giving it to him.'

'I know it's hard times –'

Mr Jensen interrupted, 'I didn't take it, I only borrow it.'

The confrontation was thoroughly calmed down now. The third man went off to his friends, and that left only the man with the club, Mr Jensen, my mother and myself.

'Look at them,' said my mother very loudly, 'frightened of a defenceless woman with a sick child. Cowards, that's what you are!'

The three men went into the bushes, falling about and even laughing.

'Mrs Pennington-Worthy'd have shot the lot of you by now,' my mother said after them.

'Ma'am's not like the other ma'ams,' said the man with the club.

Mr Jensen coughed a lot. My mother told me to go inside and shut the door. Then she and the man with the club hauled him into Euphemia's outside laundry room.

My mother came in to get two blankets from Aunt Rosemary's room, and then she finally returned and washed her hands and got back into bed.

I was sitting up in my cot, my face burning and cross-eyed.

'Go to sleep now,' she said, 'and in the morning we'll discharge the other patient.'

And I obeyed.

By the morning I had temporarily forgotten about the night before. I was quite used to waking up in agitation; I would always be in that strange, unfocused state of illness. Most of the children in Silver Town were better and Miss Kettley's was re-opening. I think I preferred to stay in my cot with mother hovering by than get up and grow and go to school. I was more frightened of Miss Kettley than of a gang of drunken Coloureds with golf clubs in their grip.

'He's not very advanced for his age, Mrs Esslin,' Miss Kettley would say.

And my mother would curl her lip and be silent.

'You should take him to a specialist. I think it's a problem of co-ordination.'

'These little things are sent to try us, Miss Kettley,' my mother would say.

'Yes, but some little things are more trying than others. I know, I've been in children for years.'

I had also forgotten that Mr Jensen, the hunchback, was in the laundry room. My mother reminded me by bringing in the other tray with a bowl of porridge on it. 'You take it to him, Jimmy; I can't go dressed like this. That's what he needs, not that terrible methylated spirits.'

I sat up and stared at her, all the memory of the night coming back to me.

'It's quite all right,' she said. 'You're getting really well now. Thermometer's right down. Well, go on.'

I put on my twisted, cold dressing gown and took up the tray. Now I was to face Mr Jensen, the guardian of the lagoons. It was before Euphemia came, and I knew she would have something to say about that. He was a bundle of torn garments and very smelly. His skin was so worn in places it had scabs. Where they had hit him on the head he was bruised, with stains of blood. My mother also said I must come back for a bowl of warm water and Dettol. I put the tray beside him where he'd see it when he sat up.

I went back into the kitchen and my mother gave me the bowl and poured Dettol into it, and it spread through the water like healing fingers. Without slopping it, I got the bowl to the door of the laundry. Mr Jensen was sitting up and he'd pulled the front of his overall open, where the skin was paler and there was a scabby wound.

'My mother says you must clean yourself and have breakfast,' I said.

Mr Jensen looked at me and was very quivering. 'Dankie, kleinbaas,' he said.

'That was bad, for them to hit you,' I said.

'They skelms,' he said. And he put the spoon in the porridge to test it, as if he didn't know what it was.

'My mother says you not going to live long because you're a hunchback,' I said. That's what everyone said about Mr Jensen, but he looked very old already.

'Yes, I'm going to die,' he said. 'But the Lord mus' wait a bit till I get them back firs'.' He dipped the spoon. 'Ag, the ma'am's a good ma'am.'

'She's not afraid of Coloureds,' I said. 'Only Japanese.'

'When the Japanese is coming they going to get those caddy-boys firs', I'm telling you.'

I wanted to ask Mr Jensen about other things. Could it be that he had forgotten our wordless rituals out there in the no man's land past the Silver estate. 'Mr Jensen,' I said. 'Do you remember – do you remember when –'

'All I remember is I had a bottle in my hand, and next thing they beating me, bloody skollies.'

'But you didn't die last night, you didn't.'

'When my time comes, kleinbasie, nobody'll beat me then, it'll be flames and honey, I can tell you.'

'Not last night, before, before –' I said.

'Oh, it's happened plenty times before.'

'No,' I said, 'not that. Not the skollies and the beatings. Before the posters, before the flying boat. Almost when my father was here. When I used –'

'They were beating me for a bottle still then,' said Mr Jensen. He dipped the wad of cotton wool in the Dettol and carefully poked it at his thumb. It oozed against the skin and his face went contorted.

'Does it sting?' I said.

I could hear my mother calling for me.

'Just a minute,' I said.

'Come on, Jimmy, your porridge is getting cold,' she called through the flyscreen door.

'You better finish up,' I said to Mr Jensen, "cause Phemie's coming and you making the washing dirty.'

Mr Jensen gave me a smile, and then went back to hurting himself with the Dettol, putting on a big act for me.

'You're just pretending,' I said.

'Come on, Jimmy, I must go to work.'

I rushed inside and shovelled back my porridge because mother was in a hurry and when the milk went into the tea it spread like Dettol.

'That's better,' said my mother, 'if you're well enough to have breakfast up, you're on the road to recovery. But you stay inside today; you can get a relapse. One of Miss Kettley's had a relapse.'

'What's a relapse?' I said.

'It's like a collapse,' she replied. 'You have to start with being ill all over again.'

At that moment the one caddy, the gang-leader, who had the club the night before, came to the French windows and said he would fix the creeper.

'Just as well,' said my mother, 'otherwise I'd take the lot of you to the magistrate.' And she went to supervise.

So I slid away from the table and returned to Mr Jensen. As soon as he'd heard the skollie, he'd prepared to go, throwing down the porridge and messing the bowl of Dettol. He was standing at the laundry door, sheltering his eyes against the sun.

'Don't go, Mr Jensen,' I wanted to say. 'Tell me about the –' It was so important to me, and I couldn't say it in words. That would destroy it.

He focused on me briefly. 'You mean the big fish?'

'Yes.'

'Oh,' he said, pulling the front of his overall together. 'Them. They gone now.'

'You mean – gone? They dead?'

'No, they not dead, kleinbasie. They gone out like submarines on patrol, man. Gone out for food, because they get hungry. There isn't food for them in the lagoons. But don't you worry, they'll be back. It's not the breeding season now.'

'So they not dead?'

'No, I told you.'

'Mr Jensen, you mustn't die,' I said.

'Also you,' he said. 'Stay strong, kleinbasie, then I'll send you a message when they come back.'

'And no one'll know?'

'Not if we're lucky,' he said.

He shambled off along the side of the house, avoiding the front where the gang-leader was. At the corner, he peeped round. I was following close behind him, but he had forgotten me. When the coast was clear, he nipped past the fruit tree and retrieved the wedge of bread my mother had shoved through the hatch the night before. He dusted it off, then tiptoed into the milk-bushes.

I went towards the veranda and saw where my mother and the caddy were hauling up half the bougainvillaea on a length of rope. I watched them, and the caddy's jacket slid up his back as he was pulling, and my mother's belt tightened up her spine with the effort of getting it up on the pergola.

'All right, thank you,' said my mother. 'And don't you ever do that again.'

'Yes, ma'am,' he said, touching his cap, and he was off.

Then Euphemia came with all her bags and my mother said that I would tell her all about it, and then Blackie arrived to give my mother a lift to the golf club. Then the man came to fix the phone, because it was broken, and Euphemia talked to him all morning, and I coloured in. Then Mrs Pennington-Worthy came and put her powdered face with the little white curls in through the window and said she'd heard there'd been a riot last night, and I didn't say anything. Euphemia said my mother was out at work, and they didn't have any parcels. Then I had an early sleep.

The source of the news about the incident of the previous night could only have been my mother, and she would not have melodramatised it. But by the time Euphemia went up to the tearoom café to buy more bread, it had travelled from the golf club to there; Mrs Feverall asked Phemie, as one woman to another, because the latter was a 'good native', if she wouldn't stay with my mother at night, in case there was a further outbreak. Then she could run secretly up the avenue to the Pennington-Worthys for help. But Euphemia said she had her own troubles. Meshack had a relapse with his scarlet fever and they might send him back from school.

Mrs van der Westhuizen was most likely the cause of the amplification in the story, as she kept phoning us to see if we were all right, although it was broad daylight and, anyway, we had settled the business. What with Mr Pennington-Worthy calling to see if everything was in order, and Mr Lotter driving down in his bakkie, and Freddie on his bicycle even though he had no post, and Sergeant Thoroughwell with his siren going and everyone having tea that Euphemia gave them on the veranda, it was a busy day. I stayed in bed as I was meant to be ill.

By the time my mother came home from work, this whole lot converged on her once more by way of a deputation. First, Sergeant Thoroughwell, who had a guilty conscience for being unavailable when the affair occurred, explained that the telephone had now been repaired and would stay repaired. He demonstrated several times by getting his wife to phone us. She delivered advice and commentary over the receiver all through the following.

Second, Mr Pennington-Worthy said we must all stick together, and implored my mother to carry Mr van der Westhuizen's old gun. My mother refused to have a gun in the house as she was a woman of peace, and the gun would only end up shooting the wrong person.

Third, Mr Feverall, who had another cup of tea, proclaimed that he for one was on twenty-four hour guard and that, by Jove, it reminded him of the Bambata Rebellion. They had lots of women and children to worry about, and you never knew where it would break out next; keeping a round-the-clock watch was vital to their security.

My mother said she was sure he would like something stronger than tea, and he said, yes, whisky, but we had only some wine Aunt Rosemary sent us.

Fourth, Mr Lotter said the only thing was to herd them into the yard and cut their throats. The black man who worked for him knew how to do that, so he would send him down with the cleaver at a moment's notice.

That was all right for cattle and for Japanese, said my mother, but the whole business was becoming inflated and this was a small matter between our own people; why, it was no more than the desperate feelings of a few of our fellow citizens.

'Who were not observing the curfew,' said Sergeant Thoroughwell.

'Or the new law about their carrying offensive weapons,' said Mr Feverall.

'Victimising an old beggar – one of their own kind,' said Mr Lotter.

'What sticks in my throat,' said Mr Pennington-Worthy, 'is that it happened on my property.'

'Nevertheless,' said my mother, 'it was a minor domestic incident of no significance and I thank you all for your help.'

Mrs Pennington-Worthy arrived, parking in the middle of the road so that there was a traffic jam, and I knew poor mother was lost. She came under the pergola with her cigarette holder and her hairclips falling out, telling the men not to get up. She wouldn't sit down and they shouldn't stand. She had to keep her distance because of the peppermints; she could catch fire if she smoked in a closed environment.

She said, 'Well, as I see it, the woman cannot be left alone. That's the trouble with wretched war – the chips are down and all your lines of communication cut. You're a target, Sarah dear, and you don't even know who's aiming at you. I've lived through enough wars to know that by now. It's not the bugles and the marching feet you have to beware of, it's the lousy little leftover sniper in the twilight, in the trees, over there.' She gestured, and everyone looked at our milk-bushes which continued to the Pennington-Worthy fence.

'But –' said my mother, 'I go down the path there to work every day. It's perfectly safe. If there are any Coloureds or natives there at all, they are quite courteous to me.'

'Courtesy?' said Mrs Pennington-Worthy.

'Yes, courtesy,' said my mother. 'What else would they show?'

Mrs Pennington-Worthy gave my mother one of those pitying looks. 'When, Sarah dear, you've been out here as long as I have, well –'

'I've been out quite long enough, Mrs Pennington-Worthy. And, if you must know, I consider this my home now; it's where I married and where I belong. There's no need to turn Silver Town into an armed camp, either.'

'I'm sure the Japanese would be pleased to hear that point of view,' said Mr Pennington-Worthy.

'Thank you,' said Mrs Pennington-Worthy to her husband, 'thank you for backing me up for once.'

'All the Japanese'll understand is bang-bang-bang,' said Sergeant Thoroughwell.

'The Japanese are your problem, sergeant, not mine. I will look to this house and my son and myself. It wasn't me who got bashed last night, but Mr Jensen, and he is a Silvertonian!' That was my mother's strongest plea, and she was shaking. 'Now go,' she said, 'all of you. Thank you for your help, but just please go.'

Mr Pennington-Worthy looked awkward. 'I'm sorry, my dear,' he mumbled, 'we all know how you feel.'

'Yes, you have my sympathy,' said Mr Lotter. 'Ever since my wife died I've missed the way women can say things we men don't even think of.'

'I would like to be left alone, if you don't mind,' said my mother, and she was on the very edge.

'Yes, um,' said Sergeant Thoroughwell, 'my wife says –' and he rushed to the phone where her voice was curling into the still evening.

'Of course, we do know how you feel,' said Mr Feverall. 'Can't have been easy all these months. Sticking it out is the worst part of war. That's how you win, in the end.'

Sergeant Thoroughwell put down the phone and came back, signalling to everyone with his nose in the air that they had better leave my mother. They all reached for their wine glasses, and then for their hats.

'Oh, I am sorry,' said my mother. 'I really didn't mean to be such a bad hostess. I do appreciate your concern. Forgive me.'

It was the only time we'd had a party since my father left for the war, and now, instead of a party, it had turned into the Silver Town Vigilance Committee, meeting on our veranda.

'We'll be off in a moment, Sarah dear,' said Mrs Pennington-Worthy, stubbing her fourth cigarette out in the pot of marigolds. 'But before we leave, do let me say what I feel. You should take immediate precautions. Give up the job for a start –'

'Hear, hear,' said her husband. 'It's not good for a woman to be out of the house all day.'

'But –' my mother was amazed. 'How do I make ends meet otherwise? I have to pay you rent, I have to provide. Besides, the club is doing quite well now, admittedly thanks to the defence force, but I wouldn't like to let our club go downhill again.'

Mrs Pennington-Worthy looked at her husband, who looked at Sergeant Thoroughwell, who looked at Mr Feverall, who looked at Mr Lotter. Old Mr Lotter the butcher wasn't really part of the committee, but this time he spoke for all, 'Yes, you're doing a good backroom job there. You've made it flourish.'

'It is a most pleasant place now,' agreed Mr Feverall. 'Just as well it's members only, or our poor old hotel'd have no guests at all.'

'Well then, if you insist on being resolute, my dear,' said Mrs Pennington-Worthy. 'Avoid those bushes. Take the main road, where everyone can see you.'

'But it's not the daytime we're worried about,' Sergeant Thoroughwell told her.

'Main road at all times,' Mrs Pennington-Worthy waved him aside. 'That's my advice.'

'And at night?' said her husband. 'Alice, that's the point.'

'Take a lodger,' concluded Mrs Pennington-Worthy. 'Isn't there a stairs going round the back of Peter's Lodge to the roof? Yes, there is. Sarah, there you are. He can come and go without disturbing you, and if there's any trouble you just knock on the ceiling. Look, he can fire from all corners of the balcony. Then you're perfectly safe.'

My mother bit her lip and looked glum.

'She has got a point, Mrs Esslin,' said Sergeant Thoroughwell. 'A woman alone is cause for great unrest to us.'

'Hear, hear,' said Mr Pennington-Worthy, 'should all be rounded up.'

'Oh, not them – her, her, dear,' said Mrs Pennington-Worthy.

My mother raised her voice. 'I've asked my sister to come, but, you see, she has her own family now. She said I should go and stay with them and the children, but I don't want to do that. I'm sure you wouldn't like to evacuate your houses, would you?'

'Sarah, the last thing we're suggesting is that you admit defeat. Just get yourself some solid company, that's all we mean,' said Mrs Pennington-Worthy, stroking my mother's shoulder.

'But as long as the lease holds, that is my husband's study upstairs,' said my mother. 'Don't you see? I'm keeping it for him. All his things are there, just as he left them, and so they shall be when he returns.'

'Into Cyrenaica now; it's going to be an awfully tricky campaign,' said Mr Feverall, 'once they really get to grips with Rommel and his thugs.'

'But there's a side room,' Mrs Pennington-Worthy pointed. 'Look, I can see it from here. Perfectly adequate for a lodger, and your husband's things need not be disturbed one bit.' She was blowing smoke on the lawn.

My mother completely changed her tactics then. 'And while we're all gathered here, I do have a few ideas of my own,' she said. 'The Coloureds and natives of Silver Town are in a wretched state. I think we should start our own home effort. Stop sending aid overseas and concentrate on what's happening under our noses. There should be a soup kitchen, because they're starving. First the shark-oil closed, then the quarry, and now the bait is licensed, and you've taken out your orchards, and Mr Feverall – Mrs Feverall's sacked two of your waiters and two servant girls, and Mr Lotter – they aren't buying meat, are they? They have nothing to buy it with.'

'They're not buying meat,' Mr Lotter agreed.

'But they're buying liquor from Mr Feverall,' said Mrs Pennington-Worthy.

'Only half-jacks these days,' Mr Feverall confirmed.

'They can't afford even to buy stamps at the post office. At the club we get a string of them applying for jobs every morning. Quite respectable ones. I have to turn them away, and it breaks my heart to see them.'

'I think the fish are running in the bay, Sarah, so they are adequately provided for by nature,' said Mr Pennington-Worthy.

'Not like they used to,' said Sergeant Thoroughwell. 'It's the worst season since 1932.' He looked quite pleased at having contradicted Mr Pennington-Worthy.

Mr Pennington-Worthy looked irritated. 'Well, I don't like it – charity,' he said. This time he did put on his hat and prepare to go. 'You coming, Alice?' He extended his arm towards his wife.

'I have my own car, dear,' she said, 'and I shall leave as soon as I'm ready.'

He smiled at everyone and went down the path to his driver.

'I think –' said Sergeant Thoroughwell, 'you've got half an idea there, Mrs Esslin. We should commandeer that useless old church hall. Haven't had a service in there since Reverend Fowler died in 1937, and then they sent Mr Creswell up to Northern Rhodesia. You haven't got half an idea.'

'That's what half of my meat's only good for,' said Mr Lotter, 'making soup. But a nourishing soup, with Miss Kettley's vegetables, and fish heads; you boil it all up together.'

'Yes,' said Mr Feverall, thinking of dinner himself, 'that'd make quite a brew. I dare say Mrs Feverall would know what to do.'

Then Mr Pennington-Worthy's driver was hooting because Mrs Pennington-Worthy's car was in the way. 'Heavens, and he's late for a meeting in town,' Mrs Pennington-Worthy exclaimed. 'Arms contract.' She pecked my mother on the cheek, and staggered towards the traffic jam, but came back, interrupting my mother, 'Oh let them wait,' she said. 'This is so exciting. When shall we reconvene?'

Sergeant Thoroughwell stood up again and said quite spontaneously, 'Well, Mrs Pennington-Worthy, may we have the honour of making it tomorrow at the club, at sixteen hours? We would be absolutely delighted if that were convenient for you.'

She smiled very graciously. 'My husband shan't be back by then, but I shall represent him.' And off she went.

Their reversing and shuffling around effectively broke up the gathering. Mr Feverall and Mr Lotter seemed most exhilarated, and thanked my mother very warmly, each giving a slight bow.

Sergeant Thoroughwell concluded the proceedings by telling her she was a brave girl and to keep her chin up.

Then I helped her clear the cups and the glasses and the bottle, and we went into the kitchen to make supper.

10

The soup kitchen, run by Mrs Feverall, became a regular feature of Silver Town life. The re-opened church hall was active all day with the comings and goings of organising women and the malnourished and unemployed. A reporter for the city took a photograph of our Mr Jensen, receiving the first bowl of thick gruel and a slice of national loaf.

Calm and routine reigned. With the catering of the area in the hands of Mrs Feverall up on the hill and of my mother at the club end, things had never run so efficiently. The hall being open made a new social focus in the community and in that lowly context all of Silver Town came to know its fellows. There was not mere charity at work, but an atmosphere of mutual need and dependence. As long as the Japanese threat hovered, Silver Town was a model village.

Euphemia and I would take what we had up to the hall every morning. The nannies' union moved in there effortlessly. For me, the village opened up across trestle tables selling jumble and dispensing aromatic beverages. Now, instead of commenting on my height odd people in the main street commented on my usefulness. Although I had no official role to play, I was everybody's scout.

I think I must have talked an inner language mostly, but I always understood what needed to be done. Speech came out of me only rarely, and I no longer minded if they failed to comprehend what was becoming clearer to me. Because of the mixed nature of Silver Town lingo, I began to annex words from Afrikaans and Xhosa – 'Hou vas, wetu' was my favourite.

Miss Kettley wouldn't approve, and didn't. Came the day when my fete was to end after the dry New Year and I went to school.

'Ah, the Esslin boy at last,' Miss Kettley said. I came to a dead halt on her school veranda, my shoes at the point of her stick. My hair was licked down under my new cap, my front buttons done up correctly, my grey shorts a size too big so that I would fill them out, my grey socks held up with black elastic bands which Euphemia had sewn for me, and the shoes, they sparkled, as I had trodden softly on the dust. My mother waited at the gate in the Christmas thorn hedge; Miss Kettley was expecting me.

'Quite presentable, aren't we?' she said. 'Well, see that we stay that way. Quite orderly and tame for a wild lagoon boy who's always full of mumbo-jumbo. Keep your language to yourself while you're in my school, James. Do you hear? I don't want you to frighten the girls. Today, for you, James, I'd like you to start with colouring in – you know how to colour in?'

'Yes, Miss Kettley,' I said.

'Come on, James James Morrison Morrison, see if you can colour in a whole giraffe. Go on, help Sheena in the sun-room.'

'Yes, Miss Kettley,' I said obligingly, taking my satchel with my lunchbox.

'He'll be all right,' said Miss Kettley, waving her stick to my mother.

A feeling of desolation washed over me as mother turned at the gate; she was going, she was gone. I had to face Sheena and Miss Kettley on my own. I stepped from my world into theirs. I was not happy there. For the entire time I was a prisoner in Miss Kettley's Beginners School of Silver Town I did not feel at ease until the schoolbell rang and I was released.

Later in the morning Miss Kettley came from the spelling class next door to supervise Sheena and myself. Sheena had done most of the labour, leaning over the table with heavy concentration. She was making the giraffe look as if it wore military camouflage. I passed her the coloured pencils, and she'd look up and take them without saying anything.

'Yes, that's quite good for a giraffe,' said Miss Kettley, putting down her stick and swivelling from the hips. She held the giraffe up to the window. 'In fact, one of the best giraffes I've seen. Good boy, James,' she said.

I didn't say anything; I never said anything.

When Miss Kettley had gone again, to see if they'd memorised the spelling chart, Sheena pulled the giraffe from under my elbows and took it to the other end of the table with all the pencils.

School followed the general rhythm of the town, so that when the church hall bell went for the kitchen officially to serve lunch, we slithered down from tables and lined up on the balcony. Miss Kettley arranged us in a line by height, so that Michael Longford, who was the senior child in the school, came first, and then Jenny Green, who was the brightest, and then the two Feveralls, then Lettie Lotter, then Kettley major and Kettley minor, then Sheena and me last. Little Marie van der Westhuizen was missing because her parents were still on holiday in Cape Town where her great-aunt lived in a big house that could take all of them, and we left a gap for Little Marie.

Miss Kettley pronounced she was satisfied. We fell to opening our lunchboxes in the garden under the pine tree. The sandwiches inside mine had curled up, and the peanut butter tasted like glue, and I couldn't eat it. All I had was the bottle of fruit juice with the taste of greaseproof paper on the rim, but I closed the box as if I were finished. The box had the writing for Sunrise Toffees, but there were no toffees inside.

After lunch Miss Kettley gave us a talk about saving food, because in Great Britain there was rationing. One whole family of four could have only one Mars Bar a week with a coupon, and they had to share it. It cost $2^1/_2$d. They shared it by cutting it with a razor blade. So we were very lucky indeed, and had abundance. Look at Kettley major and minor, whom Miss Kettley's brother had sent out for the wartime; they had whole handfuls of chocolates out here. In England they would have a sixth of a Mars Bar weekly.

She asked us what sweets we'd had for Christmas. Jenny Green said she had Cadbury's, and the Feverall twins each had a box of chocolates also, and Michael Longford had a whole Christmas cake with a pine tree like the one outside on it, and Lettie had some frosties her dad bought her with wrappings, and Sheena had jujubes and jelly babies, and I had the Sunrise Toffees. Did anyone know what Little Marie had? I knew what Little Marie had – a tin of Humphries Mints and a tin of butterscotch – but I didn't tell them.

The next day after lunch for conversation we had where we had all been for the holidays, but I didn't say anything. This lasted for many days, because Jenny Green had been to the Giant's Castle in the Drakensberg, and she was very descriptive, and Michael Longford had gone all the way to Middelburg, the one that's in the Cape where all the famous South Africans are born. After that we had fishing, and we had picking up litter, and we had the feeding habits of the blue crane. Then we had fishing for kob again, but nobody talked about the mantas.

As the shyness crumbled within me, so the mantas disappeared. By a process of hours and days I was being broken into a social being. Whereas I had been at the centre of my world, I was now on the periphery of theirs. Whenever I looked at the lunch-time parade, I realised how much growing I had to do and how many years would have to pass before I headed it, when Michael Longford and everyone else had gone to Junior School. But for the moment we were caught like that, lined up for Miss Kettley. My previous existence rolled up inside me and went to sleep.

Miss Kettley started Sheena and me on lettering with pothooks and hangers. Pothooks were like the ones Euphemia had down in the Pits, to hang her three-legged cooking pot over the fire to boil mealies. Hangers were like the ones we had in the cupboard in my mother's room. This is where I began to have difficulties that could no longer be concealed. I did a row of the pothooks like the letter g, and then a row of the hangers like the sign you use for a question mark. Then they would all come out upside down and back to front. I do the same today; I have to think very carefully before I place the nib on the page.

But then it was easy to pretend the one was the other. If I looked along a whole line of them in the exercise book with my mother's powder mirror, they came right. This took most of the year to sort out. There was a gap between my potential and my performance, between what I thought I was doing and what others perceived I did.

The next obstacle was numerals. Miss Kettley showed me how to write the date, 1942. Also my age, which was six. The nine and the six became the focus of my confusions. I wrote

1642 and that I was nine, which meant I'd come before Van Riebeeck and had all of South Africa to myself. I wrote 9142, which meant I was many thousands of years old and lived on Venus, under a glass dome. I could play the dates out to make myself anything but a six-year-old living in Silver Town in the middle of a war. My mother consulted Dr Walton's wife about it; she said it would come right, but it didn't. When Miss Kettley marked my homework, I still got nought. That was one symbol I could understand. There was no point in copying from Sheena, who always got ten, because it was in the act of copying from her or from the blackboard that I made the mistakes.

It was thought best that I should leave history and adding until the following year. Sheena was going to go on and join the proper class. At that, a cloud passed over my life. I was frozen on the threshold of promise, kept back by my ineptitude. I could tell from the way the other children talked that I was to miss a world of knowledge because I couldn't grasp its curves and swoops. From then onwards I lost all desire to grow. For homework in the evenings I just did more colouring in. Everyone said I had a very good sense of colour.

After school one day Mr Lotter told Lettie to tell me to go to the post office, as Miss Bester had a parcel for my mother. I went immediately to Miss Bester, and she leaned over the counter and said that Freddie must have taken it, but he hadn't because he told me he hadn't. I stood there, waiting to see if she could find it. But Mrs van der Westhuizen came in then; she was driving Blackie's jeep to get the club's provisions they'd forgotten on the native bus. She said Mrs Feverall had the parcel at the soup kitchen, because she was going down to Peter's Lodge in the afternoon to pay out the proceeds, and would deliver it then. I went to the hotel and Mrs Feverall had gone down already.

So I went home in the normal way, scuffing my shoes in the sand. I tipped out the crust of my sandwiches where the birds congregated at the overflow from the mountain stream, and they scuttled towards me, and waited till I was gone. Mrs Van had said it was a parcel addressed to me; the censor had opened it, so everyone knew what it was, but they weren't telling.

Euphemia had put it where she put all my father's letters, on the windowsill in the living room. The parcel was big and flat, even bigger than my satchel. It was addressed to me in my father's handwriting: it said Master James Esslin, Peter's Lodge, Silver Town, Cape, South Africa. And it came from Major A Esslin, 1st South African, Reggio Camp, Sicily, Italy. They had put the string back on it. When my mother came home, she said it must be from my father for me, and she cut the string off, and it was an album of drawings.

I couldn't fit the album in my satchel except sideways, and I carried it to school, and to the shops, and down to the harbour and to the club, and back home again. I showed everyone, and they all said that's where I got my colour sense from. They were drawings my father did for me, and they were of pumps and buildings and dark people in Arab clothes working on a pulley which was called a shadoof, and at the back there were drawings of landing in Sicily with metal planks on the beach.

He'd coloured them in with watercolours. In the letter he said he caught the idea from Aunt Rosemary and she must advise him on what watercolour kit was best for us to get for him for Christmas, although Christmas was past. And I knew that when I sharpened the crayon with a razor blade, cutting a tiny peel off the tip, my technique would improve once I had a brush and a jar and a tray of watercolours like my father, because my mother would get two sets, one for each of us. I stared at my funny hand, with chips of red colour sticking in my fingerpads, and put it flat on my father's watercolour, not dirtying it. I knew that his big hand had been there, doing such accurate work.

I didn't go to school one day, even though it was Friday. Mr Jensen came. He tapped on the flyscreen door. He didn't go to the soup kitchen anymore, and so he was filthy. I had my smartest clothes on. Euphemia was out in the laundry at that moment, and my mother was fetching her coat.

'Psst, Master Jimmy,' he crooked his finger.

'I can't come now,' I said.

'Remember what I said I'd tell you about?' he said.

I adjusted my belt, and said he must go away. My new belt was elastic with many colours, and it fastened with a clasp that hooked in a loop. 'I'll get into trouble if I come now,' I said.

'Jus' don' say I didn't tell you,' he said. 'They there. You don' wan' to miss them.'

'We are going to Cape Town,' I said in an upperhand way, as if we went there regularly. In fact, I had not been in Cape Town since I was born there in the Great Depression, and I had no idea where or what that was.

He whistled, phew, Cape Town.

The trip started with Mr van der Westhuizen getting my father's car into action. He and Little Marie were going to drive us to the station. Marie had the first part of the morning off from school, as well; this wouldn't set her back too much. The car was so full of dust we could hardly see Silver Town, but we caught a glimpse of the other children going to Miss Kettley's. Mr van der Westhuizen, who drove very well, was going to keep the car for the day and then drive to the station again to fetch my mother and myself in the evening.

We made it up the pass with the car gushing out smoke, which settled all over the scrub. Mr van der Westhuizen said it was dangerous to drive as my mother had forgotten to renew the registration for 1943, and she had to do that immediately at the council before the train came in. That got us off to a bad start, as she was very irritated at the fine she had to pay. Little Marie said that her mother said we must have morning tea at Hildebrand's in Saint George's Street, where they had morning tea every single day during their holiday. So we were all set for Hildebrand's.

The sky was magenta-coloured, and the rails were silver beneath the rusty platform. When the train came in I felt ill because the last time I'd seen it was as a military train. It was black and silver and the coaches were a gritty, sparkling brown. We were in first class only, which was in the front, and there was only one first class carriage.

No one else was there that morning; you could see because the green seats were vacant. My mother put me at the window on the south side, so that if there was any ocean I would see it first. With a heave the train went forward, and we passed the station-master with his red flag and the platform ran out, and we were going quite smoothly. Smoke kept leaking past the window from the steam-engine, but it cleared up and you could see properly. There was a patch of raw rock with steam squashed against it, and then we were past the houses and you could see the open.

My mother was very properly dressed, with a warm scarf in case it was windy in Cape Town. Somehow Cape Town was always so remote and immense in my imagination that I couldn't believe it was possible for a child to go there. We all knew it from the photographs on calendars; we had at Peter's Lodge an annual review with Table Mountain and the daisies on the cover. But my mother said we weren't going to approach it from the north like that, but across the Cape Flats, so we'd see the side of Table Mountain. She had many memories of Cape Town, because that's where she had first steamed into the bay. Then she met my father just after. Then we had a tunnel.

The Cape Flats were very flat, with puddles of rusty brown water everywhere, and wattle trees like at home. The Coloureds lived in the bushes, and you could see the backs of their houses from the train, and they were so used to it they didn't even look up. It was a long-distance train, so we didn't stop at all the intermediate stations. The train kept this rhythm: karoo karum karoo karum karum. Then at a crossing it would go tchum tchum tchum. When we got near a settlement the whistle would blow, and a swooping cloud of smoke would come over the window. Then it was dazzling again.

Cape Town started slowly with many houses. Most of them were solid and strong, with gardens. Then there was another block and another, with cars parked on the pavements. We went past a factory, and another factory where they make the blankets, and a whole row of factories. One of them was Mr Pennington-Worthy's. You could see the side of Table Mountain, bluish and green right above them, and then it was Salt River where we did stop. My mother opened the window and I hung out, and most of the other passengers from the back got out there to go and look for work in the factories and warehouses. They had bundles of all their stuff.

Then we chugged forward, and my mother grabbed me, and all the couplings were straining and tugging; it wasn't uphill, but the engine was running out of steam. As if it were floating there, the mountain turned round to meet us. The engine slackened, and we leaned forward. My crayons shot off my lap and spilled over the floor. The conductor came back then, and helped me pick them up. My mother put them in her handbag and gave the conductor the one half of our tickets. He opened the door for us and jumped out even before the train had stopped. We alighted when it was safe.

In Cape Town, everything was bigger and echoed. The station concourse was so enormous I couldn't see from one corner of it to another without turning my head, and they had places to put your shoes if you wanted them cleaned. When we emerged from the station, there was traffic going up the one way and down the other, and horsedrawn taxis, and lorries loaded with vegetables and many bicycles with bells ringing, dodging in and out. With all the people it was hard to walk, so I clung to my mother's hand – 'Watch where you're going!' said a policeman in his uniform, and I jumped back on the curb. A crush of shoes and sandals and army boots and newspapers and wheels and high-heels with the toes coming out the front, and there were Malays wearing their slippers. I walked with my other hand in front to make way. My mother was hurrying because we were late. She showed me the clock on the tower of the City Hall and we had three minutes.

She asked an old Coloured woman, who was selling dried flowers on a little patch of the pavement, where the Darter's Building was. 'No, ma'am, you jus' go straight.' So we followed her instructions and there was the Darter's showroom with black grand pianos. We didn't have time to go to the Grand Parade where we could buy books about Libya and Italy, because we had the appointment. We walked in the revolving door, and I had to let go and it was quite heavy; I thought I was getting stuck in a glass sandwich. Then we walked through the grand pianos with their lids up, black and white keys open.

The salesman said this was Darter's itself, but we had to go out again to the side entrance where the lifts were. So we went through the revolving doors again, and they were less stiff, and moved along the side of the building to the portico where the lifts were with brass crisscross doors. We had to wait for one to come down and the inner door to match the outer door. Then the liftman opened both doors and we could go inside. The inside of the lift had a decorated lamp in the roof and mirrors on the walls, so that I could see a row of my heads stretching through the side in the one direction, and the other way there was a row of my mothers with their handbags clasped under their arms.

We reached the fourth floor. You could tell it was the doctor's because of the spectacle frames on his notice, with a golden hand with a shirt cuff, and the finger pointing to the left. We were absolutely on time, but he kept us waiting. My mother explained to the receptionist why we had made the appointment and filled in all the forms with my name. My mother said was there a toilet she could take me to, but I didn't want to go in case we missed the doctor. He wasn't a doctor like Dr Walton and his wife; he was an eye specialist. He must have made the glasses for the receptionist, because she was wearing them to read her magazine.

A girl who was the same age as me came out of the doctor's room with her mother and had cotton wool over her eyes. The girl was crying because she couldn't see at all now. She took deep breaths, and her mother led her to the seat.

There was still another patient before us; he was a very respectable Coloured boy in a suit, and he had a boil in his left eye. His mother spoke to my mother when she addressed her; it was a sty; he got it from eating too many sweets. The Coloured lady said we must go first because we'd come from so far, but my mother said she was a believer that everyone must take their turn. Are you English from England, said the Coloured lady, and my mother said yes, but it had been a long time ago.

'You wouldn' like to go back now with the war, hey?' said the Coloured mother.

No, said my mother, because she thought if people behaved decently in South Africa it would come out better here.

Then the receptionist took off her glasses and said the woman and the boy with the sty must go through, and she started talking to my mother, saying it was all right if they were decent, but some of them.

She seemed quite decent to my mother, even if they lived in very disadvantaged conditions.

A sty was nothing, said the receptionist, some of them had much worse, from living in such lack of hygiene.

It's all the sand on the Cape Flats, blows into the eyes, my mother said, and in District Six.

The girl who looked like Little Marie stopped crying and her mother held out a handkerchief for her to blow.

Then the respectable Coloured boy came out with a patch on his eye, and my mother didn't say anything, but his mother said goodbye to my mother, and we all said goodbye. The receptionist took the Coloured lady's money, but left it on the desk, because she had to show us the way in.

'Come through, please,' she said to my mother. I followed her.

The specialist's room had blinds, so the light was quite clear in strips. Michael Longford told me a joke about how do you make a venetian blind – poke him in the eyes. They were venetian blinds to control the light in the room. The specialist put me in a high chair with my arms on the rests, and turned me round. I was facing different letters from the alphabet on an illuminated screen, starting with a big A. He told me to read them slowly, and I did.

'Out loud so that the doctor can hear,' said my mother.

'He's a shy one, is he?' said the specialist. And he turned to me, 'And where do you go to school, young lad?'

'Miss Kettley's Beginners School,' I said.

'Oh my goodness,' he said. 'That's a long way away. You've had a big journey. Where did you say you come from?'

'All the way from Silver Town,' said my mother.

'Now, you can read that, can't you?' said the specialist.

I kept staring at the screen. I read out loud the A, and then the O and the E and the I, and the rest of the letters right down to the bottom row.

'You did that very well,' said the specialist. 'Now, I'm just going to swing this –' He lined up a big metal pair of spectacles on my nose, and pulled up two peepholes and dropped lenses in them. He asked if I could see anything, and I could see it all, and read it out the same.

Then the specialist dropped two more lenses into the frame, and asked me to read it again. I read it, remembering it clearly.

'Good, Jimmy,' said my mother.

'Nice part of the world, that,' said the specialist. 'I have friends who go deep-sea fishing there.'

'Oh yes,' said my mother. 'But there's not much of that these days.'

'Try these,' said the specialist, and he dropped two more lenses in. I could see the screen but I had to focus very hard. I went A, and the O and E and I, and the rest I could remember, so I rattled it off all in one breath.

'Good, Jimmy,' said my mother.

'Some go for tunny,' said the specialist. 'Think it's overrated. Prefer a nice galjoen myself.'

'Tunny's impossible to keep frozen,' said my mother.

The venetian blinds and the slats of light were all wavy. The specialist put my head against the frames. He dropped in two lenses that were like looking through cloudy water and very yellow, like staring at urine in a pot. He said I must read A, O and E and I – could I? And I could, but because he said it, not because I could see them.

Then he put in two that were like looking out of the train in the tunnel, with only an aperture of light at the end and seething shapes on the sides. I said I could see A on top.

My mother said I could look better than that, because he had changed the screen and there were two halves of a circle, and I must tell him when the top half was matched on the bottom half. I told him when they fitted like an orange.

He took the frame away and turned the chair round so that my mother was in front of me. Her clothes had gone streaky. Her blouse looked as if it were blown up on the washing line. The metal clasp of her handbag shone like a fish-hook. I thought it would stick in her hand, and she was going to be reeled away.

'Shark-oil's so rare now,' said the specialist.

My mother said nothing. Her breasts were too swollen to speak.

The specialist swung a little tray in front of me, and it had a microscope on it. He said it was a spectroscope. I was meant to look at the prism with the left eye first, and then the right eye. Both times it was wonderful to see, because light split up in a rainbow of straight lines and colours that I'd never seen before.

'You like that, do you?' said the specialist, and I said yes. He said were there gaps in it, and I said no gaps.

He asked me to describe the colours, and I could do that perfectly well through the left eye and through the right eye. Those colours went straight inside me, and I would always remember them.

Then he discharged me from the chair, and my mother gave me her handkerchief and he said he was happy to tell her my vision was perfect.

'But doctor –' said my mother.

'No need to worry about a thing,' he said. 'Doesn't need glasses. No ophthalmia, no glaucoma in your family or your husband's?' He took up the card my mother had filled in. 'No, perfectly all right.'

My mother seemed dejected, as if, having paid for the appointment, some results must be found.

'He'll be all right. Corrective glasses wouldn't help – there's nothing to correct.'

'You mean he's perfectly normal?'

I wiped under my eyes smartly and my mother told the story she always told about Miss Kettley's pothooks and hangers.

'Well, it's not an optical problem,' he said, and he made a gesture for us to be welcome to go.

'Thank you, doctor,' said my mother and I could hear that she was anxious.

'Nothing to worry about,' he said, holding his hand to the side again.

'But doctor,' she said, 'he reads upside down and back to front. He can't accurately transcribe what he sees.'

'Ps for Ds,' said the doctor.

'And Bs for Qs,' said my mother.

'You'll need a child psychiatrist for that, I'm afraid,' said the specialist.

'But they're so costly, doctor, and we live so far away,' said my mother.

'There is a cheaper method. Get him a piano. Give him half-an-hour's sight-reading a day. Very good for hand-eye co-ordination.'

'Yes, yes, I see,' said my mother.

'Save you a lot of baloney, to be quite frank. He'll grow out of it. What was your school?' said the specialist.

It seemed so distant and tiny. 'Miss Kettley's Beginners School,' I said, trembling.

'Well, you become the school pianist and play all the hymns. You'll be right as rain in no time,' he said, and waved us out into the city.

The lift went down and once we were out of the colonnade we faced the glare of the street. We walked a few paces, and my mother didn't take my hand. The pavement was empty. She turned at Darter's window and put her face against the glass. I gazed at her, not at the glass.

'Well, Jimmy-boy,' she said, 'we better skip the Grand Parade. It's too hot now.'

I turned from my mother and put my forehead on the glass. I cupped my hands against it: there were the grand pianos on their pedestals. One of them was revolving slowly on a platform, with the piano stool in place. There was a cardboard display of Fred Astaire dancing; it glided away, and came back into view. I had a very quick dream – the front piano opened its keys like the mouth of a manta, and it butted me gently through the glass and the window crashed in smithereens and we flew down Adderley Street to the harbour where it wanted to go.

Then I got a fright, because there was a lot of bad feeling in Cape Town during the war. The midday gun went off on Signal Hill and the echo rolled down Adderley Street, and everything came slowly to a stop – the street-collectors and the pedestrians and the carts and the American sailors on shore leave and the trackless trolleys with everyone seated. We all stood with our heads bowed for two minutes to commemorate that we were going to win the war. I stood with my arms at my sides.

There was a bunch of rowdies from up-country. They were wearing Stellenbosch blazers and not military uniforms. They wouldn't keep still because they didn't agree with the war. They were intentionally laughing and strolling. Everyone glared at them. Then my mother joined in what the other people were doing, quietly forming a cordon around them from all sides with our heads down, shuffling so that it didn't look as if we were disobeying. Malays and Coloureds and the traffic policeman and just ordinary business people, we closed in on them, getting tighter and tighter until they couldn't make a peep. Then the time was up and Adderley Street went back to normal.

My mother said it served them right and we could fit in Hildebrand's if we hurried, so she took my hand and we crossed Adderley Street at the pedestrian crossing. And a huge bus started up, but it had to wait for us. Then we went past Stuttaford's and across Saint George's Street, and a delivery boy on a bicycle nearly got banged into by a trolley. They were loading barrels of beer, and we went down the stairs alongside the shoot, and it was quite cool in Hildebrand's.

We ordered tea and anchovy toast, and a milkshake for me, and the service was very slow. I wished I'd brought my sandwich box, because the toast was very bitter-tasting. Then we had to go to catch the early train or we'd be home after dark, but I had to go to the toilet and my mother led me into the women's toilet, which was pink, and I pretended to go but didn't properly.

It was the same first class carriage, but the conductor was different and there were some people. My mother put me against the window again, and the engine started, but this time it was at the other end. When we were out on the Cape Flats my mother put her scarf back on, and she said she wondered if we could afford a small piano, not a baby grand but an upright ship's piano. She said there were all different styles besides the grand pianos. But we never could afford even a ship's piano, because my father sacrificed most of his income for the army; anyway, we never got a piano, and Miss Kettley didn't have one in the Beginners School. There wasn't a piano even in the golf club, since Silver Town was very unmusical. It was no use having a piano at sea level because it went out of tune, and the goggas ate the hammers. I forgot about pianos soon enough.

Mr van der Westhuizen and Little Marie were there to meet us at the station. When we got in the car Marie asked me if I'd been to Hildebrand's, and I said I'd had an anchovy toast and a milkshake; she said she used to go and have scones and cream. She hadn't been inside Darter's Building, round the side. But she'd been many times to Greenmarket Square where the Afrikaners went since there was a candyfloss stall on weekdays, and we didn't get there. And she'd been to the harbour, which was just like Silver Town's, only it was one of the busiest in the world.

'We're on the Indian Ocean, but that's on the Atlantic,' said my mother, and Little Marie looked at her.

'Ja, but it's all the same if you have a coastline to defend,' said Mr van der Westhuizen, and he braked, and we went down the slope towards Silver Town.

11

An official letter came from the Red Cross, saying that Major Andrew Thomas Esslin was reported missing, presumed dead. Several months had elapsed since he disappeared – those were the weeks we had not heard from him, and my mother had gone frantic.

And so the death was now certain. That was after Florence. He was a brave and noble man, much esteemed by his fellow officers and men alike. We accepted their condolences. A memorial service would be held at the end of the war for all those lost in action.

I was in school when my mother received the letter. She took me home early and explained it to me. We sat in the lounge with the sun coming in, but she didn't open the windows or turn on the wireless. We had a nice tea, which we hadn't ever done at that time in the morning. She told me that my father was gone and wouldn't come back. I said I understood. That's why Miss Kettley had been so kind to me, since she knew. Also Mrs Feverall; and her husband said, 'Copped it, has he – poor old Andy.' A letter from the Red Cross could only mean that. Even Miss Bester who found out first, said it was terrible.

My mother wouldn't have one of the biscuits; she was choking on it. So I thought I shouldn't, either. I put back the Baumann biscuit.

'It means no more stamps on the envelopes, Jimmy,' she said.

'Yes, I understand,' I said.

'And that album – that's the last one, so treasure it till your dying day, my Jimmy,' she said.

She nearly burst, but she was very controlled. She lifted the teacup to her lips, and then put it down in the saucer. 'And to think – to think,' she said.

'Yes, mamma, I understand,' I said.

'All this is for him – this house, and keeping the car in order, and the garden, and looking after you. Oh Jimmy, if only he'd seen you once before –' she said, and she put her hand on my head and stroked my forehead where the temperature had been.

'Mamma, we'll be all right,' I said.

'Yes,' she said, pulling me towards her, 'we'll be all right all right, but what about him? Poor, poor Andy. To die on a battlefield for his country, for a measly pension for his wife and child. My, Jimmy,' she said, 'it's rotten, isn't it? And he enjoyed his life so much. He was a very active man, always enjoying what he did. And everything he did was so personal, Jimmy. The way he used to – ' She curled my hair up the back of my neck. Her warmth seeped into me, and we could have stayed like that for hours.

But she held me away from her. 'You know what, Jimmy,' she said, 'you must be very brave now, brave and strong like a good soldier. Remember, he always used to call you that. Except I don't want you to be a soldier; but it means be resolute, be firm, be strong. Do you understand what I'm saying?'

'Yes, I understand,' I said.

'Whatever happens, you must be as he'd have wanted you. Not a hoodwinker, and a little shark – but honest and true. Isn't that what he'd like?'

I agreed with her. She was going to be like that as well.

'It isn't us who'll really suffer, either. It's him – he's done all the suffering for us, and what is it all for?'

I began to grasp some of the implications of what she was saying. 'Will you go back to England, mother?' I asked, firmly thinking that now her South African days were over, she would return home. For some reason I thought I wouldn't; I'd stay in Silver Town.

'What on earth makes you say that?' she looked at me.

'Aunt Rosemary went to England when poor Bonzo died,' I said.

'Oh, Bonzo. But that's completely different. Aunt Rosemary wasn't a Jamaican, and she didn't have a child by Uncle Bonzo. Now she has children she'll stay where her real family are.'

:'Yes, but we don't have a family without father,' I said.

'I see what you mean,' she said. She took my hand and held it in her lap. 'Yes,' she said, 'you're a clever, clever boy. But we are our own family – you and me. We'll have to learn to fend for ourselves. We're really good at doing that already. I was going to get a raise anyway, Mr Lever said, and the house is ours for as long as Mr Pennington-Worthy owns it, and there's the pension. We'll make ends meet, yes we will. It'll be all right for the two of us, it really will, I promise.'

'Promise,' I said.

Euphemia came bustling in, all full of surprise that we were home. She had a feather duster and was going to beat up a cloud right where we were. She stopped still as if she had walked into a fridge, and then my mother told her. It was terrible the way she took the news. She burst into big, shaking tears and stood there. Finally my mother put a chair under her and said she must look after her heart. Euphemia was very upset, and she said she thought my mother would fire her, but my mother said there was no question of that, and Euphemia sat there in the best chair, picking the feather duster to pieces.

'Euphemia, please go and do the other rooms first,' said my mother.

'Ow, he was a good man,' she said, and a piece of the feather went up in the air and curled where the draft was coming in from the kitchen. 'I can never forget him, Master Andy.'

'Andy, poor Andy,' said my mother. The way she used the name brought all the sadness to Euphemia.

'And Master Jimmy, you don' remember him properly. He went when you still a little, little boy,' Euphemia said.

'Yes, I know,' I said.

'Never mind,' said Euphemia, putting her hands squarely on her knees. 'One day I tell you all about him. He was a good man, your father.'

'Yes, now Euphemia, please I have to write a letter,' said my mother. We were both dismissed, and I would carry the letter that afternoon to the cemented-in postbox with enough stamps on it for my grandmother in England.

Despite the way I might have behaved towards my mother, and to Euphemia and to the rest of the world, I don't think any of the real impact of my father's death had touched me. I was a boy cut off from the life around me, exhibiting the most adult and sensible behaviour. I was not sure what the meaning of any of it was for myself. I took to my own secret rituals once more, in an attempt to find for myself where I stood.

Most of my reactions were controlled by fears – of Miss Kettley and her stick, of Miss Bester and her sabotage of the English-speakers, of drunks down at the harbour, of the caddy brigade at the club, of the Pennington-Worthys most of all. I had only Mr Jensen, whom I met barely a half-dozen times – and he was the village reprobate. And Mr Jensen had said the mantas had come in, which was my private secret. The mantas which were mating in the lagoons a few hundred yards away. And that family of mantas was my true family.

My father's death, then, was a stroke of luck to me. When she got over her grief, my mother moved my cot out of her and my father's bedroom and back into my room. Euphemia and she took the sides down, so that it was now a proper bed. That meant, when my mother had stopped crying at bedtime, I could put on the bedside light and read about the mantas. While at school I was kept down on account of pothooks and hangers, at home deep into the night I was teaching myself to read.

From my father's study I borrowed a book. It was about creatures of the deep-sea. I kept it in my old satchel, because I had a new one now, and the old one was stored away with the blankets. So clever was I at hiding it, that if Euphemia or my mother had ever found it I would have considered I had betrayed myself. I would tiptoe with it to bed, and cautiously steal my hand over the bedside table with its cotton covering, past the eyedrops and the scissors and the comb, and up the stem of the lamp until I had the switch.

As they were so large, the mantas or greater sea-devils were easy to find. Family Mobulidae, Genus Manta, fig. 17. Devil-rays occur singly or in pairs. Occasionally they are found in small schools. My finger stuck underneath each word. I could spell the word out first: Manta. Then the word before: Genus. And remember both, and then remember them in sequence, and draw my finger under the two words: Genus Manta.

In a long sentence I would take the short words singly, without 'the' and 'is': disc, long, tail, short, slender. The disc is

. . . than long; tail short, slender . . . The disc is broad, broader than long. And the tail comparatively. Comparatively short, slender and . . . Genus Manta.

The disc is broader than long, and the tail comparatively short, slender . . . whip-like. Whip-like tails. The mouth is very wide. The front parts of the fins . . . pectoral fins . . . are . . . are separated . . . off to form distinct . . . or head-fins. Distinct. Cep . . . Cepha . . . Cephalic or . . . separated off to form distinct cephalic. Or head-fins. Which. The front parts of the pectoral. Fins are separated off to form distinct. Cephalic or head-fins, which project. Forward. As a pair of horn-like . . . on either side of the mouth. Appendages. Horn-like appendages. Genus Manta.

This enormous creature . . . more has been written . . . their fearful reputation . . . their reputation. Because they are extremely large and powerful, they must be treated. With respect. Competent. Scientists report. To be rather docile. They can fly . . . like a cannon-shot. Swamp a clinker-built boat. Little is known of their distribution. Pups spread wings. Plankton feeders.

Pushed back to the ship over the bow of a ten-man rubber liferaft. Dissections of this kind are messy at best. Shoot out of the water and sound like a cannon-shot. Stopped rowing. The largest of all the rays, and are found in tropical or . . . subtropical seas. Dissections of this type are messy at best. 3000 lbs. 18 ft. wingspan. Pearly drops of water iridescent, as the monster emerged.

This took several nights to decipher. I memorised the phrases, returning to them over and over again. Family Mobulidae, Genus Manta, fig. 17. Broader than long. And the tail comparatively. Pectoral. Pectoral. Cephalic or. Cephalic headfins. Horn-like Genus Manta. They are also . . . ovo . . . ovovivi . . . ovo . . . ovovivipar . . . parous. The pups are hatched within the parents and born flying, straight into the clear water, flipping its pectorals. Fig. 17. From underneath they come, and make a Family Mobulidae with the mother and the father. Like the lagoon school.

My neck would ache and my eyes sting, and a month of night-times passed in this way. If I heard my mother's bed creak, the light was out in a second, and I nestled with the book under my arm, a perfect imitation of a sleeping child. And she'd open the door to check that I was asleep. She'd tuck in the side of my bed, and she knew I'd been awake, because the lamp was warm, and she'd go to bed and leave me to replace the book.

One night I had it planned. The moon was resting on the telephone pole. There was no wind. I was prepared to revisit the lagoons. The window was open enough. I slipped out of my pyjamas, and the moonlight was coming in like water. I pulled on my clothes without the silver belt-buckle clinking. I slipped out of Peter's Lodge like a pup out of its mother, flying over the lawn. I passed the fruit tree, put my towel in the branch for when I returned. There was the heron; it picked its legs up and went sideways and I went round it. The night smells different to wild things, because they are free.

When I came to the trespassing notice, I could now read it, but I did not have the time to stop. I could draw, I could read, I could count. I was counting my strides. Briefly I looked back and counted my footprints in the sand: six, seven, eight. They went into nine and ten where my feet were pushing in the sand in the shadow. I made many footprints where I pulled the barbed wire up and slid through, too many to count – dithering. Straight strides. Four, five, six . . . To where the dead people were.

It all seemed shorter and easier now that I was bigger. My ribs heaved with hot breath. I knew the reedbeds but they had gone black and white, with firm crests and sharp edges to the leaves. Then I nearly fainted; I had disturbed a nesting kiewietjie, a plover, and it charged across, shrieking and shrieking. I stayed on my side, panting and panting until I returned to normal and the bird went back. If I crept forward I could see the Pennington-Worthys' bay-window in the moonlight, and they were asleep with no inside lights on.

I crossed the jetty of the boathouse, my feet sinking in the mud and coming out with plopping sounds. It would have been easier if I took Mr Pennington-Worthy's dinghy and rowed. He never used it and it was rotting. After that was the path where the horses went; no more horses because of the war. It was overgrown and closing over. I was safely out of sight and walked to the palm tree. I didn't hide, because Mr

Jensen would recognise me. But I didn't want to see him. I wanted to see the dead people who planted that palm tree and built the observation platform. I sat there regaining my breath, for a long time, and no one was following me.

The dead people. Now my father was among them. They didn't bring his body back to Silver Town and bury him in the cemetery, because his body was lost. If they found it, it would be too expensive. He was walking around where they couldn't find him. The dead people would help him, though. They went fishing at night, so he could go with them. The dead people were good people; they didn't go baitpicking and making holes in the lagoons, and they didn't disturb anything. The dead people could float over the water without making a ripple. They lived on the foam. And they went riding on the devilfish with their mouths open, and their noses and foreheads didn't even get wet.

The lighthouse was very close now, owing to the moon. The lens in the tower was off because of the war. But the silver dome was clear in the moonlight. The shaft went up tapering and I wondered how they got bricks that built in a slope. From the lighthouse there were bushes all the way to the clubhouse, and behind that was the golf course on the promontory, and behind that the Indian Ocean which was connected to the Atlantic where Cape Town was. At the clubhouse I could see Blackie's jeep parked on the edge of the gravel. Blackie said it was best to go fishing at night, but Silver Town was too sleepy for that.

Only the dead people went fishing at night. But they didn't eat fish; they were plankton-feeders. Why did they call them dead when they were so alive? I was wading out to meet them. I didn't go too far, because I hadn't learned to swim; there was no swimming pool in Silver Town to teach me. It was a scandal in Silver Town how few people could swim. The fishermen who went out from the harbour couldn't swim. They trusted to God, but if their boats went over God wasn't much help if they couldn't swim; they drowned like ninepins. There were also Coloured dead people.

I had told the dead people that I had an appointment to meet the mantas. I was not a dead person, but they carried messages for me very speedily. The dead people were not always reliable, so I waited, wondering if my message had been delivered. In wading out to meet the great couriers of the dead I was detaching myself from all earthly things – from the property and people of Silver Town, the bonds of my mother whom I had temporarily forgotten. I had a deep fear that this time they wouldn't come, that no gliding messengers of the deep-sea with their horn-like . . . on either side of the mouth. Appendages. Genus Manta. Scientists report. One report had recorded that mantas played with a lone child, letting him ride upon their backs. I was not the first. But in the vast wastes of the Indian and Atlantic Oceans that far south I was the only one at that time.

I raised my hands, closed my eyes. I did my shuffling, awkward little dance for them. I talked directly to the dead people, requesting them to gather across the lagoon, and see my plight, and come my way. And they could move so speedily, they answered my request instantly. I could feel from the puff and buffet of current that they were there. I don't think mantas can see very well, but they can feel a presence through the waters, and they know when to come. They are curious, just as we are. They are so ignored in real life that they have dreams, too – dreams of knowing about the beyond. All they cannot do is climb out of their element for very long.

But they did on that night, briefly and triumphantly. When all else fades – the thought of my grief, my dependence, my loneliness and my terrors – when all that is gone, I will have this memory only: of a devil-ray sliding out of the undertow before me, carving through the surface, its broad disc transforming into wings, and ascending the dark, silvery air, holding breath, curving, flying, its pale underside lifted out of its element, and my dancing and singing kept it there aloft, turning in the same air which filled my lungs. And its pale, gleaming belly with its whip-like tail wheeled forward, and three tons of it landed like a cannon-shot, and a whole crater of foam opened up to engulf it. And the waves from its landing shook me, so that I felt weak in the power of the lagoons.

'O devilfish, O manta, O messenger, fetch me, fetch me,' I chanted, feeble and exhausted. I blew my nose on my hand, waited and waited until the cold was inside my bones. But the chief manta had given me its message already: your father is not among the dead people here and has never ridden me as you have. You are alone. Go home and tell no one – they will call you a liar and a failure. But you have your secret, and that makes you richer than anyone. Your father is not dead.

I pulled myself out of the water, half hoping that Mr Jensen would be there, but he wasn't. I fell on the salty platform, and breathed and breathed until I was calm again. I covered my body with my hands, trying to rub warmth from my palms into my chest and kidneys and thighs, and I wiggled my feet until they stopped feeling like metal. I had to relieve my bladder, coiled like a hosepipe frozen within me. I wouldn't take my eyes off the lagoons, even though I knew it was over.

From the manta I had one last commission. With my big toe I scooped into the sand my father's name. Doubtless I got the N back to front or the D upside down. At any rate, I wrote in letters so big that I could not see the beginning and the end of them, ANDY. When my graffiti was completed, I was dry and I dressed. Quiet and subdued, I set off for home. So exhausted was I that I walked the distance in my sleep.

I came through the milk-bushes and avoided the dumb, sleeping heron. The moon was considerably higher and no longer shone on my towel in the fruit tree. The house was perfectly asleep. When I had my hands on the metal window-frame, I knew I was back again. I was too without a will to know what I thought of being home. I had mine and others had theirs. I was back in bed as smoothly and silently as if I had never been out of it.

But the next morning I had to continue with my secrecy. I forced myself to burst out of deep sleep, and to act as if it were a normal morning. At breakfast, with my satchel and exercise book and all my homework done, I performed as usual, although I felt I wasn't inside my body at all.

'You're so sweaty, Jimmy,' said my mother.

I shrugged it aside. 'It was hot,' I said.

'You haven't been reading all night, have you?' she said.

'No, mother,' I said.

'Well, that's good ' she said. 'A boy of your age needs his sleep.'

I put the spoon into the porridge, even though my hand was shaking.

'Tell me, Jimmy,' she said, 'do you miss your father very much? Do you?'

'I can't remember him,' I said.

'But surely you remember how he used to take you for long walks around the lagoons – just you and him?' she said.

'No,' I said.

'Hoisting you on his shoulders and off you two'd go?'

'No, mother, I can't remember.'

'And put salt on his porridge. That was some deep, dark Scottish ancestry showing, you know.'

'No, mother,' I said.

'One day we'll get the photo album out and I'll show you,' she said. 'You used to light up when you heard the car, just because it was him coming home. Don't you really remember?'

I said nothing, as if I weren't interested. If I'd agreed with everything I would have had no mind of my own.

12

While I was nuzzling around inside my fantasies, other events were occurring in Silver Town.

Meshack was back from his school for the Christmas holidays. Meshack was in Standard 8 and almost a man. He had hard skin, and my mother complimented him on his English, and gave him a fountain pen. Euphemia had a small savings account at the post office for Meshack, and she could take money out of it if we wanted to buy a second-hand fishing rod. Thus, Meshack and I went fishing while Euphemia was busy with the house and my mother was frantic, catering for all the guests anticipated at the club.

The rod was a big bamboo one. We went to the men's beach between the clubhouse and the lighthouse, where my mother could keep an eye on us. The first time Meshack cast, the hook went in the sour figs and I had to fetch it. I lay flat every time he cast, because he was a terrible caster. Then, when the old men packed up for lunch, Meshack and I would go round the heads beyond the lighthouse and look at the tide going into the lagoons and Meshack offered to share his cigarette. Meshack didn't have a bathing costume, so he swam in his underpants. I was forbidden to swim or even take off my shirt and my hat, because of sunburn. Meshack also got very sunburnt, in spite of his skin. I guarded the line and the tin of bait while he swam, rolling around, and then he would come out and dry his big hands and finish his cigarette, and offer me some. I held it in my mouth and blew it out.

Blackie came to visit us quite a lot in the evenings to have supper. Blackie was very tanned, with skin like leather. My mother said that was because he had South African blood. Blackie came to help my mother sort out the heavy work in the house, because Aunt Rosemary was coming down. They carried all my father's clothes up the stairs and put them in the cupboard in the small room next to his study. Then my mother moved the carpets and the beds so that it would make quarters for Aunt Rosemary and her babies, and Blackie put a gate at the top of the stairs so that they could crawl anywhere upstairs and not tumble down. As payment my mother said Blackie could take whatever clothes of my father's would fit him, and he took the very smart brown suit. My mother left him to try it on while she finished supper, and he came to the table wearing it and looking very pre-war.

Aunt Rosemary arrived, and the first thing she said was how pleased she was the tablecloth was still there, although we had only put it back for her sake. She had a sleep-in nursemaid who was only a young girl; she was kept in the laundry and went up and down the stairs. She didn't open the gate because it was stiff, but she climbed over it with the babies' bottles and then she'd come down with the nappies. She was called Caroline and she did all the washing for Aunt Rosemary's party.

Mr Westerley came down from the drought where he was farming, and he pruned our fruit tree, although it was far too late, and we all had a family reunion for Christmas at the club – Mr Westerley and Aunt Rosemary and my mother – and we had toasts. Aunt Rosemary held my mother's chin in her hand and said it would be better as the years went by, and Blackie took a group photograph of us with me in front and the babies sitting on my shoes.

Uncle Roy didn't do any jobs for us, as he was preparing for a deep-sea fishing expedition. We drove with him down to the harbour to fit out Mr Olivier's boat with provisions and tackle. It was the only boat left because all the Oudeskip farmers were out, and the yachtsmen were far out at the end of Long Beach having a regatta.

'And what about the compass, Roy? You'll certainly need one,' said Aunt Rosemary.

'I've got a compass, dear,' he said, 'what do you think this is – a clock?' He was screwing it down on the wood in the wheelhouse.

Uncle Roy took Meshack and me out for a test run in his new boat. My mother had bought me a windbreaker for the occasion and Meshack had his blazer and scarf with the stripes on it. Uncle Roy didn't have to do all the operation, as Mr

Olivier still operated it, starting the engine and steering in the wheelhouse. Uncle Roy was in a hurry, because a ship of the line was due up the coast and we could see it if we got out far enough.

The fishing boat heaved and shook, taking the swell with a lot of force, and then bucketing down on the other slope. Meshack was sick and lay down in the stern. The swell was so enormous that when we were in the trough, we couldn't see out. I held on to the rigging, and Uncle Roy pointed to a school of dolphins, which he said they were using as submarine detectors, with radio sets on their backs like jockeys. Uncle Roy was a typical British settler. He told Mr Olivier which way to go all the time, but Mr Olivier just went his own way. We came smack down the side of a roller, and Uncle Roy said it was worse than polo.

Then we came into a calm patch. We did see the ship of the line. It was the *Arundel Castle* and we got very close to it. Meshack was groaning, so he had to see it from flat on the deck. But Uncle Roy and I climbed onto the wheelhouse roof and stood waving. The *Arundel Castle* had all its passengers come to our side and watch us. There were ladies in white with sun parasols, and men in white as if they were playing bowls, and children in bright clothes who ran between the lifeboats and stared at us, and sailors like the one on the Player's with beards, and on the lower deck at the back all the Indians, and the cook who threw a hamper of scraps overboard. We rocked madly in the wash, and their stern came into view: ARUNDEL CASTLE, SOUTHAMPTON. 'Good old home,' said Uncle Roy. And the seagulls wheeled and screeched over the potato peelings.

The way back was even more treacherous because the swell was running against us. Meshack was sick as a dog on his scarf, and Uncle Roy grabbed it and threw it overboard; that was stupid because Euphemia would have liked to wash it. I squatted in the lee of the engine. I wanted to get home and draw the *Arundel Castle*, starting with its anchor and the sharp bows. It was as tall as the buildings in Cape Town, but with round portholes in rows all the way along. Eventually I did draw some creditable versions of the luxury mailboat.

Mr van der Westhuizen came round to talk to Uncle Roy. They were going through my father's shed to find something, as Mr van der Westhuizen was repairing the propellor shaft for Uncle Roy's boat. I went with them to see they didn't disturb too much; the Elgin party had already turned everything else upside down. Uncle Roy pulled all the canvas off my father's store, and Mr van der Westhuizen squeezed past the car's bumper, and started pulling out all the stakes and poles that had been so carefully stacked.

'Jimmy, come out of there – snakes, remember,' said my mother.

'But they're stealing daddy's gaff,' I whispered to my mother. He had a wonderfully honed spar with metal fittings with prongs and hooks. I talked to my mother in confidential whispers these days, so that no one else would hear.

'They have my permission, Jimmy,' she said, and shepherded me off to Marie. She was standing near the climbing geraniums, trying to look pretty. 'You two go and play, and don't you come back until it's drinks time,' said my mother, calling for Euphemia, who had gone early. Before New Year there never were any servants to speak of.

Little Marie took me by the hand and led me to the milk-bushes.

'There's a heron's got a nest in here,' I told her.

'Wat is dit?' she turned her nose up. Marie had a freckle on her nose, and she was wearing an Alice band.

'It's a big white bird,' I said.

'Oh that,' she said. 'We've also got one.' Marie had a Malmesbury accent like her father, and when she spoke English she also used it.

Marie sat down under one of the bushes, and she said Listen. So I said what, and listened. She giggled. I said she mustn't giggle, or the heron wouldn't come. She said she wasn't wearing any panties, and I said did she throw them away, her mummy would smack her.

She lifted her dress and she didn't have any panties on. Also, she didn't have anything there to show me.

I said it was because she was Afrikaans she was born without it, and she said, Sies! I must show her in return. So I undid my belt and showed her, and I was burning with embarrassment because I did have one. And she said that meant I could go to the toilet standing up, and she had to sit down when she went. That wasn't because she was an Afrikaner but because she was a girl. And I showed her how an English-speaking person does it upright, but that wasn't because I was English, rather it was because I was a boy. So that was sorted out.

Mr van der Westhuizen and Uncle Roy were having beer on the garden veranda, and Aunt Rosemary and my mother gin and lime. Marie and I got barley water with a lump of ice in each.

Uncle Roy said he disagreed, a show of force was necessary once in a while, bring them round.

'Well, in my opinion,' said Mr van der Westhuizen, 'that's the last thing we want now. Feelings is inflamed enough. You can't control the whole population less they willing.'

'Just a few hotheads,' said Uncle Roy. 'When the last of them's in detention we'll have peace and quiet.'

'But you got to respect a man's feelings.'

'It's war, my friend. That's a peacetime luxury.'

'That's no excuse. I'm a neutral, Mr Westerley; as long as they leave me alone I shall remain so.'

'You know, I believe my Ella can actually think, Sarah.'

'Oh, I shouldn't doubt it for a moment.'

'She sits up and – you know, I can see her frowning.'

'Usually that's a sign. These days a lot goes on in their heads.'

'It's all a matter of perspective. You can't have your armed forces overseas and insurrection back at base.'

'You'll volunteer for a home guard, I suppose. Guard yourself against the Afrikaner element, who are your neighbours and closest friends.'

'Do you know, Roy, I think she actually thinks.'

'Shouldn't be surprised, darling.'

'I wouldn't say think; I'd say perceive.'

'They're not meant to until they're three.'

'Young Jimmy's helping Little Marie along so nicely with her English, Mrs Esslin. Pity they going to be split up now.'

'Rachel's a different proposition altogether; she feels.'

'Well, you'd hate them to be carbon copies.'

'Nouja,' said Mr van der Westhuizen, pushing his beer mug across the table. 'Thanks for the drinks.'

'See you tomorrow, Van,' said Uncle Roy.

'Ja, and oh yes, a very happy New Year to you all. Sê dit, Marie, my skat.'

Marie said a happy new year, and they went and we waved.

'Don't say goodboy,' said my mother, 'say goodbye, in proper English.'

'You could plough a field with Van's accent.'

'Sounds like a real little South African,' said Aunt Rosemary. 'Clips his vowels.'

'Nothing that can't be cured,' said my mother, slightly offended.

The order of importance in the house was: Aunt Rosemary, Uncle Roy, my mother, Ella and Rachel or Rachel and Ella, myself, Meshack, Euphemia, Caroline, Freddie the postman. He came round to the back door for his Christmas box, and this is the order in which the money went: Uncle Roy fished it out of his pocket and gave it to Caroline, who gave it to Aunt Rosemary, who gave it to Euphemia (who was there that day), who gave it to Meshack, who gave it to my mother, who gave it to me, who gave it to Freddie. Freddie said he'd earned it with all the extra mail he'd carried; he was very drunk.

One evening, desperate with the displacement I felt, I simply walked out of the kitchen door. I was properly dressed. There was a light wind, so you couldn't hear Ella and Rachel crying upstairs. I went past Uncle Roy's car and the side of the house, pulling myself up as I faced the front. Then I marched up the steps and rapped on the door.

I rapped again with my knuckles, very heavily. Aunt Rosemary got Uncle Roy to switch the wireless off. I could hear my mother put down her glass.

Presently she came to the front door. She opened it.

'Oh, Jimmy,' she said, opening it more fully.

'I'm not Jimmy,' I said.

'Oh yes,' she said. 'Well, what are whoever you are doing out there?' She opened the door a little more.

'I'm Andy, and I've come back from the war. Don't you recognise me?'

'My, oh yes, well . . . Come in, Andy, of course I recognise you perfectly well.'

'Everything all right there?' Aunt Rosemary called out.

'Yes, yes. Rosemary, Roy, guess what's happened? It's Andy and he's back from the war.'

I could hear them mutter, then keep quiet.

'Yes, I've come back and you weren't expecting me,' I said boldly.

'Well, no. The Red Cross traced him and the Saint John's Ambulance confirmed you're dead, but I'm – I'm glad you're not.'

'You look very dressed up,' I said.

'That's because we're going to the New Year's Eve party at the club. We can squeeze you in, there's no trouble about that.'

I hesitated. Then I said boldly, 'No club for me, but I'd like to see Jimmy. How is he?'

My mother let go of the handle and stroked her cheek. 'Well,' she said, 'Jimmy's got a bit of a temperature, so he's going to bed early.'

'I see,' I said, clapping my side, as my father used to do. 'There's nothing seriously wrong with Jimmy, is there?'

'No, I told you,' she said.

My poor mother. I stared at her, and thought I should cannon into her front and cling to her, wrapped around and squeezing her.

Aunt Rosemary came to the living room door. 'Oh, it's Andy,' she said. 'I always thought that meant trouble.'

Uncle Roy stood behind her, craning his silly face over her shoulder. 'Andy back, is it? Have to speak to the Red Cross about this,' he said.

I heaved through their legs and hips and fought free of them, like a monkey skimming over their smart clothes, and was inside the broom cupboard under the stairs before they could catch me. I jammed the dustpan in where the handle stuck out.

'Come on, Jimmy, come on Jimmy!' they rapped on the wood.

Panting and crying, I crouched there.

They discussed among themselves what to say next. Aunt Rosemary was elected to speak. 'Now, Andy,' she said, 'do you realise I've never met you? Come and join your sister-in-law. I'm really fond of South Africans – look, I've married Roy who's just about one, just like your mother, and I'm very fond of your son, Jimmy.'

There were dead people's voices, they were helping me. So many of them whispering and telling me what to do.

Aunt Rosemary tried again. 'We love South Africa now, it's our country, too. We're very proud that you have had to die for it.'

'I'm not properly dead,' I said. 'And you don't really love me or you'd never have sent me off to war.'

Aunt Rosemary said, 'You try, Roy, oh do.'

'Just a minute,' said Roy, and he clumsily moved them round in that small space.

I pushed the dustpan further where it wedged the door, and I could feel he was tugging it open, but trying not to show me that.

'Um, Andy,' he said. 'You know it really isn't rather like you – to cower under the stairs like this.'

'The dead people are here. They're not afraid,' I rapped out.

'Yes well, be that as it may, Andy, old boy. I was really rather thinking – you know that old boat I'm thinking of purchasing. Well, we've fitted it out now so that you'd hardly recognise it. I thought – you might like to join us on a fishing expedition. Wouldn't you like that?'

'No,' I said. 'I prefer it as it was. So does my father.'

'Ah,' he pounced as if he'd caught me out. 'Who's your father, then, come on. Tell me who's your father.'

'My father is John Andrew Esslin, after whom I am named. He died in 1920, and I am his son, and Jimmy is my son.'

'Clever little brat,' said Uncle Roy.

'Mamma, send them away!' I cried, and in the silence that followed my mother moved Aunt Rosemary and Uncle Roy back into the lounge, and I could hear Meshack had come into the kitchen. A long time passed while they discussed what to do, and I could hear my mother making Ovaltine.

Their combined thinking decided that the game should now be called off. My mother was using a no-nonsense tactic. She came back to the door of the cupboard, saying, oops she'd spilled some.

'Now Jimmy,' she announced, 'we know you're upset and I've made you your Ovaltine. So come out and have it like a good boy.'

How that voice and that logic could cow me. The spittle was running out of my mouth because I was terribly thirsty. I waited and waited. I wanted to be far away from her.

'Meshack's here and we must go or we'll be late,' she said. It was her business-like voice, with no affection in it.

I moved against the door, so that I could talk softly with no one else hearing. Mamma manoeuvred round so that her head was at the level of the keyhole.

I was just going to say what the dead people told me, when Rachel and Ella started fighting, and Aunt Rosemary ran up the stairs, making a noise above my head. Then Caroline ran up, and then Uncle Roy.

'They're out of the way, Jimmy,' said my mother in her cooing, friendly way. 'Come on, soldier, tell me.'

'Mamma,' I said.

'Yes, dear, what is it?'

Then I said very carefully, 'There are dead people under the stairs with me.'

'Is that Jimmy talking or is it Andy?' she said.

'No,' I said, 'no, it's me, Jimmy, but father is here and he talks with the dead people.'

'I understand,' she said, and she adjusted herself to sit.

'So tell me Jimmy – I do believe you – what do the dead people look like?'

'They don't look like anything,' I said.

'But they must look like something,' she said.

'Dead people don't,' I said. 'That's the whole point.'

'These dead people, Jimmy, where do they live?' she said.

Aunt Rosemary was coming down the stairs. 'How's your colloquy?' she said, and ran into the kitchen.

Caroline came down as well, and she said, 'Good evening, madam.'

Uncle Roy came down. 'We're going to be incredibly late,' he said, and went into the kitchen. There he found Meshack and said, 'Sorry about the scarf. Ask your mother how much it cost and I'll replace it, eh.' Then he closed the kitchen door.

'Mamma,' I said, 'I wish they'd go away.'

'So do I sometimes,' she said.

'They live at the lagoons,' I said, 'where nobody goes.'

'Oh yes,' she said. 'So it was you who drew daddy's name on the sand, that night you were so flustered?'

'Yes,' I said. 'The dead people told me to.'

'I don't think it's very safe to go there on your own, Jimmy, but still, you're a big boy now. Promise me, promise me.'

'I promised the dead people I would,' I said.

'It's better to make promises with living people,' she said with a kind of finality. 'They're the ones you have to be with.'

'Yes, mamma, I promise,' I said.

'Mr Jensen told me you have that secret place,' she said.

I felt achingly tired and disappointed. I wanted to give in, but didn't know how.

'Will it be all right if Meshack reads you a story?' she asked. 'It's getting so late now, and your Ovaltine's got a scum on it. Jimmy, will you come out?'

'Yes,' I said, and I pushed the dustpan aside and the door came open of its own accord.

She stood back, and I crawled out without looking at her and walked stoically to my bedroom. I took off my shoes and socks, and my shorts and shirt, and climbed into bed, lying with my face to the wall. Then Meshack came to read me a story, but I didn't want to listen. At least, not until the adults were gone.

Meshack sat there. He was with me for the rest of 1943. He said didn't I want my Ovaltine, but I said he could have it and he drank it in greedy gulps. He said he had special permission from my mother to listen to the wireless until midnight, then he was to sleep in the lounge. He went to turn the wireless on and found some hot music. It was a danceband playing, like the one they had for the night at the club. There was a saxophone. I went to close the door under the stairs and joined Meshack. The living-room looked like a real nightclub – there were glasses on all the nesting tables, and a bowl full of cigarette ends where Aunt Rosemary had smoked. The Christmas tree was looking dry and faded. Meshack was very responsible, but he couldn't resist dancing on the Persian carpet to the music. He was dancing quietly, with his head back and his hands in his blazer pockets.

Did I want to dance, he said, because it was easy, and I said, no, I wasn't in the mood. I said he had better stand still because the King's voice was going to come through again, as it did on Christmas day, and it wouldn't be good to be caught during that. But he danced to himself while the music was on, then there was a programme about how it was New Year already in New Zealand and Australia, and then Burma and India, but not here yet.

Caroline came down and sat on the stool next to the Christmas tree. Caroline spoke Afrikaans at home, and she didn't understand much English, so we looked for the Afrikaans programme for her but couldn't find it, and I got the needle back to Ceylon. It was the darkest hour, but everything was bright there. Then there was more dance music because it was a long time to midnight in South Africa.

Meshack seriously asked me if I wanted to dance, and I said no, because I didn't know how. Caroline didn't want to dance because she didn't have the right shoes; she only had slippers with cat's faces sewn on. She played with the wax that bulged out on the holders of the Christmas tree candles. Then there was a really strong saxophone playing very hot, and Meshack took a stompie from the ashtray and stuck it in his mouth, and danced around. Meshack was very tall so we only saw his chin with the bit of cigarette and his hips going.

Meshack persuaded me, and Caroline laughed and had a big cough. Meshack held my shoulders and told me to put my slippers on his nicely polished shoes. He lifted them one after the other and I was walking backwards with him. It was one-two one-two, and then we did a turn and I became completely messed up. One-two one-two – no man, I bashed Meshack a shot because he went too fast.

'You must go with the music, look,' and he did it once very slowly, and then he got back into the music and did it all over the place. 'You do it, you do it.'

I put my hands in the pockets of my dressing gown and lifted my chin, and did one-two one-two turn. Caroline thought that was all right, and Meshack was pleased.

He grabbed me and landed me on his shoes again, but that didn't work because I had to do it backwards. 'You the girl now,' he said, 'so you go that way.'

'I am not the girl,' I said, 'I can only go forward.'

'But every pair has got to have one that goes forward and

one that goes backward,' he said, and he showed me backwards.

'You go backward since you can do it,' I said.

'You try, you just try.'

Then the music was off.

'No man, Meshack, you be the girl,' I said. 'You know how to do it.'

He waited there, putting down the stompie and wiping his brow with a new handkerchief.

'Ah, Glenn Miller,' he said, and a very smooth song came on.

Caroline went and put the book-ends straight where they were letting the light out.

'It's the same, but slower,' said Meshack, and I said I could manage that. So we danced with my ear on Meshack's stomach, and I could do it without having my feet on his shoes. We danced very solemnly for all that time. It was wonderful, and when we were finished Meshack did a big bow to thank me, and I bowed to thank him, and we sat down. Caroline got a duster and she polished Meshack's shoes.

Then you could hear they were drinking champagne in Aden, and Meshack went to get us three glasses and we had lime juice and water, with some ice left in the bucket. We sat on the carpet with our knees touching and Caroline raised her glass first, and Meshack lent her his handkerchief because she was running, and then I raised my glass and we elected Meshack the champion dance instructor, and Caroline said, 'Hy's goed nè?' We drank it all down. They were also having champagne in the Union Buildings in Pretoria, you could hear, and they were singing 'Auld Lang Syne' in the clubhouse, too, all holding hands, so we stood up and held hands, but we didn't know the words.

The New Year was moving on to London, then, but we'd had our ceremony, and Caroline went upstairs to watch over Ella and Rachel who'd been as quiet as lambs, and Meshack started taking the tobacco out of the cigarette ends with a toothpick. I fell asleep on the couch and he must have carried me back to bed so that the adults wouldn't see we'd had a party as well. Meshack got special pay for that, even though he had as good a time as the rest of us. The New Year dancing was good because it put the loss of my father out of my mind; if he'd come back then it would have spoiled everything.

Came the day of Uncle Roy's famous fishing trip. We all went to see the men off. You'd think there'd never been a fishing expedition before. Uncle Roy had a way of behaving like an aristocrat, so that everyone did things for him, even though he was just a plain apple farmer. Sergeant Thoroughwell was the worst of all, for he ducked as he passed Uncle Roy. Mr Olivier was a bit the morning after the night before, and all the Coloureds looked as if they were half dead. My mother was very deliberate in her movements and wore her dark glasses. Aunt Rosemary looked as if she wanted to be sick, even though she didn't set foot on the boat. They'd all had poisoned champagne the night before.

Meshack and I decided it was all more than we could take, so we went off to walk home, even before Uncle Roy and Blackie and Sergeant Thoroughwell and Mr Feverall and the whole crew cast off. My mother said to Aunt Rosemary I had a real crush on Meshack, and Aunt Rosemary said I'd get over it. This was unfair because Meshack gave up his whole holiday to be with me, when he should have been preparing for Standard 9. There were no other jobs for him to do in Silver Town.

Meshack wanted to go past Oudeskip and buy cigarettes at Mrs Feverall's, but I said the craving couldn't be as bad as that; anyway, he didn't have any money, and I didn't. So we decided to go along the coastal road and pick up his fishing rod at his home. We came to where the tar road crumbled at the verge and all the gravel went down the sand towards the Pits. The wattles were scraggy and khaki-looking. Everything had that burnt-out look. I'd never gone down there to the Pits before.

There were puddles all over the Pits. The houses were of corrugated iron, very low in the wattles. They were assembled like card houses, with stones on the roofs and fertilizer bags from the council. Some of them had window frames in four quarters. There were lots of old cars without wheels and children were living in them. And the chimneys came out of the back like in *Hansel and Gretel*, the stoves going with heavy yellow smoke. This was called a shanty town. Some people came through on bicycles, and one skidded because of the rut in the main road. They shouted at Meshack, but he said I mustn't be frightened. We had to climb over a fallen tree, and then we were at Euphemia's place.

Euphemia said something to Meshack in their language, and then she said to me everybody had been drinking. They didn't drink because her family was church-going. Euphemia went inside to make tea and I sat on a stump. She left the door a bit open, so I could see a picture of Jesus above the sideboard. Meshack went to get his fishing rod, but I could tell Euphemia was furious with him for bringing me, so we couldn't go fishing or swimming.

Meshack had to help his father outside, and he came fully dressed with a hat on. He raised his hand to me and I stood up. 'Sit down,' he said, and he sat in the rocking chair that had no legs. He was a builder in Cape Town, but now he had tuberculosis so he had to come home. He said, 'Yes, master, master's mother is a good woman,' and he spat in a big handkerchief.

Euphemia came with a smart tray with three mugs on it. She had sold the cups Aunt Rosemary gave her, and mugs were better. She didn't need to put the milk bowl and the sugar on it, because she knew how we all liked our tea. She had four tennis biscuits on a saucer. I took my mug first and the handle was very hot. Then Meshack sat down between us on a log, tucking the back of his blazer up so that it didn't get muddy. There was a gum-tree above us, and when the wind blew it shook down pellets of seed, and it reminded me of when Euphemia used to take me to the post office. Euphemia stood there, with the pollen coming down on her hair; when she wasn't working, she didn't wear her doek.

'Meshack's doing very well at school, Master Jimmy,' said his father, and Meshack looked shy.

'Oh, he's a champion,' I said, and Meshack put his hand over his face.

'He's going to work in an office,' said Euphemia, and she belted him on the back of the head, and they both laughed.

'Aikona wena,' said Meshack's father, and they stopped laughing. 'And Master Jimmy, you getting so big now. What you going to do when you grown up?'

I looked at Meshack's father, with his wrinkled jaw and white hairs around his ears. 'I don't know,' I said. 'I'm going to work in an office.'

'But your father, he didn't work in an office. He was always outside like me. I live outside because it's more healthy. Artisan's work.'

'Master Jimmy, he's going to work in a skyscraper in Cape Town with all the windows open,' said Euphemia, and I said yes.

Meshack said the wind up there can blow you out, and Euphemia cuffed him on the head again and they laughed, and his father said, 'Aikona wena.'

I said I'd better get back to the quay because the boat might come in any moment, and Euphemia said it was far too early for that, and Meshack's father said it was because I was shy.

'I just wanted to say Happy New Year,' I said, and the old man laughed and said it back.

Euphemia joked with Meshack, and they both laughed, then she said, 'Now what's all this I hear about you learning to dance, Master Jimmy?'

I said very seriously, 'Yes, I can do the foxtrot.'

'Yes, Meshack told me,' Euphemia said.

'And I can do the waltz. Meshack showed me,' I said.

'And the waltz,' Meshack's father said in amazement.

'And I can do the jitterbug,' I said.

'Yes, Master Jimmy,' Euphemia laughed, 'like your mother was doing at the Club Ball.'

'You not going to be in an office, you going to be a dancer, aai, Master Jimmy,' said her husband, and they all started laughing again.

'Who was my mother dancing with?' I said. 'You have to have somebody to do it with.'

'With Master Blackie,' said Euphemia.

'But he's only a Sergeant,' I said.

'He's still the number one champion of Silver Town,' said Euphemia.

'She wasn't dancing with him,' I said.

'Oh yes,' said Euphemia.

'How did you know?' I asked.

'Oh, everybody knows – they won the jitterbug championship,' she said. 'There, ask Mrs Kreli – you know her from the kitchen.' Euphemia asked Mrs Kreli who was passing by in her uniform, and Mrs Kreli said everybody knew they were the winners, just ask anybody, so I had to believe it.

'When you coming to the club again, Master Jimmy?' said Mrs Kreli, and I said I didn't know, and she said, ag shame, it was because my father died. And we all shook our heads.

This reminded me that we were due to go back to the house, so Meshack said goodbye and I said goodbye, and we went there, not wanting to fish or buy cigarettes any longer. There was no jitterbugging, either, as those who were waiting for the fishing expedition were in a very hungover mood.

When I woke the next day Meshack had his long, thin arm in the window and was tugging my pillow. Then the phone rang and it was the harbour-master to tell my mother they were back. He told her they'd got a very big one. I said I was going ahead with Meshack to see, and dressed like a fury.

'If it's tunny, tell them I can't get it in the fridge,' my mother said, and Meshack and I sped off.

Along the harbour they were winching the big catch into the air to weigh it, and already I knew what it was. They had caught one of the giant devilfish of the lagoons, far out to sea, and had brought it back to land. I said I didn't want to go.

Yes, come on, said Meshack, it's a very very big one.

Family Mobulidae, Genus Manta. Named after the Spanish (female) for a blanket.

It's so big, Meshack said, like a camouflage tent over the guns at Cape Town.

It was like a blanket, a huge heavy soggy one, hooked on a washing line.

'Come on,' Meshack shouted.

No, Meshack, I stumbled and pretended I was very out of breath.

The disc is broader than long. A huge swell accumulated in the rollers, and headed for this side of the harbour wall. The manta came out of that, underneath, where it was weightless. The wings didn't work when it was out of its element.

Meshack got behind me and pushed. 'Oh, what can it be?' he said.

Shoot out of the water with a rush and land like a cannon

shot. When the carrier was dead, all the dead people left it to its fate and went somewhere else and were very frightened.

We came to the harbour-master's, and the electricity was still burning inside from the night. He let us through and Uncle Roy didn't even see us in the excitement. Mr Feverall asked Meshack if my mother was coming, and he said she was dressing; Mrs Feverall couldn't come and see because she was running the hotel.

A photographer from the *Cape Times* came in his car; he was on holiday at Oudeskip, but he had his camera and tripod with him. He was standing on the quay at the end, while they lowered the manta onto the cement, and it covered the whole block. Under Sergeant Thoroughwell's supervision Blackie and two Coloureds were heaving the one wing straight out. He was signalling them like a traffic policeman. They heaved it round and got it aligned. Then the cameraman signalled that Uncle Roy and Mr Feverall must come, and also Mr Olivier, who took off his woollen cap.

Meshack and I went to stand behind the photographer, and I avoided looking at the manta, but I looked at the fishermen. They seemed tiny at the end of the big fish. They stood with their chests out, but there were too many people coming to see it. The photographer went round the manta, clearing them away like shooing geese. Then he went behind his camera and put his head under the black cloth. Then he pulled the cloth off his head and said this would put Silver Town on the map. Nobody was in Silver Town that morning; they were all at the harbour.

They had forgotten their fishing rods and the gaff. Blackie went to get them where they were lying against one of the old dinghies. He came back and held the rod upright in the air, but then Uncle Roy took the rod and gave Blackie the gaff, and Blackie put his boot on the manta because he was the one who first stabbed it. Mr Feverall put his hands in his pockets and picked up his tummy, and Sergeant Thoroughwell said could he have a copy for his wife's album. Then the photographer took it.

He took another one with the four of them having their arms over one another's shoulders, with the fishing rod and the gaff arranged over the manta's back. Meshack put his arm over my shoulder, as if he had caught the manta himself, and I watched, and then shoved him away. He said I couldn't catch a fish as big as that, and I said I didn't want to.

Then everybody screamed because a roller split its top right against the quay, and some people got soaking. They were there at their own risk, but nobody really minded.

The photographer stood on a crate to get an aerial view, and the four gathered again behind the one wing of the manta, and the sea came thundering up, and I thought it was angry and planned to reclaim the manta, and sweep all the people away.

My mother came running down with Aunt Rosemary, and Aunt Rosemary gave Uncle Roy a big kiss and put her hat on, and my mother gave Blackie a big kiss, and she didn't have a hat, but they both got in the photograph, and there were hundreds of people standing all in the background.

'It's never been seen in these waters before. Must have strayed off course,' Uncle Roy was dictating to the photographer's friend, who was writing the story for the *Cape Times*. 'Mr Roy Westerley of Elgin', she got down.

'And a final one, everybody, for posterity,' yelled the photographer. 'Yes, giant devilfish, three and a half tons!'

His assistant waved her pad to get people to stand in line. My mother saw me and she had her one arm around Blackie and she signalled for me to come. Meshack put his hand on my neck to push me. For me it was impossible.

Meshack was just going to shove me when I broke loose and elbowed my way through the crowd and skidded. But I was through the harbour-master's gate in a flash, and ran along the Oudeskip Road and went on running, and dived into the wattles and stayed there by myself, grieving for my manta.

13

Meshack said he would write from school, but he never did or Miss Bester lost the letter, and I couldn't write back, so I forgot about Meshack. Euphemia gave me news, and it was always the same – unlike me, Meshack was very accomplished.

Because he had killed my manta with the gaff, I would not talk to Blackie. Since I would not tell him, he never knew why. Blackie would talk to me and I'd just stand there. Sometimes I had to say something, but it was never willingly. Blackie came round to fix the car so that he could do deliveries for my mother, because they were fed up with his using the jeep for non-military ends. Blackie was just part of the community now, like everyone else who'd washed up in Silver Town, and there was nothing special about him. My mother said that the UDF had gathered so many men they must have mislaid Blackie. The Japanese scare was over, since they had had news from HQ that there were not enough of them to effect a landing; they were going to America instead. I thought that meant Blackie would be sent to America to defend them.

Blackie came one afternoon in the jeep, so it meant business. My mother was in the front seat and she called for me to get my hat and tell Euphemia to close up. We were going to see where they'd done sabotage on the railway line. My mother tied my hat on tightly and I sat on the back seat. We drove right out of Silver Town and Mr Lotter came, too, in his bakkie and even Mrs Pennington-Worthy had a rendezvous with us in her Daimler at the top of the pass. We went in convoy to the scene of the explosion. It was on the main line, just before the tunnel, and very hot up there. They did it at night. The embankment had come away and rolled with the sleepers and rails into the gorge. It was near the very same bridge we crossed on the way to Cape Town, but they missed the bridge.

'Who did it? Who did it?' said Blackie.

'Ask Miss Bester, I should think she'd know,' said my mother.

Blackie opened his door and came round and opened my mother's and gave her his hand as she climbed down. I climbed out, and when they weren't looking down the gorge I threw my hat over, and it went floating into the chasm, and they didn't notice. There wasn't a train in sight, so there was no damage to passengers, and the station-master had his red flag, so none would come now. Everybody had to take the bus until the line was repaired.

Miss Bester was so suspect that, by popular request, she was transferred by the Postmaster-General to another office in the Kalahari where she could do less damage. Everyone thought she had been in touch with the saboteurs. I didn't mind her so much. She said 'Totsiens' to me and was crying, because she had to pack up her single quarters where she kept her picture of Hitler hidden in her dressing table, and Mrs Feverall said good riddance to bad rubbish. In the Kalahari they were going to build a home for Hitler to rest after the war, and Miss Bester was to be the caterer. She showed me the picture when she was packing, and it had a moustache; no one in Silver Town wore a black moustache because of Hitler. Miss Bester also had one of his metal swastikas, and it could roll like a tumbleweed. They never had any evidence against her.

One day we had a half-day at school because someone important had died; I think it was the head of police in the Union, and he'd been head since 1919 under Smuts. So I went down to the club and Blackie was raising the flag only at half-mast. I talked to Little Marie's mother most of the morning. 'Wanneer kom jy 'n koppie koffie saam by ons geniet, Jimmy?' she said, and I fixed it for the next Wednesday afternoon.

I went on my own to Mrs van der Westhuizen and Little Marie and Little Marie's sisters were out playing, and Mr van der Westhuizen was down at the harbour. I had been inside their house before, but never into the lounge for coffee. It came in a tall pot and was very black. 'Stinnie, skink maar,' said old granny, who was sitting in the corner. So Mrs Van skinked it in.

'Is jy nou Mevrou Esslin se seuntjie?' said granny, and I nodded. 'Ga,' she said, 'en jy praat nie Afrikaans nie, en Esslin is mos 'n Afrikaanse naam.'

'Ja,' I said.

'I always say to Mrs Esslin she must learn, Ouma, nè,' said Mrs Van.

'Maar dis nie Mevrou Esslin wie moet leer, dis haar man; hy's die een met die van. Jy weet mos dit gaan so,' complained the granny.

'Nee, Ouma, hy kannie lesse gee nie, hy's dood,' said Little Marie. 'He can't give classes 'cause he's dead.'

'O-o-o,' said Ouma. 'Verskoon tog.'

Mrs Van said it was all right.

'En waarvandaan kom jy, Jimmy?' sê sy vir my.

I was baffled. Toe sê ek, 'Nee, ek kom van Silver Town,' en sy lag met plesier.

'Jy het 'n goeie, suiwer aksent, hoor, my kind,' en sy klap haar hande.

She spilled some coffee because she was elderly, and Little Marie had to bring a lappie om af te vee. En toe is ek huistoe om my huiswerk klaar te kry. And Little Marie gave me an extra biscuit, a ginger snap, so that I didn't want much supper.

I thought a lot about what Mrs Van told me; that Aunt Rosemary thought Blackie was not the right sort of person, but for Blackie she herself had nothing but respect. He was a man in the making and Afrikaans men were the best because they were of the veld and the land.

Eventually Mr Lever went away for a long weekend and a honeymoon and he came back with a wife which, at his age, was quite an achievement. There wasn't much room for Mr Lever and his wife in the club – only the flat overlooking the new lot of agapanthus, where he could keep an eye on the people coming and going from all over the isthmus. My mother thought she and Stinnie would be demoted, because a wife of the manager was automatically superior to them, but they stayed on the same salary, only they now didn't have to spend all hours of the day at the club. From helping out, my mother had risen to being unofficial manageress, but now there was a proper person to do that. Mrs Lever came from a hotel in Paarl, and she wanted to make Blackie's room into her office, because she had had one there, so Blackie moved in with us.

This could have caused a big scandal, but Blackie was only to use the outside staircase and his quarters up there, and the gate was to stay across the top of the stairs so that we didn't go up and he didn't come down. The caddies were getting very unruly again, and the Relief Committee recommended that my mother not have another night attack, so the army billeted Blackie with us on their instructions.

He parked his jeep in the space where my sandpit used to be, to allow access to the garage where my father's car was, so now we had two vehicles. The first thing Blackie did was take my mother out along the coastal road in my father's car to give her a driving lesson, and as the tide was low they went over the edge of the embankment and did reversing, stopping, forward, turning and parking all down the beach – you could see the tyre treads for days afterwards. My mother got lots of practice, because she drove Blackie to work in the mornings and brought him back at night, or sometimes she would drive along with him following in the jeep if he needed it for patrolling. I always walked to school because I had an extra half hour.

Then in the autumn, when the days were mellow and the leaves were turning, and the water in the lagoons was still warm, my mother decided that Blackie must do me a favour. We couldn't do anything in that house without Blackie – go shopping, fix clothes, have a meal, listen to the wireless. Euphemia wasn't fond of Blackie, either, because he made extra washing for her, and she and I were in league against him. She opened the gate at the top of the stairs and brought down the bedside table from my father's study and put it in my room, so that the bedside lamp could go on it and I had my own desk. My mother said that was a good plan, so in the evenings I usually drew at my desk and left them to it in the living-room. Anyway, the scheme was that I should have some male company instead of always being with the women, and Blackie should take me on Saturday and Sunday mornings to the lagoon to learn to swim.

Blackie was in his trunks and he had a dark skin and black hairs and was very strong. He was quite short compared with my father when seen at a distance, but very big close up. I went with him through the milk-bushes, and we came to a cove near the Pennington-Worthy fence. 'Now,' Blackie said as if he owned the place, 'the first thing is to put on your costume, otherwise you won't float.'

Very funny.

I became acutely shy, because my limbs were so rubbery and feeble, my skin so chafed and pale. I pulled down my shorts and underpants, and put on my costume underneath my shirt-tails, then pulled off my shirt and was ready. I got goosepimples and clutched my hands under my armpits.

Blackie was stupid; he didn't realise I knew the lagoons far better than he ever would. Still, he was very solicitous of my well-being. He was out there scooping the scum off the water to make a clear patch for the lesson. He got a big stick and harvested it along, swinging green bags of it onto the shore. He was doing this not for me, but so that I would tell my mother and she would be impressed. He said I'd go all green like a Martian if he didn't do that. Very funny.

Then he told me to wade in, and I did to where he was standing up to his knees. I had no thoughts in my head about any previous experiences of the lagoons; they had always been my safest, happiest refuge, but now every step I took was closer to doom.

Blackie crouched down beside me with a stupid grin on his face, and said gently now. He didn't tell me what he was going to do, so it was horrible. He picked me up and balanced me from my stomach, with my face an inch from the green water. I turned my head on the side, and he said keep my mug out of the water. Then he lowered my legs which were already wet into the water and said I must kick with a scissors movement, and I gave three sharp kicks to get above the water, and my head end went under. He pulled me up and said no, man, I must keep my head up, but I couldn't keep that end up when the other end was up. We tried again, and this time I also got a complete ducking. Very funny.

'You trying to drown me,' I said.

'Very funny,' he said.

'I don't trust you,' I said.

'Well, you must,' he said, and he took me by the belly with

his hands eating into my sides, and I squirmed out of his grip and stood opposite him in the water.

'You just think you own the place,' I said. 'Ow, you hurt me.'

'You too big for your boots,' he said.

I stomped in a circle around him and went home, so that our first lesson was not a success. But they weren't going to leave it at that, because my mother put me on the warm stone of the veranda and showed me how to do the dogpaddle on dry land, with my legs going in a scissors movement and my hands scooping the air towards me. It was like digging sand. Then I could go to my room.

The next morning was a Sunday so we listened to the church service over breakfast, and they were singing 'Rock of Ages' in Saint George's Cathedral. Then I couldn't go swimming on a full stomach, so we waited till eleven o'clock. Then Blackie went through the milk-bushes with me for a repeat performance. The scum had not fully grown back round our lesson area, but he did a massive dive, trailing it out after him, making it about double the size. I sat on the dune, watching him. Suddenly I remembered Meshack and how he threw water at me, and I missed him. Meshack learned to swim in the reservoir behind his school.

Blackie told me to come in and not walk out this time, but I wouldn't promise anything. 'Come on, man, be a real water baby,' he said.

I wanted to do it on my own, but if I put my front down my bottom would stick out and I couldn't breathe. If I lay back I'd just sink. Blackie sat down in the water opposite me, and made me crouch and try the scooping of the dogpaddle.

'That's right,' he said, 'dig it out, man. Go on.'

I crouched down again so that everything but my head was submerged, and dogpaddled with my hands.

'Keep them even, man,' he said, and I churned up quite a froth, and he was pleased with that.

'Now let me hold you,' he said, standing up with water cascading off him.

I said no, I was all right.

'Yes, man, Jimmy,' he said. 'I'm not going to hurt you. Just let me hold you.'

I said no, and turned away and dogpaddled but I was actually walking.

Then he did what he shouldn't have done; he grabbed me by the waist, and my face was full of sand from the bottom and my throat was full of water and the taste of grapefruit which we'd had for breakfast. I came up, wiping the water from my face like liquid glass.

'Sorry,' he said, 'I only wanted to support you, hey.'

I stomped around him and said nothing, taking my towel back to the house where it was easier to dogpaddle on the veranda. My mother said I was improving, but I thought it was getting worse.

All the weekdays went by without any lessons, and then it was Saturday again, and the scum had grown right across the swimming lesson patch and Blackie walked around getting it on his legs and trailing it off like a Martian.

I was in my costume and it was already looking quite well used, with creases developing above my hipbone. I half-stood and scooped the water towards me and made quite a froth, and Blackie showed me to do it more gently, but I was going like a windmill in a south-easter. Time it with your breathing, Blackie said, and he went heave-ho, heave-ho, and showed me how he got it to match his wrists going in strokes.

'Just don't be frightened, man,' he said.

The water was so cloudy that day you could hardly see the bottom. Underneath there the bait was breeding, and the baitpickers weren't allowed to dig it out until it grew bigger, otherwise there'd be no more in the whole lagoon. Just beyond us was an old rusty buoy where they used to tether their dinghy.

Blackie came alongside me and said he wouldn't touch me, he swore. 'Just watch,' he said. And he started the dogpaddling, and then pushed with his legs and went forward so that I could see only his legs kicking, and he went in a circle and spat out water in a spout, like off the edge of a boat.

'Come on, it's your turn,' he said, but I pretended I didn't hear him. I crouched forward and went heave-ho, heave-ho. He watched me for a long time and then shouted, because I was making such a splashing, 'Jump forward and kick your legs, man,' but I couldn't hear.

'All right,' he said, and he waded towards me.

He was going to pluck me out if I went in the drink, but that only made it worse. I started skimming off some weed he missed, and I could do it with my fingers apart because it stuck together.

'What's the matter, Jimmy, don't you trust me?' he said. I didn't trust him. I took my towel and went into the bushes and dried myself there.

The next day was Sunday so we were due for another lesson. At eleven o'clock I said I hadn't digested yet. I said that to my mother, because I wouldn't talk to Blackie; she could tell him.

'Now just what is the matter?' she said. 'You never let up.'

'The grapefruit comes into my mouth so I can't have digested fully,' I said.

'Between Blackie and you,' she said. 'I want to know why you never give him a chance.'

'He doesn't give me a chance. He holds my head under when I should be breathing,' I said.

'Nonsense,' she said. 'Everybody has difficulties learning to swim; that's why I've arranged for you to have proper lessons.'

'He's not a proper instructor,' I said.

'Jimmy,' she said, 'Blackie won the freestyle when he was doing his basic; you can see he's a swimmer – look at his arms and look at his legs.'

'I've had enough of looking at them,' I said.

'Well, if you don't learn from him, you'll learn from no one,' she said.

Blackie clattered down the outside stairs in his sandals and bathing costume, with his towel, and came to the veranda and looked at his waterproof watch.

'Now shush,' said my mother. 'Blackie, here's the unwilling pupil. He'd better learn before the weather turns, that's all I can say.'

'He's doing fine, Mrs Esslin,' said Blackie. He turned me round and gave my mother a big wink.

This time we both waded into the water together, and to tempt me Blackie launched very slowly into a dogpaddle and went round and said it was lovely. I didn't say anything, but I did my paddling exercises with my chin up high, ignoring him completely.

'Look, I'll show you overarm,' said Blackie. 'It's a bit shallow here.' He waded further out and swam across with one arm coming up behind his shoulder and an armpit of hair showing, and the weed pulling over him like a net. And he broke through it and picked up quite a speed. He came up and spat as if he had tuberculosis. I didn't notice how he breathed when he did it.

Before Blackie could get back, I decided. With a heave I launched forward and kicked my legs and dogpaddled as fast as I could go, and it was true, for a few seconds I remained buoyant and went forward, and then my insteps hit the bottom and I was walking again.

Then the siren went at the club, and Blackie had to go immediately and change and take the jeep round. I thought I could swim on my own for a while longer, but my mother would come running down to see I wouldn't drown, and I just sat on the sand next to the clump of sour figs, and dug my ankles in, and waited. In due course she did come down with a hat, and put it on my head. She sat beside me.

'I don't wonder you love it this side,' she said. 'It's much nicer than the sea. When the war's over they're going to turn it into a bird sanctuary, and only the Pennington-Worthys'll have access to it. But it's so neglected now, it's better that way.'

I was gazing across the lagoons at a colony of flamingoes on the other side. They were like the red line in the thermometer. They never came our end because it was too noisy, what with sirens and drunken caddies and all the traffic.

'Funny boy,' she said, 'you're a real nature lover. Growing up just like your father. I wonder what goes on inside that little head of yours.'

I didn't say anything, because I couldn't remember what my father was like. All I knew of him by then were the things I did that people told me were like what he used to do.

'Do you miss him very much?' said my mother.

I didn't know whether I missed him or not.

'Jimmy,' she said, 'I miss him very much too. But we've got to become accustomed to the situation. We just have no choice, you see.'

'Mummy,' I blurted out, 'are you going to marry Blackie?'

'Why, what on earth –' she said. 'Marry Blackie, don't be absurd. He could get posted any moment.'

'You mean posted like a letter?' I said.

'Yes, well – sent away. There are terrible losses and they need everyone they can get; they won't forget Blackie in Silver Town for much longer. Then where would we be? I've already been through all that with your father, thank you.'

'If you marry Blackie, you can make a baby like Aunt Rosemary and Uncle Roy.'

'Why, Jimmy,' she exclaimed.

'Yes, you could,' I said.

'Yes, I know I could. That's perfectly true. But it wouldn't be the same, Jimmy. We don't really want a brother or sister for you. You've got a seven year start, and babies take a long time coming. You'd never be able to be friends, really.'

'Then why's Blackie in the upstairs?' I said.

'Because –' said my mother, and she gave me a look as if she didn't want to go through all that again.

'Why because?' I said.

'Because because,' she said.

'Why because because?' I said.

'Oh Jimmy, you ask far too many questions,' she said.

'Miss Kettley said it's wrong,' I said.

'Oh, did she just? Well, you tell Miss Kettley to keep her nose out of other people's business.'

'You tell her,' I said.

'Yes, I will,' said my mother. She pointed, because one of the pelicans was cruising in like a flying boat.

'I'm sorry I was angry with you, mamma,' I said.

'That's all right,' she said. 'Forgiven and forgotten.' She patted my hat and got up to go home for lunch.

'Blackie must have had a telephone call,' she said.

I shook out my towel and bundled up my clothes.

'So, how's it going with the swimming?' she said.

'Very well, thank you,' I said.

All the weekdays passed once again before I had a chance to resume the swimming. When Blackie and I went down on the Saturday, I felt quite sorry for him that I was such a bad pupil. I didn't tell him anything, but I resolved to kick forward while he was watching and surprise him that way. There had been quite a storm during the week, so the inlet was completely clear. The water was pearly grey. There was lots of flotsam on the shore, and the jetsam was out at sea. One of the women from the Pits was collecting the flotsam for firewood – bits of orange-box, branches and timbers. We waited for her to trail off.

Then Blackie waded out and this time I took his hand; the water was getting chilly. 'You not frightened?' he said.

'No,' I said, and I gave a shiver.

'You just better learn quickly, 'cause it's the end of the season,' he said.

Immediately I crouched down and launched forward, my hands scooping and my legs cutting up the water. He stood with his arms folded and didn't react very much. I thought it was on account of the water being unclear and he couldn't see.

'You know what, Jimmy,' he said, 'you doing it the wrong way. You're doing the left side all together and the right all together, so you're rolling like a 44 gallon drum, man, no wonder.'

He demonstrated for me, standing on one leg. The arms and legs had to synchronise across; he kicked with his left leg like a dancer and drew with his right arm, then he hopped and did it the other way. He said there were blokes who marched the way I was doing, and they were pitched out.

I was angry with disappointment, then. He could throw me out, because I was no good. He could also keep his opinion. 'I did swim,' I said.

'But you wasting your energy; your body must work across, otherwise you're wasting your time and my time. Come, let me show you.'

'I did swim,' I said, defying him.

'That's not swimming, that's drowning in slow motion,' he said.

'It is not. Who do you think you are?' I said.

'Damn it, come here, and I'll show you properly like a grown-up,' he said.

'You're just a – just a Nazi,' I said.

'And you're just a baby,' he said.

'I am not!'

'A silly English milksop, that's what you are.'

I stamped my whole body in a rage.

'And you're stubborn and you don't listen to me,' he said. He was getting impatient.

'Because you don't show me how, and I can't do it.' I was defiant with my hands on my hips.

Another woman from the Pits was raking along the shore. 'Môre baas,' she said to Blackie.

'Môre, Katie,' he said back.

'Is dit nie koud nie, baas?' she said.

'Ja,' said Blackie. 'Come on, man,' he turned on me. 'Brass monkey weather, and you're still wondering if you've got it the right way round.'

'Mind your own business,' I said, and I leaped aside.

Blackie was furious, and he caught me up and I gave a blue murder yell as he forced me round and struggled all wet and frozen with me. He gave me a clap, but quite a gentle one, and then he took my sides and held me face forward so that I wriggled loose. My fear changed within me into demon energy, and I complied furiously. I pulled with the right arm and kicked from the left hip right down to my ankle and then, while he held me up, reversed the procedure.

'Good. Do it again,' he said.

I did, methodically and concentrating.

'Good. Do it again,' he said.

I took a breath and repeated it.

'Good,' he said. 'Once more.'

'Sounds like you in the army,' I said.

'Don't you get cheeky with me,' he said. 'Do it and keep it going,' he said.

I did, with my eyes closed and my chin straining forward, beginning slowly to feel that he was holding me all right, and it was all right having the drink so close.

Then he put me down and said that was fine, just have a breather. 'Gee, you got a temper,' he said.

I panted with no energy to spare for a reply.

'All right,' he said, and I nodded. 'Now we going to swim.'

He picked me up and I didn't resist, and this time he held me with my chin on the level of the pearly water. And I swam, not as if it were myself doing it, but some power from outside me. With wonderful concentration I kept going, and I could feel Blackie slacken his support, and when he let go I could feel myself sinking in a disaster, but this time I knew what he meant.

I jumped up with water in my eyes and ears and mouth, but I didn't mind.

'Don't let go,' I gasped.

'Don't you tell me what to do,' he said.

'Well, hold me then,' I said.

'No,' he said, folding his arms. 'You're going to try it on your own.'

I gave a cough, and took a deep breath to last me. I could do it for about six strokes, and then my tail sank.

'That'll teach you to be so stubborn,' he said. 'Now you just do that ten times more.' He struck out himself, going overarm as fast as a dolphin. He was swimming out to the buoy.

I did my exercises meanwhile.

He got to the buoy and his voice came booming across the lagoons, 'How you doing, Jimmy?'

'Very well, thank you,' I shouted back.

And at the end of the lesson we were both exhausted and found a sheltered place behind a bit of dune, and sunbathed there to get dry. Beside Blackie I was so helpless; my arms were like bamboo poles compared with his, and I had no bulk on me to generate warmth. From the strong patches along his chest where the blood was pumping he made body heat. I was shivering like an old rattling tricycle and my joints were blue with cold. Blackie took a handful of sand and trickled it onto my back and it landed there like milk.

'Where's your hat?' he said. 'Better get it or your ma'll chew me out.'

'It's not hot today,' I said.

'Yes, but you know what she says. The ultraviolet's just as strong as the infrared.'

'You're not my father,' I said.

'Never mind, just do as you're told,' he said.

I fetched my new hat, which was quite a tolerable one, and crawled back alongside Blackie. 'You don't wear one,' I said.

'That's because I've got dark skin,' he said and he put his arm against mine. 'Dark skin's an advantage for sunbathing,' he said, and he rolled a bit.

I took a handful of sand and trickled it on his shoulder blades and he just grinned, as Blackie always did, a big grin with his teeth clenched.

'And you know what?' he said. 'Tomorrow you're going to swim right out to the buoy, all by yourself. Then you'll be a real swimmer.'

We went home for lunch because we were starving. After lunch Blackie showed me how to get the water out of my ears with the little finger, and you shake and it dribbles out, then he went to his quarters upstairs. But the whole evening and night it sounded as if my head were gargling, and I could shake it like a cocktail.

The next morning I was ready for our Sunday lesson and, even though my body ached from my neck down, I was all set long before I'd digested.

'I'm going to swim to the buoy today,' I told my mother.

'Jimmy, that's very good,' she said. 'Blackie's obviously a very fine teacher.'

'And I'm a good pupil,' I said cockily.

'Where's your hat?' she said.

'Ah ma –' I said.

She had to turn the roast in the kitchen, so she put down Blackie's shirt; she was unpicking the stripes. Blackie came down the stairs in his sandals, and he was wearing a jersey today. She didn't go inside.

'I heard Jimmy's going to swim all the way out to the buoy,' she said.

To avoid any trouble, I belted into the house to fetch my hat.

'Soon you'll have to come and see,' said Blackie. 'He's getting a real water baby.'

My mother held Blackie's new stripes against his shirt where he had it over his biceps, and Blackie made a hang of a fuss when she pricked him with a pin.

'Oh Blackie,' she said. 'Don't be such a cretin.' She had more pins in her mouth because Blackie had had a promotion. 'Just tell me when I can come and watch this great feat,' she said, and one of the pins came out.

Blackie and I were down on our hands and knees, retrieving the pin from the lawn. Then we went for the lesson.

We walked through the milk-bushes, putting our feet in almost exactly the same places as we did every time. I took Blackie's great hand; there was a pile of roots where he jumped over and I usually had to scramble, but he just hauled me across.

I said to him, 'Blackie, why do you smile so much?'

'Because I got more money from the army,' he replied.

'No, not that. You're always smiling.'

'Then it's because I have a happy nature,' he said.

'Oh you,' I said. 'You always teasing me.'

'Well, I'm not like you; you've got a very sulky nature. Just like your mom. She's a very bitter person,' he said.

'Then you shouldn't smile in her presence,' I said.

'Ag man,' he said. 'It's my birthday, don't you know? Everyone smiles on his birthday.'

'It's not until tomorrow,' I said.

'Yes, but tomorrow's Monday, so we celebrating it today.'

We got to the inlet and I didn't feel like smiling at all. The water had cleared a lot, but my sullen, brooding fear came back. The lagoons were so immense if you looked beyond the dunes, and even the buoy was very far out. The sky was a deep grey again.

We changed behind our sand dune and left our clothes lying in a bundle. I put my hat underneath so that it wouldn't blow away. Then in we went without saying a word.

Blackie wanted to go immediately, but I thought I'd better do some exercise first. I swam in a semi-circle around him, grabbing onto his bathing trunks and spitting out water to one side. He was very patient with me, because he knew that if I got frightened I wouldn't go.

'That's the style,' he said. 'Hell, you can wriggle like a real nipper.'

'Blackie, will you be my father?' I said. It blurted out.

'Well,' he said, 'that all depends on your mother.'

'No,' I said, with the blind confidence of a social need, 'it depends on me, not her.'

Blackie washed the sand off his hands, and said, 'Well, Jimmy, that's not how it works. She has to decide, not me or you.'

'Mrs Feverall said it was a shame to let you get close to us if you not going to tie the knot,' I said. I had no idea what that meant. All I knew was, and I repeated it, 'Will you be my father?'

'But you've already had a father,' said Blackie, looking as if he didn't want to talk about it.

'He's dead,' I said.

'But he got in first, so how can I be your father?' said Blackie.

'I mean my new father,' I stamped with impatience. Blackie could be so stupid sometimes.

'Well, I don't promise a thing,' he grinned, 'but if you – if you, Jimmy, can make it to the buoy before lunch gets cold, I guarantee at least I'll consider it.'

I looked hard at Blackie, and he was smiling uncertainly. That was his challenge and, even if there were no likelihood of my bribing him into it, I had to accept. I turned and took a sighting on the buoy and started swimming at a level where I couldn't see it. Blackie waded alongside me, giving me instructions, 'Take it calmly, just keep a rhythm, no, this way –' and he'd nudge me over without my losing the stroke. Once I swallowed a clot and had to sink down, and my toes could just touch the soft bottom, but I pulled them up and kicked.

Blackie swam alongside me, doing a few strokes of crawl and then treading water, and I kept going and he prodded me over. 'You're doing well,' he said, 'keep going, keep going.' He made some waves and, when I bobbed on one, I could just see the top of the rusty old buoy. The sun was coming down on the back of my head, a trickling, salty winter sun, and the water was just on my upper lip and I blew out. I swallowed a brown mouthful and got a shiver, but I kept going with heavy, tired, aching arms. Time slowed down, and the current was running out there, much colder. Blackie advanced on me, then waited, but if I ignored him I caught him up and began to pass him as he lunged forward again.

'No, Blackie,' I gasped.

'Yes, man,' he replied. 'Nearly nearly there.'

For the last lap I was coughing and felt heavily sick, and I went on mechanically. There seemed to be no pleasure in having to do it. I was overwhelmed with exhaustion. I craved Blackie to put out an arm and support me; I had no option but to endure. I didn't dare let my feet sink, in case they plummeted down with my body behind them, and it became darker and darker and I rolled into the sedge where there was no air. I heaved onwards, making far too big a splash.

Then I had a shudder of panic; I thought Blackie had deserted me, and I couldn't look for him without drowning.

'Nearly there now,' came his voice. 'Not far now.'

The last length I don't remember at all, or how I persuaded myself to get to the buoy. My elbow slid off it. I grabbed at the chain underneath it, and tried to lunge out of the water to be on top of it and never swim in the water again. It hardly sank under my weight, and I slid for a complete dunking. And I grabbed for its warm, dry surface, preferring that to anything. I fell sideways and ribbons of bubble came out of me alongside the slippery, green chain, and I put my feet round it and stayed upright that way.

Blackie came alongside, and I was too clapped to do anything but a pounding breathing. There was an old piece of rope coming like a tail from the fitting at the top and I clutched that with one hand and bashed my forehead on the buoy itself and drifted there, my flimsy, disconnected body somewhere around in the water, and just my nose and hand against the buoy. Blackie must have said something, but I remember only my hand with the brown stain of the rust and a stinging patch inside my nose where the salt was eroding it.

Presently Blackie said whatever he had to say, and my hand came off the rope and went round his neck, and he did a slow breaststroke all the way back with me trailing over his shoulders. He stopped and kicked, and forced my hands around his chin because I was going to strangle him. He hadn't shaved and I could feel the bristles on his jawbone. Then I had him by the Adam's apple again, but it wasn't my fault because there was no strength left in me. When we got to our lesson area, he prised me off and I knelt where I fell, my knees firmly in the silt.

'That's what you get for ducking me,' he said, and I didn't even see it coming. My face was forced under the water and a spectrum of colour came out of my mouth, and cruising under the surface like a dead log I decided I definitely didn't want Blackie as my father if, at the end, all he could do was push me under. I tried to breathe and my throat was stopped. I drifted sideways and came up, heaving in a huge mouthful of water, and I couldn't even spit, so I sat there, swallowing it bit by bit, and wiping the hair out of my streaming eyes.

Blackie was up at the clothes and everything went wrong for me from there. He was signalling and calling me, and with exhausted obedience I flopped forward. I dragged myself onto the shore, and fell into the sand, vomiting up half the inlet. The trouble was Blackie had money in his shorts pocket, and someone had stolen it. The tokoloshe in the reeds took it, was my only thought.

Water came out of the side of my mouth with streamers of spittle. Blackie was trying to trace the footsteps of people who'd been there, and wanted me to help him.

He came to me, indignant. 'No man,' he said, 'that's all my birthday money gone.'

'Serves you right for drowning me,' I said.

'I'm sorry,' he said. 'But you were trying to throttle me to death.'

'I wasn't,' I said.

He gave me some slaps on the back, and my breathing pipe cleared.

'Oh well,' he said, 'it wasn't so much money. I'll get lots more next month.'

'How much was it?' I said.

'Twenty-two shillings,' he said. 'One for each year. My mother sent it to me.'

I stood up and he pointed to where we had been, and it didn't seem all that far out for all the effort expended.

'Come and get a quick sunbathe before lunch,' he said, and he plunked my hat on himself, but his head was far too big for it. He bent down and I took it off.

We sunbathed for a bit, yet it wasn't the same. He trickled sand down my back, but I didn't respond. It felt like sand landing there, and it was irritating, not ticklish.

'Hey, Mister Sourface,' he said, 'you look as if you've lost all your birthday money, not me.'

'You look like a pumpkin,' I said.

'How's that for gratitude?' he said. 'I give up my Saturdays and my Sundays to teach you to swim, and now I'm a pumpkin. You realise how many pints I could get down at the club while I'm giving you lessons?'

'You couldn't get any with your money stolen,' I said.

'Aren't you just a bit pleased you managed to do it?' he said, and he nudged me.

'A bit,' I said. I wanted to say something else – him to take me drinking at the club, to show me how to drive the jeep, endlessly to pamper and chastise me.

'That's what I like is gratitude,' he said. 'You can swim right out to the buoy like a champion. You don't need me any more. If the ship sinks, you can swim; if the whole bloody affair goes down in the middle of the night, you'll be all right. But at least you can say thank you before I go.'

I didn't know what to say, and we dried ourselves and got dressed, and Blackie put his jersey on me and it went down to my knees with my thin shins sticking out. And I could smell Blackie inside that jersey.

And we went home before the roast got burnt. And we had roast lamb with mint sauce and roast potatoes for Blackie's birthday lunch, and my mother had put little bows on the cutlery, and I had seconds and thirds as if I were dropping the food down a well, and peas and gravy, and Blackie wore a hat from a cracker, and I got a whistle which I was too tired to blow. Blackie came in with his own birthday cake, baked by Euphemia, on which my mother had squeezed pink icing, and it had twenty-two red candles, and he said I must blow them out, and I said, you do it. And I had two slices, and they had coffee as well.

Blackie was so full he just collapsed on the Persian carpet where the sun was coming through the doors, and I was so full I collapsed on his lap, and he moved me down because I was too heavy and I passed out with my head between his knees, and my mother came to sit against Blackie on the carpet and put her hand on my shoulder, and he put his hand on her arm.

14

Winter came. As the wind stirred and flopped over Silver Town, the community took to the indoors. Euphemia would arrive with her umbrella bust up and her shoes would leak over the kitchen floor.

'How's he doing, Euphemia?' asked my mother, with reference to Euphemia's husband.

'Ow madam,' she sighed.

'You really should consider the Santa hospital,' she said.

My mother was worried I would catch tuberculosis from fondling Euphemia.

Blackie took to delivering me at school because the road was in such a mess my mother couldn't manage it in our car. He never dropped me right in front of the Christmas thorn hedge, but on the corner, to avoid the gossip.

'Morning, Miss Kettley,' I'd say.

'How did you get here so dry? All the other children are soaked right through,' she'd enquire.

'It's not raining our way,' I'd reply.

'Come and sit in front of the fire. Nothing to do with an army jeep, I suppose?' she'd say.

All the best cushions were taken beside the fireplace, as usual, and I'd sit in the corner, a real dunce.

'Now, children,' Miss Kettley put her stick down and twisted into position, clapping her hands. 'Let's play father's game, until we're all nice and dry.'

'Ah, father's game,' moaned Jack Feverall, who was now head boy. Jack Feverall was always fighting with his twin sister, Joan, and she cracked him to keep quiet.

'You, Joan, father's game,' said Miss Kettley, pointing her knobbly fist.

'Yes, Miss Kettley,' said Joan.

'Well, you know the rules by now.'

The rules were that you had to be descriptive, in complete sentences, and everyone was to keep quiet while it was your turn. Then Miss Kettley could interrogate you.

'Um,' said Joan. 'My father—'

'Don't say um,' said Miss Kettley.

'Sorry, Miss Kettley.' Joan clasped her hands closed and concentrated.

'My father was always in the Defence Force and that is why my twin brother and me —'

'My twin brother and I,' corrected Miss Kettley.

'Sorry, Miss Kettley,' Joan stumbled out.

'Never mind. Carry on.'

'That is why my twin brother and I,' she stressed the correction to show she was learning, 'live in my grandfather's hotel for the duration. My twin brother Jack,' and Jack nudged her, '— is not my identical twin because, unlike me, he's considerably dumb.'

Jack looked as if a bomb had dropped on him.

'No, Joan, no, you're out. Why's she out, children?' Miss Kettley raised her eyebrows.

Everybody mumbled, 'Off the subject, off the subject.'

'Quite right, she's run hopelessly off the track. Your twin brother Jack is not your father, Joan.'

Joan cringed, and relaxed when Miss Kettley's gaze swept over to Lettie Lotter.

Lettie screwed her face up and we always had to wait a long while, then she blurted, 'My father is a veteran and he is the only butcher in Silver Town and he gets all his stock from town and he doesn't accept donkeys and he learned how to dress meat when he was on a big naval ship before he retired to Silver Town and my father married very late because he was in Germany and then he was in Canada and my father —'

'All right, very good, Lettie,' said Miss Kettley. 'What's wrong, children?'

It was always the same. Too many connecting words and no past participles.

'Sheena,' pointed Miss Kettley.

Everyone turned to Sheena, who always carried her protractor with her, measuring every angle. Sheena put her protractor in her lap and covered it with her hands. 'Um —' she said.

Miss Kettley ignored that, and smiled.

'Having participated in the theatre profession as a singer,' said Sheena.

'Good girl,' said Miss Kettley; Sheena was her pet.

'– my father retired from active work in Gilbert and Sullivan to become a choir-master, and having reached the age of resigning – '

'Resignation,' prompted Miss Kettley.

'Excuse me, Miss Kettley; he didn't become resigned, he did resign,' said Sheena.

'Very good indeed,' said Miss Kettley. 'Can you improve on that, children?' She raked her assembly with her eyes peaked, and we had no comments to add.

'Major,' said Miss Kettley, calling up her own grandnephew, about whom we all knew everything. Part of the exercise was to make it interesting with new facts.

Major had a frog in his throat and was sort of the family darling. 'Ah, my father –' he said, lolling about, 'is an infinitely superior creation to Minor's father;' which was his joke, because their father was the same.

'Oh,' said Miss Kettley, pretending amazement, 'do explain yourself, boy.'

'Well, my father was so exhausted from having me there wasn't much left in him when he came to Minor – that's why Minor's so puny!' At that we all had a laugh which was permitted when Major cracked a joke, and Minor looked red all over.

'My father –' stammered Minor.

'All right, have your turn now,' said Miss Kettley, and she made a sweeping gesture to announce him. 'And see you get him back.'

'My father's been having trouble with his – heart – ever since,' Minor stuttered and got stuck on the s, 's-s-since he first s-s-saw Major and therefore –' he stopped, because therefore was a good point to score, 'what he's lost in mobility he's gained in mental qualities which he's passed on to me!'

'There is some truth in that,' Miss Kettley nodded. But Minor continued to her face, 'But our father is Miss Kettley's nephew s-so,' another good point, 'it should not s-surprise you that we are in the family way.'

'In the family, in the family,' said Miss Kettley, holding her hands out for criticism. 'And a good family, too.'

Jack Feverall interrupted, 'One of the waitresses is in the family way, I heard this morning. Granny fired her because she isn't married to that Petrus. She's always drinking at the garage, honestly, it's a juicy scandal,' he concluded.

'I'll thank you, Jack,' Miss Kettley drew up sternly, 'not to talk out of turn. As head boy, you should know that.'

'Sorry, Miss Kettley,' said Jack, putting his head in his hands, but he knew everyone would ask him about what he said during the lunch break.

'Little Marie, please,' said Miss Kettley, 'it's your turn, dear.'

'Yes, Miss Kettley,' she said.

'And try to use your English accent. Afrikaans is for out of doors, dear.'

'Yes, Miss Kettley,' she said and gave an uncertain smile.

'Proceed.'

'My father speaks Afrikaans but his English is also excellent, therefore —' she dried up.

'Therefore —'

'Therefore comes he out —'

'Therefore he comes out —'

'As everybody's friend.' Little Marie came through the obstacles with a radiant satisfaction.

'She really is improving,' said Miss Kettley, 'and with very little prompting from me. Remember, children, when she could only say, Ag, Miss Kettley, ag?'

'Shot,' said Major, and he thumped Little Marie on the back.

'And last but not least, Jimmy,' said Miss Kettley. Everyone turned round on the floor to face me.

The fire was radiating heat and the smell of dampness had gone.

'My father is deceased,' I said, 'but having served his country on two fronts he received four medals and therefore —'

'Therefore,' said Miss Kettley.

'Therefore, having served his country, he was a credit to his family.' I stopped thinking and put my head down.

'Very well done, Jimmy,' said Miss Kettley. 'You have all our sympathy.'

'Yes, shot, Jimmy,' said Little Marie, and Miss Kettley clapped her hands for prayers in the classroom.

It was in the playground that the true versions of all our stories were current; on days when we were cooped up because of the weather it felt as if we would throttle on the official versions of our lives. Lettie's widower father drank too much and couldn't make a living in a larger town; the Feverall grandparents had long ago lost control of their establishment and it was run by Petrus who took the country girls as his just reward; the Kettley boys' mother had long walked out on them and all their father did from Wimbledon was send Miss Kettley an allowance; Little Marie's story was genuine, because she had been well brought up and her mother coached her; the only time Sheena's father sang was in the golf club bar, and so on. There was no deceit in our double lives. We merely told Miss Kettley what she wanted to hear.

The hour after lunch was assigned to the war effort. For Ouma Smuts's Gifts and Comforts Fund we battled to knit. I chose a blue muffler because that was straight, Lettie could do a red balaclava because she could already knit round corners, and Jack did socks with the four needles. We sat on stools very solemnly in Miss Kettley's assembly room and knitted with our shoulders hunched and no talking. We didn't talk, but at first we snickered a lot. When the routine took over we had competitions to see who could make the needles click most loudly.

My old problem reasserted itself, the hand not matching the eye. Miss Kettley got me a smaller pair of needles and unravelled what I had done. I was so conditioned to my miseries that it no longer worried me when, after forty minutes of diligent feeding and tightening, I had produced only a spider's web of blue wool that never lengthened into a scarf. Into my satchel it went as the bell rang. In the evenings my mother would unpick and take over for a few inches.

'It's going to be for a very small soldier if you do it that way,' she said with great tact, and closed my hands over the needles again.

Everybody's mothers were helping them, and even Miss Kettley cheated for Major and Minor, so there was no special disgrace in receiving assistance. Only Lettie had to do it for herself, and she turned into a very professional balaclava-maker. This early training paid off, I suppose, as in the 60s she became one of the first women to manage a clothing factory in Salt River.

I became more and more hamfisted, and the prevailing disillusion over my abilities dampened my zest for life; I had no idea what was to become of me. All I knew was that I would not turn into the soldier who inherited that mangy muffler somewhere in the Alps in 1944. But still, we all persisted. Miss Kettley's Beginners School in Silver Town, Cape Province, was aiming to clothe an entire regiment.

'Jimmy, you're not doing very well there, are you?' said my mother.

'It's all right,' I said.

'And she charges twelve guineas a quarter – that's shocking, that's exorbitant,' she said. 'I think if you don't move up at the end of this year, we should educate you at home. Until you're ready for Primary School. Otherwise you'll be stuck for ever.'

'Yes, mamma,' I said, knowing that Primary School meant being a boarder in Cape Town. That's where Meshack went, and Michael Longford and Jenny Green.

'You could always play with your friends after school. I'll take you round to Mrs Van's as often as you like.'

I didn't say anything, because the decision was not in my hands.

We listened to the wireless and they played 'You are my Sunshine.'

'You're not just fooling everybody, Jimmy? You really can knit quite well?' asked my mother.

'Knitting's for girls,' I said.

'I know, but with the war we all have to muck in.'

'It's always the war,' I said.

'You've got a point there,' she replied. 'But it's made Silver Town, you know. Gosh, with all the fund-raisers and functions and balls and heaven knows what. It can only lead to expansion when peace comes,' she said.

'Then why can't you afford to keep me at Miss Kettley's?' I asked.

'It's not that, Jimmy. With my salary and the pension and the money that comes in from Blackie's rooms, we're doing adequately. If you take a year off, we can really save for Primary School,' she said.

'I don't want to go to Primary School,' I said.

'No boy I've ever heard of wants to go to Primary School,' she said. 'But you'll like it, you'll see.' She put her head back and sang, 'You are my Sunshine.'

I stood up on the carpet where I was trying to assemble a railway track.

'Put that away before you go to bed, Euphemia must sweep in the morning,' she said.

It was always the same; get it half assembled and then pack it away. No train ever went around my track. I sank down with a sense of uselessness.

So it came about that I was not to return to Miss Kettley's. My old headmistress was very uncomfortable about that, because she, too, needed the income.

'Just you watch, I'll have him writing perfectly in no time,' she said with a friendly optimism.

'Oh, it's no good, Miss Kettley,' said my mother. 'It's not your fault; he just seems to deteriorate. I know you've done everything you can.'

And for me there was a kind of triumph when I took my mother's hand and we strode down those crazy paving stones of Miss Kettley's and shut the gate for the last time. Lettie and Joan and Sheena were hanging over the balcony, waving to me, and I waved back, seeing how co-operative and meek they were.

During that time my mother and I accepted an urgent invitation to tea with Mrs Pennington-Worthy, whom the people at the club had got to know quite well through all her charity work. They called her Mrs Pennypincher, or just Mrs Penny. Mrs Van covered for my mother.

We dressed in our best. Mother decided we should drive to the big house, even though it was only three hundred yards further down the road. But there was so much mud and dust that by the time we swirled into the gravel driveway it looked as if we'd splashed through a hundred miles. One of the gardeners was sweeping the gravel with a stiff broom, making it like scrimshaw work, and our tyres had scrunched it all up.

My mother alighted with her scarf blowing, and I clambered out. She looked like one of those ladies in the C to C advertisement, smoking over their shoulders. Mrs Penny's maid, who was very respectable with a white lace cap on, peeked through the curtains to see if it was us. We went to the porch over the front door and rang the bell.

Mrs Pennington-Worthy didn't come to the front door, but the one maid did, and said we must come in and wait. We were likely to be the only visitors, as of the four garages alongside the drive only one was occupied, by Mrs Pennington-Worthy's Daimler. We stepped inside to the hall and there was a stand with the mackintoshes and umbrellas and gumboots of all the people who lived there, and a dog-basket for the Dalmatian.

We could hear Mrs Pennington-Worthy shuffling in her study at the other end of the lounge, and the maid came back and led us through the hall door to the lounge where some light came in. There were French bustle chairs like the one Mrs Pennington-Worthy had thrown out for my mother's desk – four of them around a card table. And a grand piano with stacks of music on it. And lion-skin rugs and a lot of bookshelves holding books with gold letters on the spines. And a lamp with a Chinese silk shade, not on yet, and a good sofa with carved legs, and the Dalmatian obviously lay there at night when Mr Pennington-Worthy sat under the lamp in the armchair, because there was a smear of mud on the brocade where the dog threw himself down before the fireplace. We stood waiting, and my mother whispered there must be some hitch, and I said Mrs Penny hadn't had her whisky yet, and my mother yanked my arm.

Mrs Pennington-Worthy came out of her study and closed the door immediately, so that I couldn't see inside.

'Oh, don't stand on ceremony, Sarah, please, do sit yourselves down,' she said, and my mother and I sat right on the couch where we were. 'No need to be so formal these days, is there?'

'Good afternoon, Mrs Pennington-Worthy,' I said.

'Ah, Jimmy,' she said, 'so glad you could come too.'

I stood up and she gave me a kiss on the forehead, and I could tell she was sucking a peppermint.

She pecked my mother on each cheek, and then said the tea was coming instantly, wasn't I hungry, bet I was.

Then she fetched the accounts and laid them out on the low table, pushing the ornaments to one side with her ruler. 'See here,' she pointed with the flat of the ruler, and then she mumbled and lifted her glasses with the silver chain, onto her nose. 'See, Mr Pennington-Worthy donated £50 and I entered that here.'

'Under credits, that's perfect. Why, that's most generous of him, I must say.'

'Evens it up a bit,' and she pushed the binder across to my mother. 'Bit of a novice at accounting, my dear; I'd be so obliged if you'd check it through.'

'Well, all the debits seem to be in order; £12 to Mr Lotter and 5/- to Mrs Feverall for services rendered – I must say she's quite remarkable at it.'

'Oh absolutely,' said Mrs Pennington-Worthy, 'made for the job.'

'Looks absolutely in order, Mrs Pennington-Worthy. Do you want me to go through it now or could I return it to you at the meeting tomorrow?'

'Sarah dear, take it. I've gone as far as my financial brains will go. We can't all be wizards like my husband, you know.'

'Very well then. Should I find a slip, I'll just mark it in pencil above. You do have the most elegant copperplate; I don't want to wreck it with my ugly scrawl.'

Mrs Pennington-Worthy was very satisfied and folded her glasses. She stood up to ring for tea again. 'These blasted servants never come when they're called,' she said. I could hear the bell ringing about a hundred yards away through the house. 'You know, Sarah,' she turned on her grey heels, 'I do honestly feel that we've all made a sterling effort. I think our little soup kitchen has raised more funds, just locally, I mean, than all of Miss Kettley's operation. Just in this area, mind you, I've pulled in more money than old Ouma Smuts, and that's something to be very proud of.'

'Yes, and the kitchen's certainly contributed to a peaceful community in Silver Town. Otherwise we'd be crime-ridden, like in Hermanus.'

'Believe it's too dreadful there,' Mrs Pennington-Worthy agreed. 'Can't go to bed in Hermanus without having your very slippers pinched. If you don't take law and order into your own hands, the home front just does what it likes. Don't you agree?'

'Well,' said my mother, nudging me to stop fidgeting, 'I think there's a very very good spirit in Silver Town. Helped of course by gestures like your husband's donation.'

'Does he want a biscuit? Does he want a biscuit?' Mrs Pennington-Worthy said about me.

'Oh, just sit still, Jimmy,' my mother said.

The trouble was the sofa was so high I couldn't get my feet on the floor to wriggle my shorts straight.

'Or would you like a raisin bun?' said Mrs Pennington-Worthy, and she went to ring petulantly for the servants again.

'She was here just now,' I said helpfully, 'because she let us in.'

'Yes, we know that,' said my mother, 'but it's the other maid who brews the tea.'

Mrs Pennington-Worthy ran her finger along the mantelpiece to check for dust. 'I know, Sarah, you and your socialist ideals. A community where everyone knows their place is a happy one and functions in an orderly way, but that's not quite the same as saying we're all entitled to an equal share in the cake.'

I thought that meant the other maid would come in with a cake for tea, but she didn't. When the tray came with its silverware there were only triangular sandwiches and a rock bun that had glazed over. While they were pouring and distributing the cups and teaspoons and sideplates, I took advantage of the lull and ducked behind the couch to get my underpants untwisted.

The Dalmatian then came in and nearly knocked me over, and Mrs Pennington-Worthy shooed it off with a doily, saying 'Out, boy, out,' opening the bay window, and it leapt through. While Mrs Pennington-Worthy was at the window my mother jumped to me and did up my top button, then she backed and spilled some of the tea over the accounts.

'Oh,' she gasped, 'this is too much.'

Mrs Pennington-Worthy wasn't distressed at all, and rang the bell for the first maid to come with a lappie.

We had so many sandwiches after that, and I had the rock bun, with the result that when my mother and I got home we didn't feel like a full supper, so we had toast and Ovaltine.

My mother settled in at her desk on her French bustle chair, which is where she usually wrote letters to my grandmother. She opened the account book and, like a naughty schoolgirl, grimaced at where the tea had made two splotches.

'Where's Blackie?' I said. 'I want to play with him.'

'I suspect he's having a drink at the club,' she said. Then she turned to me, 'Honestly, she's a dear soul, Mrs Penny, but she does say the most awful things. Did you hear what she said about Blackie?'

'She said he didn't have two brains to rub together,' I remembered.

'And those two housemaids, Iris and Esther, they're so stuck up. She imported them, you know, from Saint Helena. The local girls are not good enough.'

'They never wave when they go to the shop on their afternoon off.' Everyone called them the two old maids, because they never laughed or talked, they were so stuck up. In Mrs Feverall's shop they wouldn't talk to any of the other Coloureds; just bought their thread and went back to the Silver estate. Sometimes they nodded to Petrus, when he was standing with his feet on the balcony railing of the hotel, and flashing them with the sun's reflection from his tray.

'Is Mrs Penny very stuck up?' I asked.

'Oh, not as bad as she used to be. Ouma Smuts will get a fright when she hears Mrs Penny has gone into competition. But Ouma Smuts is more my type of woman – she doesn't put on any frills and fancies. Do you see what I mean, Jimmy? It's awful to sit there like a parasite while your husband makes all his money from munitions.'

'What's munitions?' I said.

'Well, bombs, shells, that sort of thing. And he doesn't employ any of the local population in his factory, not a damn,' she said. 'Thinks he can fob them off with fifty quid. It's not good enough.'

'No, not at all,' I said.

'That's why they say as cold as charity. I bet you Spot the Dalmatian has more to eat in a day than half the children in Silver Town, black and white,' she said.

'I know, mummy,' I said.

'The trouble'll come after the war, not now. And all I can say is the answer is not guns,' she said.

I thought she meant guns for all the animals that had been shot – the rhino head and the oryx horns and even the antlers from England in the sitting room – but she meant Mrs Pennington-Worthy's own gun that she kept beside her slippers.

'That's what you call stinking rich,' said my mother. 'And if you really go into it, she's not that different from the enemy we're supposed to be fighting.'

'Mummy, what's a socialist?' I said.

'Well, it's not the same as a socialite, you can put your money on that,' she said. 'A socialist believes everyone should have an equal chance, and the state should really look after us all.'

'Are they ovoviviparous?' I said.

She unscrewed her pen. 'What on earth do you mean?'

'Are they, you know, like munitions?' I said.

'Ah my boy,' she said. 'It's really bedtime for you. Come on, no arguments,' and she was going to push her chair back.

But I surprised her. 'Look what I found,' I said, and I wrestled out of my right shorts pocket my trophy.

She was absolutely amazed, and I put it down on the accounts book where she couldn't miss it. 'I found it,' I said.

'But Jimmy!' she was completely stunned, 'oh no!'

'Where Blackie parks his jeep. It must have fallen out,' I said.

It was Mrs Pennington-Worthy's sugar tongs, the ones that arrived on the teatray.

'So that's why we had to take sugarcubes with our fingers? So it wasn't Esther's fault?' She glared at me.

'I can use them for when we're steaming stamps off the letters. It can go with my stamp collection,' I said.

'But Jimmy,' she said, 'that's theft outright. You are a terrible, naughty child.' She picked up the tongs with their dragon's claws at the end and covered them as if somebody was going to come in. 'Jimmy, that is an awful, terrible thing to do.'

'It's for peeling the stamps,' I said.

'No,' she said strongly. 'Admit it. You are a miserable little thief. And what's more, Esther's going to get the entire blame for it. That's not fair and it's dishonest. Admit that you stole them. People go to jail for less than that – do you want that? Tell me? To go to jail and never come out again?'

'I don't know,' I said. It didn't seem worth it just for a pair of shiny tongs.

'Jimmy, what – what can I do with you?' she said, and she put her head on her arms and was going to blubber.

'I'm sorry, mummy,' I said, wishing with a sick feeling that the incident would blow over.

My mother opened one of the desk drawers and pulled out a sheet of tissue paper, and kept me in suspense while she wrapped the tongs and tied a ribbon round them, as she did when we were wrapping bundles for Britain.

'Now take that,' she said, prodding me with the tongs, 'and tomorrow morning you're coming with me, and you're going to return them to Mrs Penny and tell her you made a frightful mistake, and apologise to her. You do all that, as I've told you, because I will have nothing more to do with it.' She forced the tongs into my hand. 'I will not have it said that my son's a sneak-thief. Don't you ever, ever do that again. Go to bed.'

I put the tongs on my bedside table and climbed into the sheets, not saying my prayers or being tucked in. All the feelings of family disgrace worked their way into me. I was being punished, and that was fair. I didn't know how I could face Mrs Pennington-Worthy in the morning – in the corridor with the potted palms, not in the lounge with all the committee people.

I could hear Blackie coming back and closing the upstairs outside door. My mother got up from her desk and went up there. She had such long legs she could just hop over the gate. She knocked on the inner door and Blackie opened it and closed it.

I pushed back the covers and peeled my blanket off the bed. I climbed the stairs extremely quietly, knowing exactly where the creaks were under the carpet. I climbed to the corner and listened, and then tiptoed across the straight bit and around the corner, then very slowly ascended each stair until I was touching the gate. I wanted to say, don't tell him, don't tell him, because that would spread the terrible news, but I pulled the blanket round me and sat with my forehead on the gate.

Blackie had had a beer and his boots made a noise on the parquet. He shuffled this way and that way, and my mother said she'd sit there, at my father's desk. He sat on the bed, because you could hear the springs extend, then they joggled when he forced his one boot off and threw it into the corner of the door right near me. He had lost in the darts against the barman, therefore he was moody.

'Oh, the most disgraceful thing has happened,' my mother said in a moan. 'Bloody Jimmy swiped Mrs Penny's sterling tongs, just ups and pockets them. Wretched little tyke!'

Blackie got the other boot off and didn't throw it, but put it seriously down. 'Sounds like you got a kleptomaniac on your hands,' he chortled.

'It's not funny, Blackie,' said my mother.

'I didn't say it was funny,' said Blackie. 'You mean he just helped himself to the family silver when you weren't watching? Well, how do you like that?'

'Only the tongs,' said my mother.

'Mrs Pennington-Worthy's tongs,' said Blackie, and he whistled.

'It's too embarrassing for speech,' said my mother.

'Now, now, now,' said Blackie, trying to make her laugh. 'Yes, I can see how awkward it is, but if he'd nicked the floating trophies as well I'd start getting really worried.'

'Oh you,' she said.

'And if he'd really got down to the string of pearls round her neck, and her diamond ring and those moondrop earrings of hers, all while she was having her cucumber sandwich, then, Sarah, then I'd really be getting jittery.'

'Oh you –' said my mother.

'It's only a pair of tongs,' he said. 'They can use their teaspoons. Serve them right.'

'But Blackie,' my mother said, 'I can't turn his pockets out every time we go to a public place. Imagine me saying, wait while I search my child.'

'Ah come on, Sarah,' said Blackie. He stood up, because he tripped on the one boot. He must have put his hand on my mother, for she was very quiet.

Then Blackie sighed, and he said very gently, 'Please man, Sarah, it's driving me to drink, man.'

So quiet was it I could hear my mother's lips on his wrist. Then she said, 'I know, Blackie, but I've seen enough of wartime romances to know.'

Blackie shuffled beside her, and she moved the chair a bit.

'I know, Sarah,' he said, 'but it's not right – two lonely people living under one roof.'

'Oh Blackie,' she said.

'Anyway, it's what most people think we're doing. If you knew what's really going on in Silver Town, you wouldn't lose a moment, I'm telling you. You know, the barman tonight –'

'I don't want to hear a thing about that,' said my mother.

'He said I was so damn lucky, man –'

'Blackie,' said my mother firmly, 'I do not want to hear it. Please.'

'He said how lucky I was you were keeping the sheets warm for me,' said Blackie.

My mother took a deep breath. 'Well, next time he insinuates a thing like that, you just tactfully put him straight. If anyone so much as – if just anyone, they'll get such a jawful from me –' She paused. 'Blackie, I can't – I just cannot, that's all. I'm not like those other women who come from Cape Town for a weekend pass. How the Feveralls sanction it, I simply don't know.'

'They got to make a living,' said Blackie. 'Come on, Sarah, no one will know the difference, honestly.'

'Now you're contradicting yourself; you said everyone knew about something that hasn't happened.'

'So what difference does it make?' said Blackie, and he had my mother there.

She stood up and came to the door. I grabbed my blanket and started to evacuate. But then Blackie stood against her so that she couldn't open the door. I thought she was going to need help, and I'd have to get Blackie out. I crept back to the gate; they were bustling and thumping on the door; Blackie's shadow was in the crack. She pushed him away slowly.

'The difference is we have to go on living here, Blackie. There's enough disgrace with a little kleptomaniac on the loose.'

'But yourself, Sarah, please man. You can't give your whole life to a little kleptomaniac. You just said that's all he is; ag nee jislaaik, Sarah, you making a fool of yourself and of me.' He flung himself out on the bed.

My mother's shadow crossed the crack and you could hear she sat on the edge of Blackie's bed.

A long time later Blackie said, 'Well, if you don't want another child, there's a doctor in Cape Town who can fix you. All the WAAFs go to him and they only have a good time.'

'Shame on you, Blackie, shame, shame,' said my mother.

'Well how much can a man stand, I'm asking you? Now you've got me in your house and now I give your child swimming lessons and take him on rides because the school can't handle him. He's all about face, man. But does that worry me? – no. I accept him as he is. So you accept me.'

'Blackie,' said my mother, 'I know you're extremely good to Jimmy-boy, and I'm extremely grateful for every minute of it, believe me.'

Blackie sat up roughly. 'I know I only come from Pietersburg and all that, and I'm not good enough for you, and I'm younger than you, but I'm good enough for him. Jislaaik, Sarah. I don't take him out for your sake, you know; I take him out for his sake. If you just left him alone he'd be perfectly all right. Look at me – I'm a stupid bliksem from the platteland and all that, and I can only half add and all that, but it's all right, isn't it? We still people. We can still have some fun, hey?'

'Ah, Blackie,' my mother sighed, 'you really are a special person.'

Blackie fell forward into her lap. 'My English is improving, hey?' he said.

'Don't say hey,' said my mother.

'But it is, isn't it?' he said.

'Oh yes,' she said, and they both laughed.

'If it's all right with you, I'm just going to pass out,' said Blackie.

'I'll make you some Ovaltine,' said my mother, and then I had to streak down the stairs and spring on my toes down the passage and feel my way to bed. I got such a fright my heart bounded about in my throat. I thought in a huge jumble about the silver tongs and the picnics we would have, curled up like a watch spring.

A lot later my mother came and replaced the blanket I'd left on the stairway and she went to finish Mrs Penny's accounts.

15

The scene in the portals of the golf club duly took place. The wind was raging and I caught Mrs Pennington-Worthy from behind a palm. For a moment she thought I was a ghost of south-easter tugging at her sleeve. I handed her the silver tongs. Perhaps she felt I was making a gift presentation to her. I made my short speech and she thanked me graciously and tottered in to the meeting. To this day I do not know if I am absolved of the crime of theft. So much in my life had no definite outline.

But the horror and guilt I felt over that incident were soon absorbed into the next event, for we then had the flood. It came up from the ocean and down from the mountains, and we were trapped between. Everybody said it was an act of God against which there is no insurance. The whole ocean reared up and almost took the lighthouse off, and the isthmus became a peninsula where the tide broke through the sandbar into the lagoons. The coastal road was unusable, unless you wanted to resist the rollers, and the strip of tar came off like piecrust. Most of the fishing boats went adrift and landed at Long Beach, where they had to be dug out.

The rain poured – not just drizzle and wind, but as if the clouds were flying low and strafing the little village. The clouds crashed into the mountains. Everyone said the farmers would be pleased to have rain for their crops, but their crops must have been flattened. And then all the rain that collected in the mountains turned around and came back down again. The small stream on our dirt road became a rushing downpour. A new channel opened through the bushes behind our houses, and where the trickle used to seep into the dunes a dam collected, and eventually it bulldozed its way to the lagoons near the wooden bridge. The bridge itself was marooned, taking people from nowhere to nowhere.

Our sunken lawn became a muddy swimming pool. My mother had to switch off the electricity. We were isolated from Silver Town, but we had paraffin lamps for storms and a spirit stove in reserve, so we just waited until it subsided. Mother also had the phone, and everyone phoned to check that it was all right, and it was.

Now Peter's Lodge being built in the form of a ship had some meaning, for we seemed afloat. When the skies cleared briefly we went up onto the roof which my mother explained was the deck, and were monarchs of all we surveyed. The water was so brown and running Euphemia couldn't get to us. Aunt Rosemary phoned from Elgin because it had been on the wireless; thank God they hadn't bought that boat in the end.

One of the caddies swam over with a large paper bag from Mrs Feverall's and, although it was sopping wet, it contained all the items we needed – bread, milk, cheese, fishpaste, chops and a tube of jujubes. He wouldn't let us pay because Mrs Feverall said we could have it on account, but my mother ran to her purse to give him a large tip for delivering it under such conditions. Then Iris from Saint Helena came to the front gate and called, because half the groceries were meant for Mrs Pennington-Worthy, and I got in my bathing costume and had almost to swim across to her with what they were owed. Nobody would deliver to the big house because they would be trespassing, so Iris was the messenger and we were the receiving depot.

Blackie was out all day because the Defence Force came in to do flood relief. On about the fourth day he arranged with them to make a pulley and cable across the new river and he came across like Tarzan out of the wattles. He brought things from the kitchen of the club, more than we needed. He didn't sleep at all and his beard grew because he didn't have time to shave. Everybody agreed it was best we stay where we were in case the water table rose, then we could carry valuables upstairs.

Mrs Pennington-Worthy phoned us, and she was crying as her husband happened to be overseas at that time, and she could not get a message through to him, but his manager in Salt River arranged a rescue party which was like an outing for all his staff. They came past carrying their trousers above their heads and rescued her. She got such a bad shock when her whole sitting room was flooded that she was taken to Groote Schuur hospital. She didn't ask for help from anyone in Silver Town, so no one gave it to her.

Then they had a fly-past when the sun was shining, to take aerial photographs of the extent of the damage. Blackie said the divisional council came down to study the waterways, so that after the war there would be bridges over which we could walk. They needed to put a rampart around everything in Silver Town, judging by our house – the car was up to the running board, the laundry was all soaking, and inside the house the carpets were mushy. The plaster around the skirting in my room got like marzipan. The septic tank was hopelessly waterlogged, and all you saw in the bowl was the stuff you wanted to go down coming up and bubbling, so we made the whole toilet out of bounds and used Euphemia's in the back yard.

All in all, though the flood was a disaster for Silver Town in general, those ten days were all right for us. We had a constant stream of visitors, and even people we had never known. They all came over to see us and be taken on a tour of inspection.

To prevent rising damp in the house, we had to bail out the garden, which had no natural outlet. To think, my mother kept saying, the old codger who built the house plunked it down near a water course. We wore old clothes because we got completely dirty, and soon we just lived in them. My mother tied her hair in a bun and my hat looked like a cement-mixer's. We had to dress warmly down to the knees, and then we went barefoot. We used the tins which had had plants in them to pump bilge. There was a ditch among the roots of the milk-bushes which worked its way down into the dunes where big puddles had accumulated, so we had to traipse with the tins from the deepest part of the lawn to the beginning of the ditch, and tip them out. It was quite hard to carry a tin of muddy water without it slipping through our hands, so in the end we made a broomstick handle with two slings, and I had an old branch with similar slings.

This was the best time I ever had with my mother, because we went on with it for hour after hour. She got tired when I was tired, and we'd sit on the veranda with our feet still in the mud up to our ankles and have a break. She carried bigger size tins because she was stronger than me, but I made the same number of trips as her, and one would be down at the ditch knocking the contents of the tins out while the other was at the lawn, filling up. We beat our own path through where the strawberries used to be and the sandy patch with the heron's nest and through the way we used to go swimming and up the bank. We stopped making food, too, and just got on with it, sharing a packet of biscuits or having bread and dripping and honey. Mother said she was like a milk-maid in the nursery rhyme, and I was a Chinese peasant in the rice fields.

The Persian carpet was draped over the dining-room table and the corridor carpet had to come up with Blackie ripping out the tacks, and Blackie took the gate off to let us come and go upstairs. Eventually my mother and I shared the single bed in the little room up there. It was quite usual for us, when we wanted to go to the bathroom to clean our teeth, to take our slippers off instead of putting them on, and Blackie was so clumsy he slipped and went caboomps in a puddle. The phone was about the only thing we used that was left downstairs, and if it rang you had to jump down the stairs and skid across the mud before it rang off. All the old rules didn't apply any more, and the only new rule was not to put muddy paws on the paintwork, so I walked around with my hands up in the surrendering position.

We made good progress with emptying the lawn. Firstly, it was horrible to see how many animals lived in it and got flooded out. I was in charge of collecting lizards and insects and earthworms; I laid them out on the veranda to dry in different categories before burial. In the one tree next to the cypresses we found no less than four chameleons. My mother took them one by one on a twig and let them go outside. There were dead baby birds and their nests and little grass snakes that were half-dissolving. The worst was the moles that used to have parties under the lawn.

Secondly, there were some plants that could survive where they were. Others like the cannas had to be salvaged and cut back to being bulbs for when my mother remade the flowerbeds, and still others were tangled up and unrecognisable – those went on a heap where Blackie could make a bonfire once they'd dried.

One night the drizzle came on again and, as my mother and I listened to it accumulating and rattling down the gutters, we were disheartened. Then she truly missed my father, as he used to be a water engineer and he knew about irrigation and he could open a channel and get a diesel pump going so that the flood wouldn't accumulate around us. But the drizzle had stopped by the sunrise, and it just made a layer of clear water on top of the soggy, oozy mud in which we lived.

My mother said our feet had begun to think for us, and that was right. We should have worn gumboots, but the gumboots we had got waterlogged and too heavy. We couldn't turn the electricity on again until everything was bone-dry, and my mother was very angry because it would probably cost her whole fortune in rewiring.

But we did adequately with our spirit stove. It burned with a soft blue flame under the soup pot we had on the camping table upstairs. With the storm lanterns the light was all yellow. We had bean soup, and one night my mother nearly died laughing because I said the soup looked like mud and the beans themselves were like tortoises struggling in the garden. That didn't stop us having second helpings, and I asked my mother what we were having for supper the next night, and she said, 'Tortoises and mud.'

Blackie got back and had some too, and he said it was the best soup he'd ever had. Then some of us, if you don't mind my saying so, started farting because it was bean soup. I opened by mistake with a big one, and Blackie went into competition with me, and we were laughing so much my mother was fuming and said the next person who made one of those would get a whole depth charge in their bowl tomorrow night. 'An atom bomb,' said Blackie, and he gave a really massive one that sounded like when the saboteurs demolished half the mountain, and my mother said that was totally enough now. She stood up to go but did a little one too, inadvertently, so we were all paralytic.

Blackie put 'You are my Sunshine' on the wind-up gramophone he'd brought us from someone who had got flooded out and given it to him for saving her cat. Then he went off to do rescue work. I asked for turtle soup for days after that, but my mother smirked and said bad luck, it was split peas and bacon. My mother was actually pleased with me because my co-ordination was coming along with all the practice in the paddy field.

On the Sunday Blackie had time off and the sun was shining. My mother sat us both down on the kitchen chairs on the upper veranda, and got out her sewing scissors and cut our hair. While she was cutting mine, Blackie gave lots of advice how she was to do it. I returned the compliment when she put the towel round his neck. He had clumps of black hair and looked like a wild man, and she just merrily snipped it off when she'd got the ends in the comb. She said it had turned into seaweed, and mine was ridged like a wheatfield from wearing that cement-mixer's hat. We were monarchs of all we surveyed from up there. Blackie got out his shaving mirror and razor and took the beard off up his jawline. I collected all the hair with the dustpan and brush, and just threw it overboard. Blackie used his mirror to send heliograph messages to the mainland, and he spelled it out in Morse code: SOS, save our souls.

Those were our private ceremonies during the flood. Blackie brought in the news of the public world across the new river. We were so preoccupied with our own labours that none of it had any meaning for us, at least not until the weeks passed and we had examined the full extent of how Silver Town was damaged. All the important places along the ridge were unscathed and functioning normally. The harbour was wiped bare. Blackie and the Defence Force had had to open a track down past the old quarry to get traffic through to the golf club, and four-wheel drives only could negotiate that. The Oudeskip cluster of houses near Long Beach was perfectly all right, except that a gum-tree fell on one and collapsed half the roof, and then there was pillaging. The Pits took the brunt of it; Blackie said that it was completely true that you could get around the Pits only in a rowing boat. But none of this seemed real to us, because we could see no further than our own waterlogged gully. Finally it was brought home to us by what happened to Euphemia. The flood finished Euphemia.

Basically my mother had given her off to deal with her own problems. Meshack couldn't leave his school or he'd fail Standard 9, and his father was dying when the floodwaters came down. He just coughed up and he was dead. Euphemia kept the body tucked in bed, but there was nothing they could do since she was completely encircled. He lay there with his hands folded on her crucifix and she thought the bed was going to become a raft, so that he'd have a funeral like a Viking. They couldn't get him to the hall which they used as a church as the harmonium was washed out to sea and nobody would come to a funeral without a harmonium, and anyway they were all sitting on the dyke and couldn't rescue anything because the water was swirling between them and the shanty town.

The Defence Force eventually had to bring tents and they waited there with their pigs and chickens, and it was lovely weather for ducks only. Over a hundred people were sleeping in the soup kitchen under blankets from the military depot. And you've never seen the number of helpers Mrs Feverall had in the kitchen, dispensing soup just like we were eating, and the cadets had to sink chemical toilets behind Mr Lotter's butchery, because they had dysentery too, and they were queueing all the way down the main street. The Red Cross came back from the war and gave them all injections. Only the ones who worked at the club and the hotel were all right.

So Euphemia couldn't get anyone to attend to her husband's funeral. The graveyard alongside the quarry was also flooded, so even if they had had a proper funeral they couldn't have put him in the sand because he'd wash out again. The dogs had gone wild and were hunting in packs, so Euphemia stayed with the body all that time. The Defence Force had to shoot all the dogs and they burnt them with the jet from a flamethrower.

Euphemia came and said she was sorry she was late for work, and she didn't want to lose her job. At that time we didn't know about her husband and what had happened to the Pits. My mother just said better late than never and she could help shovelling. Euphemia had her breakfast first, two slabs of national loaf with butter and apricot jam. She was very hungry and tired.

'All right, let's get down to it,' said my mother, and I was already under my branch and tins, with the knobbly bits rubbing on my shoulder blades. Euphemia just looked at all the damage we were so used to, and said nothing. My mother came back and Euphemia gave her a parcel Mrs Feverall had sent with an account slip, and my mother said groceries were getting very dear. She explained to Euphemia that there was no electricity and the whole house would have to be rewired.

'Let's get down to it then,' my mother said, and Euphemia had to look round for her mop and bucket; everything was in a different place. She started with the laundry because we had had no clean clothes for ten days.

At tea we had some biscuits, and I must say I was longing for a proper meal by then. For lunch we had sardines on bread. After lunch I went down to Euphemia in the kitchen and said why was she so angry, and she just clicked, 'Aikona.' I said what did that mean, and she said, Just Oh.

After we had a rest, my mother and I got to work again in the garden, and then my mother went inside to talk to Euphemia. She was sitting on the stool, practically asleep.

'Well, you've had eight working days off without any explanation. I know it must have been very difficult for you, but you could have sent us a message,' said my mother.

'Madam hasn't been working at the club,' said Euphemia.

My mother was a bit taken aback. 'Yes, I know,' she said, 'but Mr Lever owed me a few days and I had to look after the house.'

'No Madam, I mean I sent a message to the club with Mrs Kreli.' Euphemia sat there, looking thin and tired.

'Well, I don't know, Euphemia,' said my mother. 'We've just got to clear up this mess. Have you seen how it came right through?'

'Yes, madam,' she said, looking out through the flyscreen door at the gully that came right under the house. 'It's God's miracle,' said Euphemia.

'Yes, built like a ship so all hands can work,' said my mother.

In the front we had got down to the mud and in places it was beginning to dry and crack. Blackie had shown my mother how to make a siphon by exhausting the hosepipe, and she had to suck on the end with her head on the ground until she went almost blue in the face, and the other end was under the house.

That evening Euphemia was just as filthy as we were and she went I don't know where to sleep. By then they had taken her husband's body in a sack to the council; this was done by the relief workers who kept it for her to bury over the weekend on dry land. Euphemia had never told my mother her husband had really serious tuberculosis, so now she couldn't tell my mother about his death.

When he got back, Blackie took the torch and fixed the siphon to run all night, but it must have blocked at about midnight. He set it going again, and went to work where the army was excavating part of the shanty town from the mud. He couldn't tell us about Euphemia or her husband or her house because he never knew which one it was. They had the whole area cordoned off with patrols, and nobody could look for their possessions unless they went by escort with a permit. They commandeered Blackie's jeep, so he had to walk.

When Euphemia came to work the next day my mother was so relieved because she could leave me to go to work herself. She got dressed all smartly again and hurried off, and we rushed with her to the crossing in the road and watched her as she negotiated the swing bridge that was between two rocks.

Euphemia couldn't make the siphon work either, so we just went to get the wheelbarrow from the garage shed. The stack of poles had fallen over it, and they were half waterlogged, including the gaff which came tumbling down and landed on the roof of the car. That made me very anxious; it could have smashed the windshield. I climbed up to see that it had made scratches on the paint, but they were on the top so I hoped my mother wouldn't notice. Then Euphemia screamed snake and ran outside, but I was still standing on the running board and I could see there were no snakes. So she came back in and replaced the gaff and we abandoned the idea of the wheelbarrow.

Later in the morning, when we were scraping mud with the spade from the place where the washing dried in the yard, and throwing it over the wall, Euphemia told me the story of what happened to her. Then I asked questions of her, as was the custom.

'And was he really dead?'

'Yes, Master Jimmy, with his mouth hanging open.' She tied it up with a ribbon.

'And the tea mugs? What happened to them?'

'The tea mugs I rescued, Master Jimmy.'

'All three of them?'

'Yes, that was lucky.'

'And the picture of Jesus with the heart?'

'Yes, the picture. Only the watertank went and the armchair, I told you, Master Jimmy.'

'And you couldn't leave him alone because the dogs were coming to eat him?'

'Yes, the dogs. But they were from other people. We had no dogs, Master Jimmy.' The dogs came from the flooded houses.

'Was it the big one with the long tail? I bet you were frightened of him.'

'Yes. They were very hungry because there was no food for them, and they turned into scavengers.' They were eating anything they could find.

'Why didn't they go to the soup kitchen?' I asked, knowing the answer.

'Because they didn't have bones for dogs, Master Jimmy,' she said with such patience. 'I stayed with him because it is our custom, and by then the dogs were getting very hungry, and they were eating one of the dead people in the cemetery, you see – who was recently buried, so I didn't take any chances.'

Yes, I said.

We had the spade going quite well, and I said it was a pity her husband had retired because he was a good builder and could make a proper wall for us with a rockery.

When we had lunch it was bread and cold meat, and Euphemia told me she had sent a letter to Meshack's headmaster to explain everything, and Petrus at the hotel had written the letter and charged her 1/6 for it, because it was a longer letter. She had to write to Dear Sir. And at the end she put Yours in Jesus, because the headmaster was a priest in Euphemia's church and that's why he took Meshack for no fees.

'Where do the dead people go?' I asked her, and she said straight to heaven and I said it was the lagoons and she said Aikona, that was where the tokoloshe lived.

'And did they burn the dogs, Phemie?' I asked, and she said that, like in hell, they burned them with a big jet of fire.

The next day my mother left as soon as Euphemia came, so there was no opportunity for her to tell my mother, and Euphemia got down to the dirty washing. She was taking the sheets off the line in the late afternoon in the place we had scrubbed out when my mother came rushing home and said to her why didn't you tell me.

'Ow, madam,' said Euphemia, and she dropped one of the sheets.

'But Mrs Van told me your husband had a seizure and you had to go up to the council to bury him. Mrs Kreli did tell her at the club, and that's why you weren't at work. Why, why didn't you tell me directly?'

Euphemia said when a man had a weak heart you never knew when it was going to come, and when the water burst out from the watertank the same thing happened to his heart from shock. Euphemia picked up the dusty sheet and clicked, and she put it back in the tub.

'Oh but Euphemia,' said my mother. 'It's too terrible for speech. How much did they charge you for the burial? I know they make it so exorbitant for you people.'

'No, it's all right, madam,' said Euphemia.

'And where are you staying? How can you go home if it's an emergency area? It's an absolute scandal. They will have to apportion you land out of the flood plain. It's on the agenda for the committee and I think we can form a pressure group and take it right to the top. Euphemia, this must never never happen again.'

'I'm staying at Mr Lotter's boy, he's got a room,' said Euphemia.

'And clothes, Euphemia? Oh you poor thing.'

'I've got clothes, madam.'

'All right, how much was the funeral? At least I can reimburse you that.'

'Five pounds,' said Euphemia.

'Good heavens,' said my mother, raising her eyebrows. 'Jimmy, go inside and fetch my handbag immediately.'

I did so, and my mother counted out three pounds and some silver and said she would give Euphemia the rest tomorrow. Then she explained about the rewiring again, and how that was an unforeseen expense for us.

Euphemia put the money in her uniform pocket and said Thank you, God be praised. Then she pulled out the letter she had in reply from the headmaster in Cape Town. She gave it to my mother to read, and she read it aloud for Euphemia.

'Well, my goodness,' said my mother, and she tried to sit down, but there wasn't anything to sit on, so we went into the kitchen.

'Jimmy, bring the one chair down from upstairs, there's a good boy,' said my mother.

I brought the chair down without banging the walls. They were deep in conversation. Euphemia sat on her stool and my mother on the chair.

'Don't just moon around, Jimmy. Go and get your drawing book upstairs,' said my mother, but I stayed and listened.

'In effect, it means – the Reverend Mr Tyamyashe suggests the best thing you could do is take an assistant cook's job in the refectory in the school. That's very good terms for board and lodging included, but you need higher wages to keep alive in Cape Town. I could give you the one reference, a glowing, red-hot one on notepaper from the club. He'd know from that you could be a housekeeper, too, not just experienced as an ordinary nanny.'

I thought that Euphemia might be going to join Meshack, and neither of them would come back to Silver Town.

'It's all right, Jimmy. This is grown-up talk, so go and play.'

I went upstairs and sat on the other chair on the veranda. I was too filled with foreboding to play.

That evening Blackie didn't come back at supper time and we ate alone. My mother was very sombre, and I asked her if Euphemia was going to Cape Town. She said very probably, as what else could she do in the circumstances; we couldn't match the offer and Euphemia could be with Meshack and she could sell the few bits of furniture she had left. There was no reason for her to stay on in Silver Town, except us. We had no right to push her loyalty.

My mother carried the storm lantern through to her desk

and cleared the newspapers off it and said I could sit in the shadow for a bit, because I must be tired, like her. Then she wrote the best reference possible so that Euphemia could land the job and the next morning she typed it at the club.

I knew Euphemia would get the job as, for the next few days, she worked like a fury to clean the house for us once and for all. She had relays of washing on the line and between that scrubbed the walls down and we carried everything down the stairs and left clear patches on the walls for when the electricians would come and fix the plugs.

Then the letter came from Meshack's headmaster. Euphemia sold everything to Mr Lotter's assistant who was going to get married and had a place in the shanty town which was being resurrected to be exactly as it had been before the flood. Euphemia couldn't keep her house now that her husband was dead. Mrs Kreli's brother from the Transkei and his family moved in. Euphemia didn't have to pay rent once they had come.

On the next Saturday my mother drove me up to the native bus to say farewell to Euphemia and she was in the queue with a big bundle that the driver put on the roof. Mrs Kreli gave her a box with hard-boiled eggs in it, and my mother gave Euphemia a bonus in an envelope, and they shook hands. I said goodbye to Euphemia, but I didn't kiss her because all the people were standing there and I was shy. Everyone was shouting and wearing blankets, and there were chickens on the roof and even a piglet.

'Look at Porkie the Pig,' said my mother, and I said it was going to be a big, fat one.

Euphemia got into a seat by the window and took her handkerchief and cleaned the glass. And she put her hand on the window to make a shadow and see out. And I said goodbye Phemie, and her lips said Goodbye, goodbye Master Jimmy-boy.

My mother waved and said she was always such a respectable body. And we got in the car and went home.

Thus ended that phase of my boyhood.

16

It wasn't yet the end of the war, but everyone told everyone else it had all but happened. To me the prospect of peace was daunting and unimaginable. Peace would mean further changes that would force me to grow, and I had no confidence that I would be able to do that.

My life continued meanwhile to depend on the preoccupations of my elders and betters. When Blackie was sure that he had a chance with my mother, even though she was older and more educated, he brought her a truly huge bundle of arum lilies and asked her to marry him. She put the lilies in an old brass vase and accepted.

But she made four conditions: that everyone in Silver Town whom they knew should also accept the idea before they rush into it; that Blackie resign from the Defence Force because she wasn't going to have another military husband; that he take me as his stepson but not change my surname; and that, to pay for the electrician's bill, he strip down the car so that she could get a good price for it.

After supper Blackie was under the car like a shot, but I couldn't help him because my mother sat me down and said, 'Jimmy, what name do you want to be?' and to make it easier for Blackie I said Esslin, not Rousseau.

The first person she would have to get approval from was my grandmother in London, and with the mail services the way they were that would take time. So she sat at her desk immediately and explained the position to her mother. She was not to send expensive linen this time, because the old linen was still perfectly good. She hoped she would be with us in spirit.

Then she phoned Aunt Rosemary and told her they couldn't possibly have the ceremony before New Year, so the rooms upstairs were still occupied and the Elgin contingent couldn't come down. Aunt Rosemary instantly said we must go up to

Elgin if we wanted an engagement party, and how thrilled they were that Sarah the widow, the serious one, had found her new companion. They knew Blackie, of course – no matter what they thought of him, he was a good sort.

Then she phoned Mrs Van and told her, and you could hear Mrs Van screaming over the phone.

I took his Ovaltine out to Blackie and he was already under the car with the wheels off and the body on bricks. I put his Ovaltine down on the side and he put his face out all covered in oil. He told me to get the wind-up gramophone and I did from upstairs. We played 'You are my Sunshine.'

Because there was now no Euphemia, my mother was in the kitchen and she stopped running the taps over the washing-up to listen. Then when the needle came to the label, she said put on 'The Nearness of You.' So I went upstairs to fetch the one with the purple and gold label.

We weren't expecting anything to happen, but Mr and Mrs van der Westhuizen came through the back gate with a huge bunch of daisies for my mother and Blackie; they couldn't resist it. 'Oh, my hands are all soapy,' my mother yelped, and she ran for the cloth, 'and Blackie – just look at you.'

Blackie emerged and he was simply covered in oil from the sump and everybody laughed at him.

'Please, please excuse me, Stinnie,' said my mother, pointing to the sitting room, 'we were just – having an evening at home.'

'Please excuse us,' said Mrs Van, 'but we couldn't resist, you know, surprising you.'

'Oh, aren't they absolutely lovely?' said my mother.

'They for you and Blackie, man, we're just so pleased for you – for you both, Sarah,' and he handed them over.

My mother went to get the jug because she had to put them in water, and Mrs Van sat down and showed Mr Van where to sit. Blackie went to clean his face in the bathroom and told me to get the gramophone because his hands were all dirty, so I brought it into the living room and set it up again, and we played 'So long, Sarie, so long.'

'Now you going to be a true South African,' said Mrs Van. 'Isn't it just wonderful, Sarah?'

'Well, I've been a true South African all along,' said my mother.

'Yes, but now you really will have to learn to talk like us,' said Mr Van. He produced a stick of dried sausage from his sports jacket and a penknife and sat back and cut pieces.

'That's what I like about South Africa. There's room for a dozen different accents and colours and we all have the same goal,' said my mother.

'You hit the nail crack on the head,' said Mr Van.

'Ag Blackie, jou ou donner, so you've pulled it off, hey?' and she gave Blackie a big wink. 'My, where did you get those pragtige lilies from – down at the quarry, I bet you.'

Blackie laughed, because he knew she had arranged to get them from Mrs Feverall at five o'clock.

'You know, they fly those over to Britain for society weddings and they cost a fortune,' said my mother.

'And here we just call them pig lilies and they grow in the ditch,' said Mrs Van.

My mother smiled and Blackie took her hand.

Mr Van gave me a slice of dried sausage on the end of his penknife and I chewed it.

'Well, it's all happened in such a rush,' said my mother.

'Ja,' said Blackie, 'can you believe it?'

'But in us you've got your firmest supporters, just remember that, Sarah. So if anybody gives you trouble, just send them to me,' said Mrs Van.

'Oh, Stinnie, I don't know how I would have come through without you, really.'

'And Blackie – I knew it from the first moment and I know a good man when I see it,' said Mrs Van with great contentment.

'Just spit it out,' said Mr Van to me. 'Has it got too much skin? Here, take a middle bit,' and I spat into the ashtray.

'And your floor, Sarah, how did you get it to shine again?' said Mrs Van.

'Oh, Euphemia just wiped on the Sunshine,' said my mother.

'This sausage isn't like it was before the war,' said Mr Van. Blackie took a piece and chewed it down.

'Yes,' said Mrs Van, 'that Euphemia was a maid in a million. I always said you'd never get another like her, so consider yourself lucky. Some of them – ag, my Bathsheba's getting quite good now.'

'Jimmy's been a great help around the house,' said my mother. 'Of course, it's been difficult for him, but you've been a real sport, haven't you, Jimmy?'

I nodded, and Blackie took the bit of sausage and got his fingers under the skin and peeled it all the way round.

'I must have a word to Mr Lotter about it; he's selling us real donkey sausage now,' said Mr Van.

'Hell, in Pietersburg we used to get nice sausage,' said Blackie. 'It comes in from Bechuanaland, that's the best. Really dry – droë wors. En by Kakamas se kant, koedoe biltong, you know, Oom Piet. And beer – hang, I completely forgot. Wil jy nie 'n bier hê nie? I'm sorry, you just caught us by surprise.'

'What?' said my mother privately to Blackie.

'Yes, I'd love a beer,' said Mrs Van.

'Oh good gracious,' my mother stood up. 'Please, please forgive me, Stinnie. It's just that after the Ovaltine I don't register very much.'

'That'll be fine for me,' said Mr Van.

'Oh, I am so sorry,' said my mother, and Blackie pressed her down to say that he would get four mugs and the beer supply. She went to fetch the jug instead, and set it on the nesting tables and arranged them some more.

'Yes, Mr Lotter really thinks he can scrimp and screw nowadays,' said Mr Van.

'Stinnie, you shouldn't have' said my mother, and she held her hands round the flowers as if she wanted to kiss them. 'Oh and just look at those lilies,' she added.

'Never mind, Sarah, your garden'll be back in shape in no time,' said Mrs Van. 'Ag, it's just daisies, my dear. When you think of the flowers Mr Lever puts in the dining-room these days, this lot is but a poor thing.'

'When you think what Mr Lotter picked up for cheap from the Pits when the flood was on, hey Blackie.'

Blackie had the bottles opened and was decanting the beer.

'My word,' said Blackie, 'he must have got that livestock for nothing.'

'But what a lot of fleabitten old crocks, if you ask me,' said Mr Van.

'And Mrs Lever's coming round quite nicely, too,' said Mrs Van. 'Ah, she's not a bad type. But her language – did you notice how that deteriorated when she went into the bar.'

'That's enough for me,' said my mother, and she accepted her mug, and Mr Van took his, and Blackie gave one to Mrs Van who sat forward on the chair so as not to dribble, and Blackie clinked his against my mother's, and she clinked hers against Mrs Van's and Blackie against Mr Van's and Mrs Van's against Blackie's and my mother's, and then my mother gave a final one against Blackie's.

'So, here's to VE day,' said Mrs Van, and Mr Van said, 'It's really the end now,' and Blackie gave my mother a kiss on the cheek and she stared forward and put her hand on her mouth.

'My, Sarah,' said Mrs Van, 'I know how you feel, but if anybody just makes the least trouble about this marriage, you send them to me.'

'Yes, I will,' said my mother, and she drank some beer.

'No, it'll be all right,' said Mr Van. 'That's one thing the war's done. Got rid of all snobbery. We can do what we like now, and you tell them, Sarah – class differences've gone.'

'So have the Saps, looks like,' said Mrs Van. 'They been away at the war so long they've left it to the Nationalists.'

'If you ask me,' said Mr Van, 'that's the way things are going all over. No more of this extended courtship. Stinnie and me, we had to wait four and a half years before her father said we could go, hey, Stinnie?' He put his hand over her wrist on the arm of the chair, and she moved it from under and put her hand on top of his.

'Oh Jimmy,' said my mother, 'it's way past your bedtime, my precious.'

'Never mind, it's a special occasion,' said Mrs Van.

'Another five minutes,' said my mother, and Blackie passed me his beermug and it was so bitter I pulled a face, and they were amused.

When I went to bed my mother came while I said my prayers, and she said I must put Blackie higher up the list, so it went, God bless my mother and my father and Blackie and this house, and Euphemia and Meshack were also left out eventually.

Blackie got the car in working order, and he could resign his commission because the Defence Force was voluntary. So Blackie had to take back all his uniform including his boots, which was a pity because he was due for promotion. He had to sell the car to cover himself for while he was seeking a job. When he came back from overseas, Mr Pennington-Worthy offered him one because he knew his capabilities perfectly well, so the car didn't have to be sold because Blackie would need it for the job. He was going to be a salesman for Mr Pennington-Worthy's windmills and other equipment. Blackie didn't have any qualifications, but he didn't need them because he had an agreeable personality as far as the farmers were concerned.

His first job was to convince the council that a floodwater channel should be built at the quarry so that the clubhouse wouldn't get hit next time, if there was a really big flood. So Blackie stayed in Silver Town, after all. Sergeant Thoroughwell came and put him on volunteer peace work, too, so he was connected in all ways to our little community.

My mother and Blackie went round to see just about everyone in Silver Town, as well, as a courtesy and on an informal basis, just to be sure that everyone was in favour and they were accepted as a couple. Mrs Feverall declared it was her intention to have a private engagement party exclusively for them after the season, but meanwhile there were so many small ones that we never had a big official one. After Christmas and the New Year Mrs Feverall scaled her invitation down to a Sunday lunch, and when the tourists were over and the hotel was empty again we all felt we had better do our duty and oblige.

After the fine dinner we had coffee on the balcony and I just sat apart from them in a deck chair with the view in front of me and my hand on my belt. I could feel the panoramic glass pane behind me with my free hand.

Then Mrs Feverall said goodbye and what a pleasure it was, and she shook Blackie by the hand and my mother and patted me on the head. We got into the car and it was totally baking. We had to put cloths on the seats and Blackie had to hold the wheel with his fingertips only, and he made shooshoo noises to amuse me, and we cruised home over the new road.

And I went to my bedroom and my mother said I had behaved very well indeed. She went to Blackie upstairs, I suppose to tell him that he had behaved well, too.

17

There was more to that scene than I have recorded. I was resting on my side, so heavily that it seemed as if my stomach were a parcel I had to nurse. I didn't want to burp or anything, but lay waiting, like a python with a bulge, to digest. Maybe it would take until the end of winter and I'd better hibernate.

My mother eventually came down and I called for her weakly. She came into my bedroom, showing surprise, which proved that she had forgotten me. 'Oh Jimmy,' she said, 'is anything the matter?'

There was something the matter.

'It's so hot, a lie down will do you good.'

'Mamma,' I said, and she moved one step in.

'Yes, my Jimmy,' she said, 'I just wanted to show Blackie this book. It's all right, we're just talking upstairs.'

'Is it my one?' I said.

'Yes, the one about the scorpion and the brown and angry miles,' she said. 'I thought since we had a flood, too –'

'That's my book,' I said.

'I know, Jimmy, but you wouldn't mind Blackie just paging through it, would you? Then he can read it to you sometimes.'

But I was determined to hold her. 'Blackie couldn't read when he was my age,' I said.

'Well, he's certainly catching up now. He's becoming quite a civilised bloke.'

'Do you love him because he can read?' I said.

She edged a bit more into the room. 'But Jimmy, those things are not connected at all,' she said.

There she had her choice of being angry or of calming me down. She swung with the book in her hand and put it on the desk. She sat on the bed.

'No, mamma,' I said.

'What do you mean no?' she said.

'My stomach hurts,' I said, 'so don't bounce the bed.'

'I am sorry,' she said. 'But Blackie's going to be at the quarry most of the week with the contractor from the council. You'll have me all the time, so don't worry. Sunday afternoon's Blackie's turn,' she said.

I said quite unreasonably, 'I don't care. That's my book. You gave it to me, not to him.'

She put her hand on my knee. 'Jimmy, don't be so ridiculously jealous,' she said in her hard voice.

'I'm not,' I said. 'My tummy's sore so don't shake the bed.'

'Jealousy's the green-eyed monster,' said my mother.

'And you're a dwarf with a big empty mouth,' I said, and with all my strength I rolled onto my stomach.

She left to read Blackie my poem.

I was in bad odour for quite a few days after that, and my mother held out till I should apologise. I voluntarily had no supper that night, for the reason that I would have been sick. I had no breakfast the next day and avoided lunch by going up to the post office with Freddie. I drank out of the bathroom tap and that's all I needed. My mother frequently said how difficult I was and that became boring. She said I must apologise, but I said nothing.

I went with her to the golf club and as soon as she was in her office I walked out of the back, past the kitchen where the smells were gluey and sickening. I sat in the sour figs at the end of the golf course. I moved when a team sent its golf balls stinging past me. I tried to read about the brown and angry miles, but the page blazed before me in the glare.

I became aware there was no place for me there, and I must leave. A lot of people were coming for lunch, so my mother was busy and wouldn't notice.

I had a few things to do before I left. The first was to use the key under the flowerpot at Peter's Lodge, and I hid the book under my mattress and took my jersey out of the cupboard. Then I closed the front door and returned the key, thinking what a small house it was after all, with its funny one eye, being the circular window in my father's study. I closed the front gate and turned my back on it to face the road.

The second thing I had to do was find Blackie because, if there was to be an apology, it should be to him. This was more easily resolved between men. He could sort it out with my mother later. I also wanted to prove to her that I was not jealous of Blackie; I'd rather live with Blackie than with her. Even if he was very rough, he would give me lessons and I would understand.

I paused, for two reasons. One is that I should have taken some food from Peter's Lodge, and I had no money for the road. The second was that Blackie was down at the quarry, and the quarry had always been forbidden territory. However, it was a time to be resolute.

I climbed round the back of the Marfak garage and under the edge of the lawn of Mrs Feverall's hotel, out of sight of the panoramic window. I found a rough path that the garage hands and the staff at the hotel used as a short cut. You could tell what they also went down there to do, as there were broken brandy bottles, the hipflask kind.

The path came to the crest of the quarry wall, and I had to look over for Blackie. There was an old barbed-wire fence, but the garage people had broken that down and you didn't even have to pull the strands apart to slide through. I got a fright because there was a goat grazing there, with its forelegs in a tree, pulling the tree down; I thought it was going to stop me, but it let me pass.

From below the wind was coming up like scorching whips. I crawled to just before the edge and put my hand where one of their drills had gone. The rock was brown and hard with crystals. In one hollow. was a smudge of water that the sun hadn't reached, and a springy plant growing.

Six inches closer to the edge I pulled and, as usual, was not sure of myself. I was so weak from starvation that the truth is probably I could go no further. The wind was coming in gusts, and my eyes were streaming from its warmth. My lids felt as if they were baking, with the eyes turned into marbles.

When I reached the very edge the cliffside was shaking and wobbly in my vision. It went down to a narrow ledge with tufts of bush along it, and it went down below that to a jagged bit, and down below that to a section that was carved absolutely flat, and it caved in underneath there to a hollow part where swallows were flying and echoing. Below that it went down into the shadow where the dull black water was. I remembered how my father took me up the windmill in the Karoo and how he was with the dead people in Italy, and I looked for Blackie. Blackie was no good, really; he wasn't anywhere down there, and I felt sick and weak.

My eyes went into double vision and I could see I had two pairs of hands. And a very chafed goat came near me to nibble, and it looked like two goats, one exactly alongside the other. And I looked back at my hand – the left or the right, I couldn't tell – and tried to make it become one hand with everything together. I couldn't reconcile them and my head ached from trying.

The smeary puddle opened into two halves and the plant grew twice within it. I closed that eye; the plant stayed on one side, the other one disappearing. I could feel my nostrils drooling, and everything my body did was double. It seemed as if I had split into a light half and a dark half and the sun was going down in my body from the radiant day into the darkest night. With my one eye I stared, streaming with tears, and there was a distinct stone in front of me with edges like a geometric drawing, and I couldn't clasp it.

I was completely blind with all the sights only inside my head. I didn't want to be part of that world, except in a new way, where I wouldn't have this disobedient, sideways body and things I could not master. I wanted to be easy in the world, taking it in so that I could control it, order it, connect it from one item to the next. It all needed a great adjustment, to be organised, like the structure of a windmill with a tough metal ladder leading rung above rung up stable metalwork. I had every reason to want to conclude my not being able to function.

Petrus and Rina were there, and Petrus said I must be careful or I'd fall over. I didn't talk to them because I was unable to. My voice had already left me. I think I probably had died. Petrus and Rina were going down from the hotel to the ledge. Petrus said they were having their lunch and would I like to join them. We went down to a flat bit and they had a newspaper with chips and some fried sausages.

'Sit back, hey, in case somebody throws you with a stone,' said Petrus.

Rina peeled off the newspaper where it was sticking and passed the bundle towards me. She didn't pick one out for me, but let me take it. I was so hungry the floppy fried potato chip went down so fast I didn't have to swallow.

'If Master Jimmy's hungry Master Jimmy must take it,' said Rina, and she pointed to a sausage, and I took it.

Petrus was talking in Afrikaans and he said I wasn't a bedorwe kind like some of the others, and that meant I was welcome to have a picnic with them, and Joan and Jack and all the other children weren't. Rina said Shame, I could take as much as I could eat, poor child, and Petrus said they weren't really hungry.

Then Mrs Feverall rang her drinking bell and Rina jumped up and tried to make her apron look straight. Petrus had to go too, and he nearly forgot the newspaper with chips and sausages, and he said he didn't want any more and he rushed back on duty. That left me with one and a half whole sausages and I couldn't count how many chips. I could resume my escape without any difficulty now that I had a supply.

I had only two further worries: the one was Blackie and the possibility of meeting him, I could no longer remember for what reason, and the other was water. As far as Blackie was concerned, I skirted the descent along the east end of the quarry, listening for any human noises that might tell me where he was. I wouldn't know what to say to him if I did find him. I experienced the strange feeling of forgetting him while I was searching for him. Probably he was celebrating in the golf club like everyone else that day, with the flags and the bunting out.

I skidded down to the shanty town people's cemetery which Blackie was going to have to move. Climbing along the gully where the trees were still brown with the flood, I avoided the town. The smoke from the chimneys was drifting across with a smell of rotten clothes. I had to hurry because they were lighting their stoves for the evening.

Water was obtainable from Mrs van der Westhuizen's place. I got over the fence and took my bundle and, making sure nobody could see me, crawled over the lawn to the metal tap that was dripping anyway into the delphiniums. Mrs Van's garden was beautiful, and I wondered what it was that made cultivation so different from the wilds. I drank and drank. I had to drink more than my fill, much more, to last a long time.

Putting my head out a few inches, I could see Marie. She had a big bedroom window and it was shining. Through the reflection she was squatting on the floor and screeching, 'Nee nee,' to her sisters, because they had upset the milk. Her two sisters were so stupid, and when they sat plump on the floor their dresses were so short their broekies showed. Marie hit them and said she wouldn't play if they didn't want to play properly.

At that very moment the telephone rang and I could hear Mrs Van answer. It was my mother asking if I'd gone to tea there, and so I knew it was time to continue my travels. Mrs Van was going to phone people on this side of Silver Town to put them on the alert. Sergeant Thoroughwell was going to be out, and Mrs Van had influence with the Oudeskip people, so they would be looking too, and down at the harbour. So I had to go where there were no roads.

On the east side of the fishing cottages there is a long valley before the dunes and the sea begin, and people don't go there because it is useless for farming. There are some trails the fishermen use, but mostly it is overgrown with lantana which is very prickly, so I went there and kept to the shingle path with the lantana so high it covered my head. It retains the heat in that valley, and the beetles sing so loudly it sounds as if every branch and flower is humming.

Eventually the lantana thinned out but no habitation overlooked that area, so I was safe. I was coming to some more wattles when the slight wind carried the noise people make when they're coming through, so I ducked behind a very old tree-trunk and waited with my bundle in my lap.

Some of the line fishermen came with first one carrying the rods and he didn't look back at the others but went on talking in front of him. The rest came with their catch on a pole between their shoulders and their bait cans, and one of the fish was very big, a grunter, I think, which is what Meshack always wanted to catch. A seagull landed near them and turned its head, watching them, then it flew off to watch further up. So I knew that if they were coming back so early the beach would be unsuitable for fishing, and no one would be there.

Through this tunnel in the wattles I went. That meant I had left Silver Town. I wondered if without knowing it I was really a German Nazi like Miss Bester; when they discovered I was gone they would be pleased. Nobody talked to her and she was an outcast when she was in Silver Town. I also didn't like her, but now I could see we had more in common than our differences.

But I wasn't a German Nazi because I was English-born and my father went expressly to fight German Nazis. Maybe I was a Japanese and over the dunes I'd find a lot of Japanese and take them to Silver Town to show them where everything was. Then they'd kill my mother and Blackie'd give them a good run for their money, but they'd torture and shoot him. And they'd use Mrs Feverall's as a headquarters because they could see all of Silver Town through the panoramic window. They were really desperate now, with the Americans in the Pacific. I had to relieve myself before the wattles ran out, and that lowered the water level. Otherwise I would make an easy target, like the boy in Brussels whom anyone can shoot, especially the Eighth Army now that they're there.

I wasn't a German or a Japanese or an American, so what was I? But I abandoned that train of thought with the dunes breaking out, and I had to step firmly. When I came to the crest I could see Long Beach all the way, but I didn't stop to look. I ran down the sand to where the tide would come up and obliterate my footprints. The sea was running nicely; it did that all the way down Long Beach, even if there was no one to watch it.

So, I wasn't all those nationalities and I wasn't black like Euphemia and I wasn't Afrikaans like Blackie and Mrs Van and I wasn't English English like Mrs Feverall. I wasn't any of those, even though my mother was English English and she belonged to Winston Churchill, and my late father was English-speaking and he belonged to the Italians. All I could be was what I was, and I was different from all those; I didn't want to be like Mr Lever who was Jewish and like Petrus who was Coloured. The rollers were really coming in and along the tideline mussels were digging themselves in. The one was the size of my kneecap and it had a flapping tongue and it dug with its shell jerking up and shining. I squeezed it and it squirted water, but I had to move on.

I didn't belong to Silver Town anymore, so that was that. I was part of the coastal belt from Sir Lowry's Pass to Plettenberg Bay.

Looking back, I could see my footprints stretching for half a mile, but in places the foam had covered them and they were filling with water. The tracks of the fishermen had already gone, so it was only a matter of time.

Mr Jensen I had forgotten. Mr Jensen, whose origins were a mystery and who lived alone outside Silver Town. All he had was the birds. Nobody talked of Mr Jensen these days, so he must have moved on. I would have liked to have seen him then, because he was so ugly and twisted and the only person he talked to was me. He had that terrible spine like a hanger. I asked Mr Jensen what I was, and he said he was a hunchback and I was a war child. Maybe that is correct; my category is war child. He said you don't have to be just a child for that, because even an adult could be a war child.

I doubled speed and came to a reef where a long time ago was a shipwreck. There some black women had been taking advantage of the tide when it was out, because their bucket was left with a hole in it. They were strandlopers and they wore their dresses up and didn't even pull them down when they came to the hotel to sell oysters. But they weren't there then, or they'd have also gone to the club and sold my mother the blue mussels in salt water and told her they saw me at the wreck on Long Beach. I couldn't even remember what my mother looked like anymore; she was so excited about marrying Blackie and Blackie could have her.

So I'm a war child and also an only child, I thought. Since my father is completely dead, there can never be another one made like me, even if Blackie made another child with my mother – that would be my half-brother or half-sister and, knowing Blackie, they wouldn't be only children; he wanted a whole cricket team of them.

It was nearing the end of the day and a string of cormorants flew home over the water to the really wild coast on the other side. I knew where I would spend my first night because it was not far to the old shark-oil factory. I reached the slips where they used to pull up the dead sharks, but it was all sand now, and even the offices were full of sand. The place was familiar to me, maybe because it was full of dead people, and they were swinging on a metal door and it went clang, clang. A bat came out and flew straight through where, if there had been a pane of glass, it would have stunned itself. That reminded me of something, but I couldn't tell what it was. I couldn't put two and two together, as they say.

So I went to the first cave and as I stood on the doorstep out came hundreds and hundreds of bats, and they twisted and missed me and I just stood. I didn't mind if they came in and out because it was their cave. I dropped down on a soft part and brushed the floor. My feet were pasted in my sandals with damp sand, so I took them off finally. Then I couldn't wait for it, so I opened the squishy bundle of food. I looked down on the whole of Long Beach, and I peeled back the newspaper and had the half sausage first.

Then I moved the wad of potato chips down the page and tried some of my reading. It wasn't hard to read because it was the front page and the letters were about two inches high. All it said was, HITLER DEAD, and then there were smaller words and they were so ground around with carrying that they came apart. But it was the *Cape Times* because it had that crest with the lion and the unicorn. And then I thought that if Hitler was dead that was why they were all drunk at the club at eleven o'clock in the morning.

Ants were collecting on the sausage skin I spat out, taking it away to their home. It was getting dark with the sun almost gone over the bay, and the local dead people were gathering in the foam, so I ate the potatoes while I could still see to pick them apart. I was very happy and tired. I was sleeping on the bat guano, because that is what bat droppings are called. I was tired; I was happy. I was an animal finding my own rhythm. I was beyond human society.

I woke up as everything awoke around me. The sun was coming up the edge of the ocean and about to get onto it. The bats were coming back with full bellies. I put my palms on the damp rocks and licked the moisture before it evaporated. I got an early start, scrambling up to the dirt road that led over the eastern mountains to other forlorn, desolate fishing camps like Credence and Saint George's Bay.

The dust was white and dry, but fresh-looking. As I went over the top, Long Beach and Silver Town disappeared and I didn't look back. This was the setting out and I had no regrets. I should have brought matches. I would steal fire when it came time to cook. I had forgotten my last remnants of food, but that wasn't going to stop me. My jersey dangled on the back of my knees like a hem, and I thought it wasn't only women who wore dresses. I trotted, and the jersey came down with strokes, encouraging me.

In due course I developed a stitch, but it wasn't a stitch. It was stomach pains from wanting to go to the toilet. I didn't know how to go in the outdoors. I held it in. But I couldn't hold it for ever. I squatted behind a bush and let it come out, then I felt better. I buried it so that nobody would follow me.

I didn't have words for these things any more. I no longer held the world with words; it was feelings, adjustments with the world that told me what to do. I felt relieved inside and spun back onto the road, loping over the rolling land. I was feeding on air and warmth.

Up ahead of me I saw, before it curved down towards the sea, an old donkey cart led by a shabby man. They were carrying firewood. They must have been up very early. Their tracks showed that they had already been where I was going. I slowed down. The man wasn't looking back and the donkey didn't stop. If I kept at this speed and they at theirs, they'd be turned down to one of the coves before I should meet them. I was invisible to them while the bond of those relative speeds held. Where the going was uphill the donkey stopped to make droppings, and the old man waited for it patiently.

Later the road split in two and they took the lower section to Saint George's, so they would be gone by the time I reached the division. I was not apprehensive. There was a belt of milk-bush further along where I could take shelter. No farmers were on that stretch because it was stony and barren. If the road ran out, I could guide myself along the coastline. I could not see the ocean, but occasionally a sound came from over the horizon of a door slamming in an echoing house. The breakers were angry at being halted.

Every so often I was told by the land that I was there. I was not invisible. I disturbed a kiewietjie with its white halo and red bill where it was nesting in the sand. It screamed lies at me about where its eggs were, wheeling and feinting to fool me. Then I disturbed another one, and I learned that if I didn't disturb them they would snuggle on in the sand and ignore me, let me be. All that stony, barren land was good for was raising kiewietjies. They had found the ideal place where no one went, except the old man with the donkey cart. He had gone down the bend on the lower road now, so my way was open. I ran down it and ran.

That's when Blackie and Sergeant Thoroughwell spotted me. I cut off the road towards the milk-bushes, and they were a great distance away. If I ducked and ran through the rough area I could make it, even though they had Sergeant Thoroughwell's van – they couldn't go on that terrain. I ran, not bursting, but full of air and warmth, as though I was being edged forward by a flame.

I didn't look back much, but they were being shot forward by a wave of white dust, and I was shot by fire. They were shot along the road by clouds bouncing and multiplying behind them, and I was the fire person. I was propelled into the rocks and I knew every step and ledge and gully and leapt across, carried on a wave of fire. And their pillar of dust went the wrong way and they obviously found the donkey cart and stopped for instructions. And the donkey man must have seen me, for their cloud of dust came back again, doubling up into the ghost of itself.

But I was through the rocks, running and bouncing towards the break of milk-bushes. And they stretched over the horizon like brown water moving under gravity. I did not want to be fire, or I would be consumed. I was flood-water and rain, parting the branches and vanishing into the roots. And a buck with quick strides was racing alongside me, a leaf in its mouth, and its speckled body bouncing like water and its brown eye like a puddle. I had no words for this; the buck was not scared of me, and I was scared of nothing. In the bushes you could not see far, and I followed the buck and the buck knew where to go.

And then I knew I was a wild animal and they were going to shoot me. With that knowledge, I had to escape, or I would be shot and loaded in the back of Sergeant Thoroughwell's van. And I was only good for meat now. I flung myself down on the leaves, and the buck stopped and watched me, and chewed its leaf, sharply, quickly, and I saw it was turning green leaves into meat, and it would be shot for that, once they had shot me and weighed me for meat.

I had no words for that, and I could neither laugh nor cry. I panted and my head went up and down on my chest; I was a wild thing and I went rigid and could move no more. And the buck picked its feet up and went like a brown stream to a lower part of the bush, showing me the path, but I had no words, no movement. I was stagnant, I was dead still.

Blackie came through the sand, and it was burning and white, and he didn't shoot me; he stood panting, and he said a lot and he put his hand around my wrist and dragged me off. I was limp, I was dead, I was meat to him, and my body felt like red-hot bones connected inside my skin.

And they took me in Sergeant Thoroughwell's van back to Silver Town, probing me a lot, but I didn't reply. I didn't understand why they talked; they were dead to me. I was a wild thing; I had nothing to do with them. I had my own domain; they knew nothing of it. I could not tell them of it, and I was as dead to them as they were to me.

My mother wiped my face with a cloth and wiped her own face and wiped mine, and she was dead to me. She couldn't recognise me and I couldn't her. She put me into a bed smelling of Dettol, and the smell was so strong it overpowered me. And when I could get over it I was off again, through the milk-bush and they rounded me up and my mother put burglar bars on the windows and they locked the door and I tried to get out but I couldn't.

And I wouldn't eat and I wouldn't drink and it took them several weeks to feed me, and I wasn't hungry because I longed for the fire and the water. And I couldn't talk because no one could talk the language I understand.

My mother came in and sat on the floor and she wasn't my mother and I couldn't look at her. I patted her pale hair with the palms of my hands and smoothed it down where it was rough, and I parted it and pushed it down on the shoulders.

Blackie came in with pencils and sat on the floor and he wasn't Blackie and I couldn't watch what he was doing. His hair was glossy and when I patted it with my one palm on the back of the other hand it bounced up and I patted it. This went on for a long time. Then I patted the shoulders and went back to the blanket in the corner. Everything was out of the room except the blanket and the rubber feeding bowl.

The one with the pale hair came in and I couldn't look at her and I lay on the blanket, watching the shadows the curtain made on the ceiling. They were water-shapes and they had wings so burning hot they gave out trails of sparks.

The one with the dark hair came in and changed the rubber bowl and changed my nappies and I couldn't look at him. He drew on the floor with a piece of chalk from my blanket to where he sat and the chalk was white like sand.

The one with the pale hair came in also and drew with another coloured chalk over the white shapes and changed my nappies and went away.

People came to visit and they took me by the wrists to them and I watched the ceiling and the Persian carpet and they lifted me onto the sofa and I patted my hand and the people went and I returned to the blanket.

And one day when it was very hot they left my door open. I went into the shed and took the gaff that had the sharp edge like fingernails and I took it by the empty end and went with it trailing behind me. And it made sparks on the tarmac in the dark, glinting beautifully. And I walked backwards, pulling it for the sparks.

And I saw the black dog on the steps and he stood up and wagged and licked my forehead with his tongue. And inside one of the rooms with the light was my father and I showed him how the glass could break and came tumbling down in sparks and it broke and came tumbling down and the glass smashed and the fragments bounced out with colour and flew through the air, glittering, and the window-pane cracked like a wave and showered over me with droplets of raging colour and the glass broke into a thousand, thousand rainbow-coloured fragments and fell on me like hissing water and the glass broke like a cascade and I could hear it break.

18

From there it is not hard to piece together the rest of the story. But I can do it only from hearsay, from what I learned later; I have no memory of it.

Certainly, my father did not return to Silver Town. My mother, Sarah Esslin, as she frequently told me, would not marry Blackie Rousseau until she had laid her husband's ghost to rest. I have a photograph of the ceremony on the Cape Town foreshore where the flags of many nations flew at half-mast and she received his beret. His beret had his rank on it and, tucked in the brim, one of the hairs of his head. The beret was symbolically buried, and she was free of the war and all that her years in South Africa had meant to her.

Their wedding present from my grandmother was money to bring me to England for treatment. As there were special schools for war children, I might get a place if I were not too far gone. They accompanied me from Silver Town to Cape Town and onto the ship and I do have one memory of that time – a typical one, the light reflected off the swell drawing in a wash across the ceiling of the cabin.

There were trains, and walks in Hyde Park and along Bayswater. I have no recollection of my grandmother, except that she left me a signet ring with the family crest from her father. There are photographs of me at the Peter Pan statue, with long arms and a thin face. I don't remember the camera looking at me and I certainly didn't look at it. One of these photos has the caption, 'Our Elfin Child,' because it was common at that time to think of such children as having been smuggled into another world by unknown forces. There is something in that, because I did not then belong to the human race.

My memories of London after the peace, for what they are worth: a staircase in the immense hotel with a carpet that had brass runners; a blackboard that had diagrams like triangles; a bomb crater bordered with yellow dustbins. This was my new home. I have no idea within myself of how the dustbins, the blackboard and the brass runners interconnect. I have no inner conviction that they were all part of one geography, though I know perfectly well where they were located: the Westminster Hotel with its gaping neighbouring lot, and the school where I was sent for attention, along the Northern Line at Goodge Street.

Nor have I any direct knowledge of the weeks, months and years of patience and care, routine and drill, experiment and relapse that went into my rehabilitation. I only know that many people, with wells of unending tenderness, made it their business to redeem me. I know I emerged a thorough Londoner, drawing from the new environment a fresh personality that you could have seen duplicated in any Lyon's Corner House or greengrocer's. I was taken for walks along the dowdy pavements with their sweet wrappers and treated to Wall's ice-cream between wafers.

Blackie found work in a grocer's, but I have no direct memory of that, either. He used to pine over imported avocadoes and oranges from South Africa – in post-war days South Africa was one of Britain's great providers. Once, when food started flooding back into the shops and ration coupons were abandoned, he found an apple from Elgin, and said it was so delicious he even missed Aunt Rosemary.

But my stepfather didn't flourish in England and their marriage eventually fell apart. Obviously my poor mother could have no more children, though I doubt that that was a factor in Blackie's leaving. They wrote to one another regularly and lovingly. My mother was painfully tired, never being able to rest unless I was asleep. So that I should not run away, we literally slept tied together. For her it was a harrowing, speechless bond. Blackie had helped her with me, taking his shifts with a faithful sense of duty.

My mother couldn't work with Blackie gone, but we had the rest of my grandmother's capital to live on and he sent us money. I have no memory of the flat we lived in – only a photo of the painful case with his legs apart at the end of a huge duffel coat, against a background of pines and banks of snow. I had become cocooned within mufflers and coats and jackets and scarves and Viyella and vests, sealed in by cold, an ember burning somewhere deeply inside.

When I was twelve and the year was 1948 there was a return trip to South Africa. We stayed with Aunt Rosemary on their farm near Elgin. Blackie was reunited with my mother, but it did not work out. Things were going badly in the land; with the election my mother said she would return with me to England for good. Aunt Rosemary and her husband decided to stick it out, as maybe the English-speakers would regain power. Their entire livelihood was rooted in that soil, stretched before them in the orchards.

Before Blackie finally left my mother, she and he took me down to Silver Town in their old car, which Aunt Rosemary now had. There is a photo taken by my mother of Blackie steering at the wheel like a maniac, and one taken by Blackie of my mother posing at the wheel, lifting her hair like a mermaid. In both I am distinguished as the gawky third party who couldn't stand against the bucket seat without holding on. The dusty slope down to Silver Town, the trading store and the post office, the hotel, Peter's Lodge, the golf club, the harbour – none of them drew the spark of recognition from within me.

But in time it was drawn out. It sputtered and lay dormant and smouldered for as long as it willed. It blazed out only once I had decided that whatever glass pane divided me from the rest of the world should now dissolve and release me. The process took all of the time that should have been my adolescence. Out there was a new world of peaceful opportunity to be claimed; I had only to join it. By the time I did, in 1954, I was in body an adult, with a mind that had ceased to function normally shortly after Hiroshima.

When the time came for me to cross the intervening years everyone else had forgotten them. Only I was marooned at the other end of history, beginning again, heaving my eyes together and trying to focus on where all of them stood, holding out their hands to me. One day, when I was ready, and from no particular cause – I stepped across to join them.

Little remains to be said. I'm your average British businessman now, in textiles. The old firm I work for has factories in the Cape, using cheap labour and cheaper raw materials. I commute there in my brown suit, my head against the window of another 727. If anyone wants to belt themselves in alongside me for the flight, I haul out my wallet and show them a photo of my wife and our three children. They have never seen the land of my birth.

'Have you been to Africa before?' is the question.

'Yes,' is the answer. 'As a matter of fact, I spent the war years at the Cape.'

'Ah then, maybe you could tell me. When we get to Johannesburg, we connect with Cape Town on SA211. How do I get from there to –?'

Then out comes the photograph and I pay for the round.

When it is time for lights-out, I snuggle sideways in my seat, my elbow touching her downy forearm. I know that in the morning we will wake over that tawny landscape, like a cowhide, that is the blighted paradise of my youth. With her excitement and enthusiasm beside me, however briefly, I will be able to face it and, in helping her to her destination, recover my own.